[illegible]NG DRAGONS

Taku Kuwabara

6

DRIFTING DRAGONS

Table of Contents

This is a work of fiction.
Any resemblance to real people, groups,
and events is purely coincidental.

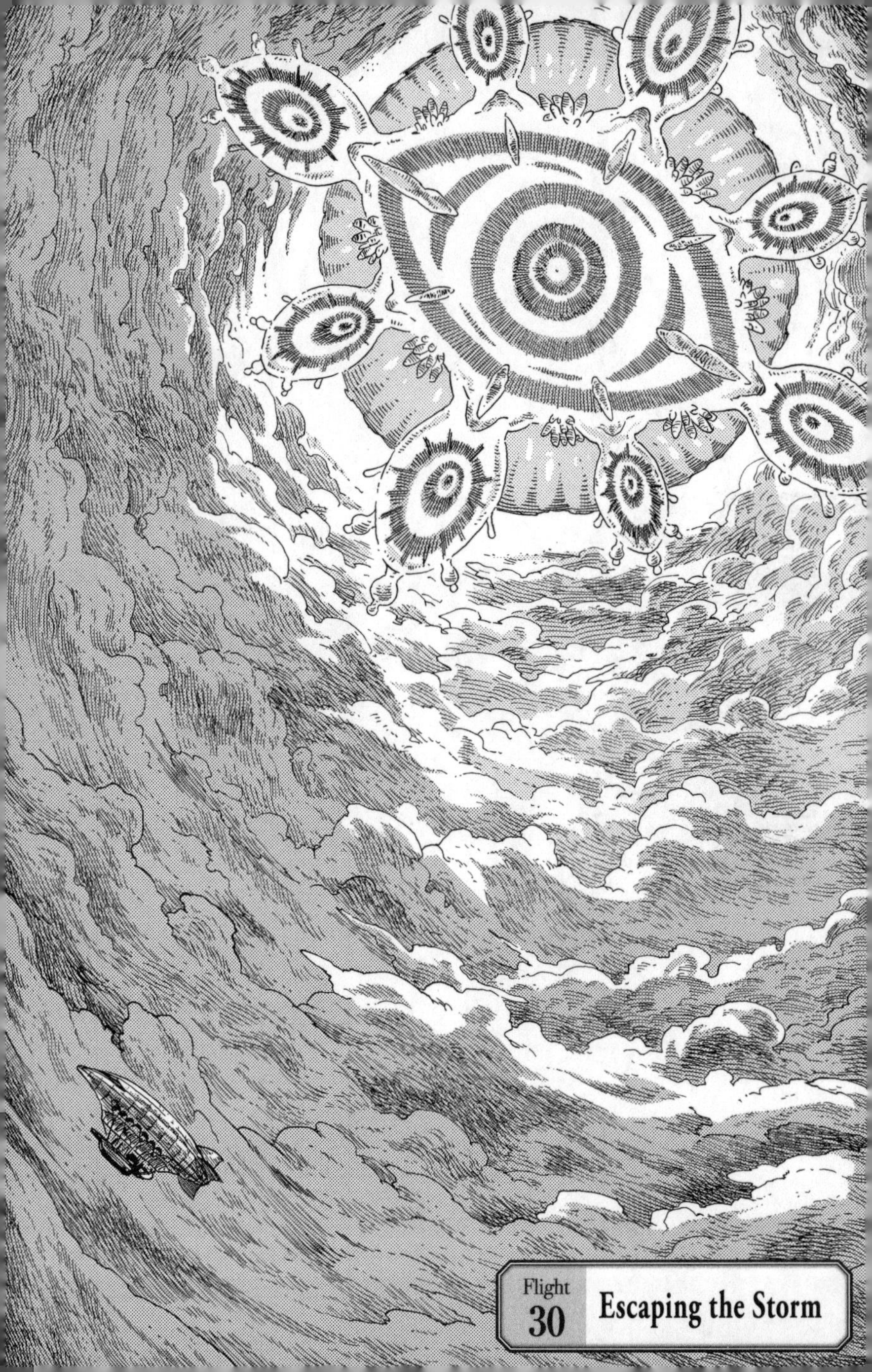
Flight 30
Escaping the Storm

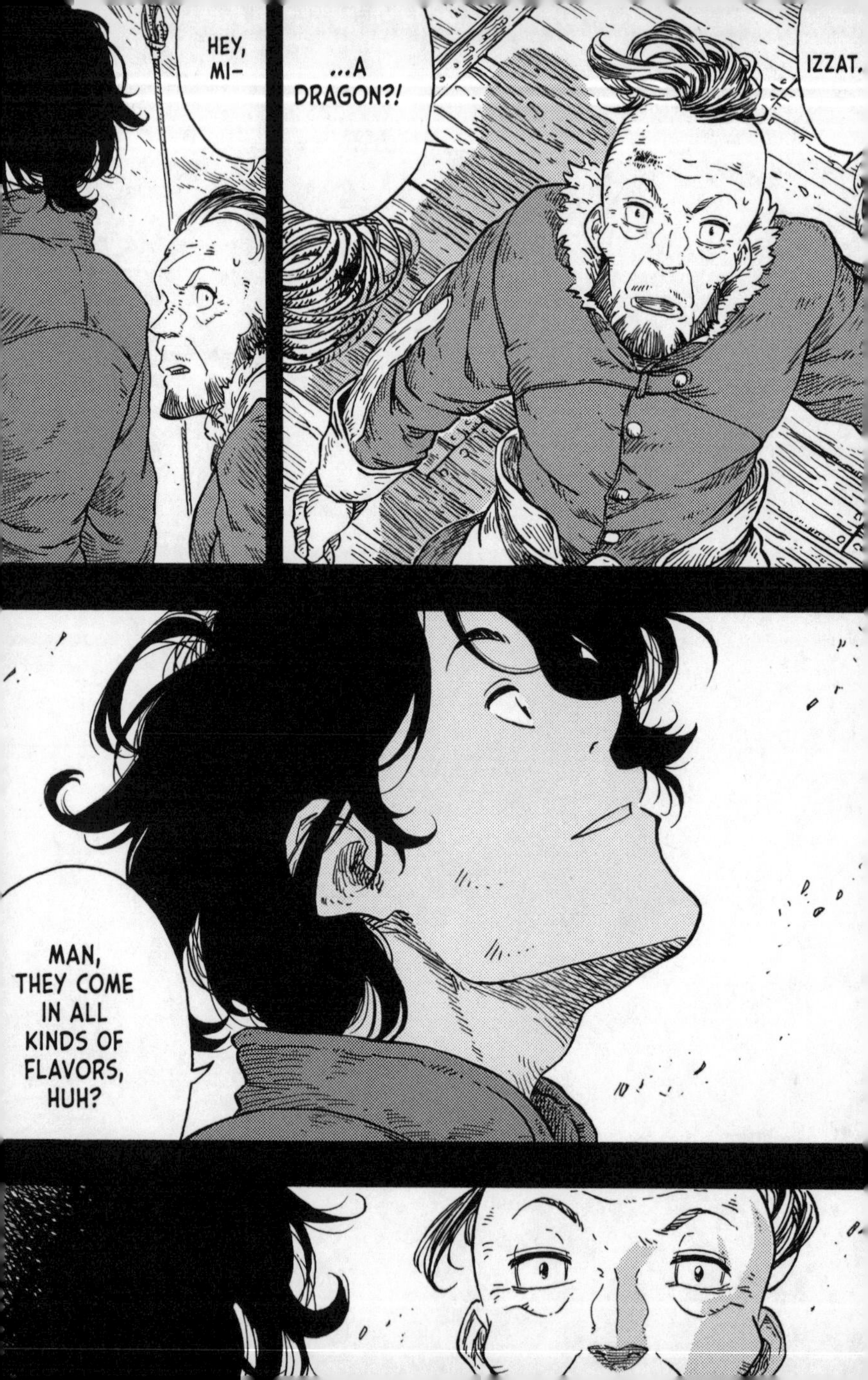
IZZAT.
...A DRAGON?!
HEY, MI-
MAN, THEY COME IN ALL KINDS OF FLAVORS, HUH?

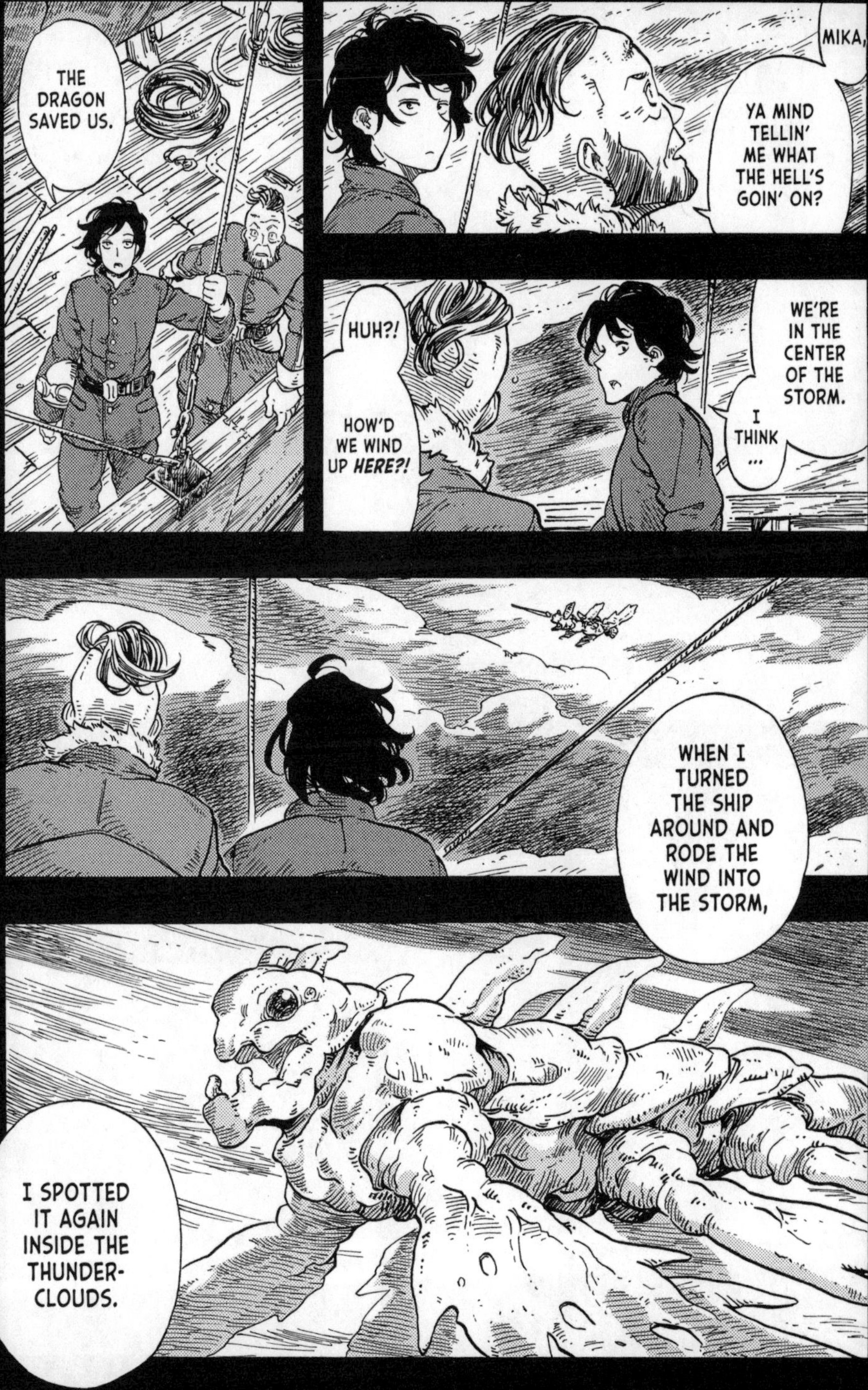
MIKA,
YA MIND TELLIN' ME WHAT THE HELL'S GOIN' ON?
WE'RE IN THE CENTER OF THE STORM.
I THINK ...
HUH?!
HOW'D WE WIND UP *HERE?!*
THE DRAGON SAVED US.
WHEN I TURNED THE SHIP AROUND AND RODE THE WIND INTO THE STORM,
I SPOTTED IT AGAIN INSIDE THE THUNDER-CLOUDS.

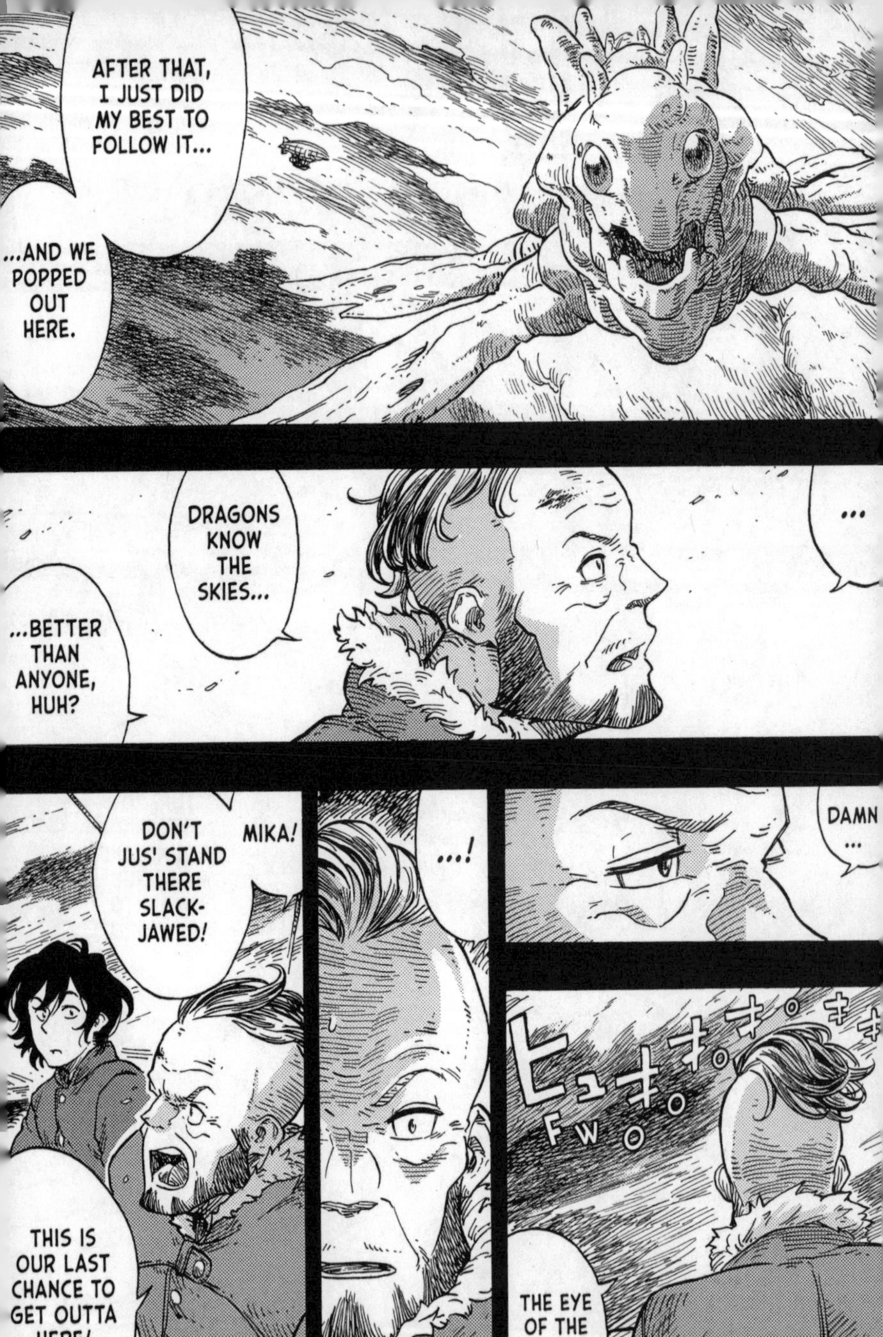
AFTER THAT, I JUST DID MY BEST TO FOLLOW IT...
...AND WE POPPED OUT HERE.
...
DRAGONS KNOW THE SKIES...
...BETTER THAN ANYONE, HUH?
DAMN...
FWOOO
THE EYE OF THE STORM...
...!
MIKA!
DON'T JUS' STAND THERE SLACK-JAWED!
THIS IS OUR LAST CHANCE TO GET OUTTA HERE!

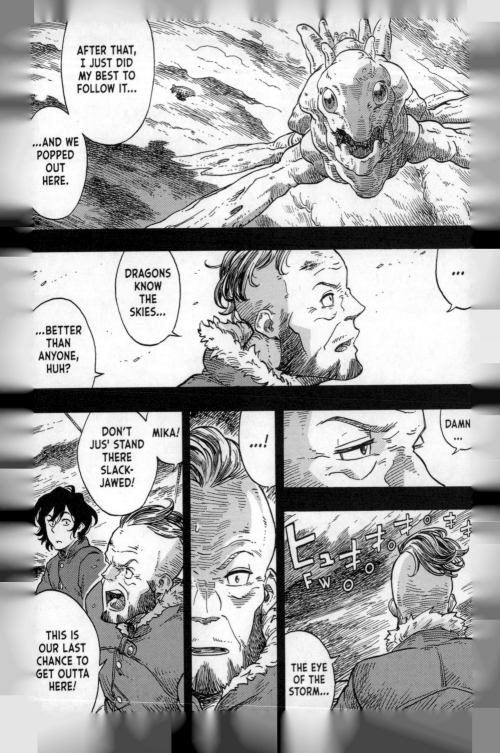

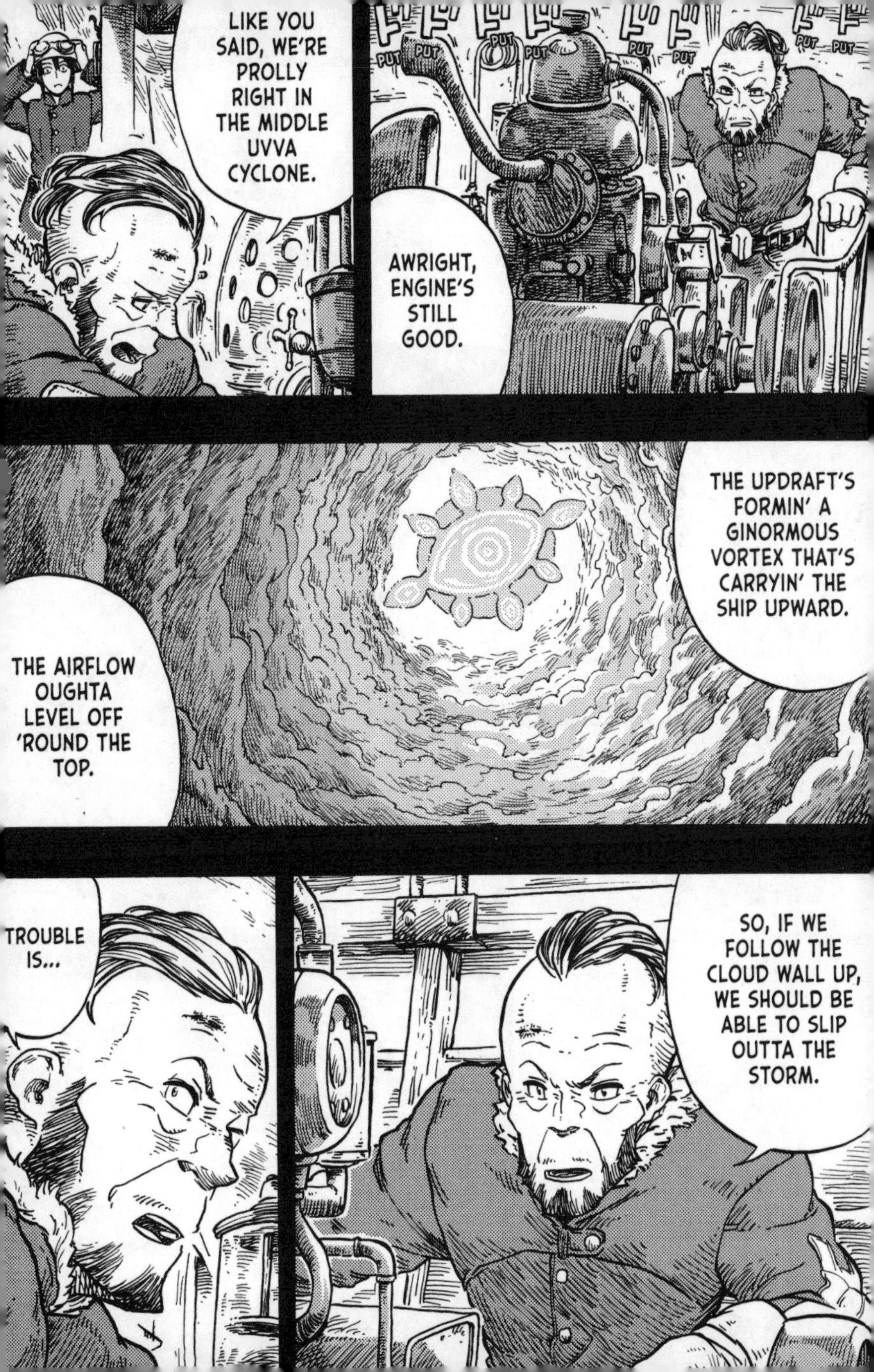
PUT PUT PUT PUT PUT PUT PUT PUT
AWRIGHT, ENGINE'S STILL GOOD.
LIKE YOU SAID, WE'RE PROLLY RIGHT IN THE MIDDLE UVVA CYCLONE.
THE UPDRAFT'S FORMIN' A GINORMOUS VORTEX THAT'S CARRYIN' THE SHIP UPWARD.
THE AIRFLOW OUGHTA LEVEL OFF 'ROUND THE TOP.
SO, IF WE FOLLOW THE CLOUD WALL UP, WE SHOULD BE ABLE TO SLIP OUTTA THE STORM.
TROUBLE IS...

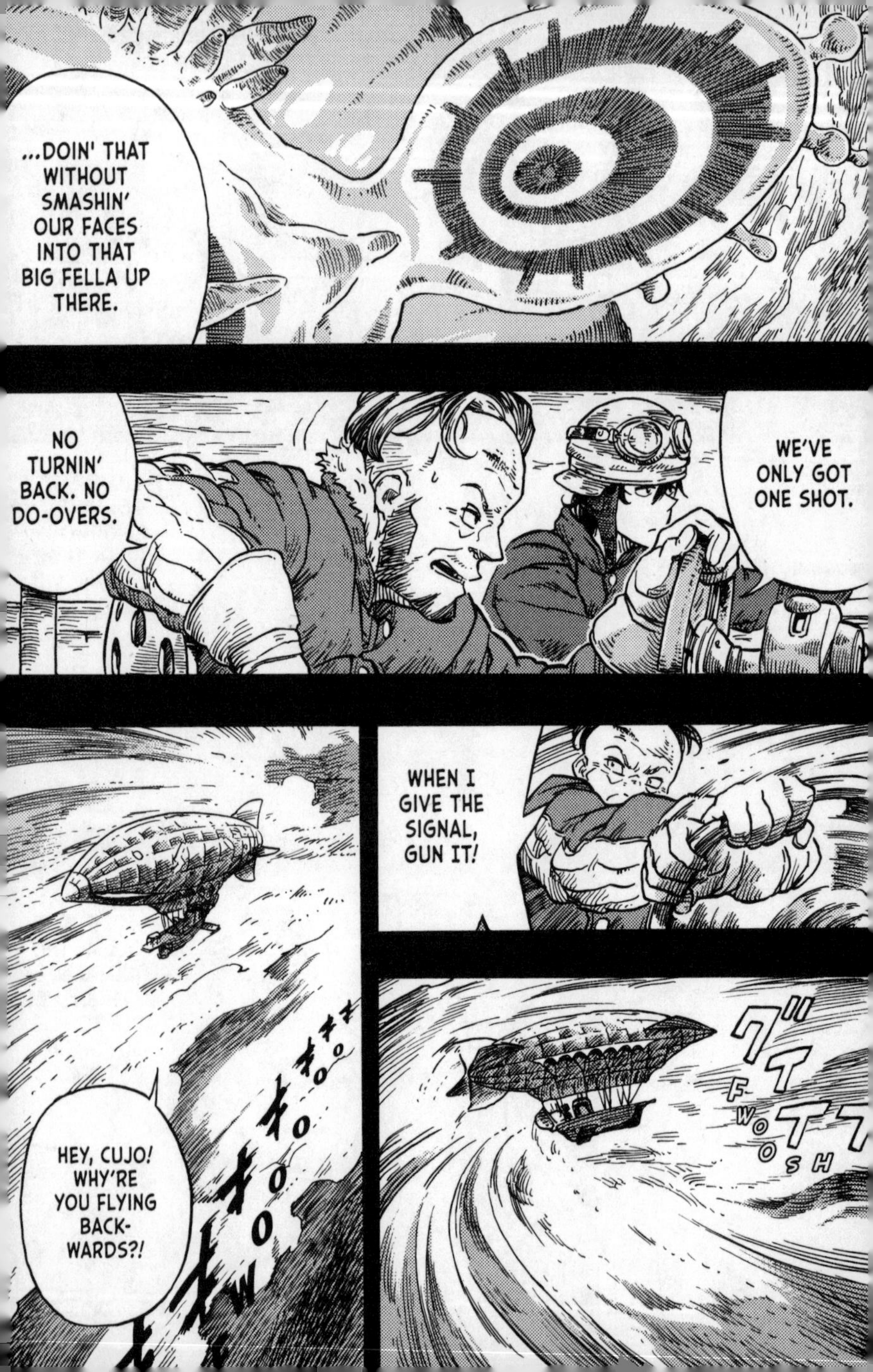
...DOIN' THAT WITHOUT SMASHIN' OUR FACES INTO THAT BIG FELLA UP THERE.
WE'VE ONLY GOT ONE SHOT.
NO TURNIN' BACK. NO DO-OVERS.
WHEN I GIVE THE SIGNAL, GUN IT!
FWOOSH
HEY, CUJO! WHY'RE YOU FLYING BACK-WARDS?!

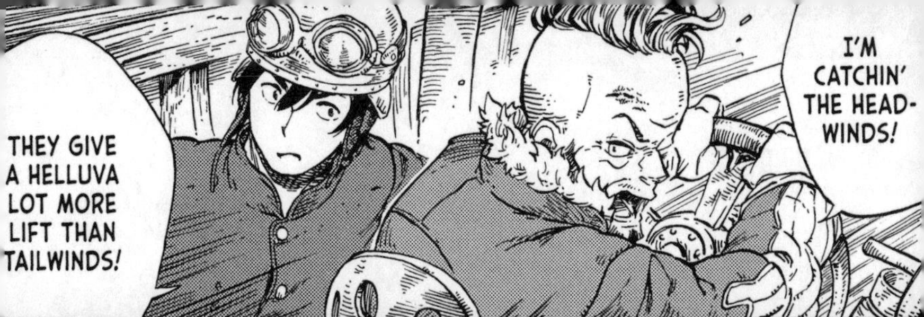
I'M CATCHIN' THE HEAD-WINDS!
THEY GIVE A HELLUVA LOT MORE LIFT THAN TAILWINDS!
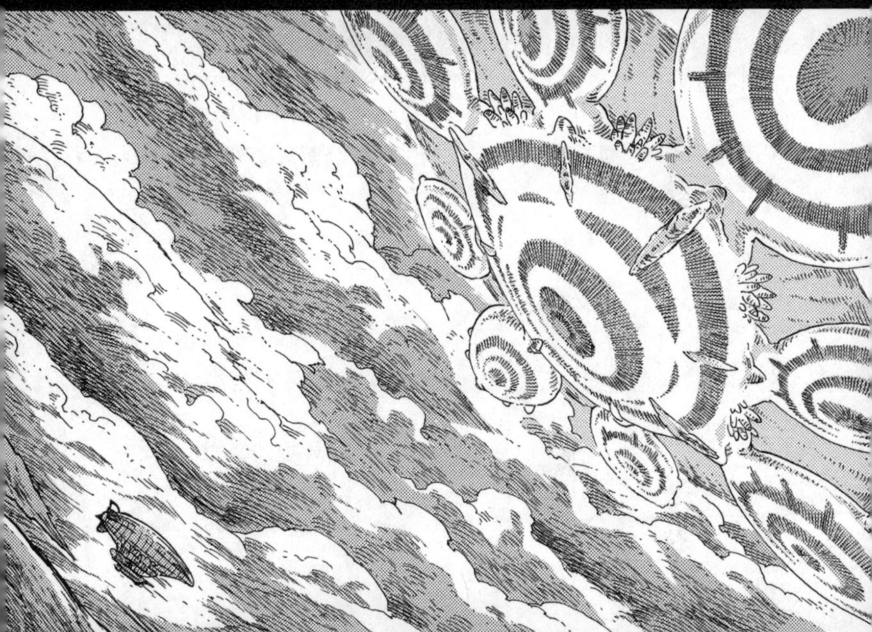
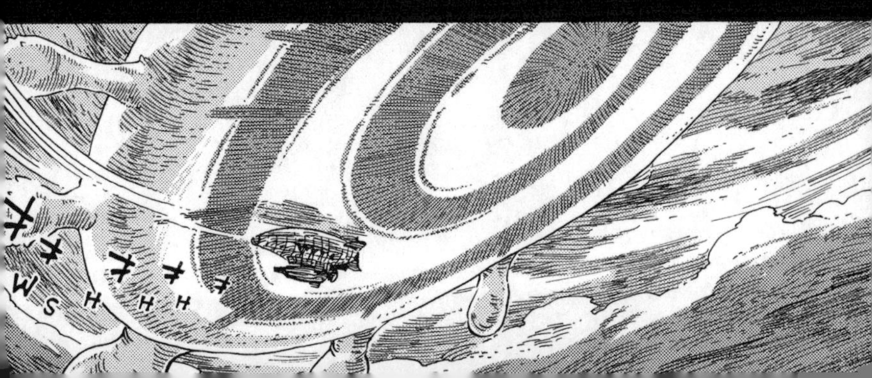
WSHHHH

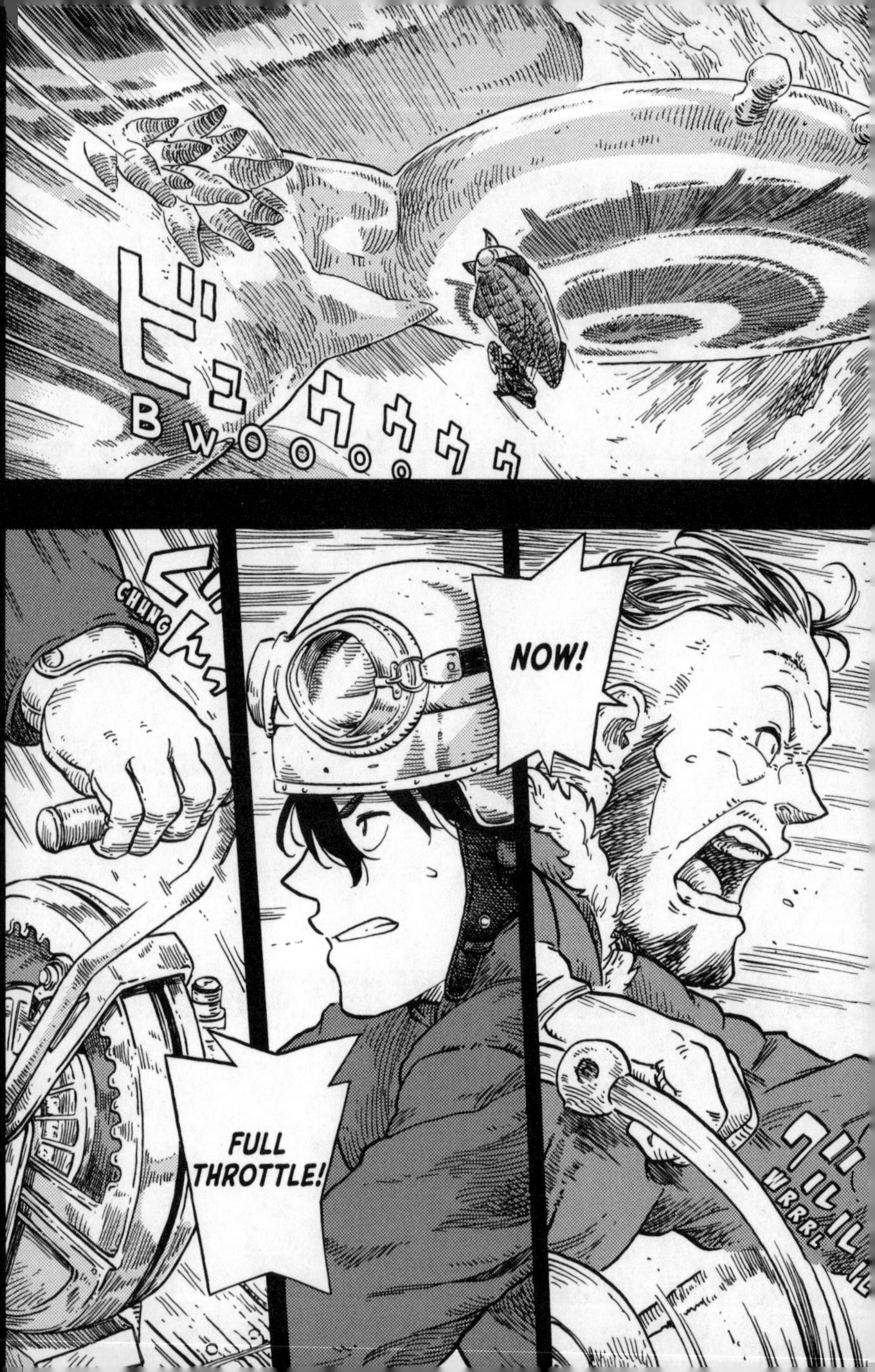
BWOOOOO
NOW!
WRRRL
FULL THROTTLE!
CHUNG

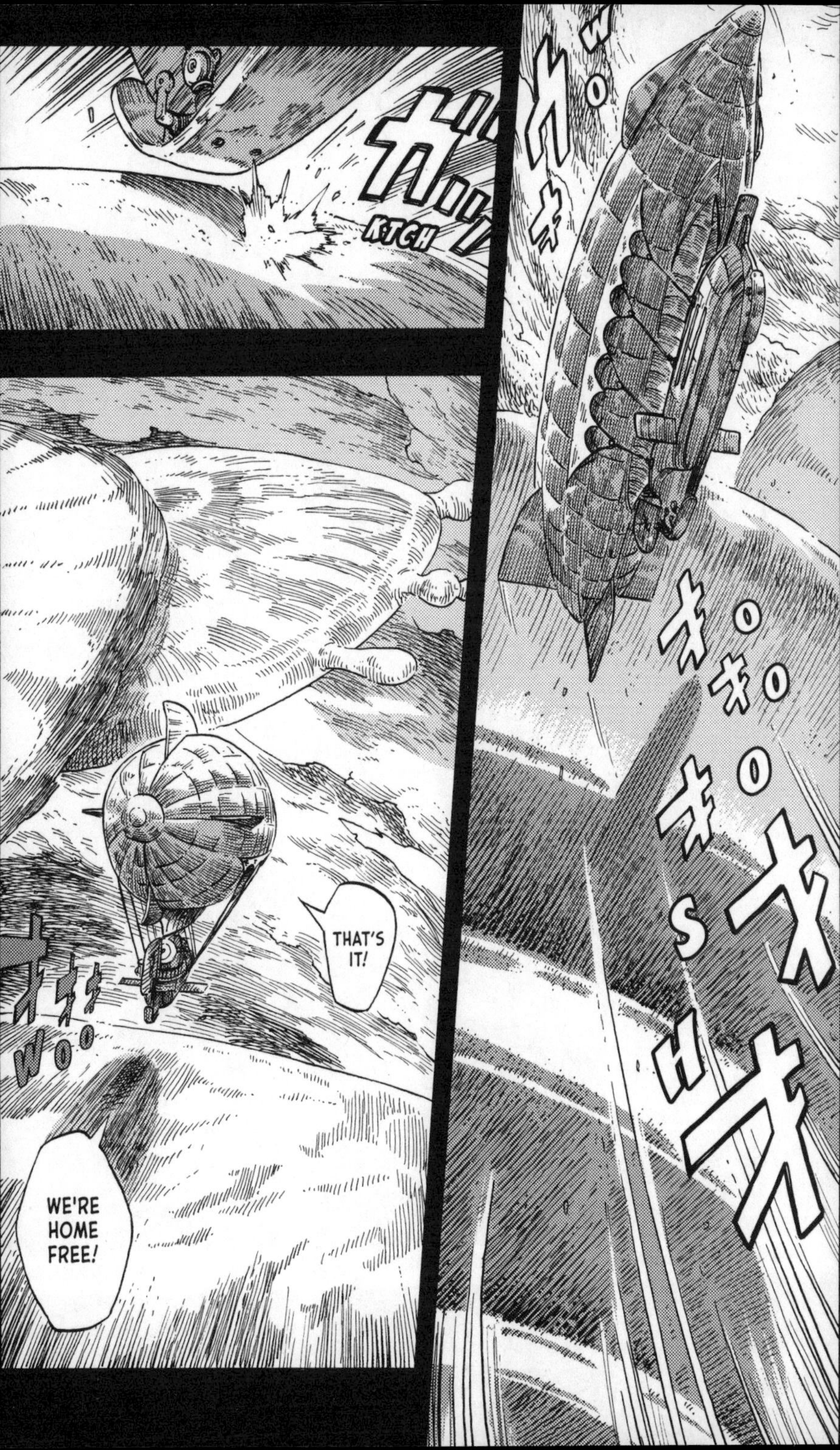
KTCH
THAT'S IT!
WE'RE HOME FREE!

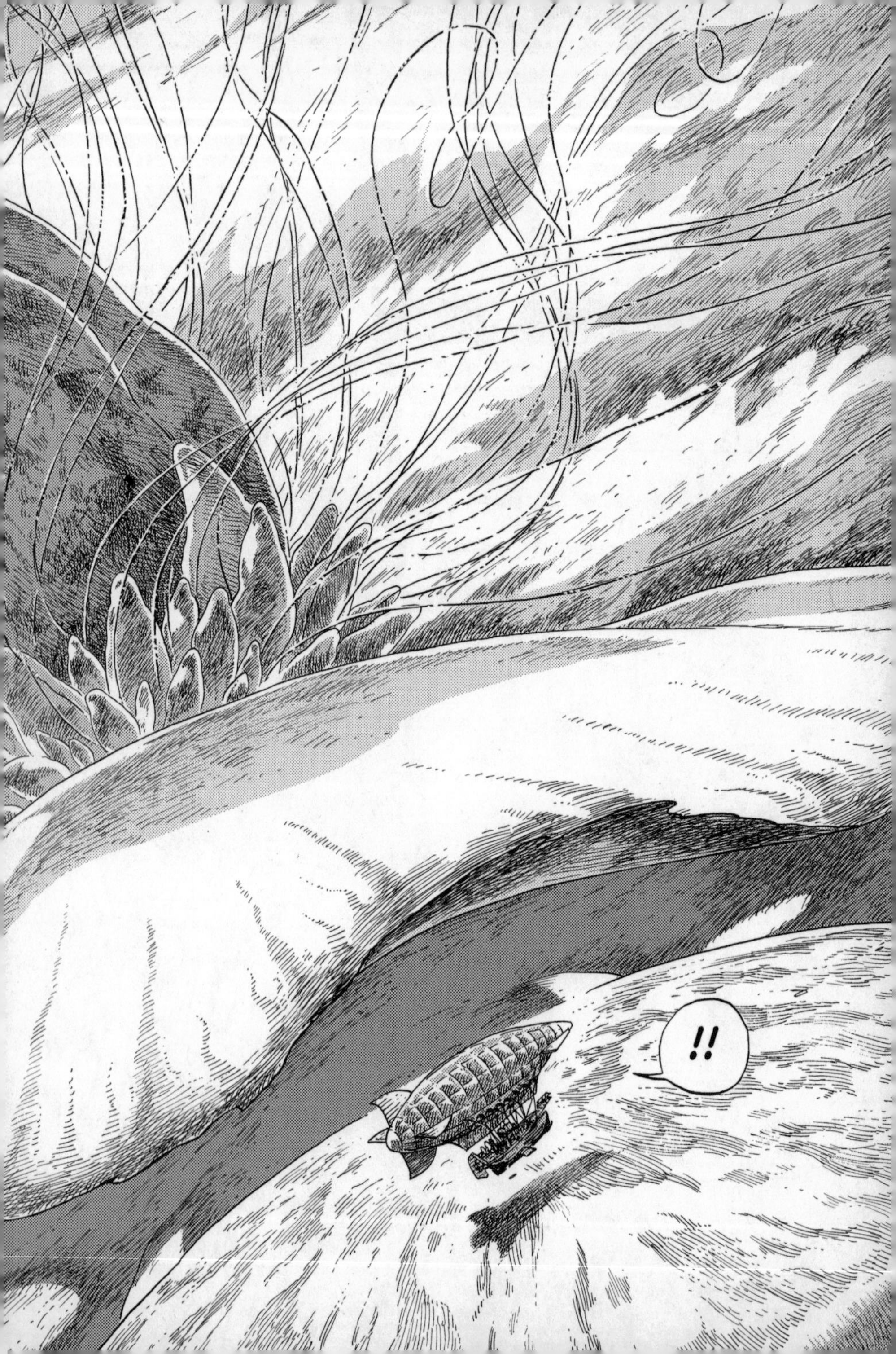
!!

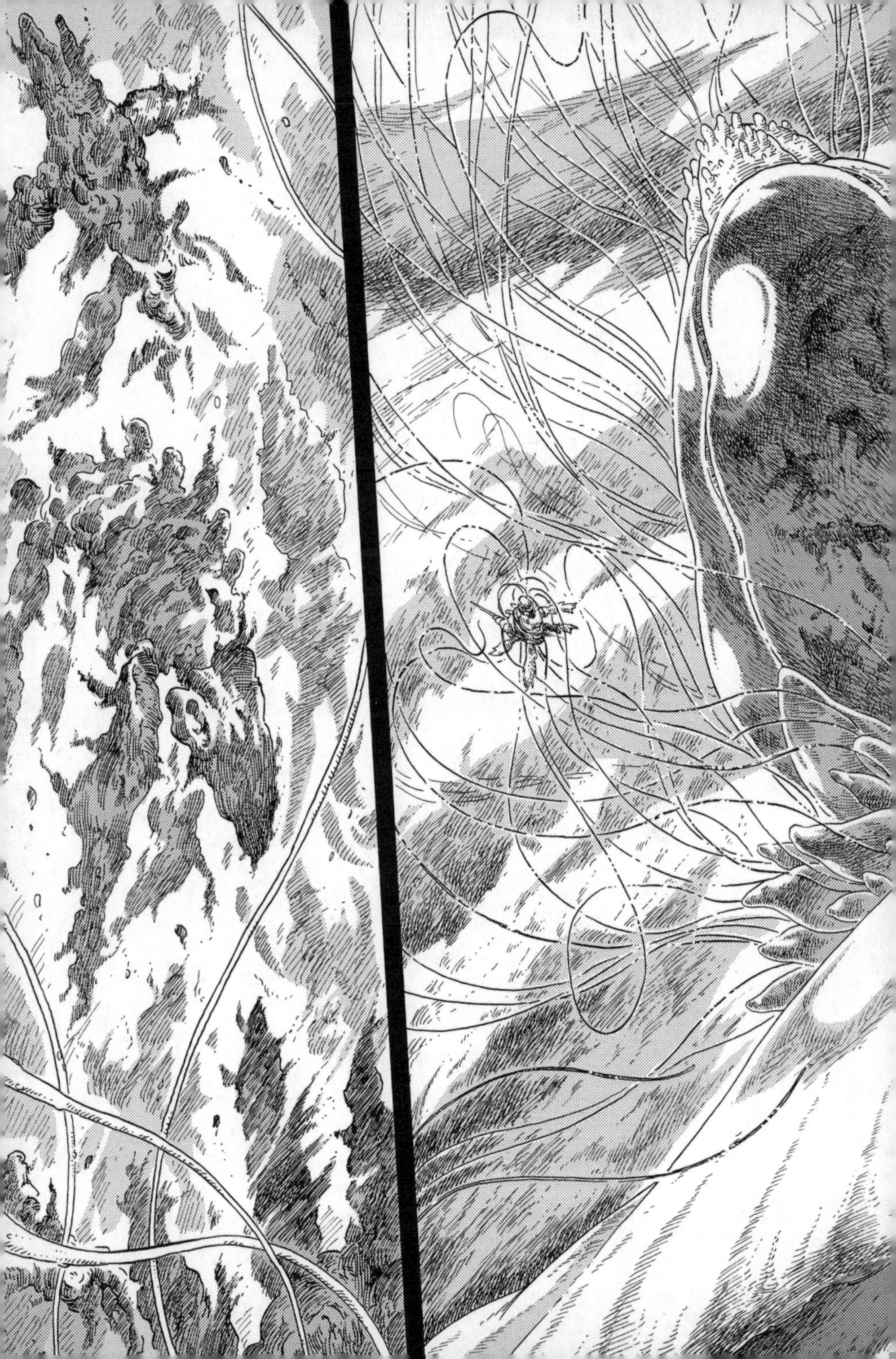

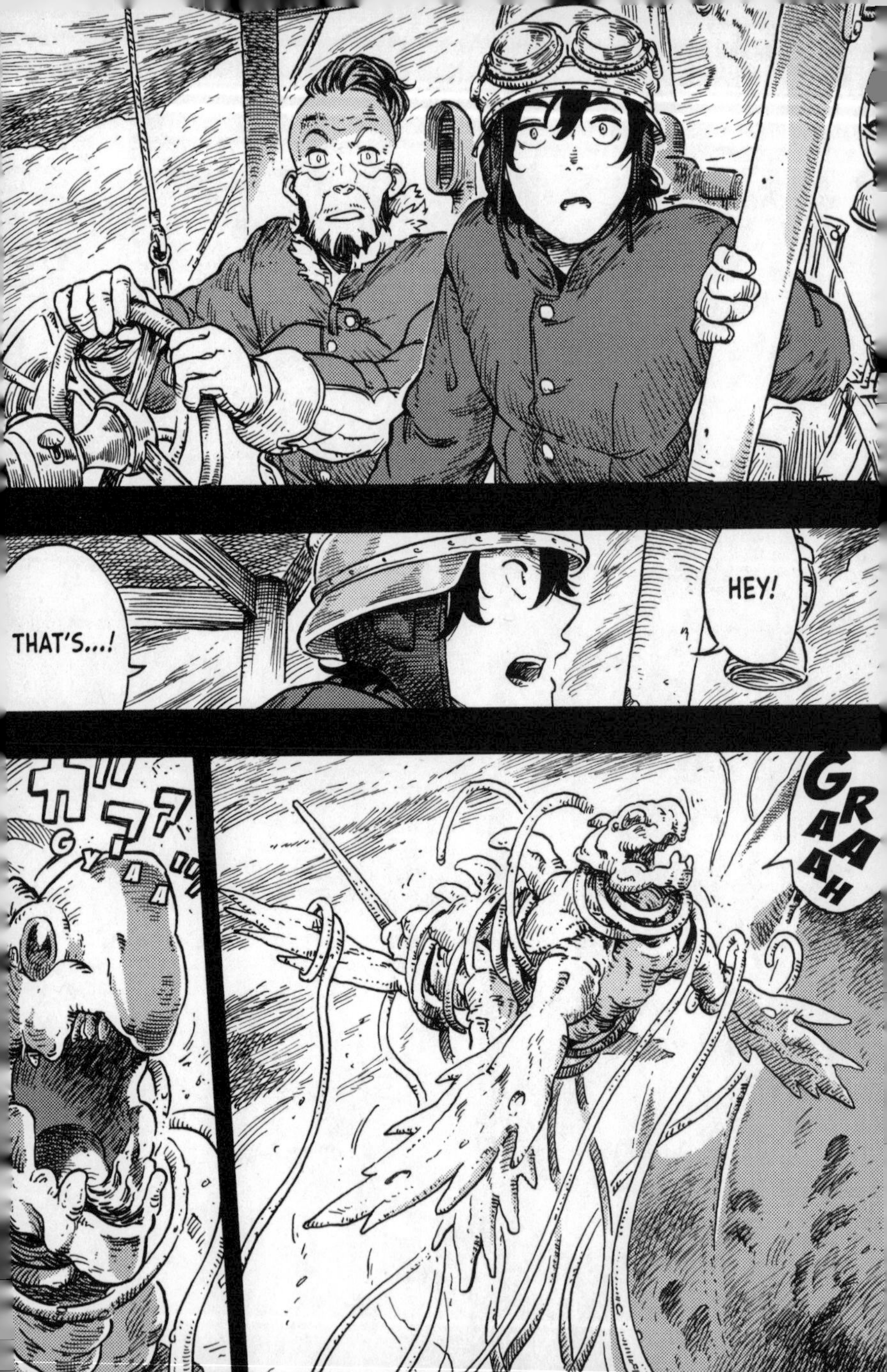
HEY!
THAT'S...!
GRAAAH
GYAA

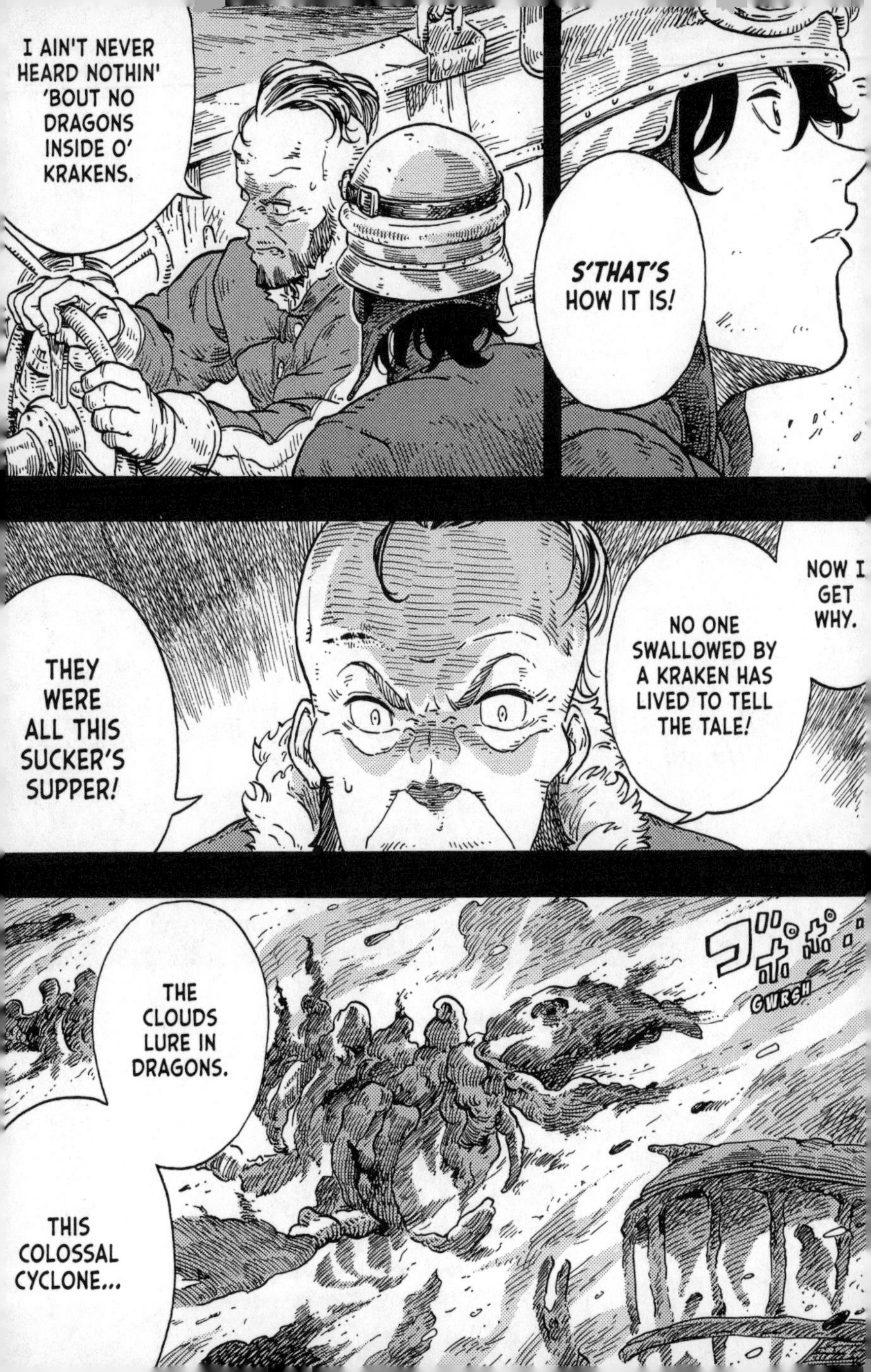
S'THAT'S HOW IT IS!
I AIN'T NEVER HEARD NOTHIN' 'BOUT NO DRAGONS INSIDE O' KRAKENS.
NOW I GET WHY.
NO ONE SWALLOWED BY A KRAKEN HAS LIVED TO TELL THE TALE!
THEY WERE ALL THIS SUCKER'S SUPPER!
GWRSH
THE CLOUDS LURE IN DRAGONS.
THIS COLOSSAL CYCLONE...

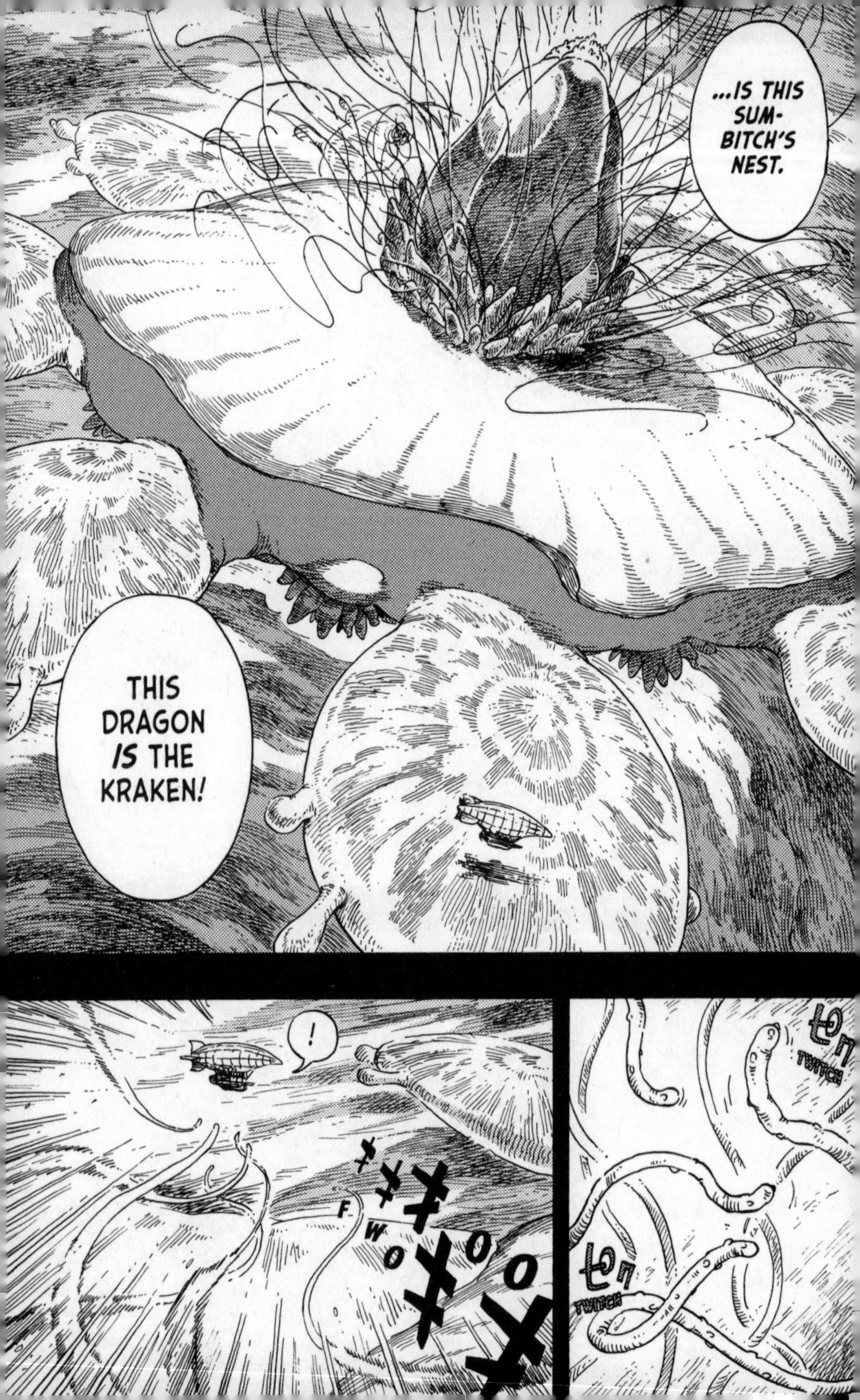
...IS THIS SUM-BITCH'S NEST.
THIS DRAGON *IS* THE KRAKEN!
TWITCH
TWITCH
!
FWOOO

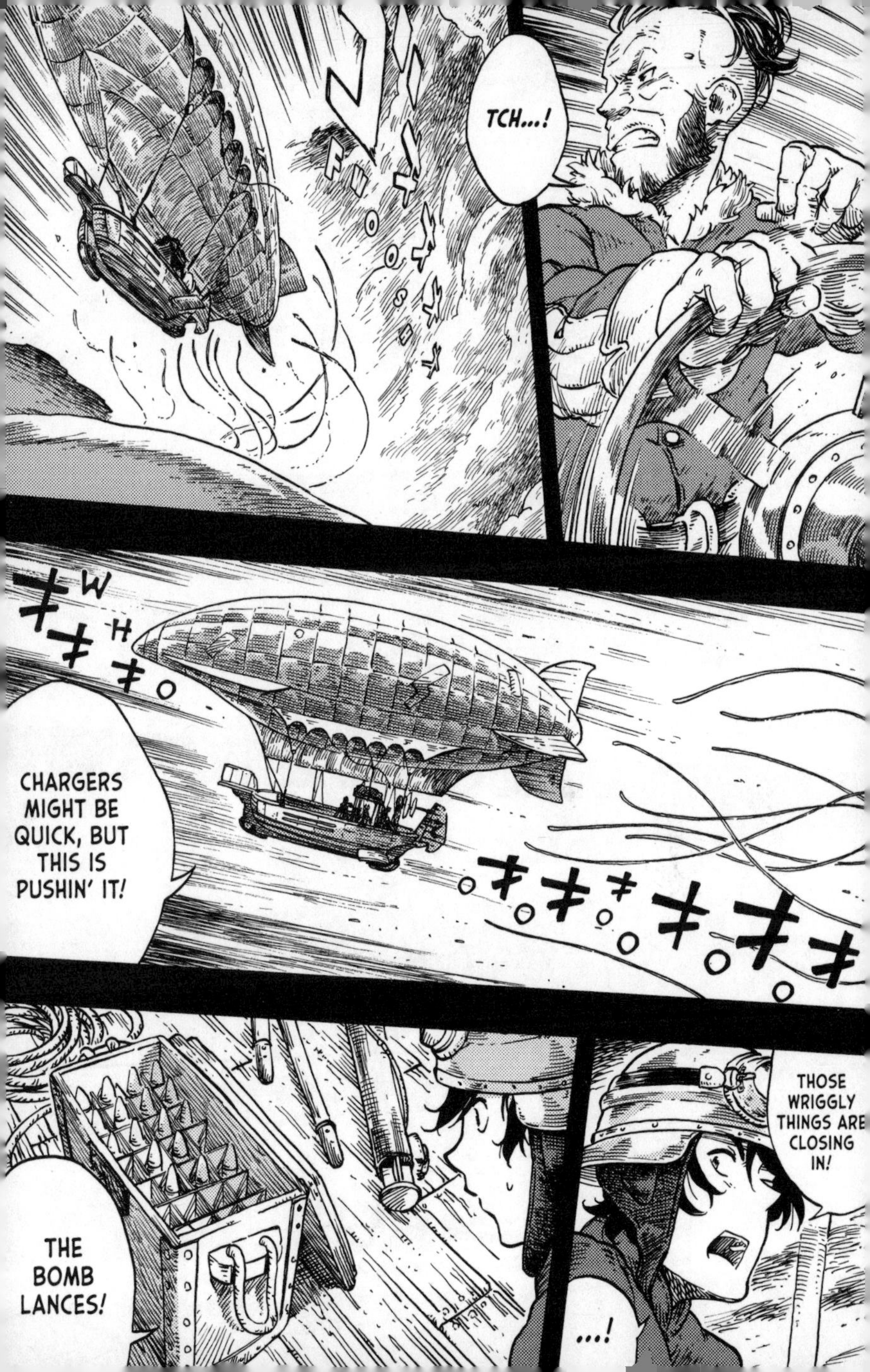
TCH...!
FWOOSH
CHARGERS MIGHT BE QUICK, BUT THIS IS PUSHIN' IT!
THOSE WRIGGLY THINGS ARE CLOSING IN!
...!
THE BOMB LANCES!

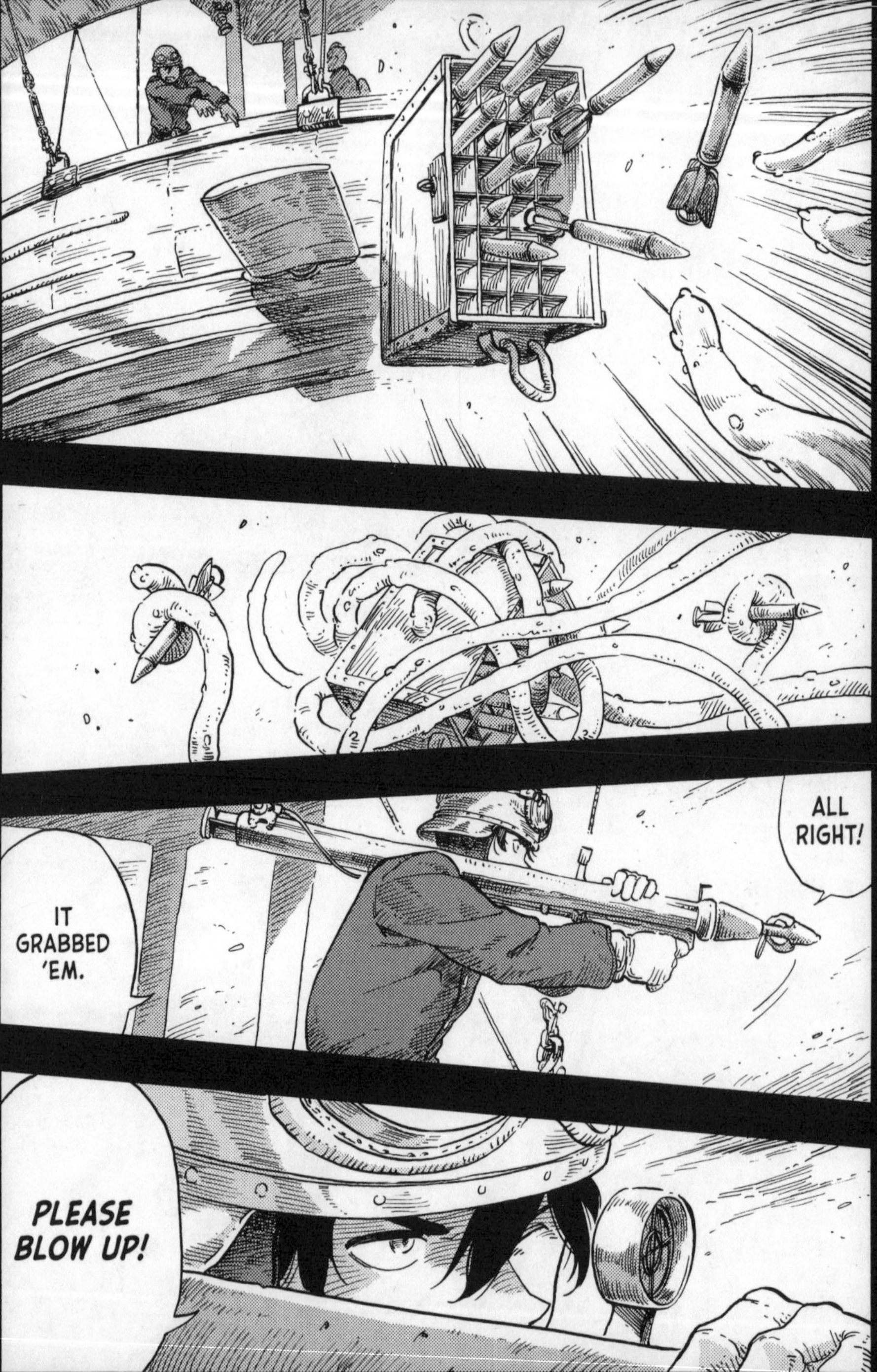
ALL RIGHT!
IT GRABBED 'EM.
PLEASE BLOW UP!

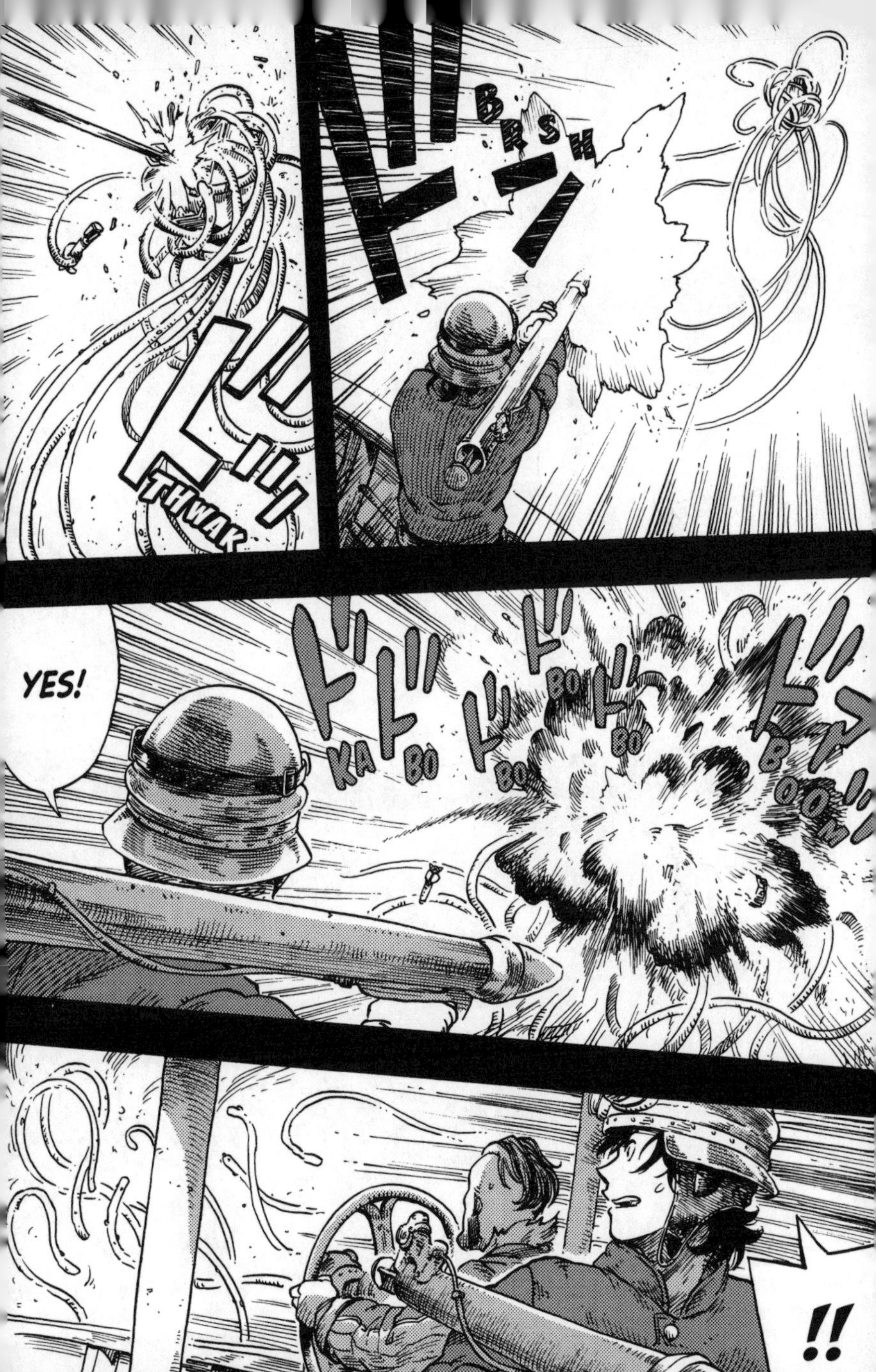
BRSH
THWAK
YES!
KA BO BO BO BO BOOM
!!

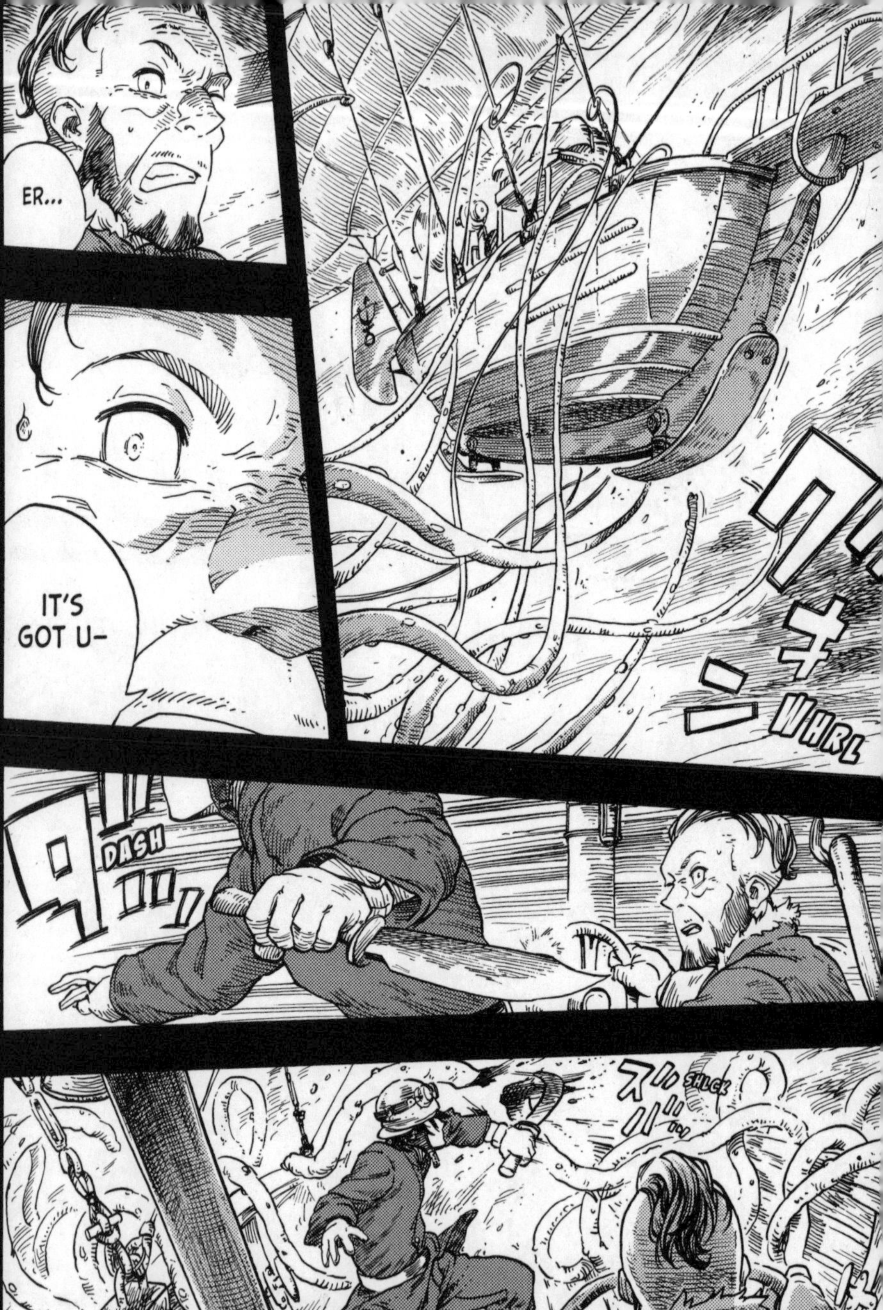
WHRL
ER...
IT'S
GOT U-
DASH
SHLCK

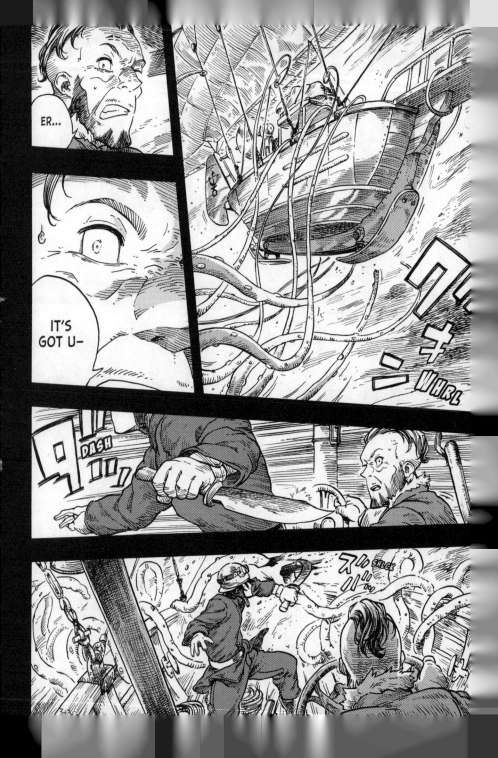

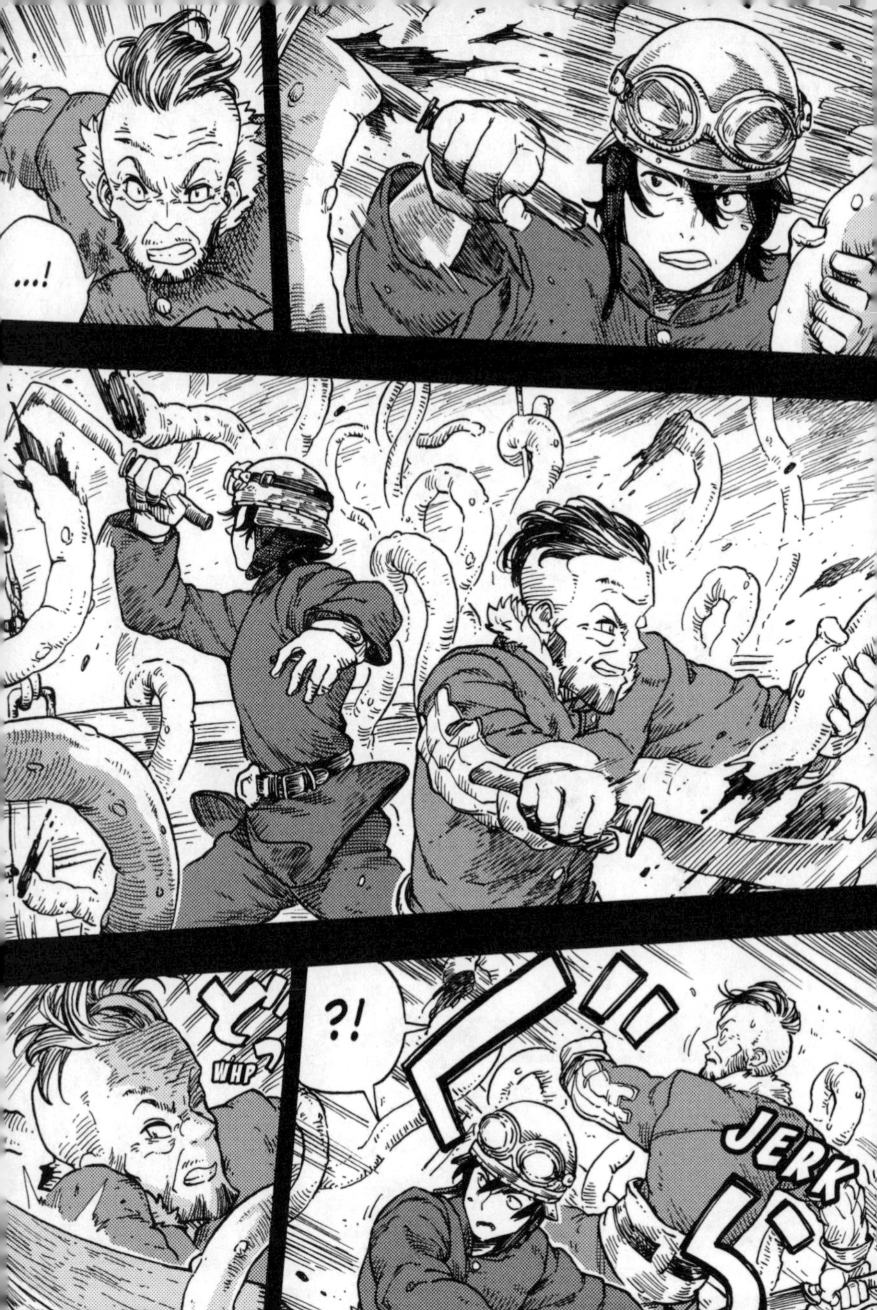
...!
WHP
?!
JERK

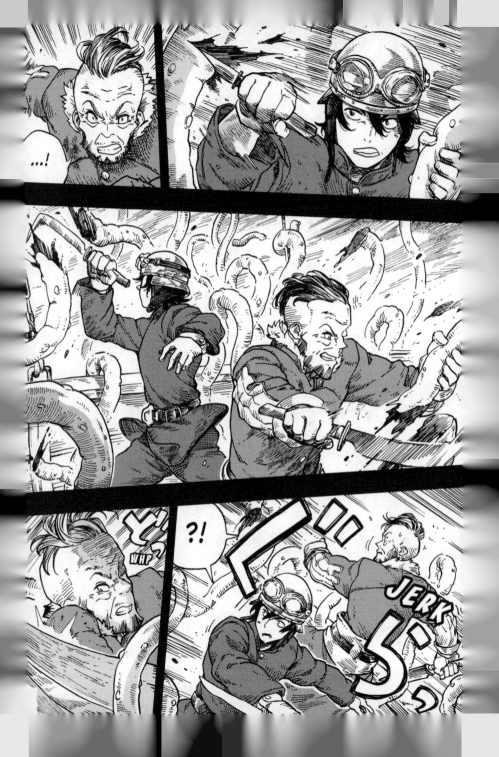

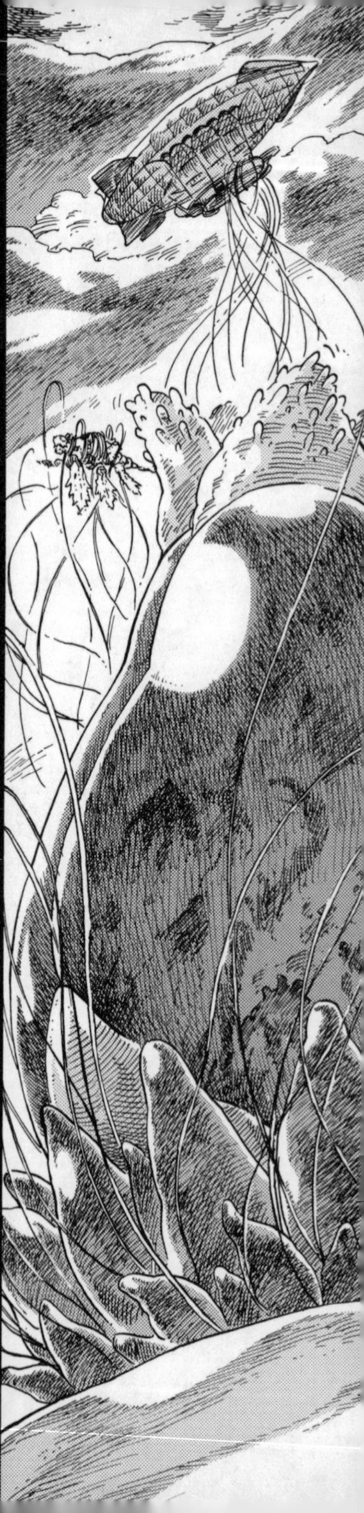
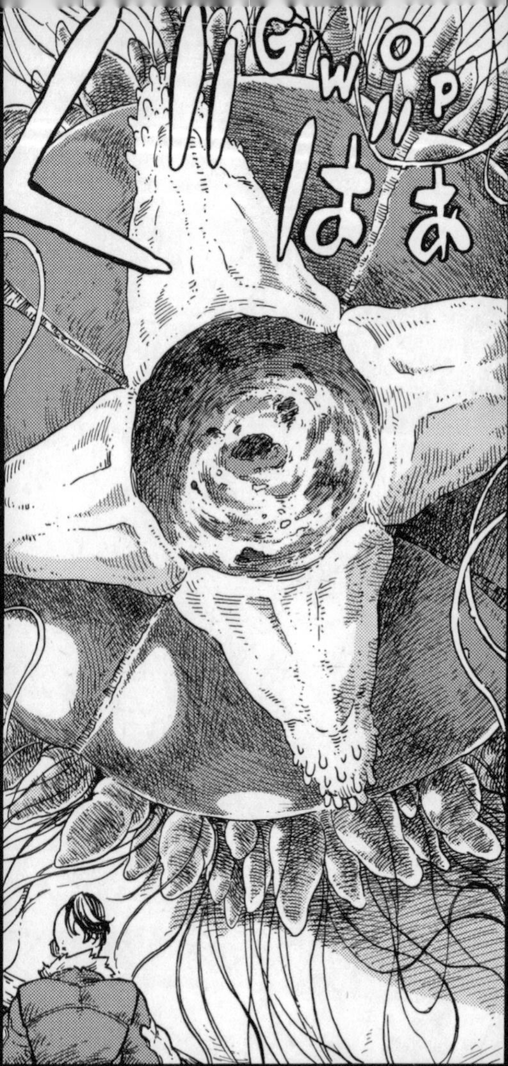
GWOP
はあ
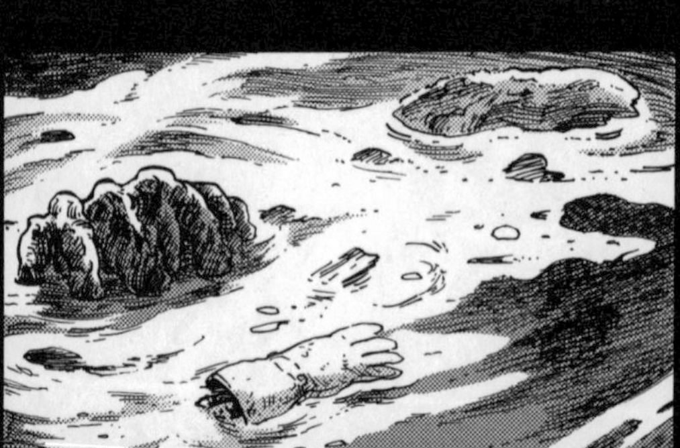

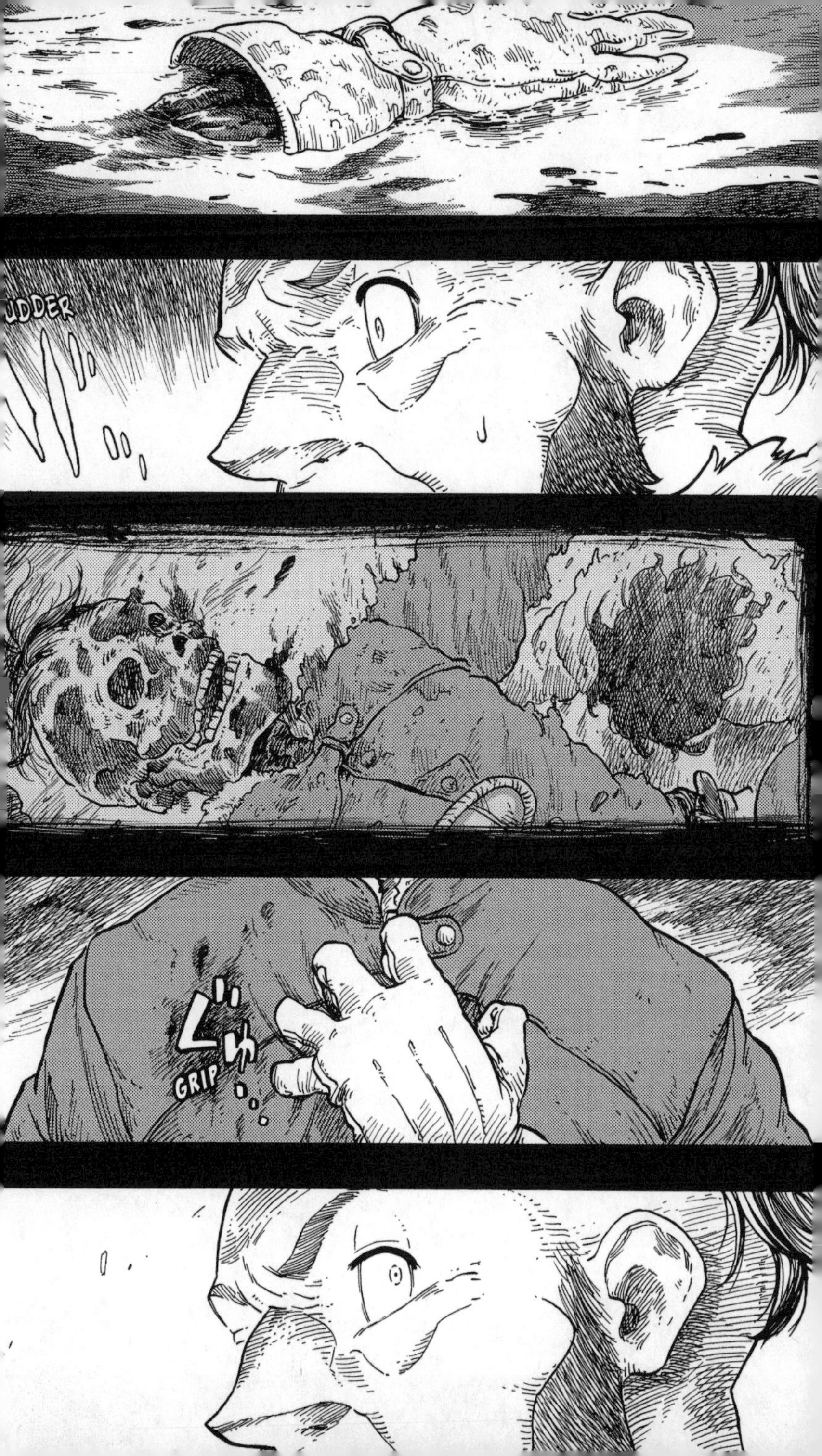
UDDER
じゅ
GRIP

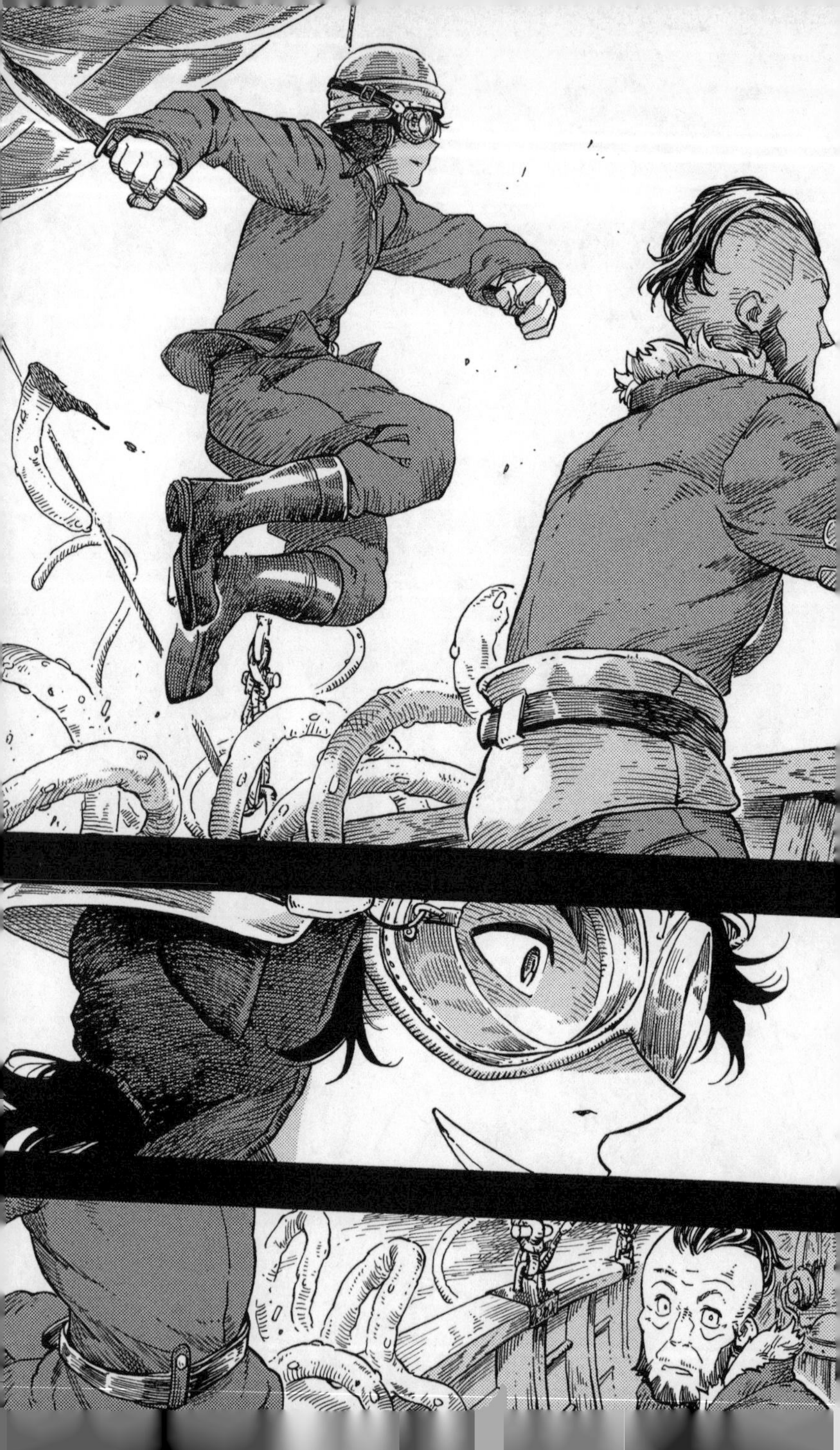

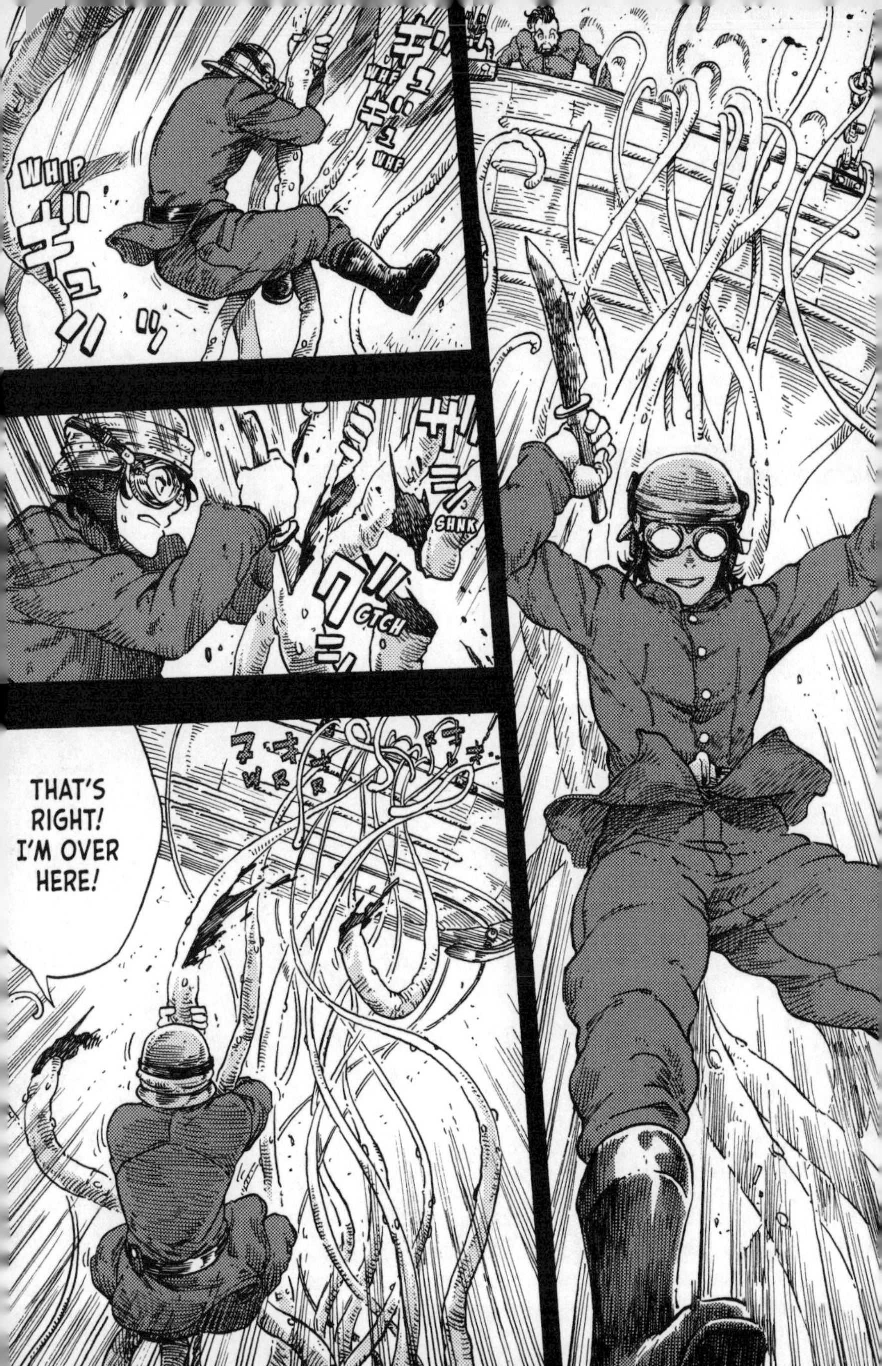
WHF
WHF
WHIP
SHNK
GTCH
THAT'S RIGHT! I'M OVER HERE!

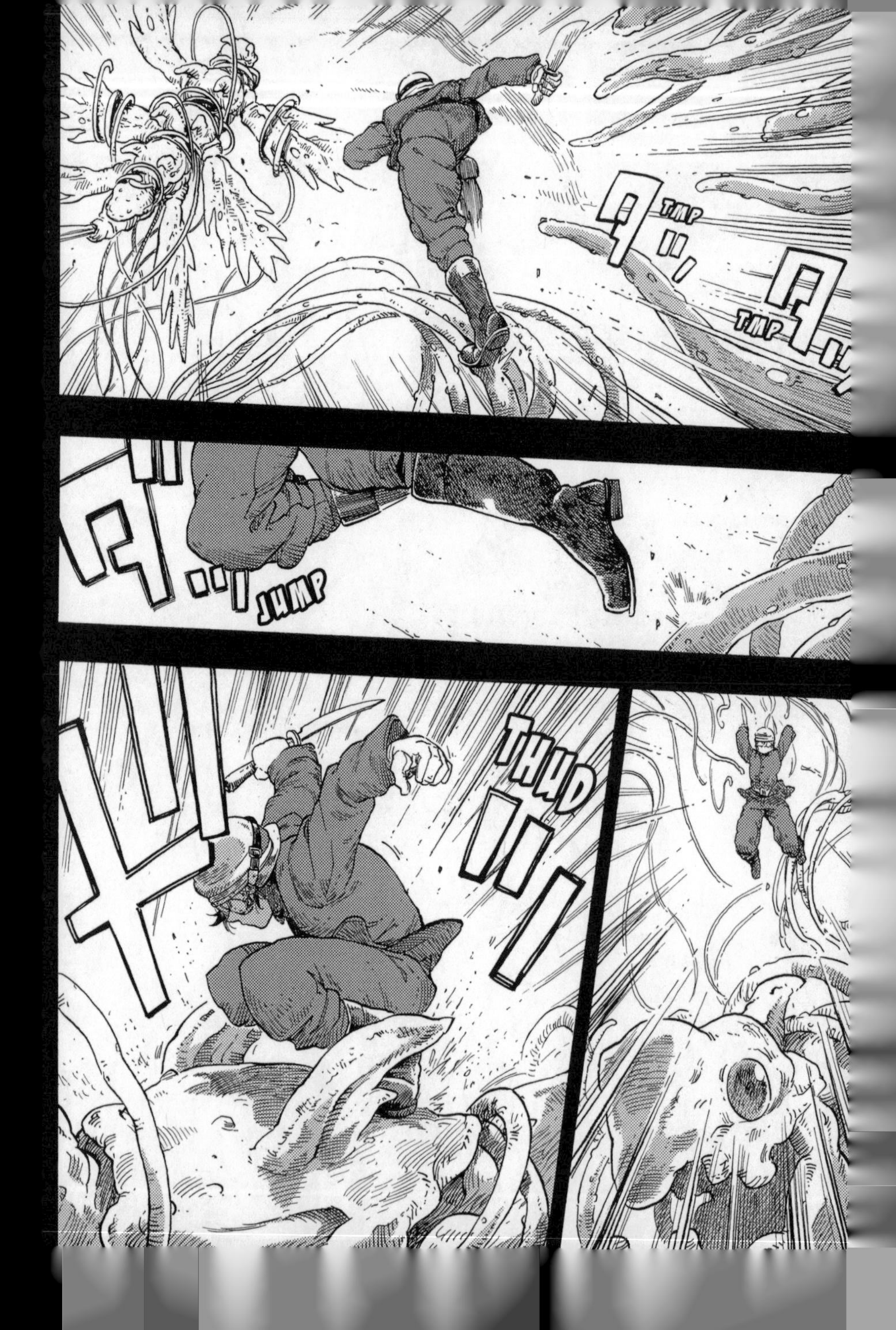
TMP
TMP
JUMP
THUD

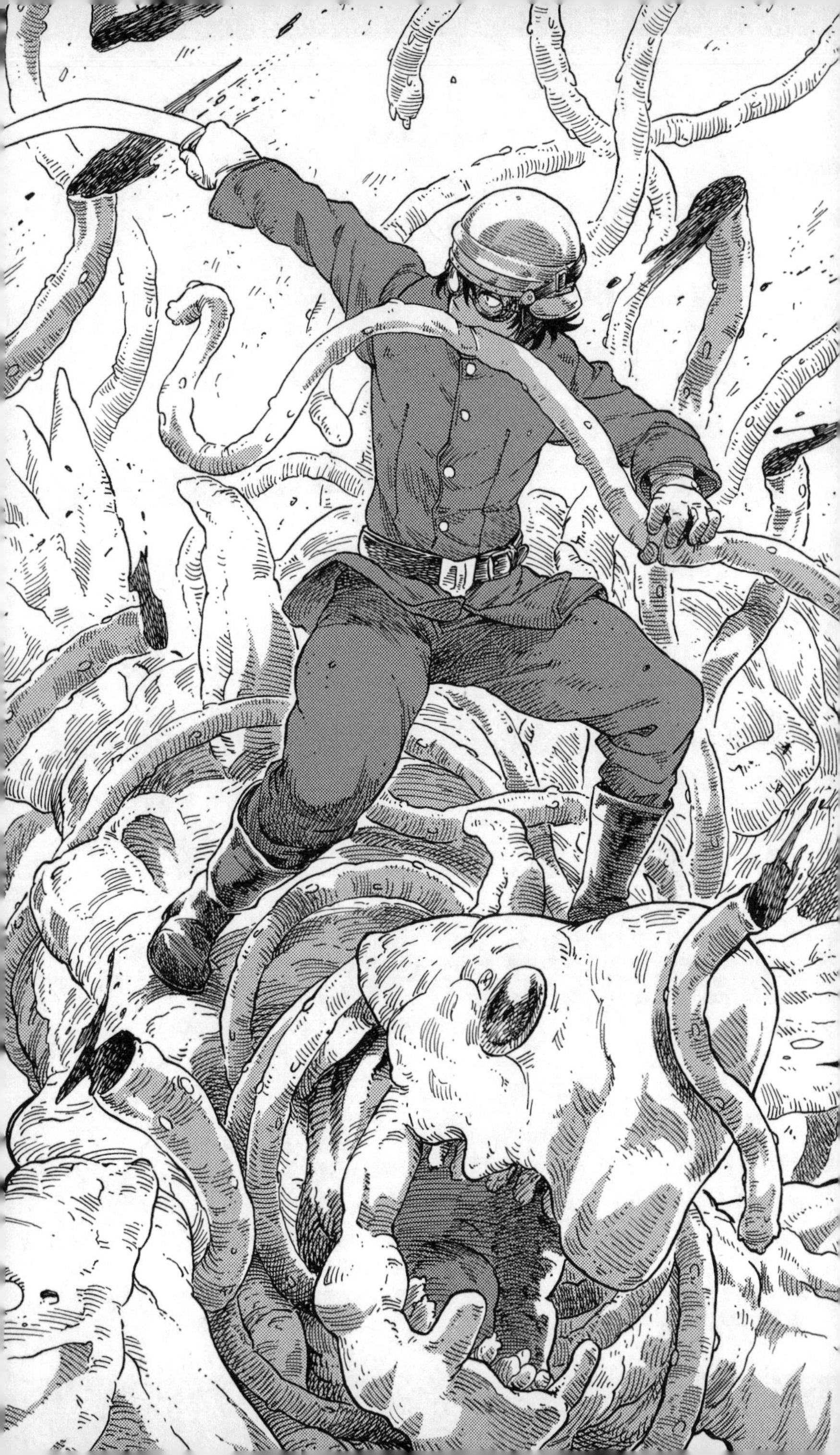

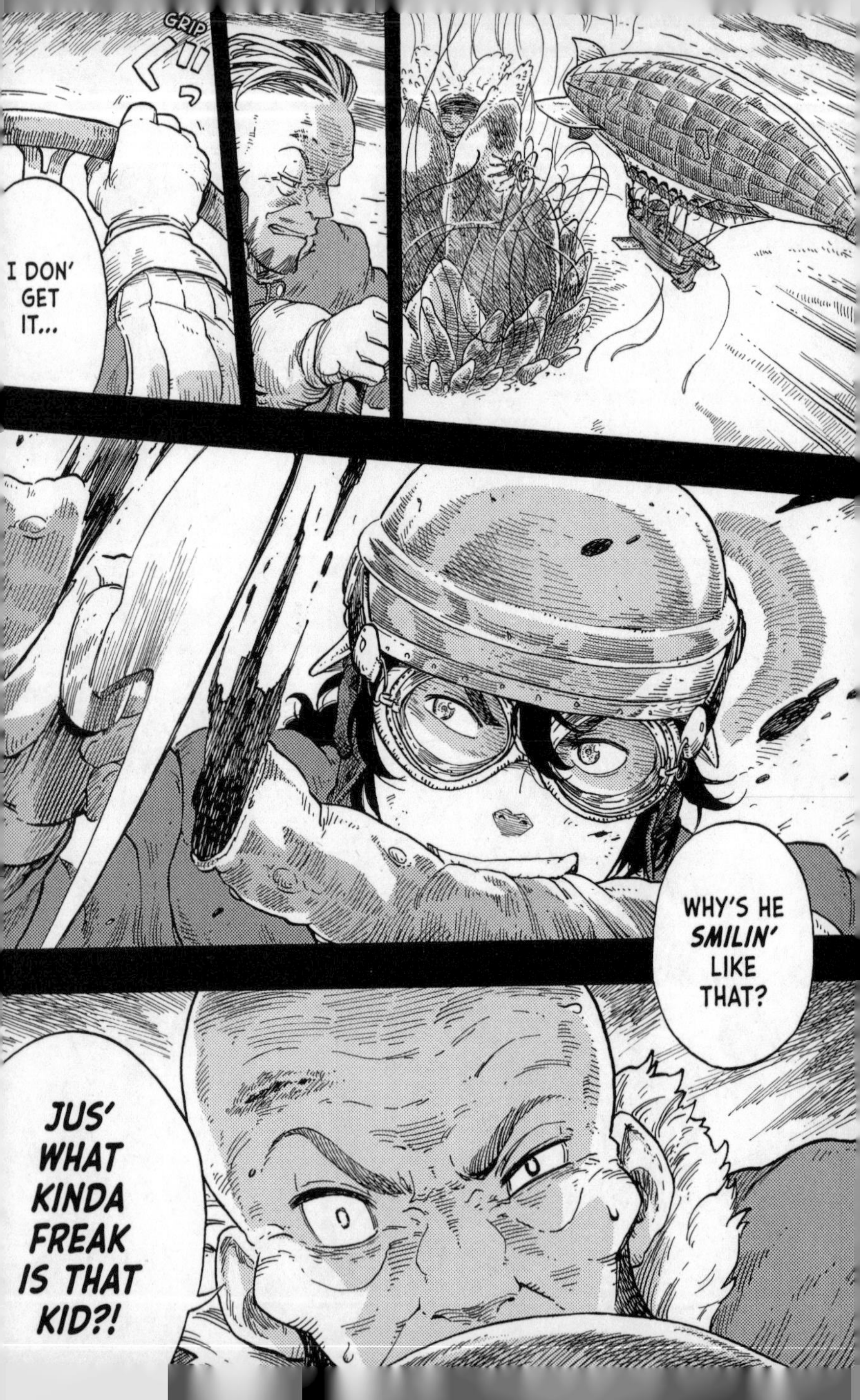
GRIP
I DON' GET IT...
WHY'S HE SMILIN' LIKE THAT?
JUS' WHAT KINDA FREAK IS THAT KID?!

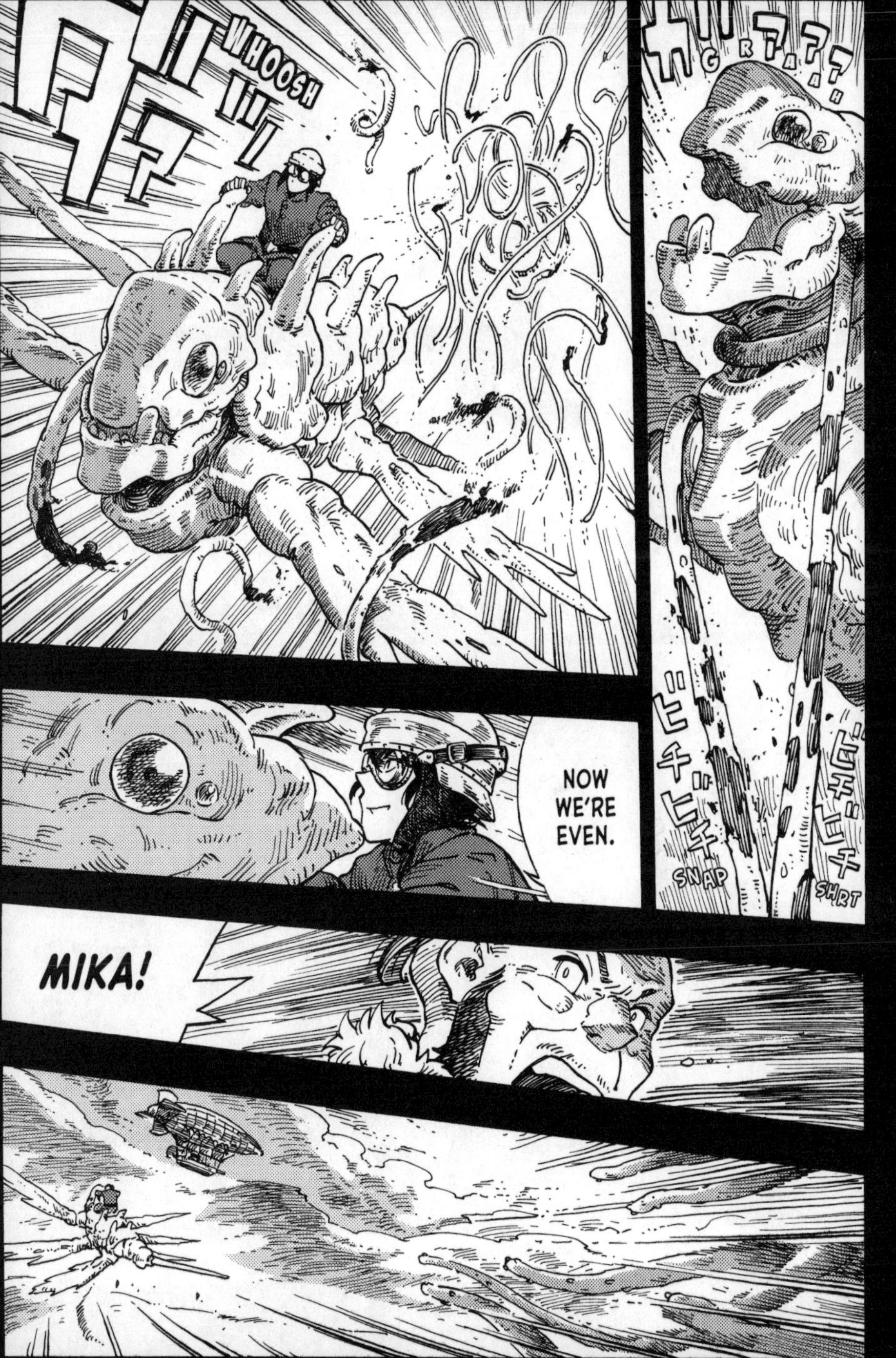
GRAAH
SNAP
SHRT
WHOOSH
NOW WE'RE EVEN.
MIKA!

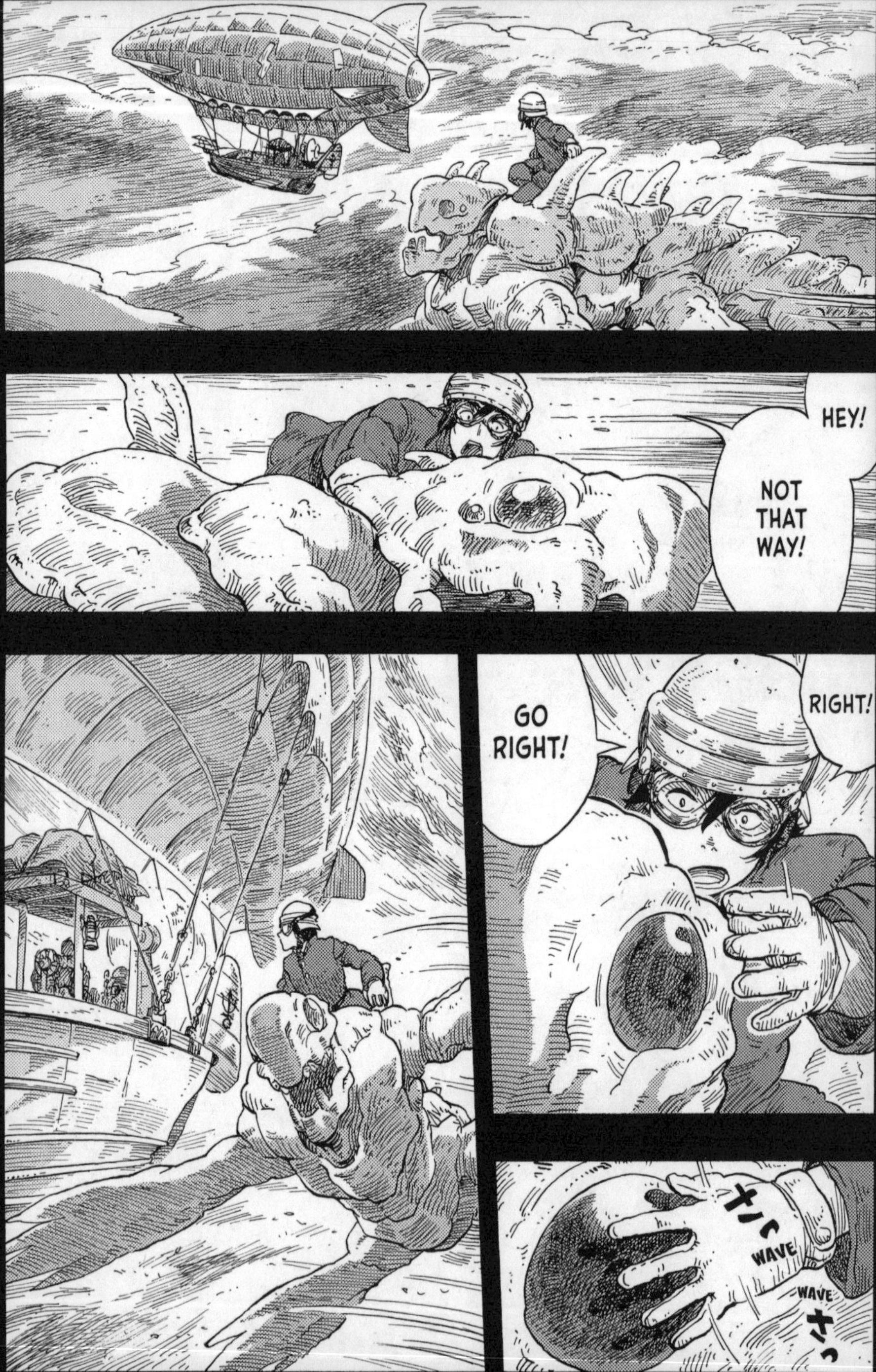
HEY!
NOT THAT WAY!
RIGHT!
GO RIGHT!
WAVE
WAVE

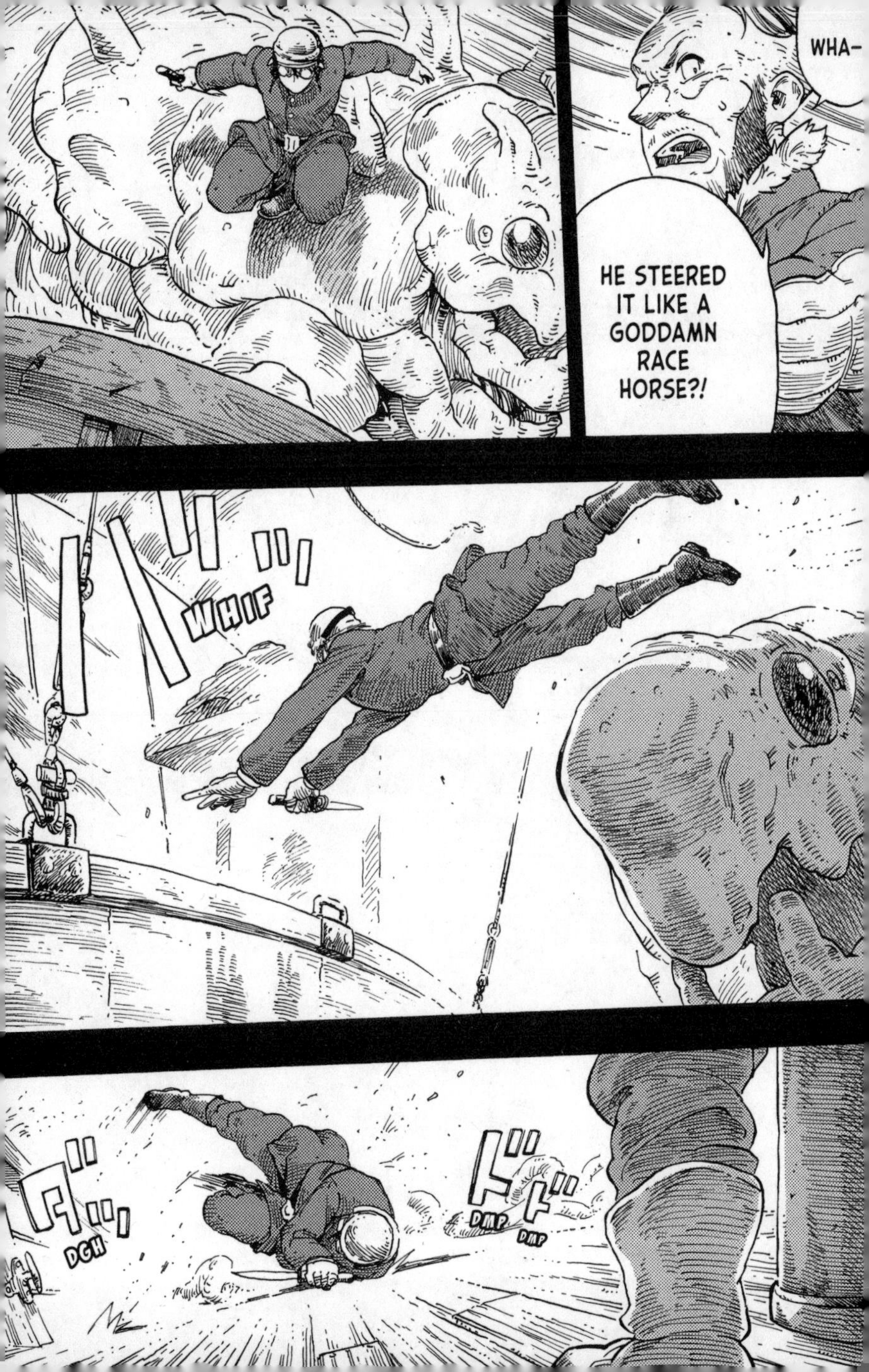
WHA-
HE STEERED IT LIKE A GODDAMN RACE HORSE?!
WHIF
DMP
DMP
DGH

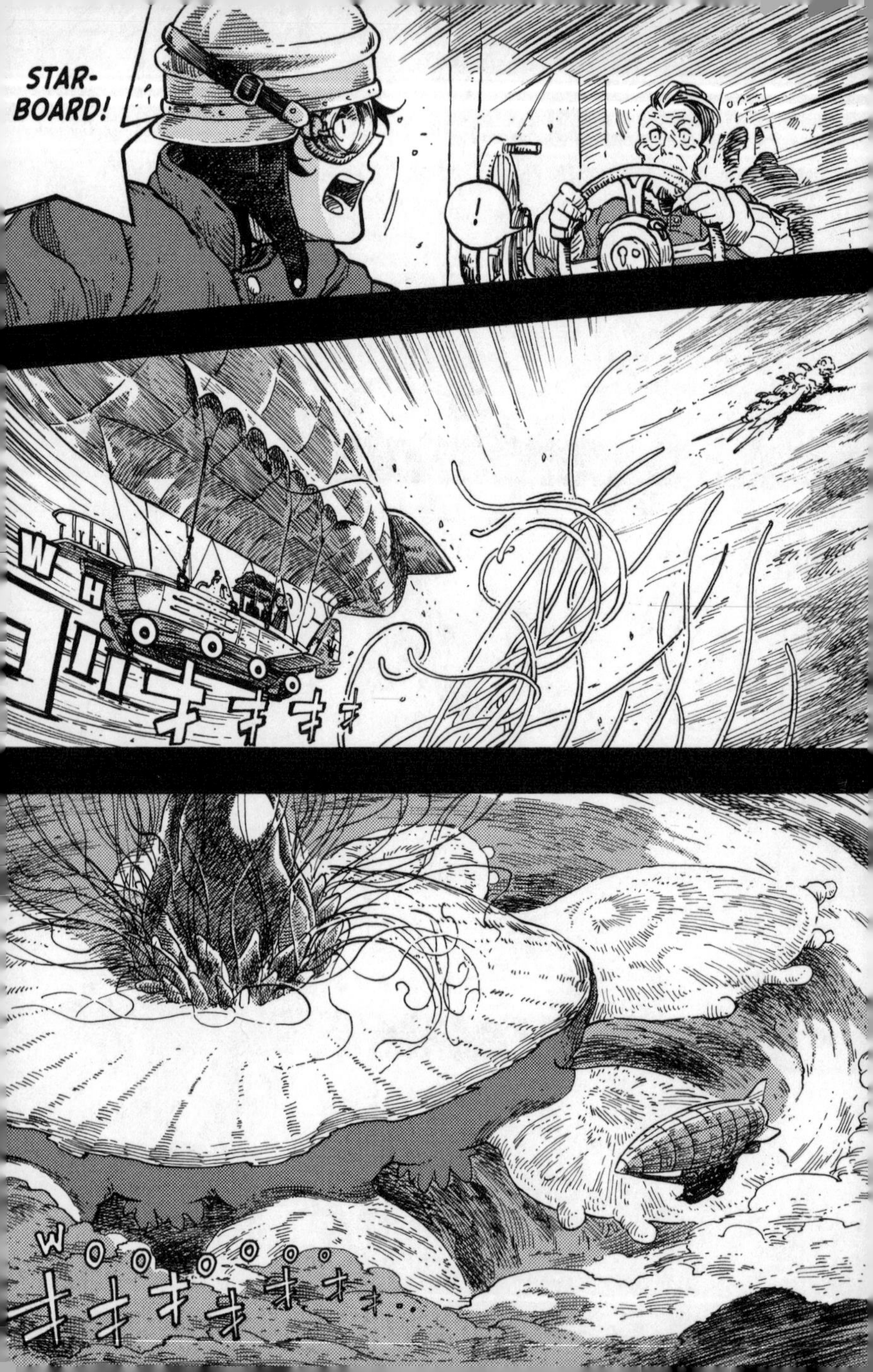
STAR-BOARD!
!
W H
WOOOOOO

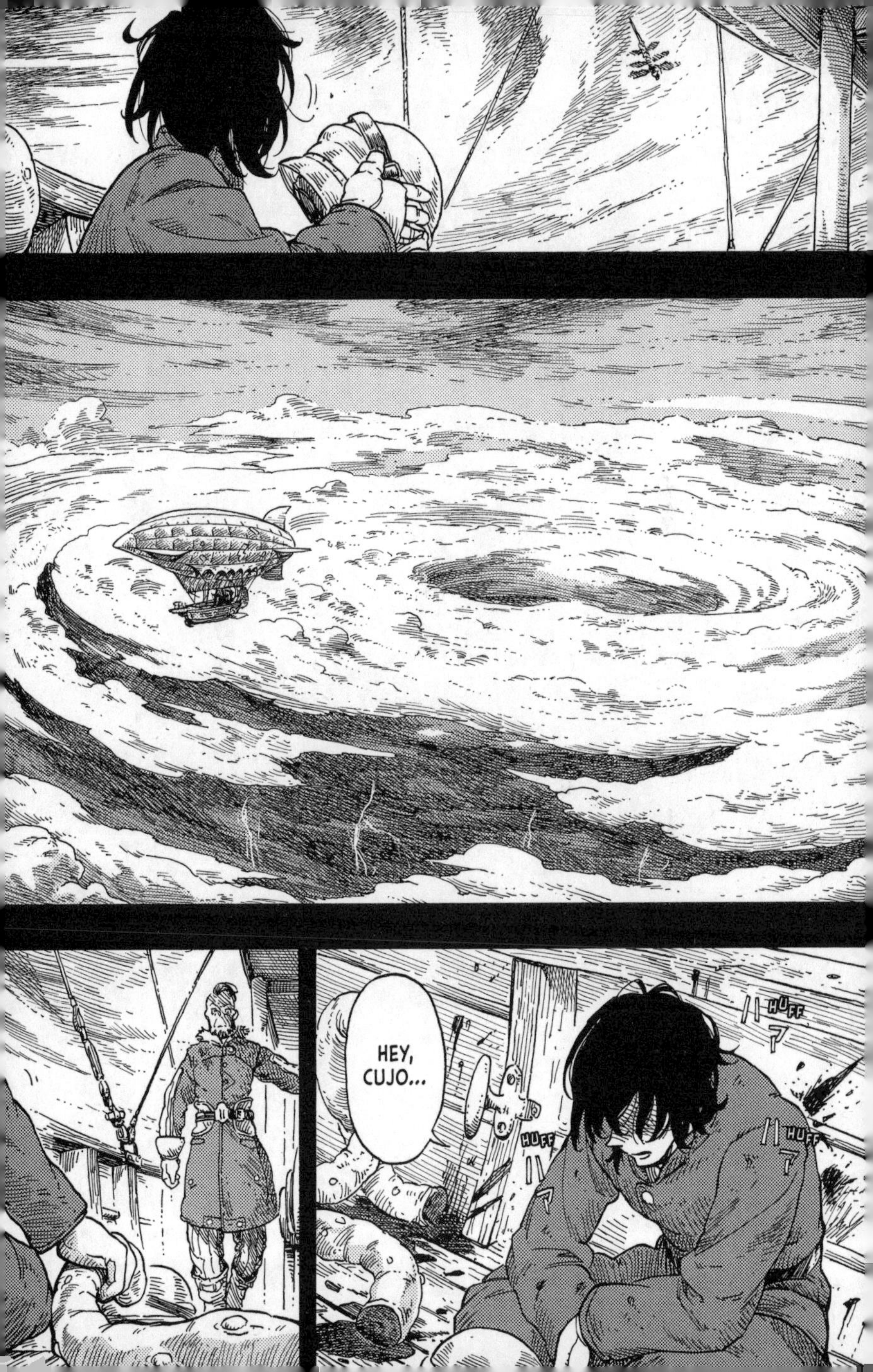
HUFF
HEY, CUJO...
HUFF
HUFF

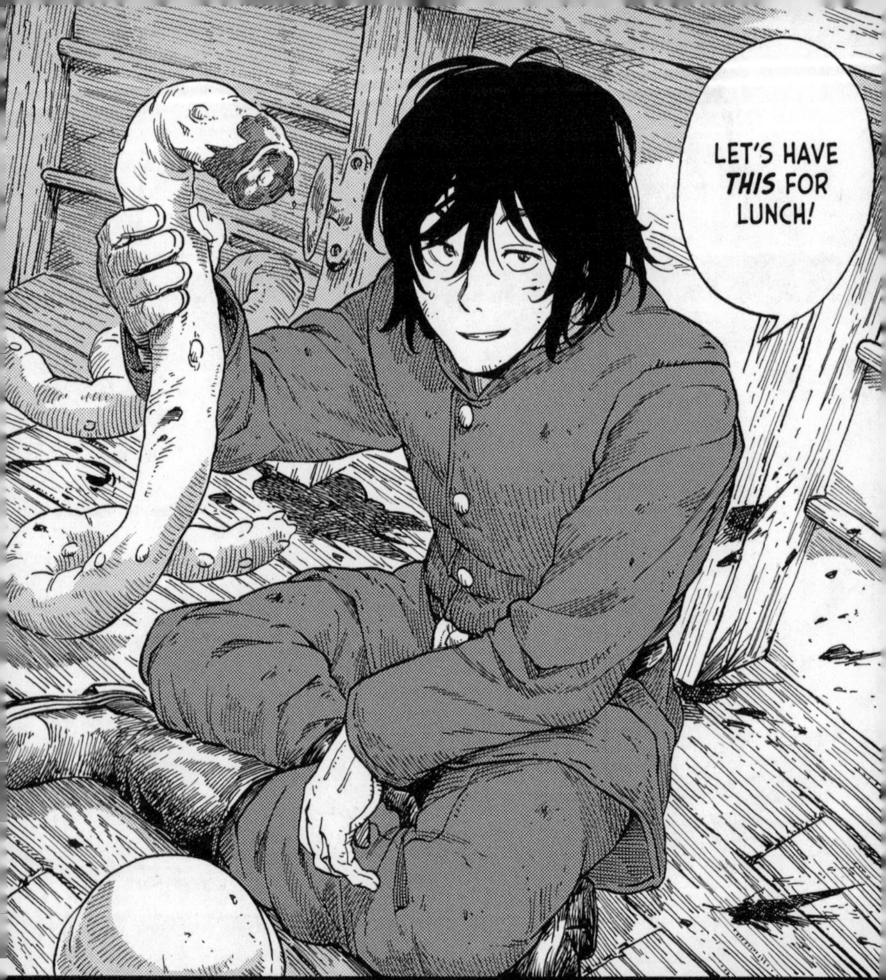
LET'S HAVE THIS FOR LUNCH!
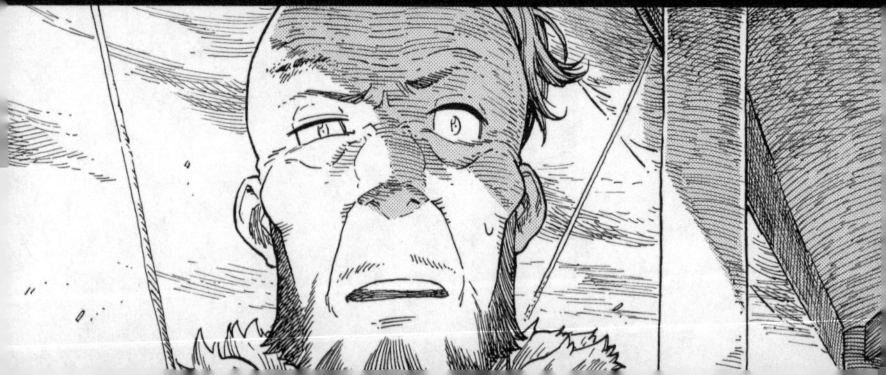

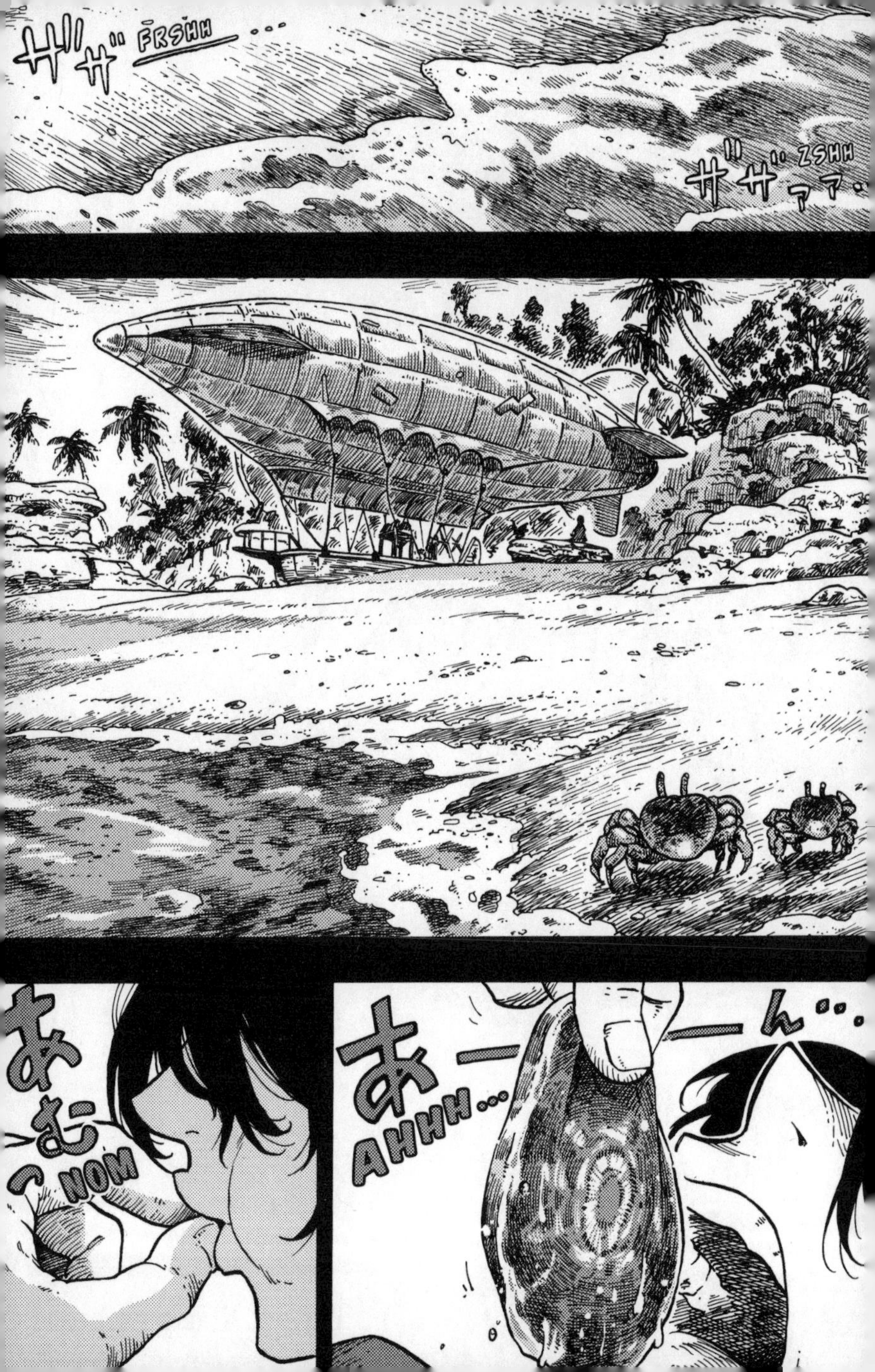
ザザ FRSHH...
ザザァア・ ZSHH
あーーーん‥ AHHH...
あむ NOM

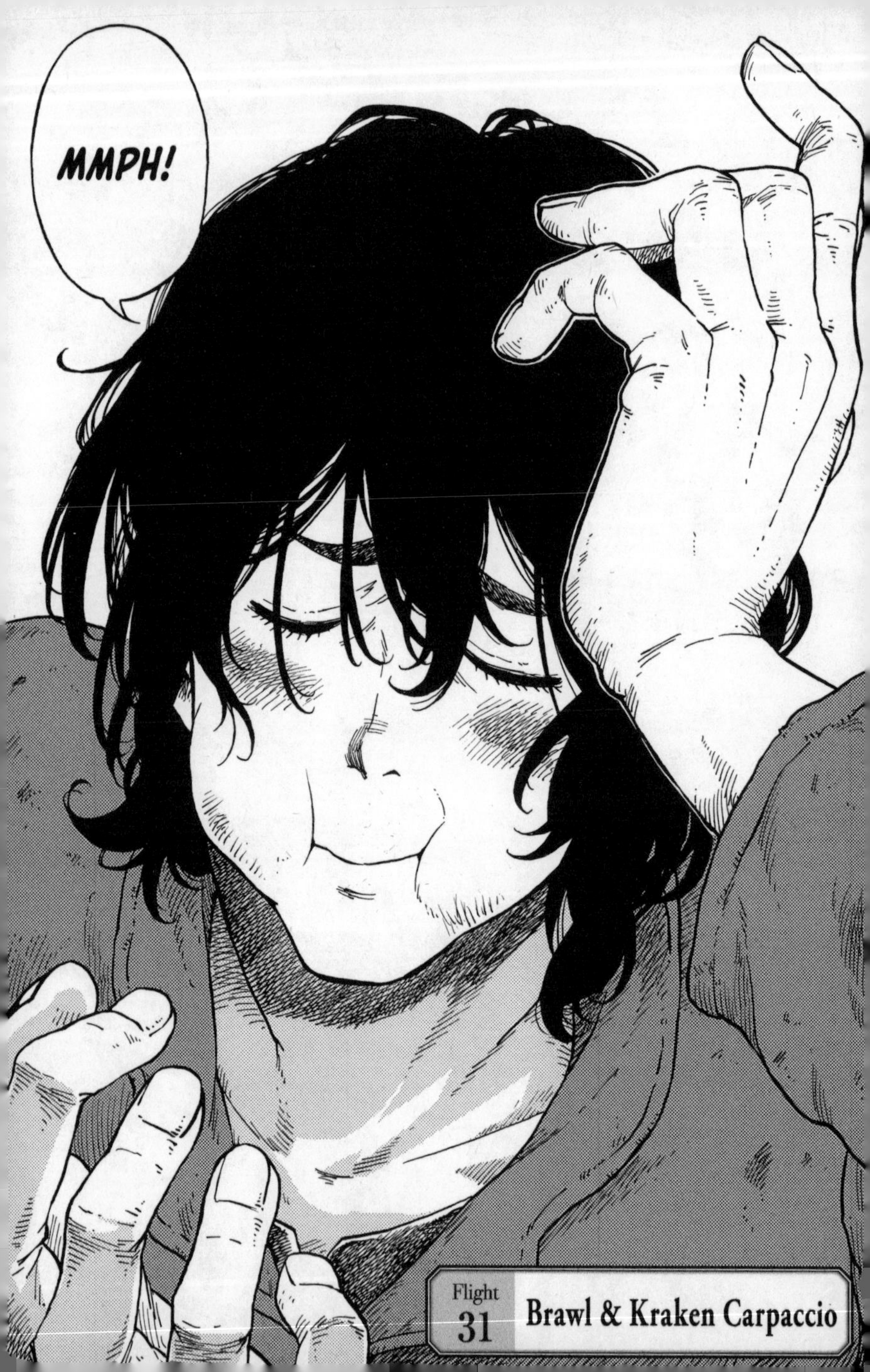
MMPH!
Flight 31
Brawl & Kraken Carpaccio

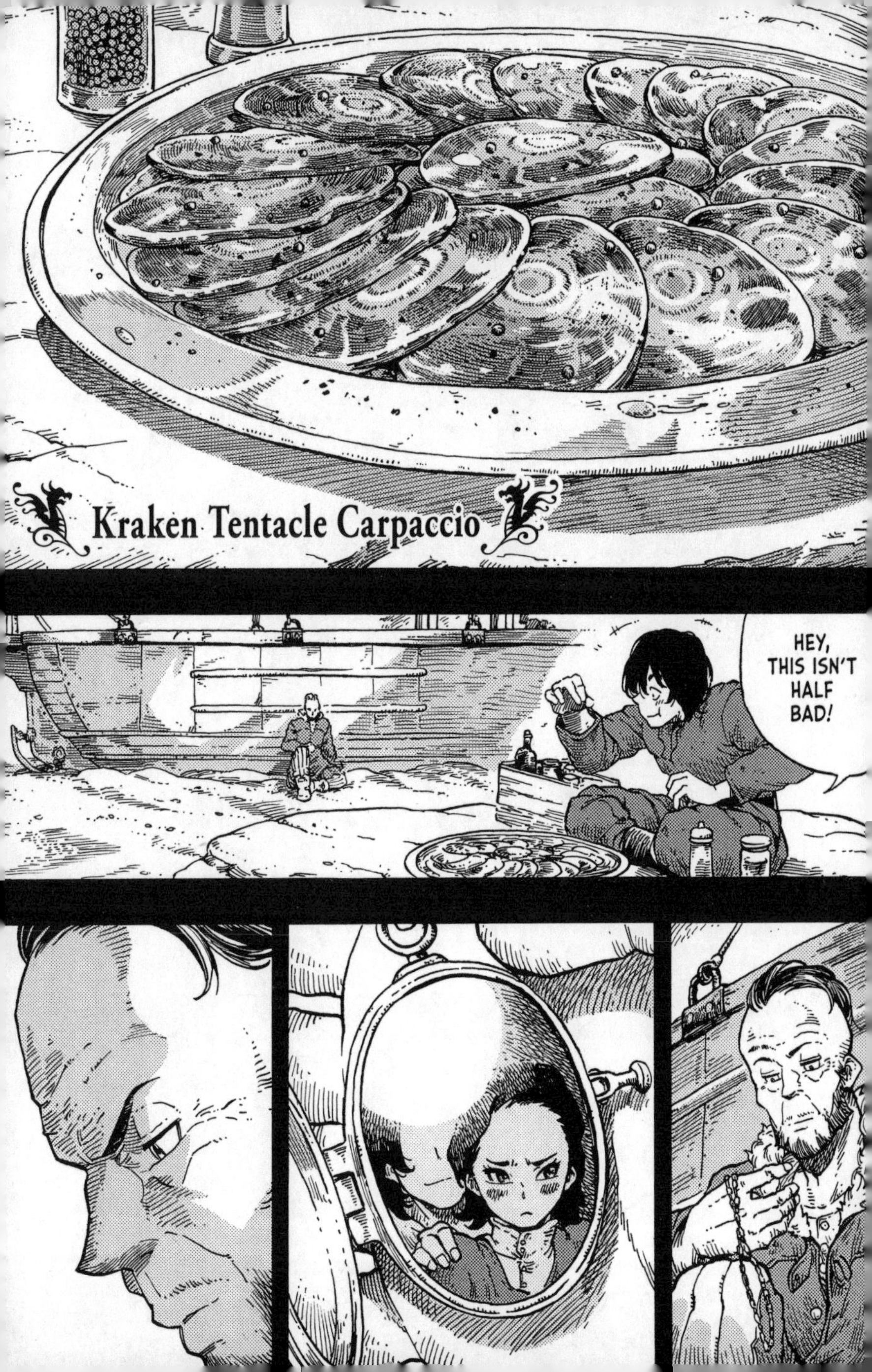
Kraken Tentacle Carpaccio
HEY, THIS ISN'T HALF BAD!

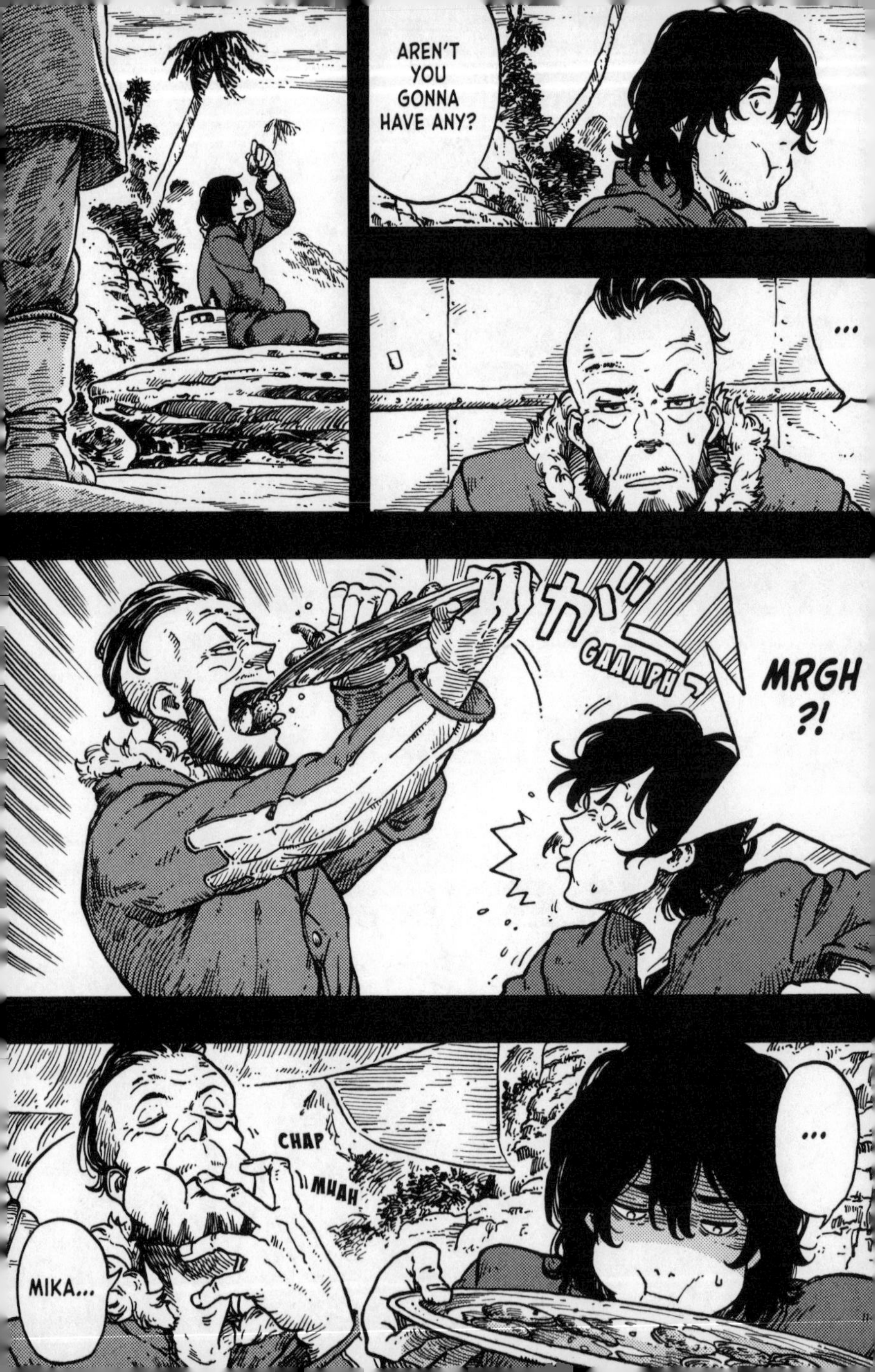

AREN'T YOU GONNA HAVE ANY?
...
ガー
GAAMPH
MRGH ?!
...
CHAP
MUAH
MIKA...

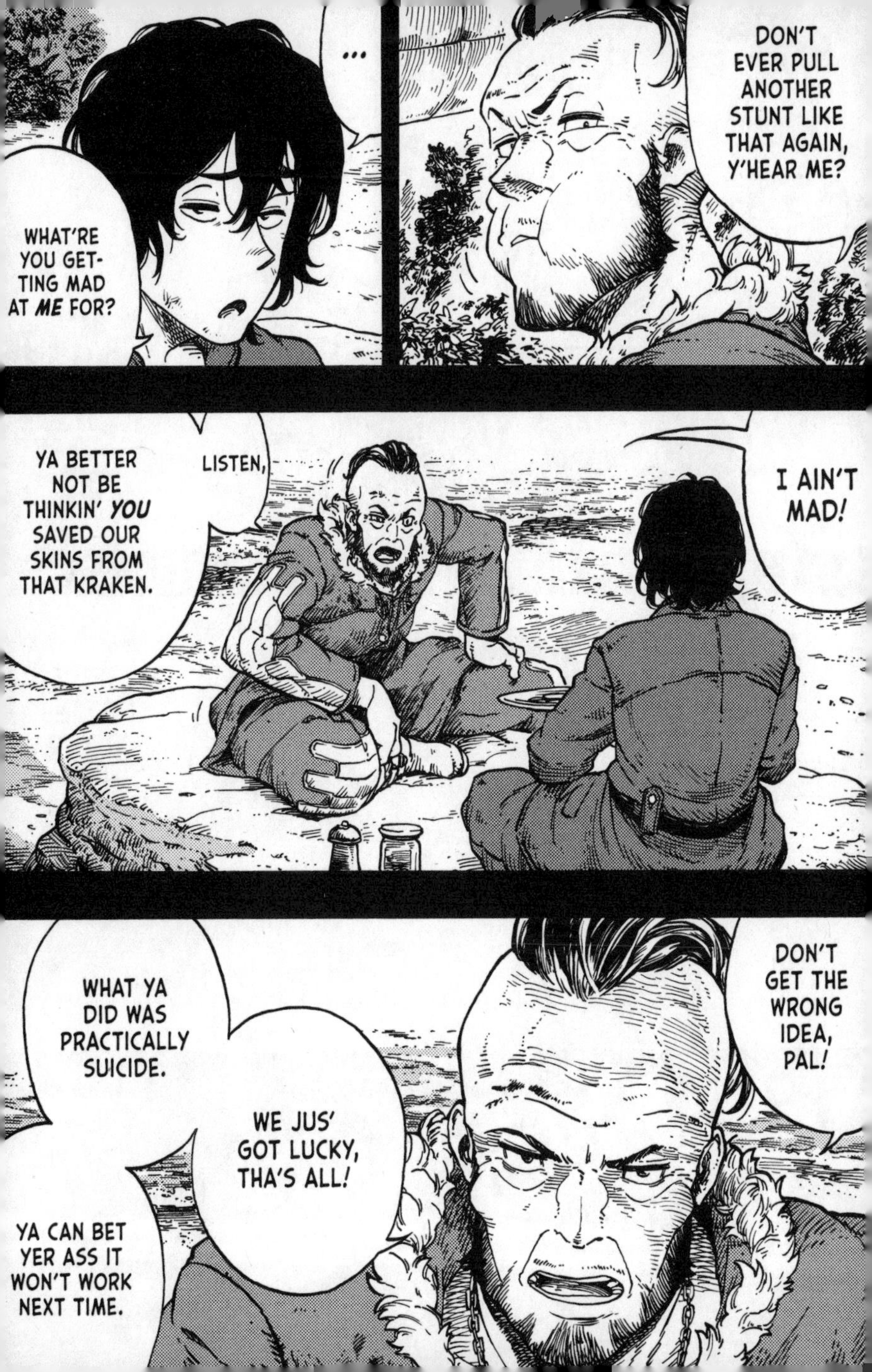
DON'T EVER PULL ANOTHER STUNT LIKE THAT AGAIN, Y'HEAR ME?
...
WHAT'RE YOU GET-TING MAD AT *ME* FOR?
I AIN'T MAD!
LISTEN,
YA BETTER NOT BE THINKIN' *YOU* SAVED OUR SKINS FROM THAT KRAKEN.
DON'T GET THE WRONG IDEA, PAL!
WHAT YA DID WAS PRACTICALLY SUICIDE.
WE JUS' GOT LUCKY, THA'S ALL!
YA CAN BET YER ASS IT WON'T WORK NEXT TIME.

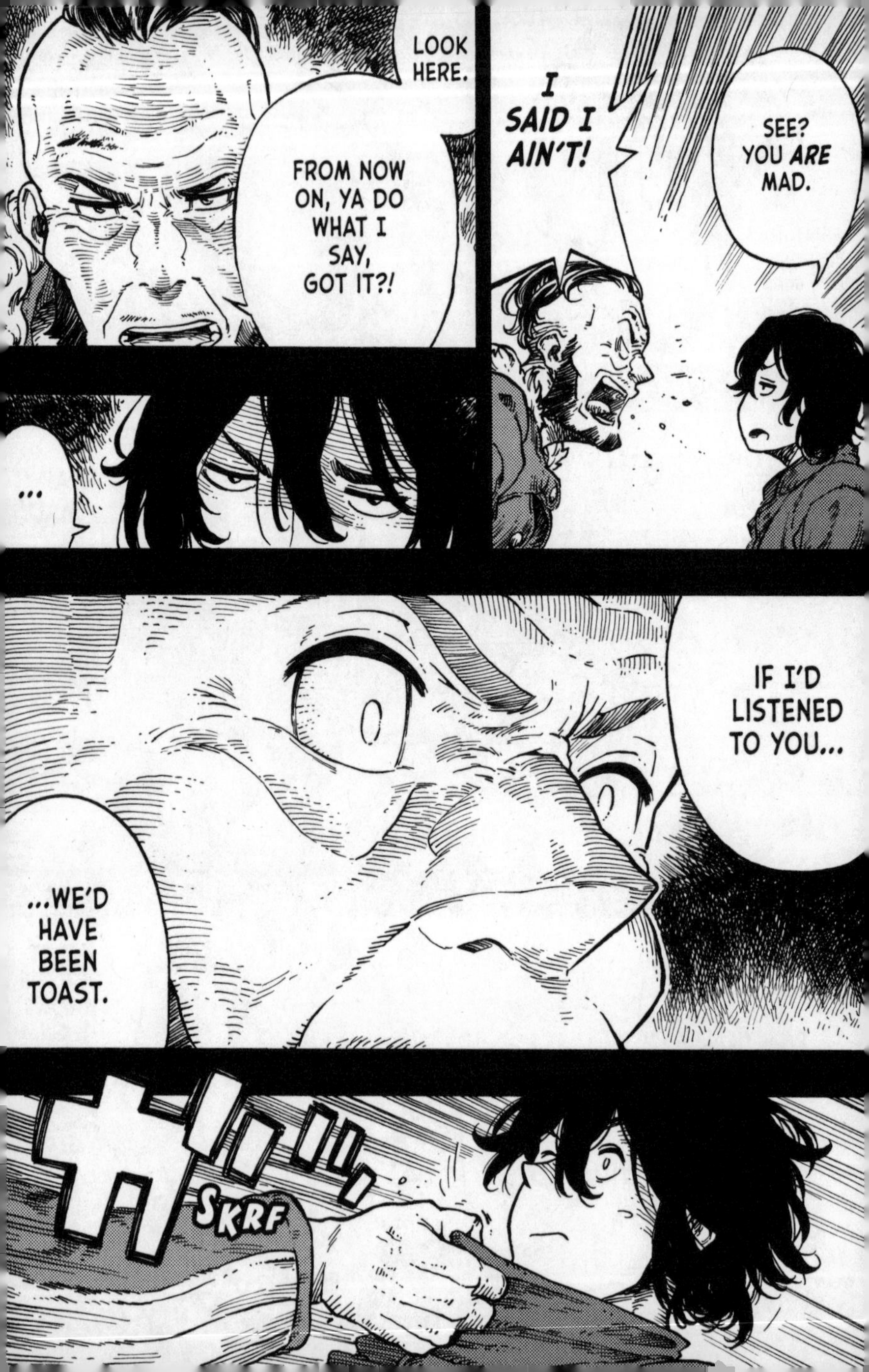
I SAID I AIN'T!
SEE? YOU *ARE* MAD.
LOOK HERE.
FROM NOW ON, YA DO WHAT I SAY, GOT IT?!
...
IF I'D LISTENED TO YOU...
...WE'D HAVE BEEN TOAST.
SKRF

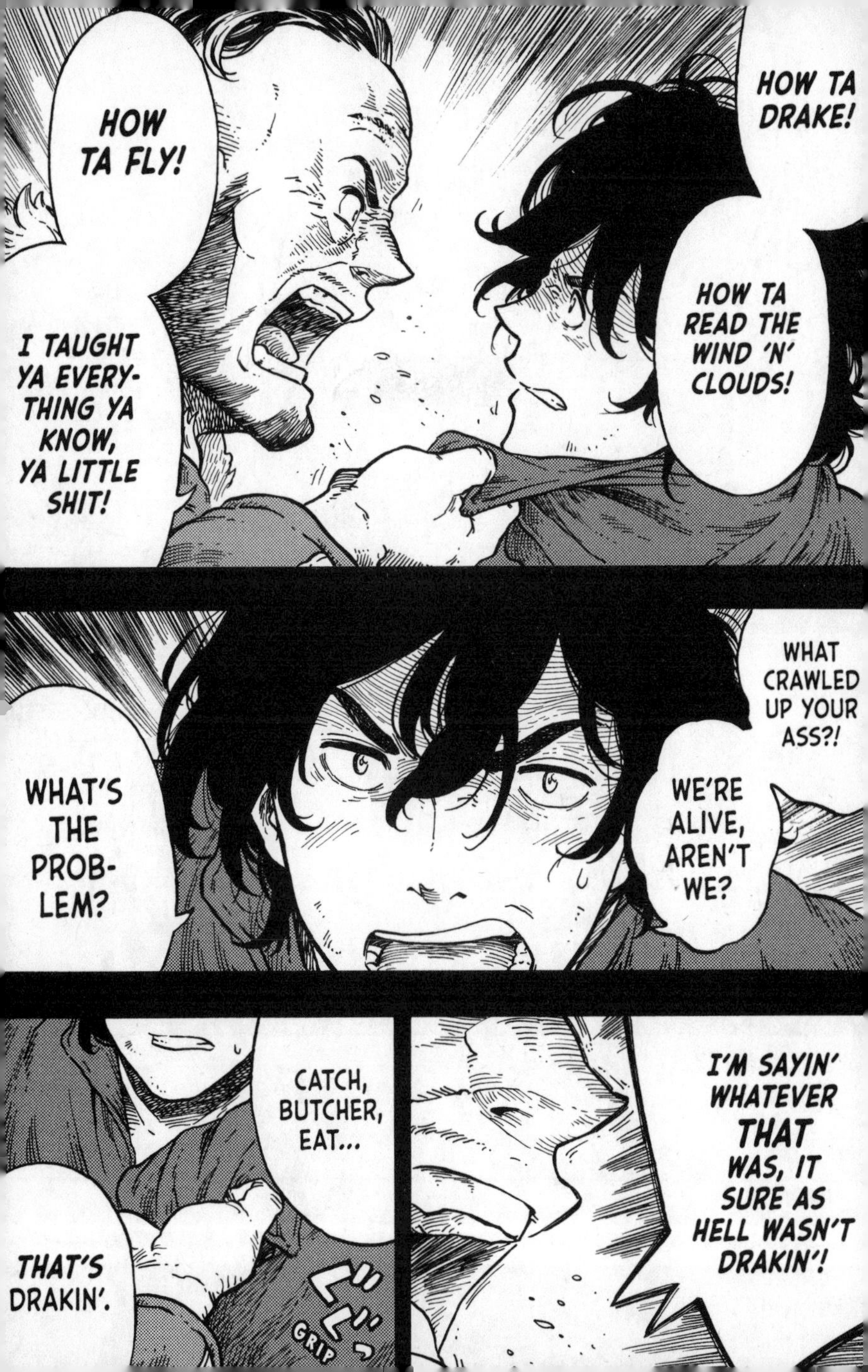
HOW TA DRAKE!
HOW TA READ THE WIND 'N' CLOUDS!
HOW TA FLY!
I TAUGHT YA EVERYTHING YA KNOW, YA LITTLE SHIT!
WHAT CRAWLED UP YOUR ASS?!
WE'RE ALIVE, AREN'T WE?
WHAT'S THE PROBLEM?
I'M SAYIN' WHATEVER THAT WAS, IT SURE AS HELL WASN'T DRAKIN'!
CATCH, BUTCHER, EAT...
THAT'S DRAKIN'.
GRIP

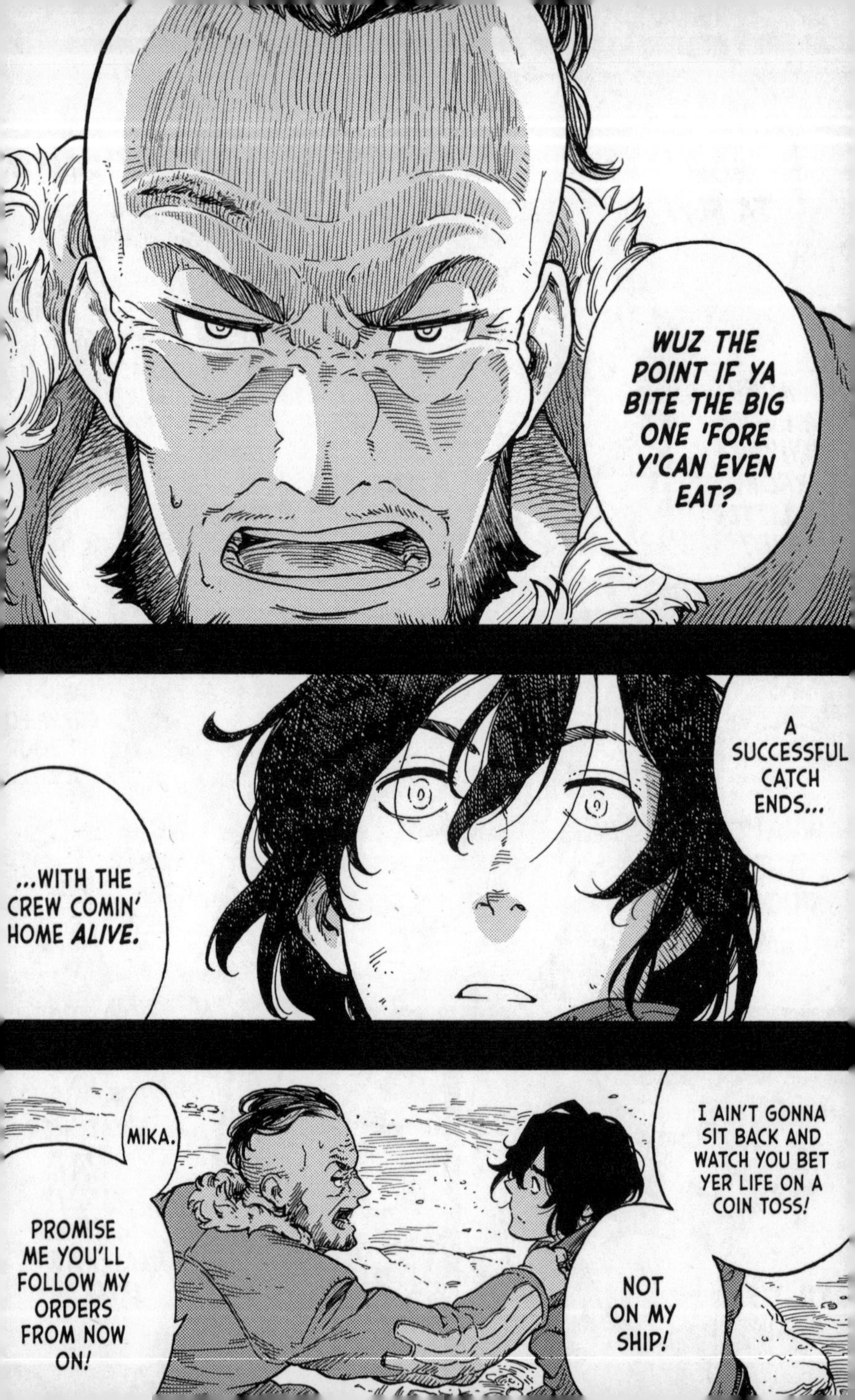
WUZ THE POINT IF YA BITE THE BIG ONE 'FORE Y'CAN EVEN EAT?
A SUCCESSFUL CATCH ENDS...
...WITH THE CREW COMIN' HOME *ALIVE.*
I AIN'T GONNA SIT BACK AND WATCH YOU BET YER LIFE ON A COIN TOSS!
NOT ON MY SHIP!
MIKA.
PROMISE ME YOU'LL FOLLOW MY ORDERS FROM NOW ON!

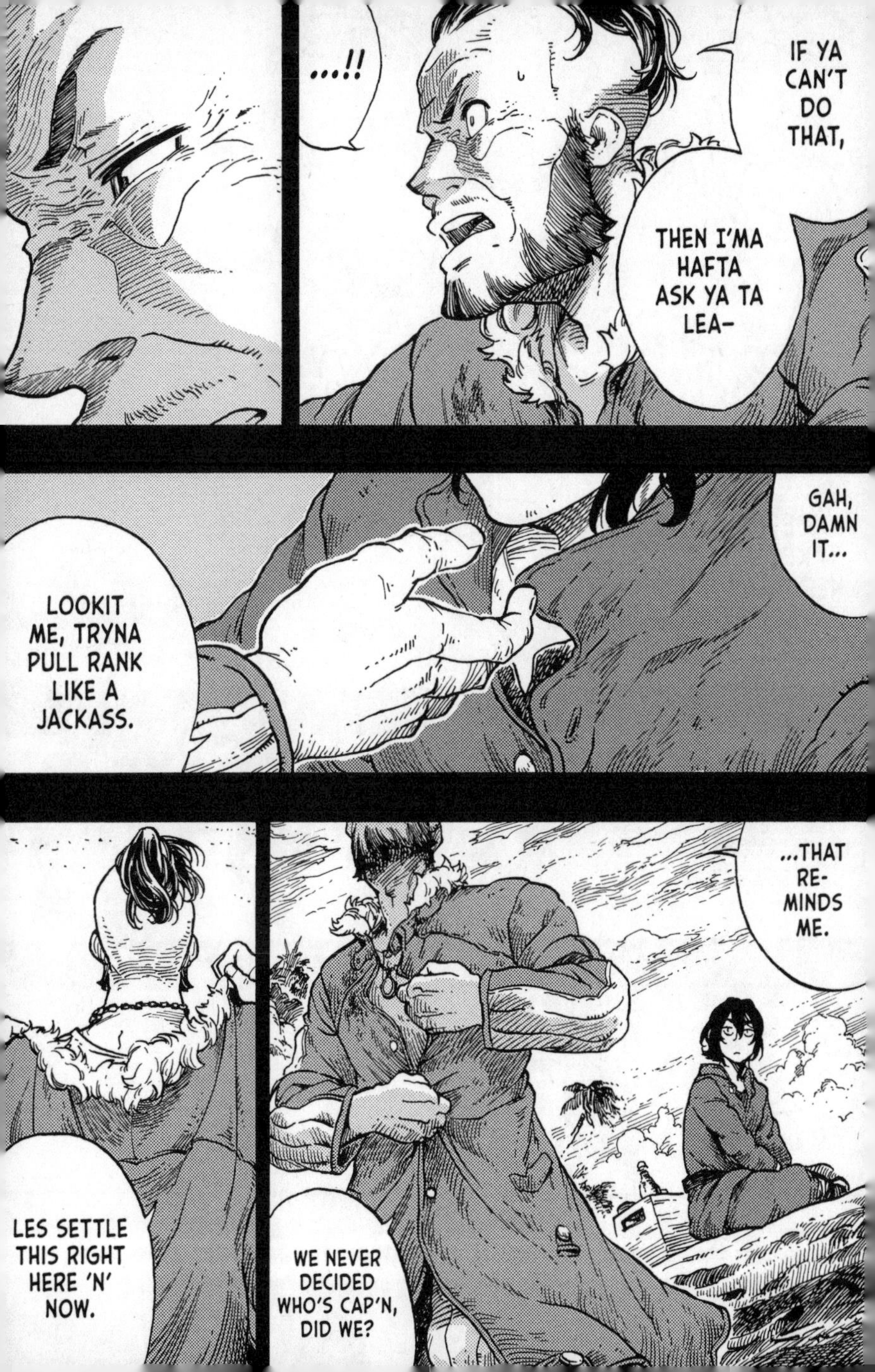
IF YA CAN'T DO THAT,
THEN I'MA HAFTA ASK YA TA LEA-
...!!
GAH, DAMN IT...
LOOKIT ME, TRYNA PULL RANK LIKE A JACKASS.
...THAT RE-MINDS ME.
WE NEVER DECIDED WHO'S CAP'N, DID WE?
LES SETTLE THIS RIGHT HERE 'N' NOW.

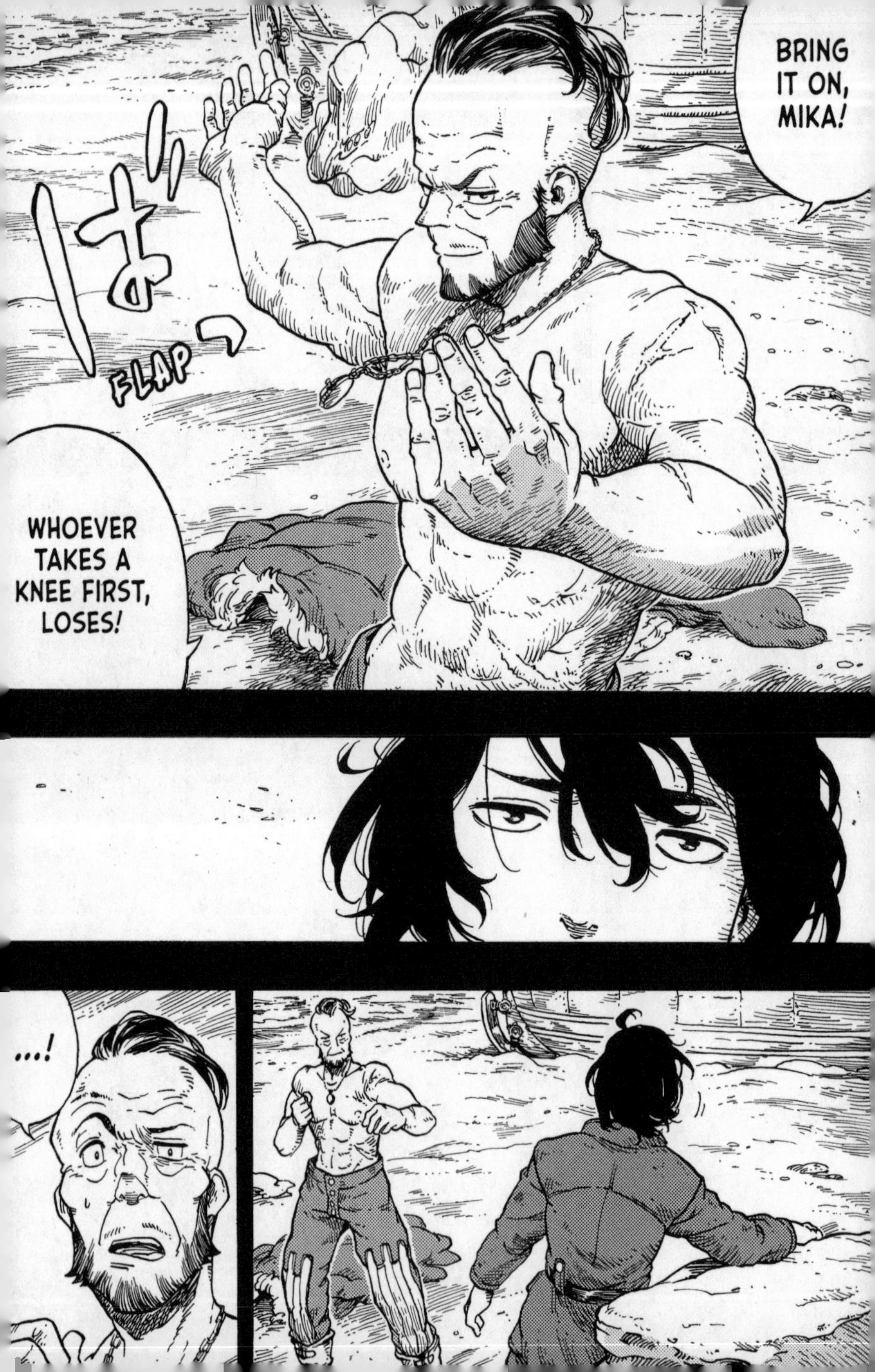
BRING IT ON, MIKA!
FLAP
WHOEVER TAKES A KNEE FIRST, LOSES!
...!

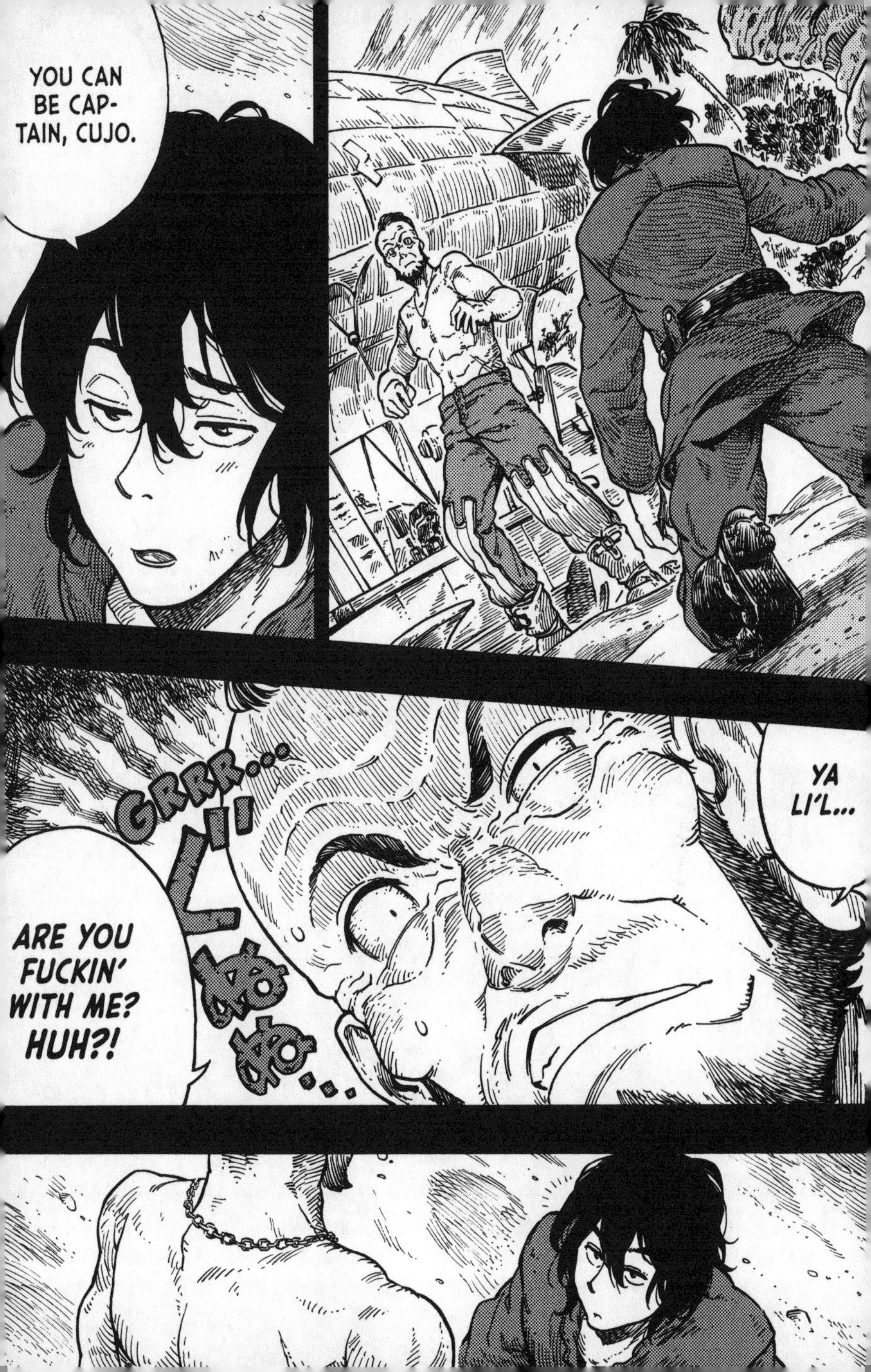
YOU CAN BE CAP-TAIN, CUJO.
YA LI'L...
GRRR...
ARE YOU FUCKIN' WITH ME? HUH?!

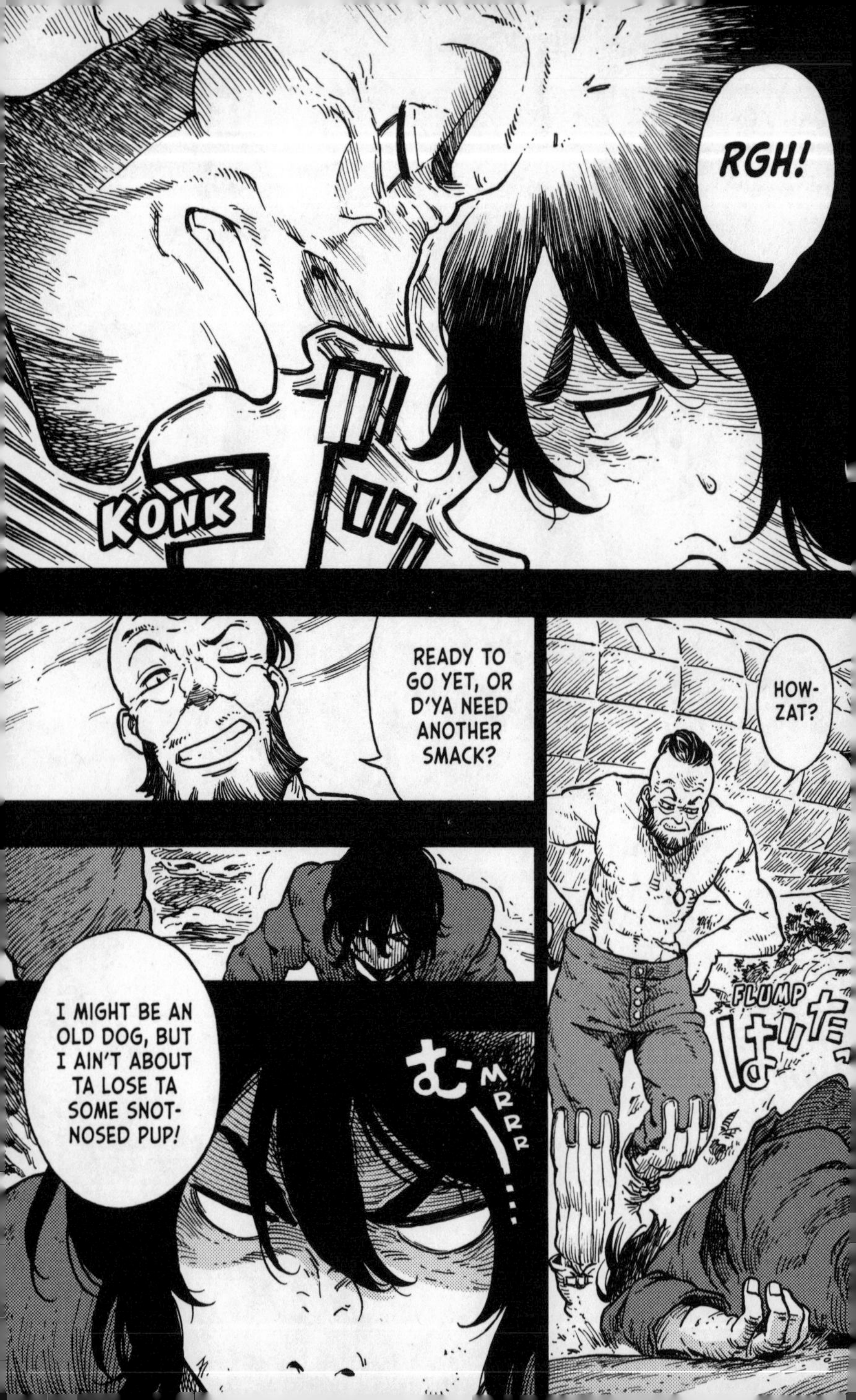
RGH!
KONK
HOW-ZAT?
FLUMP
READY TO GO YET, OR D'YA NEED ANOTHER SMACK?
I MIGHT BE AN OLD DOG, BUT I AIN'T ABOUT TA LOSE TA SOME SNOT-NOSED PUP!
むー
MRRR...

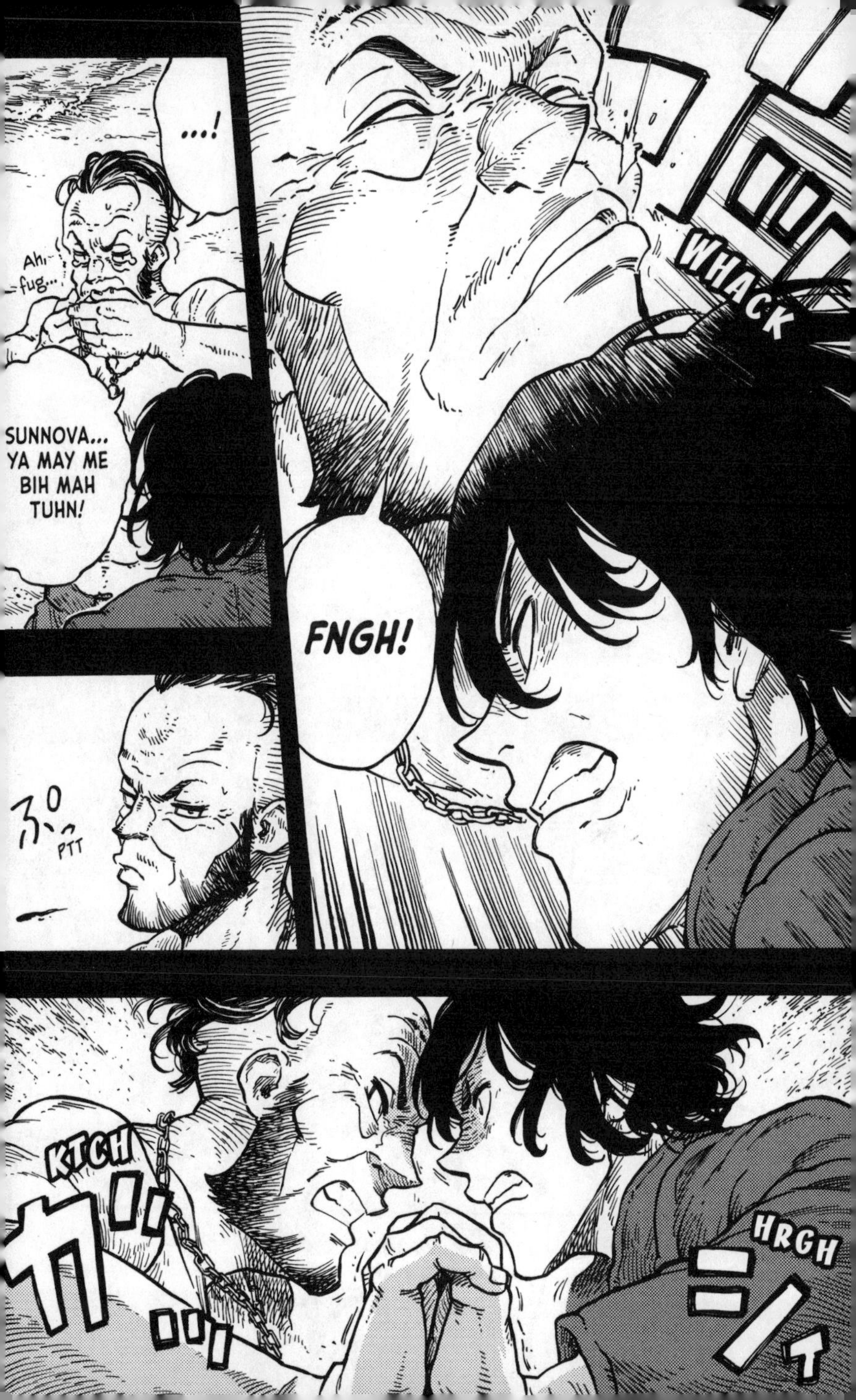
WHACK
FNGH!
...!
Ah, fug...
SUNNOVA... YA MAY ME BIH MAH TUHN!
PTT
HRGH
KTCH

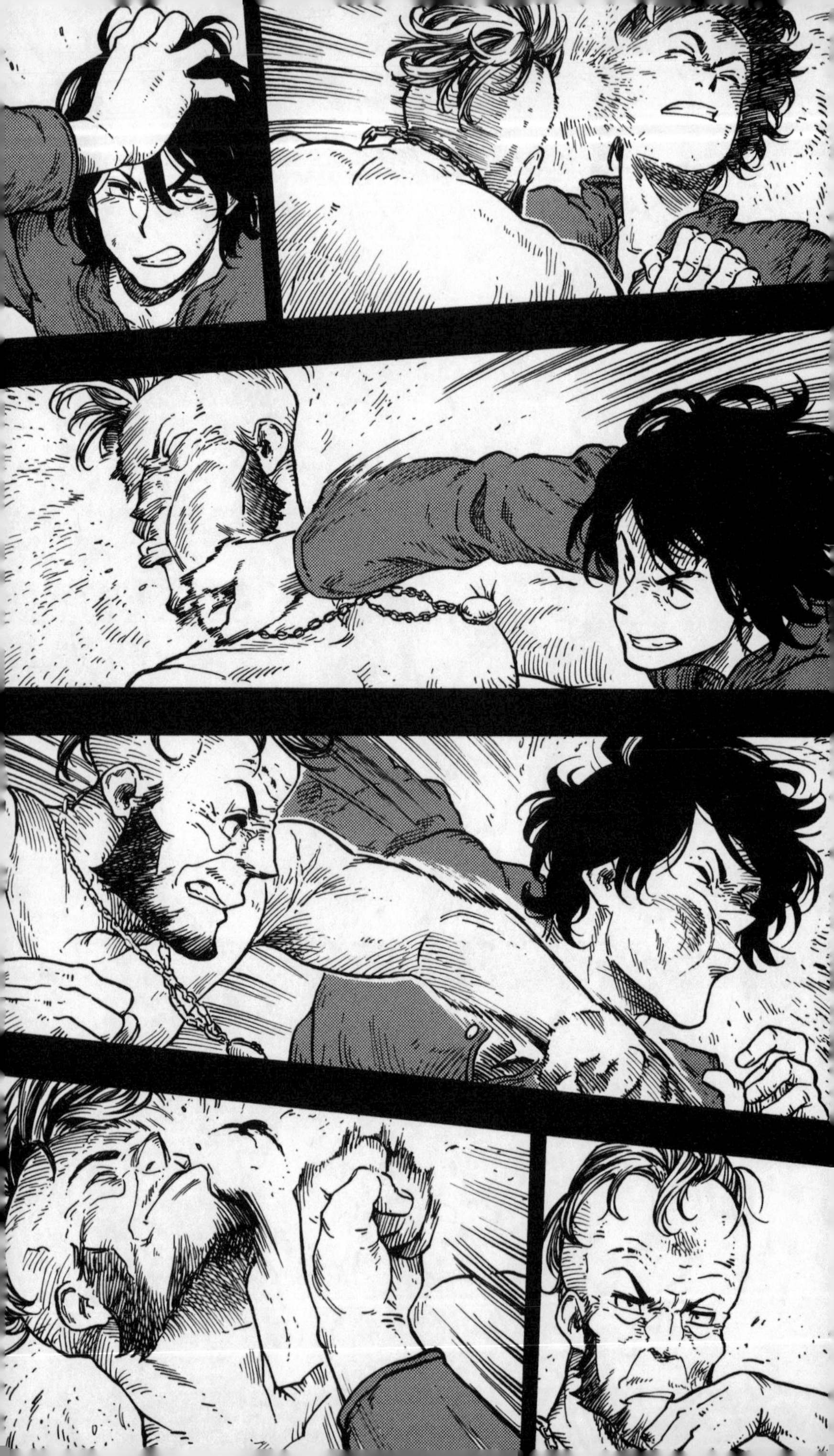

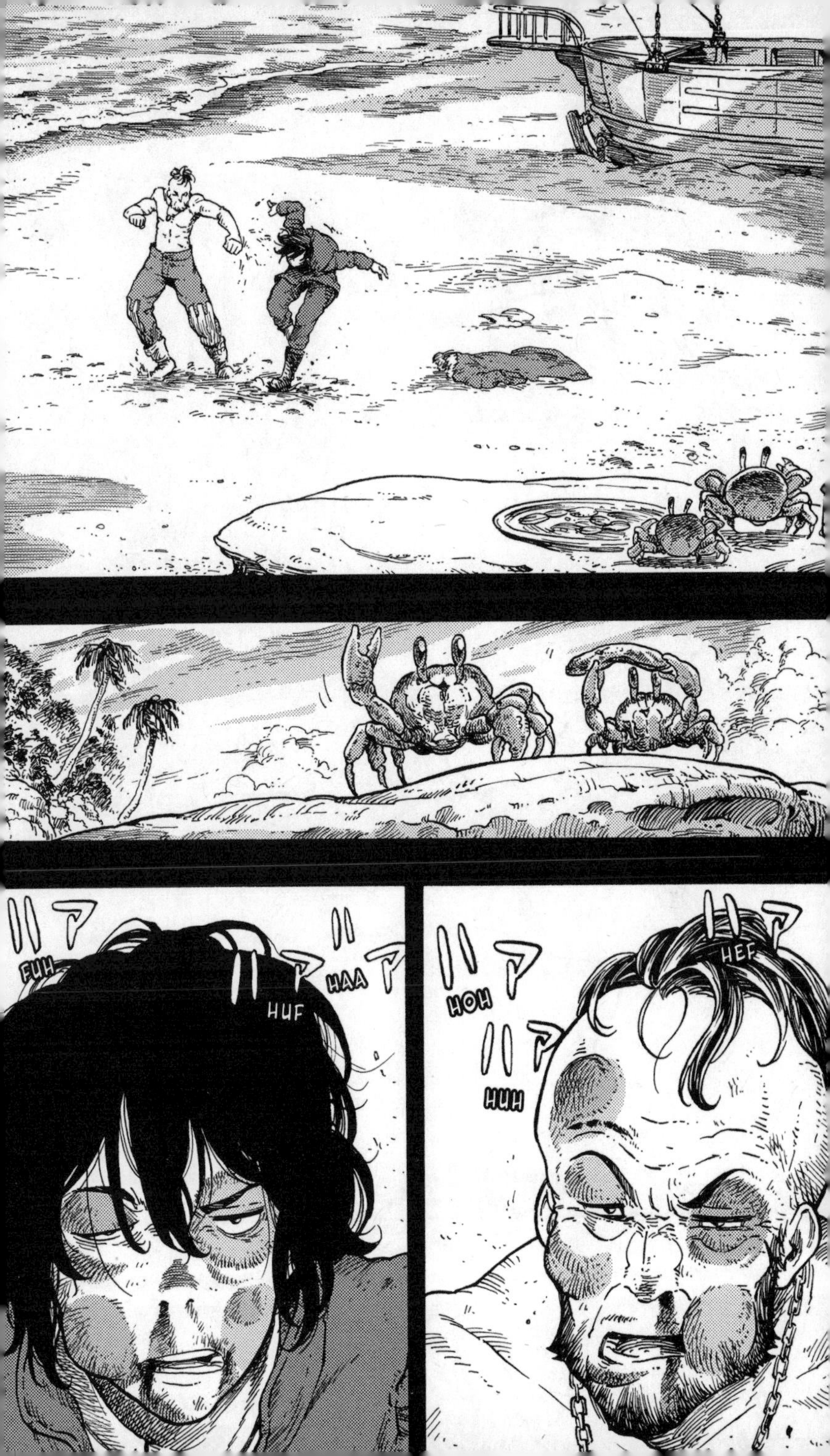
ハア
HEF
ハア
HOH
ハア
HUH
ハア
HAA
ハア
HUF
ハア
FUH

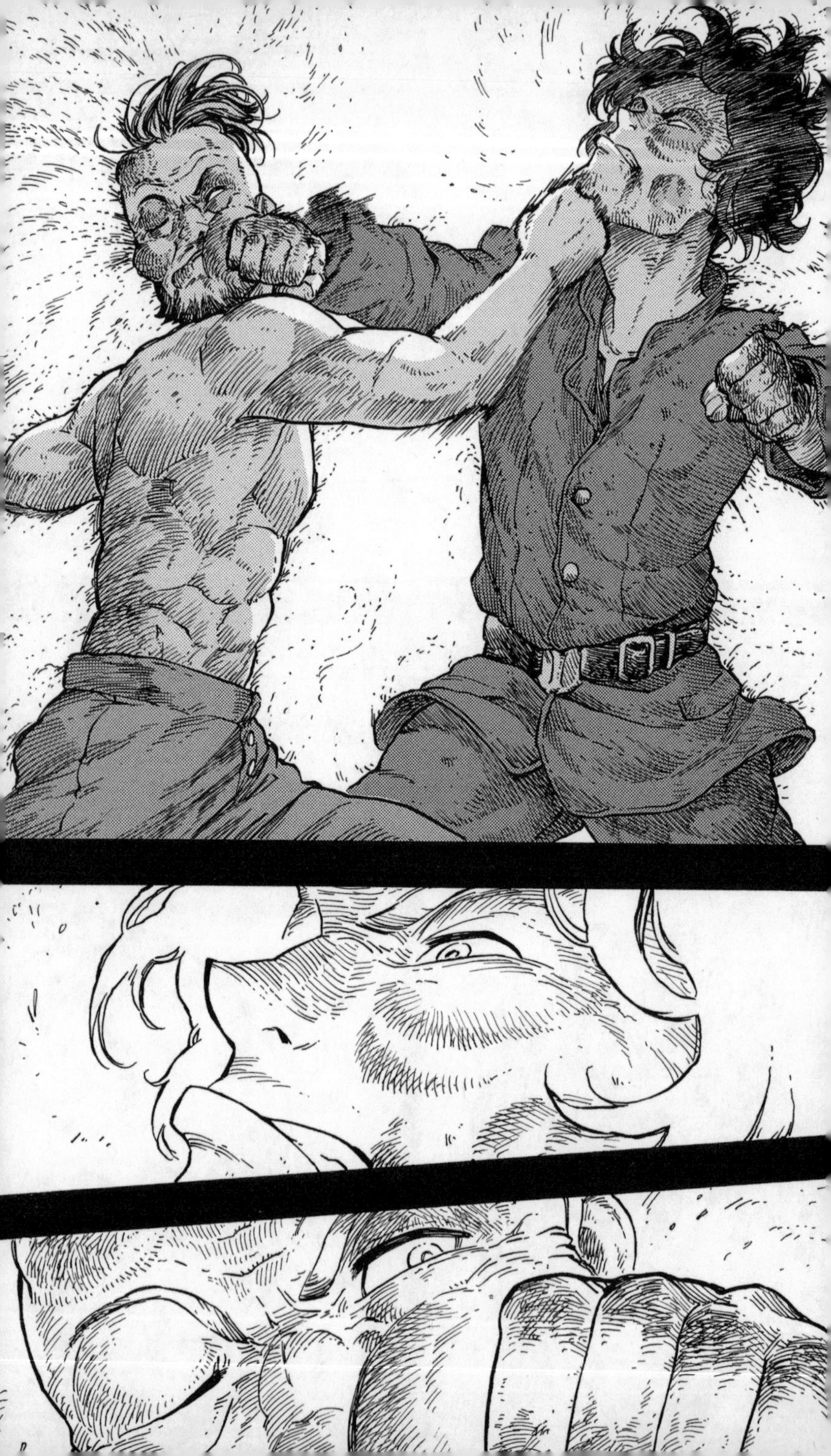

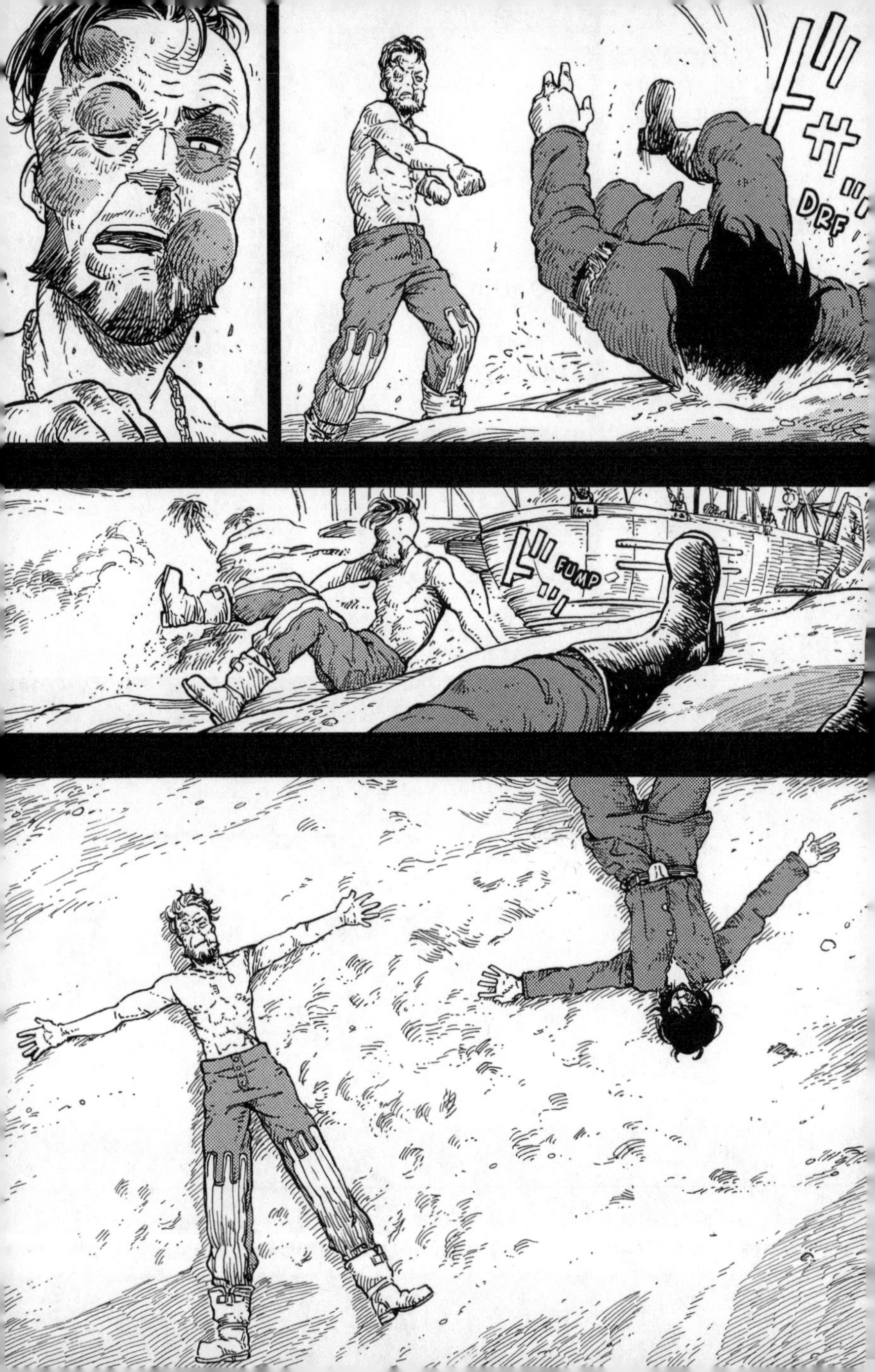
ドサ
DRF
ド
FUMP

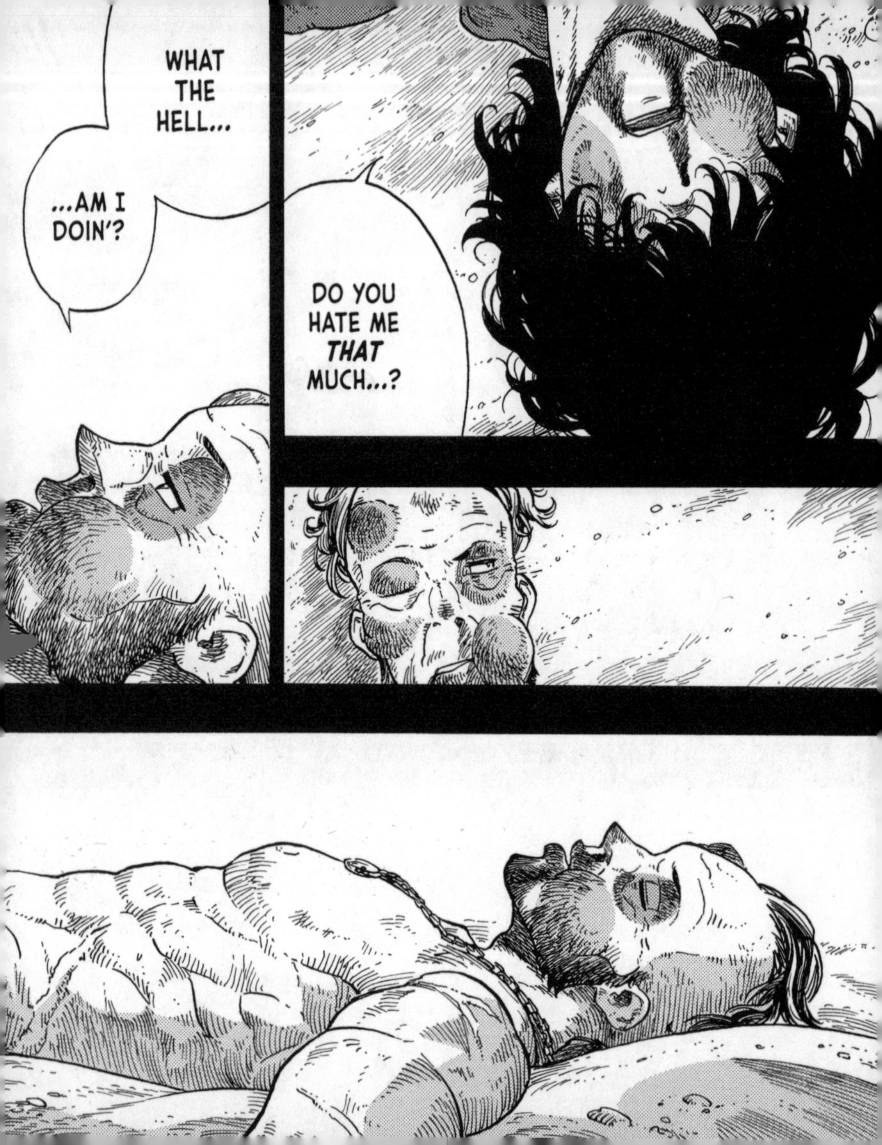
DO YOU HATE ME *THAT* MUCH...?
WHAT THE HELL...
...AM I DOIN'?

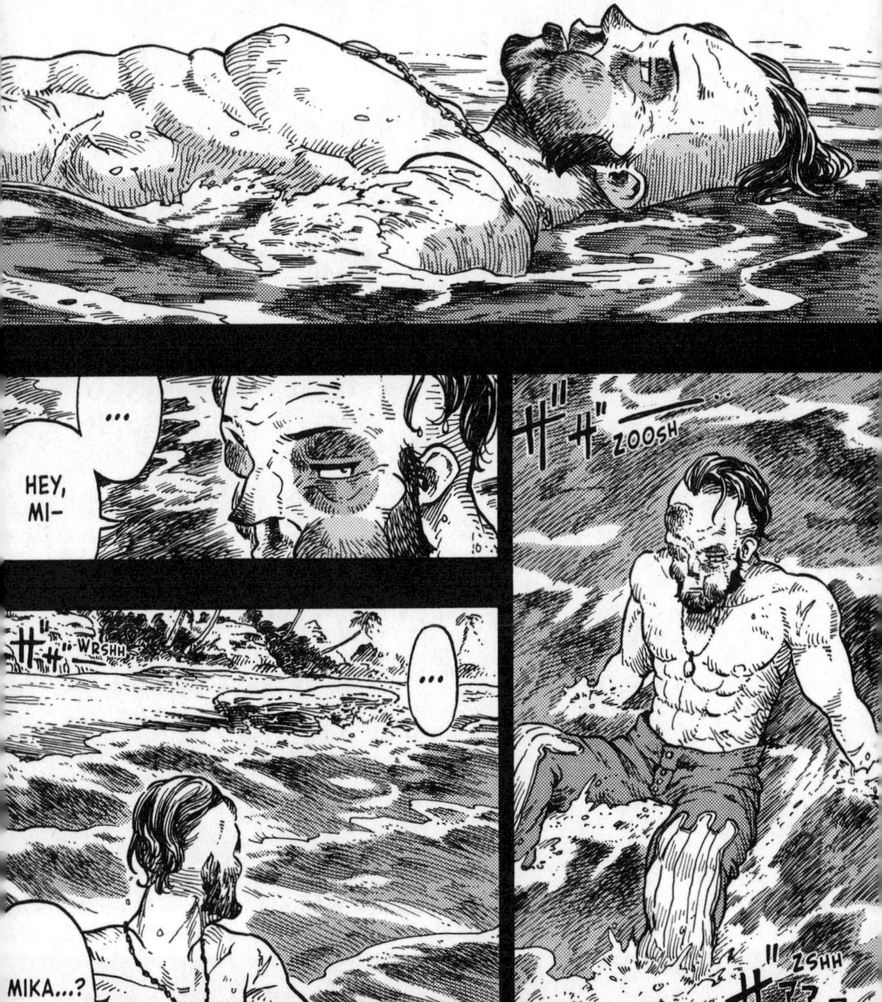
ZOOSH
ZSHH
...
HEY, MI-
WRSHH
...
MIKA...?

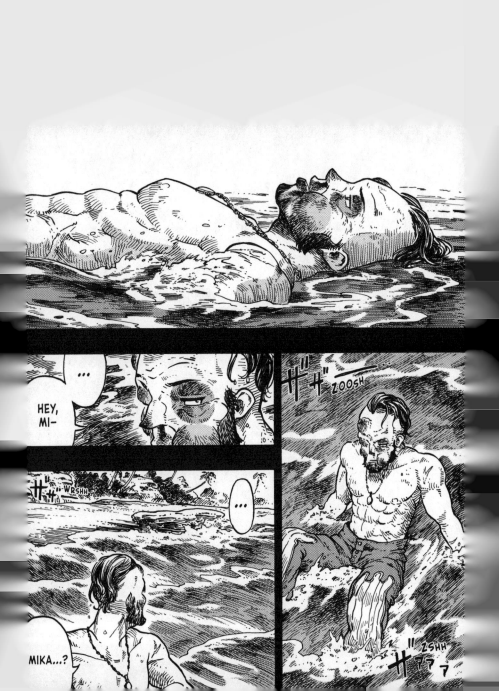

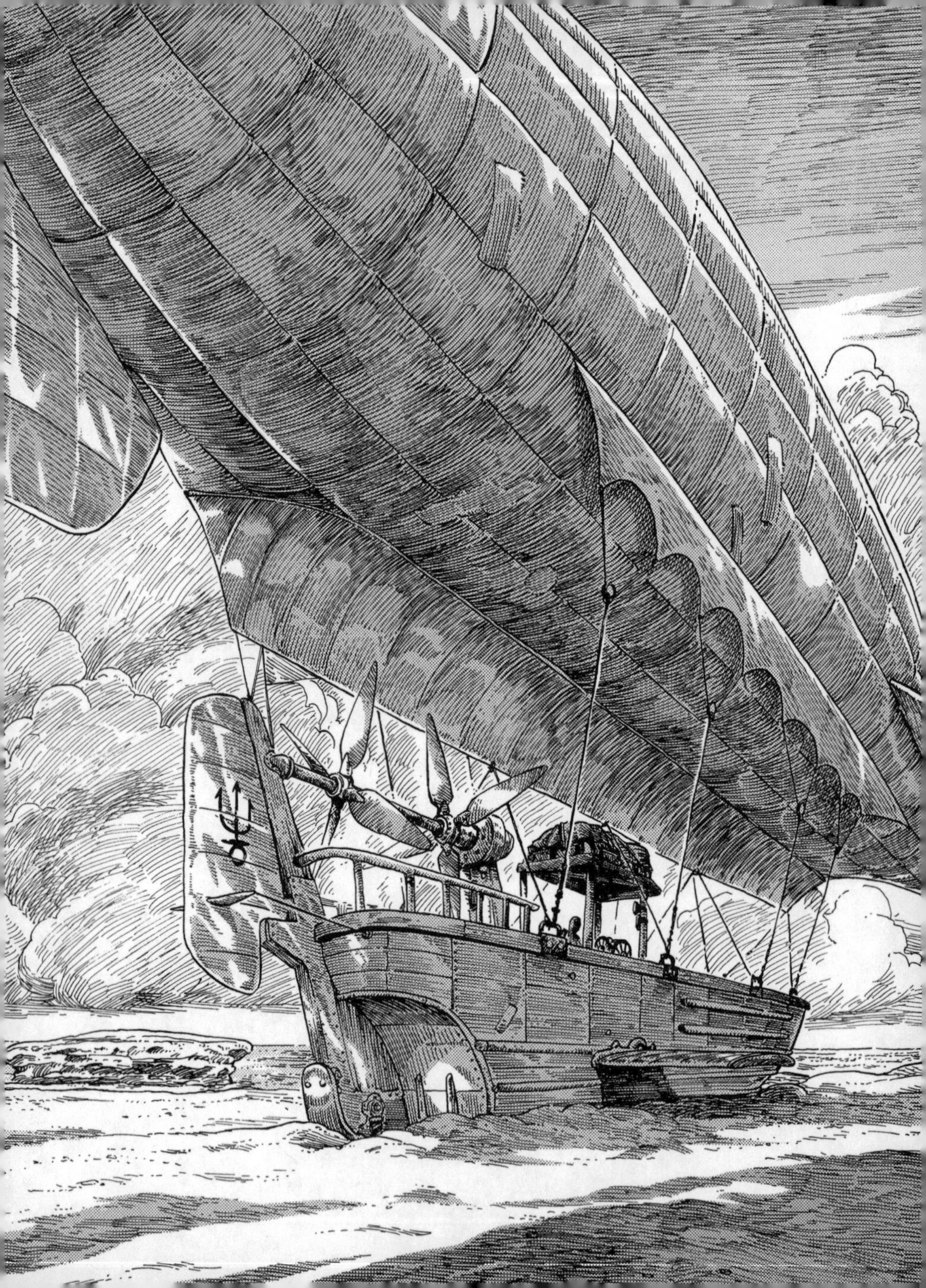

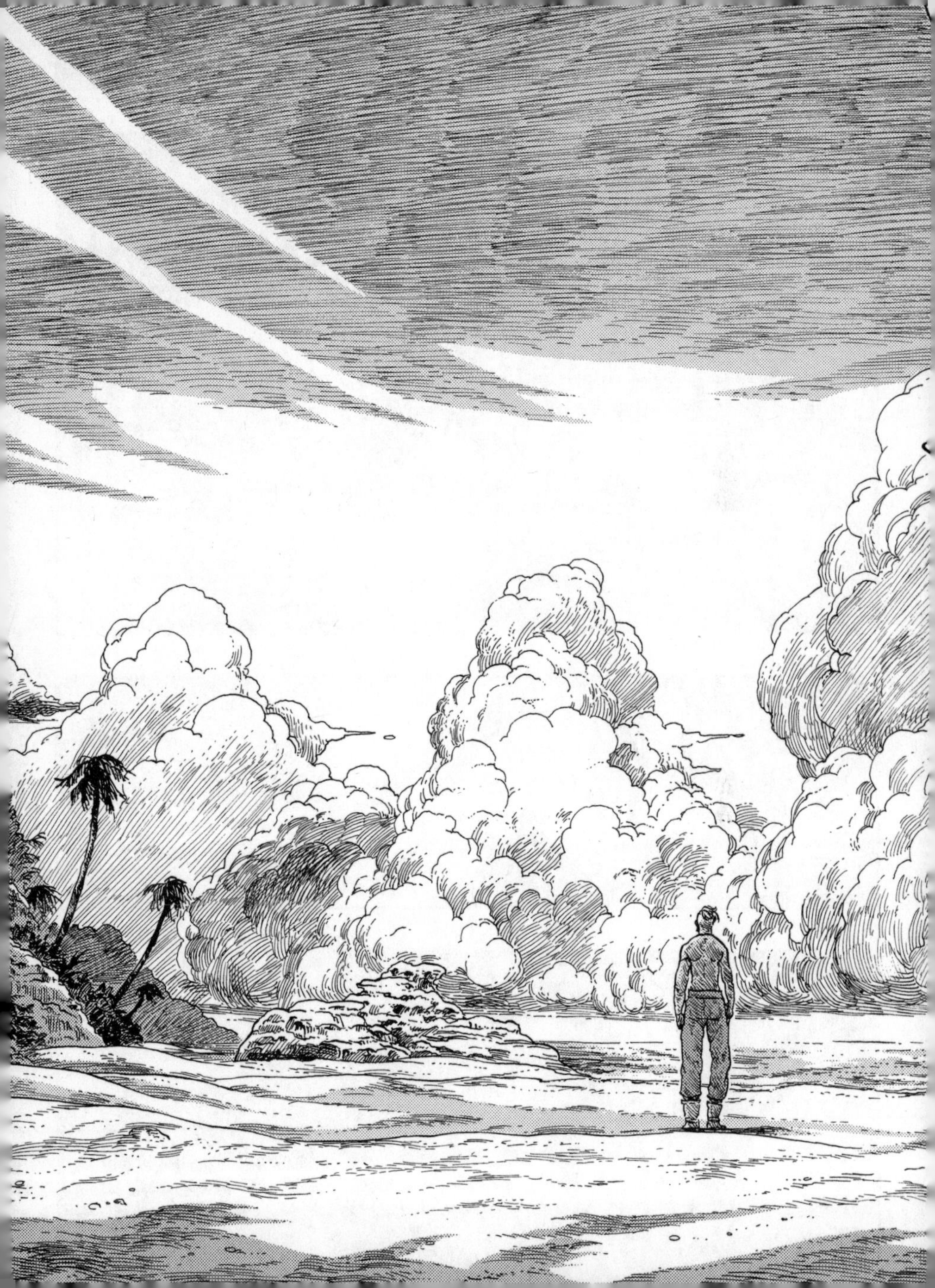

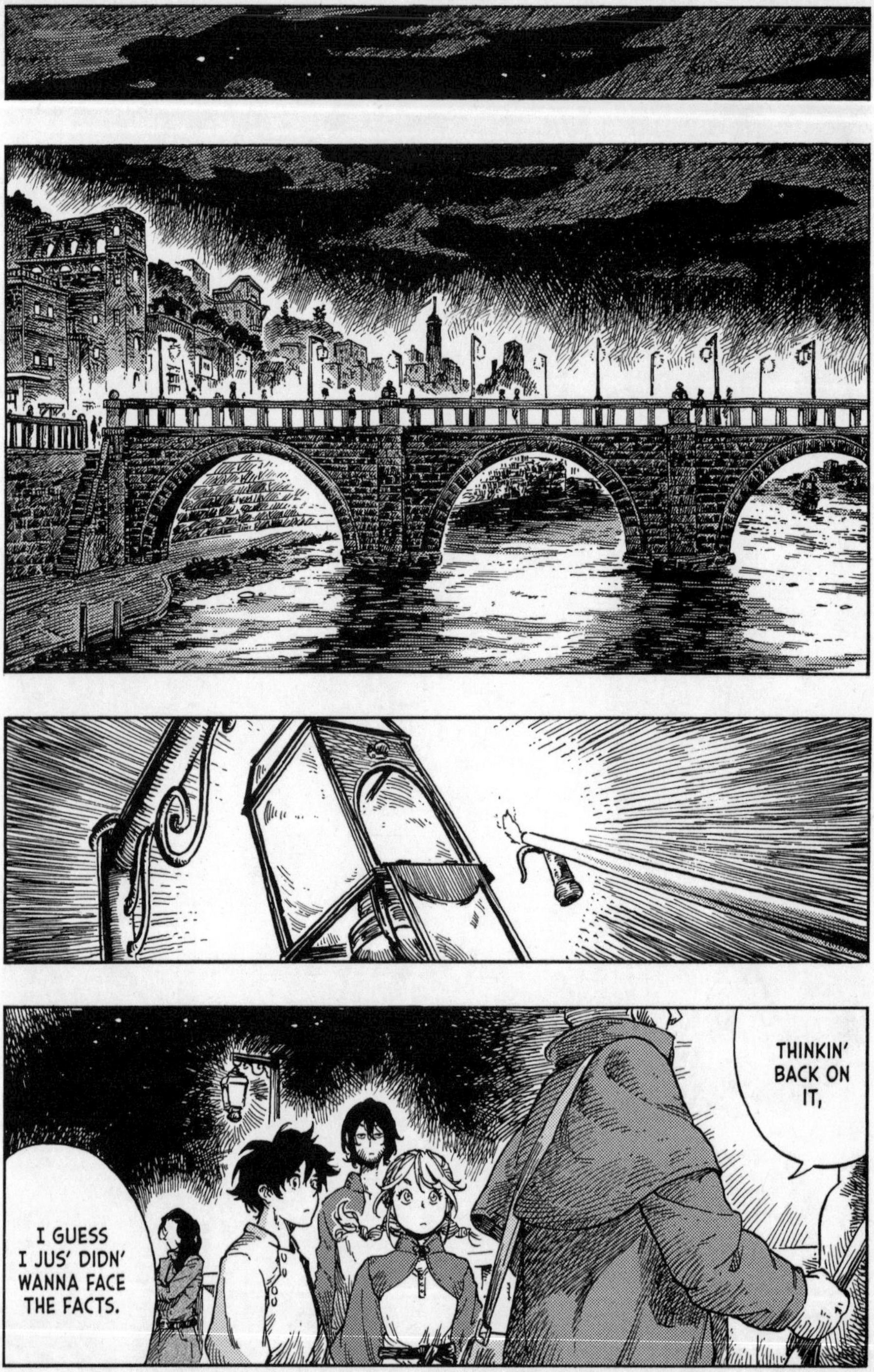
THINKIN' BACK ON IT,
I GUESS I JUS' DIDN' WANNA FACE THE FACTS.

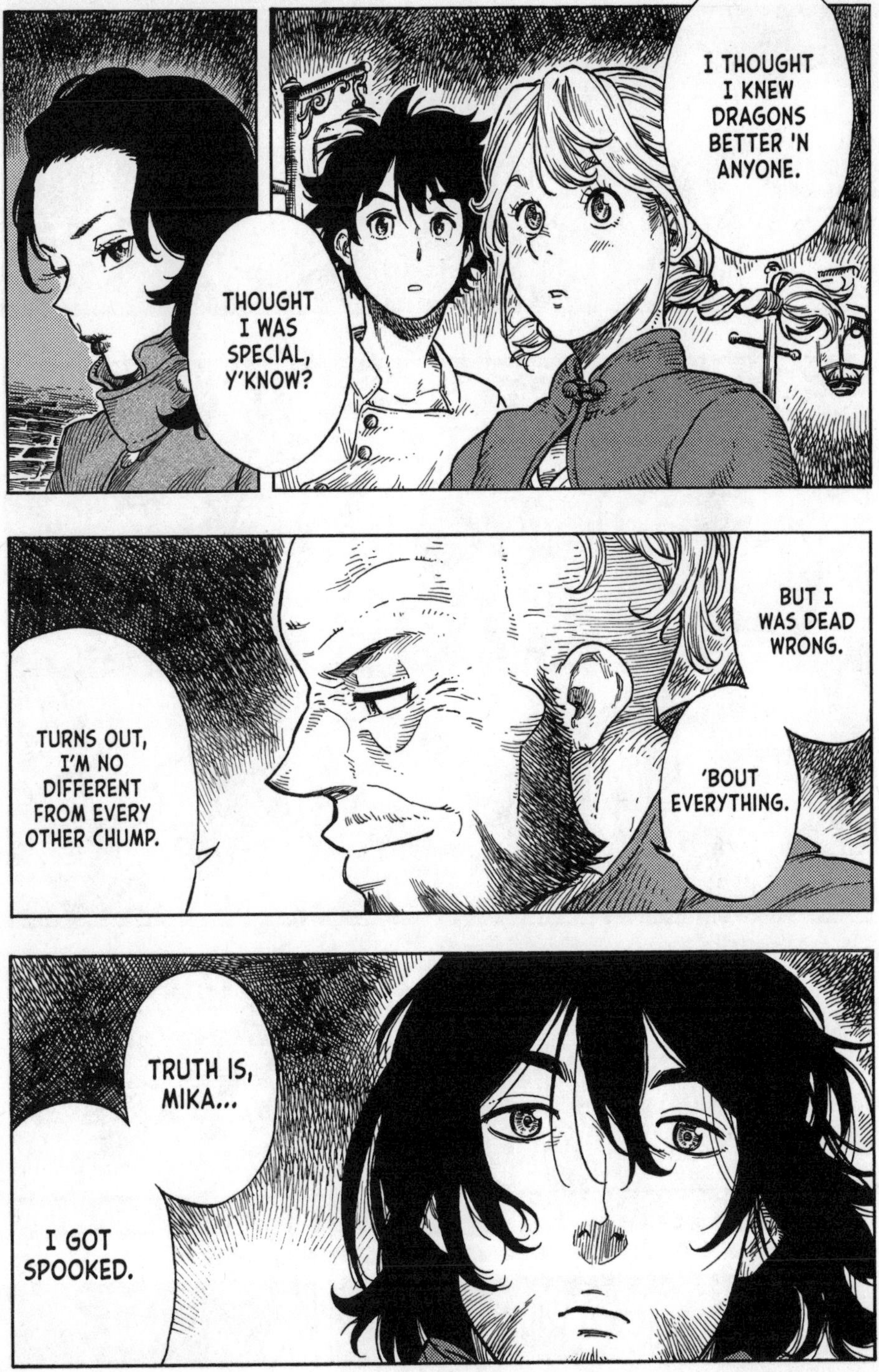
I THOUGHT I KNEW DRAGONS BETTER 'N ANYONE.
THOUGHT I WAS SPECIAL, Y'KNOW?
BUT I WAS DEAD WRONG.
'BOUT EVERYTHING.
TURNS OUT, I'M NO DIFFERENT FROM EVERY OTHER CHUMP.
TRUTH IS, MIKA...
I GOT SPOOKED.

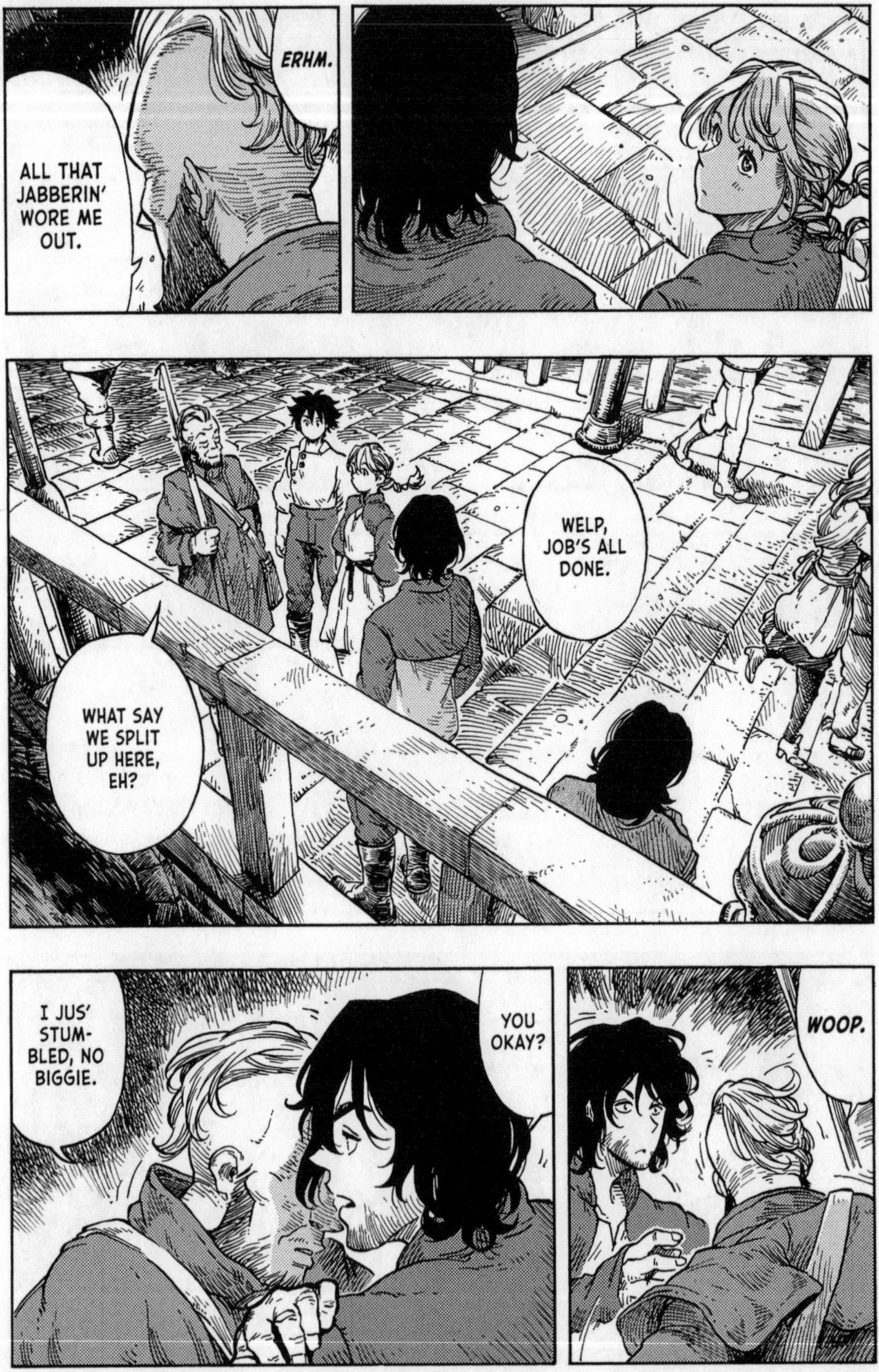
ERHM.
ALL THAT JABBERIN' WORE ME OUT.
WELP, JOB'S ALL DONE.
WHAT SAY WE SPLIT UP HERE, EH?
WOOP.
YOU OKAY?
I JUS' STUM-BLED, NO BIGGIE.

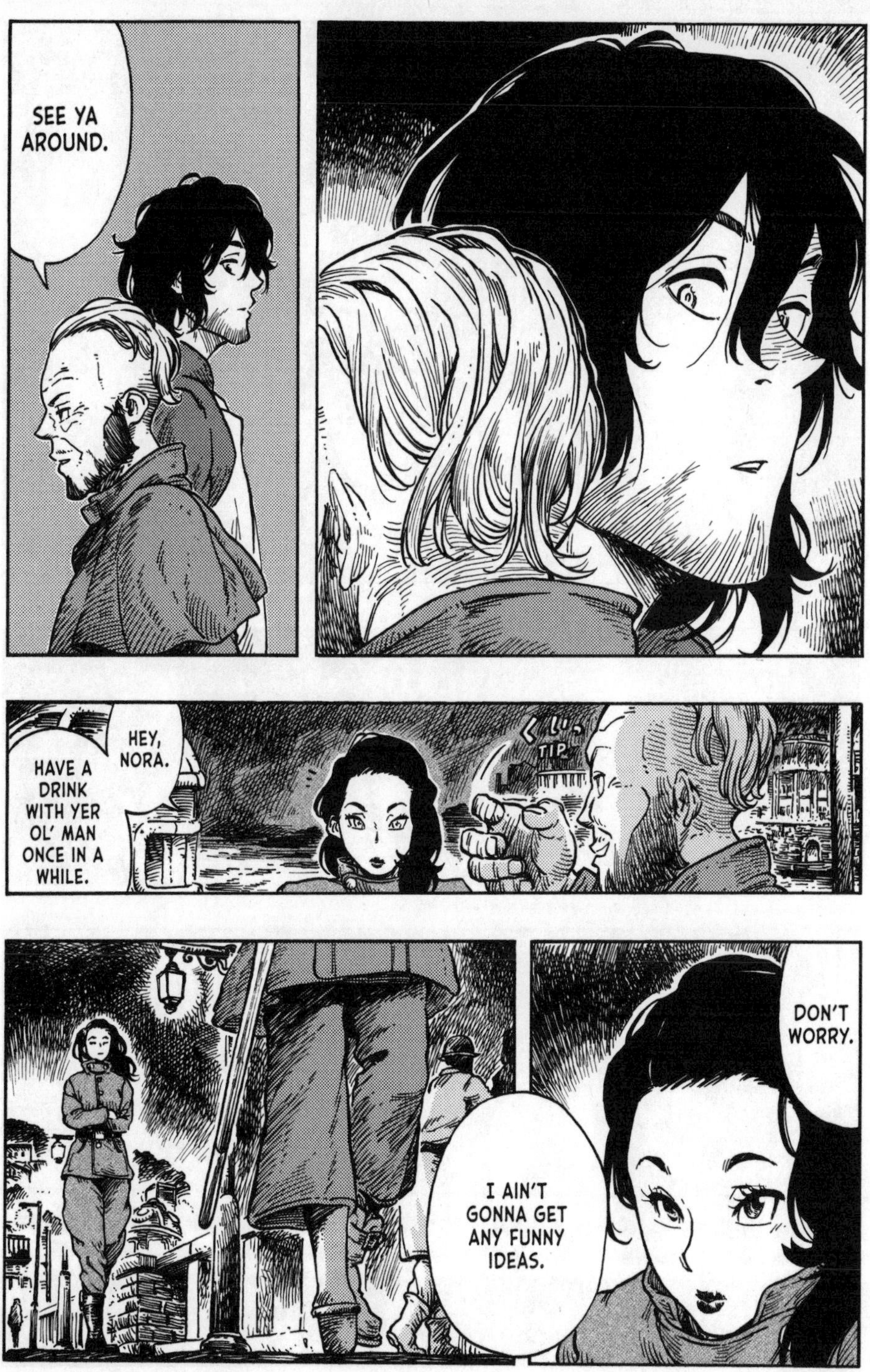
SEE YA AROUND.
HEY, NORA.
HAVE A DRINK WITH YER OL' MAN ONCE IN A WHILE.
TIP
DON'T WORRY.
I AIN'T GONNA GET ANY FUNNY IDEAS.

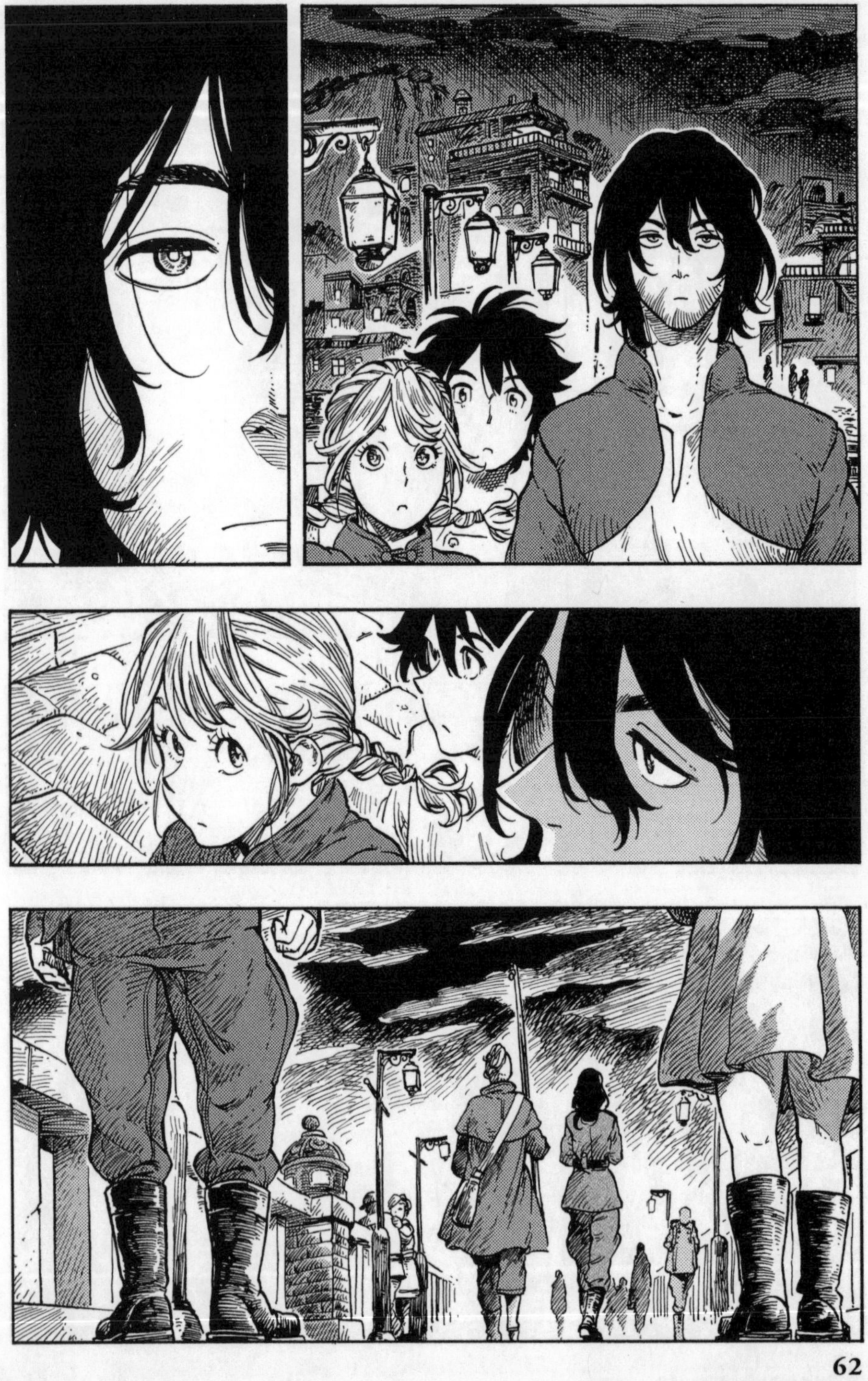

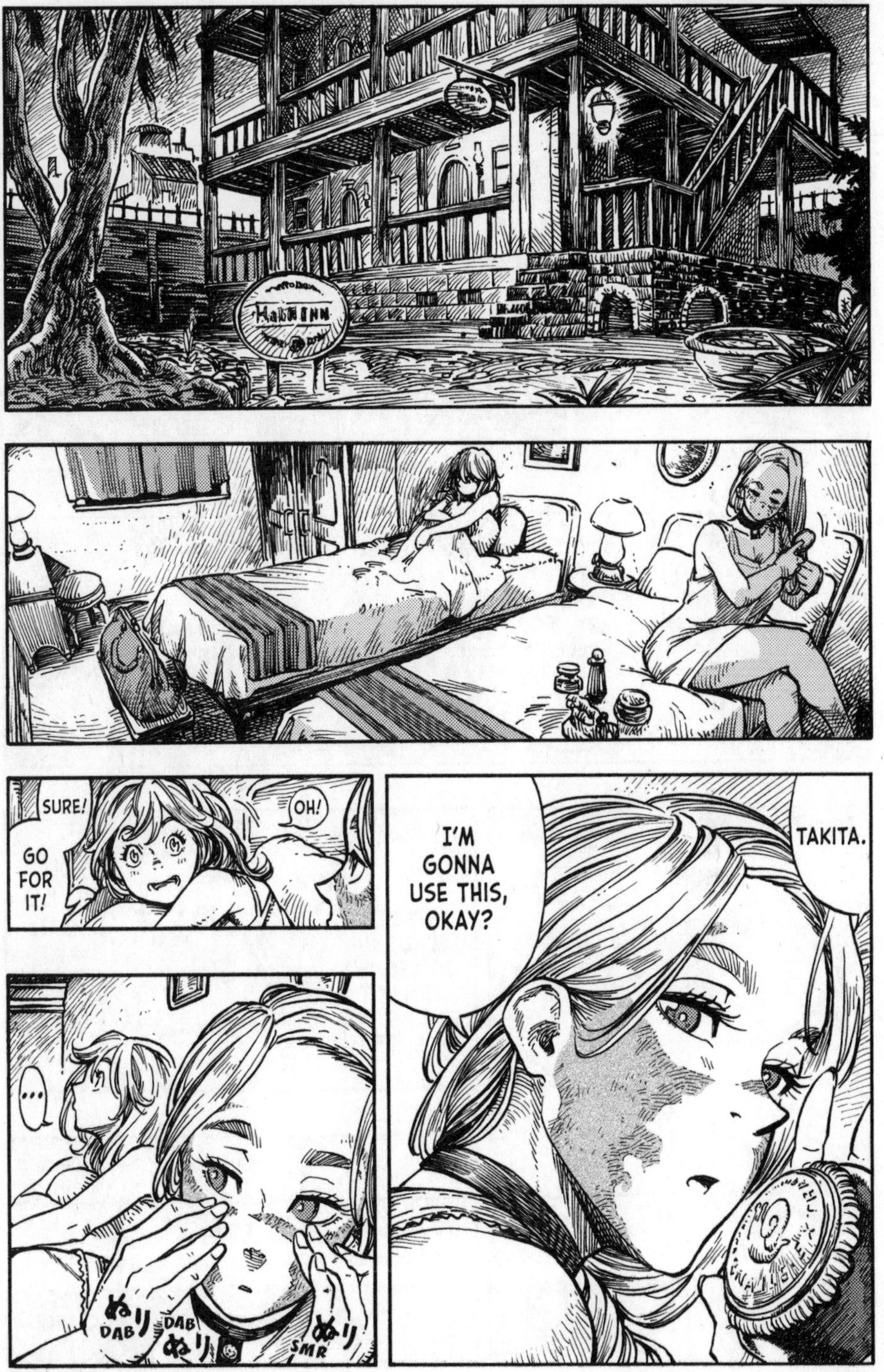
TAKITA.
I'M GONNA USE THIS, OKAY?
OH!
SURE! GO FOR IT!
...
ぬり DAB
DAB ぬり
ぬり SMR

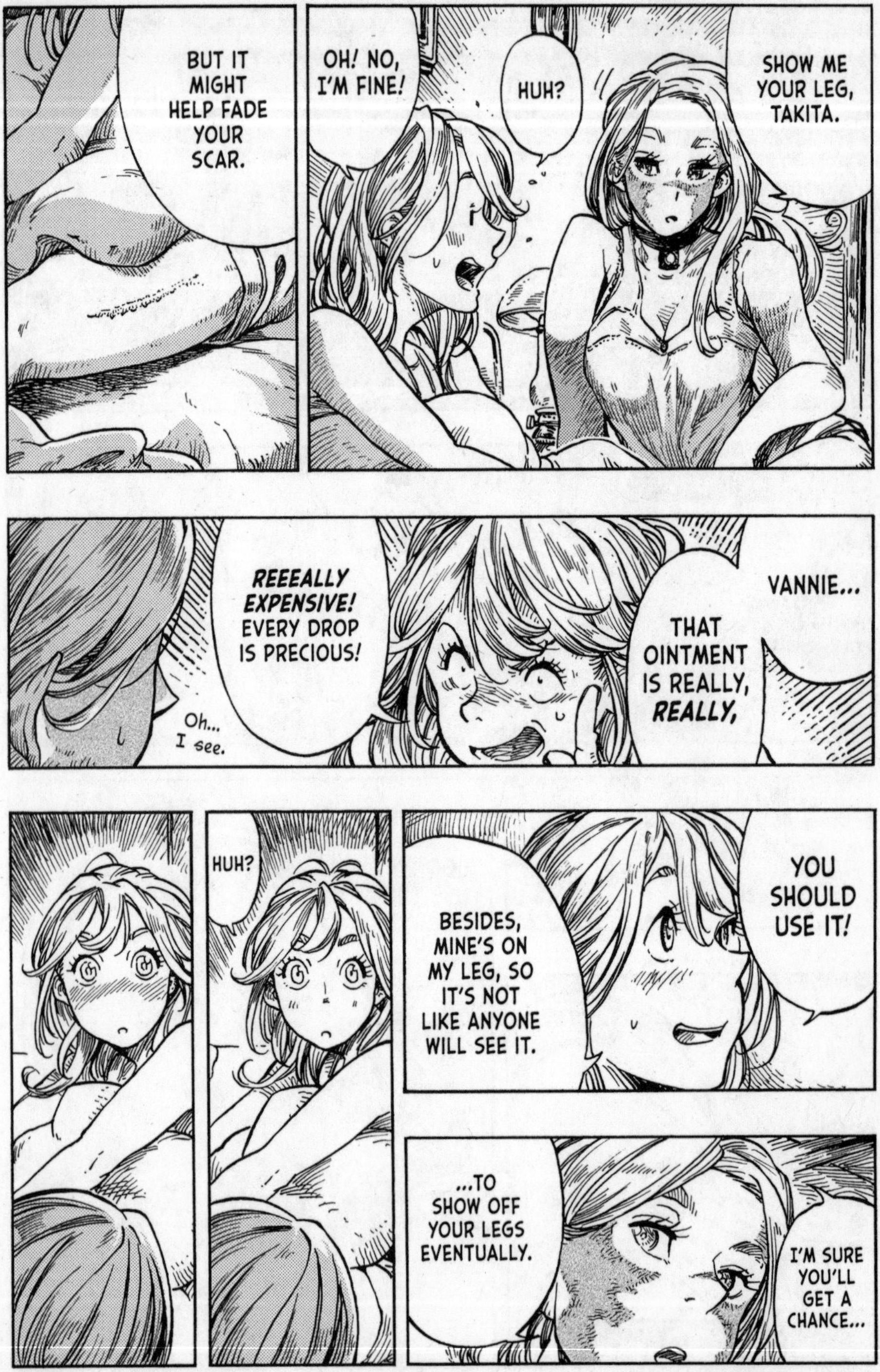
SHOW ME YOUR LEG, TAKITA.
HUH?
OH! NO, I'M FINE!
BUT IT MIGHT HELP FADE YOUR SCAR.
VANNIE...
THAT OINTMENT IS REALLY, *REALLY,*
REEEALLY EXPENSIVE! EVERY DROP IS PRECIOUS!
Oh... I see.
YOU SHOULD USE IT!
BESIDES, MINE'S ON MY LEG, SO IT'S NOT LIKE ANYONE WILL SEE IT.
I'M SURE YOU'LL GET A CHANCE...
...TO SHOW OFF YOUR LEGS EVENTUALLY.
HUH?

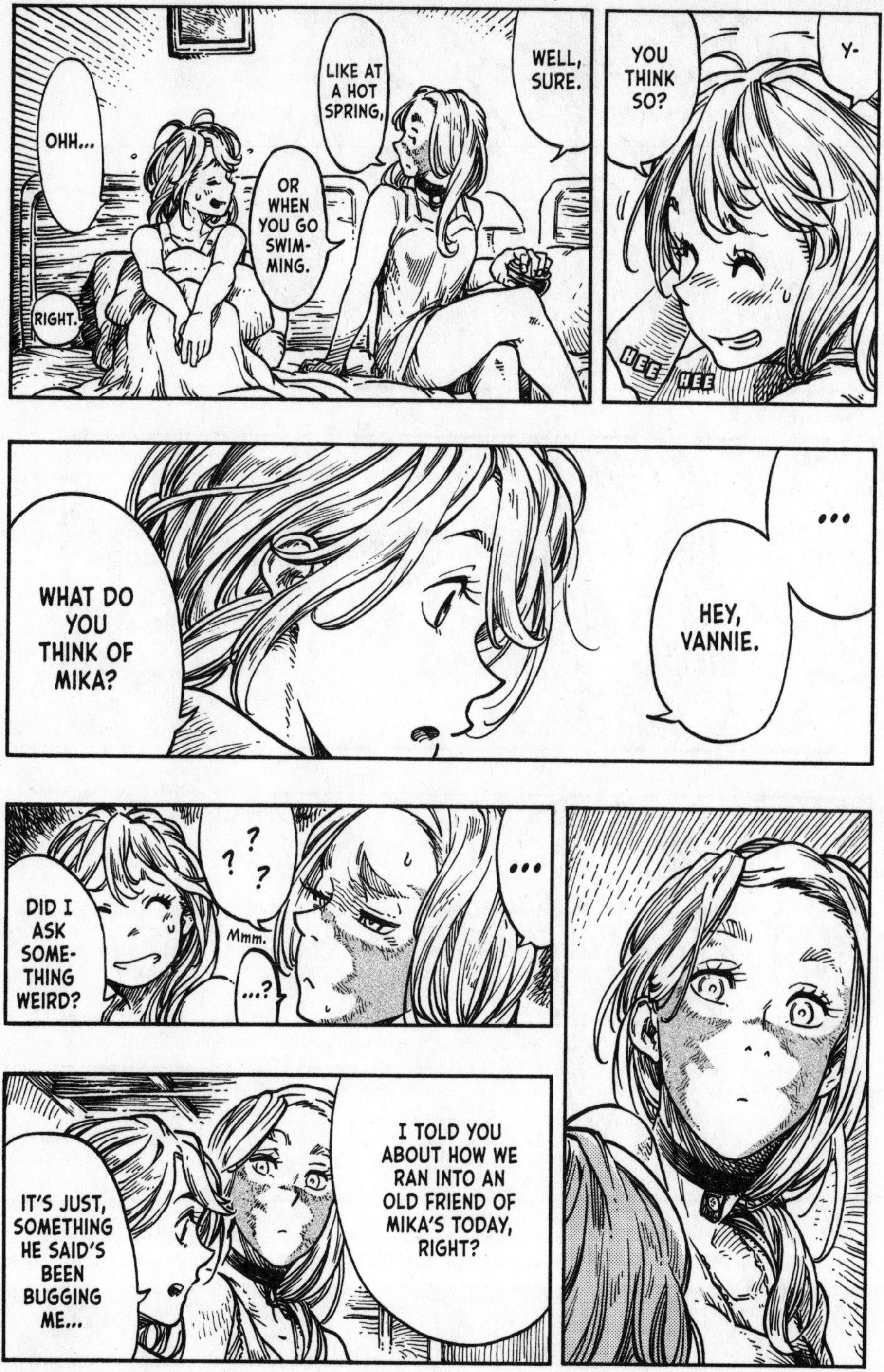

Y-
YOU THINK SO?
HEE HEE
WELL, SURE.
LIKE AT A HOT SPRING,
OR WHEN YOU GO SWIMMING.
OHH...
RIGHT.
...
HEY, VANNIE.
WHAT DO YOU THINK OF MIKA?
...
? ? ?
Mmm.
...?
DID I ASK SOMETHING WEIRD?
I TOLD YOU ABOUT HOW WE RAN INTO AN OLD FRIEND OF MIKA'S TODAY, RIGHT?
IT'S JUST, SOMETHING HE SAID'S BEEN BUGGING ME...

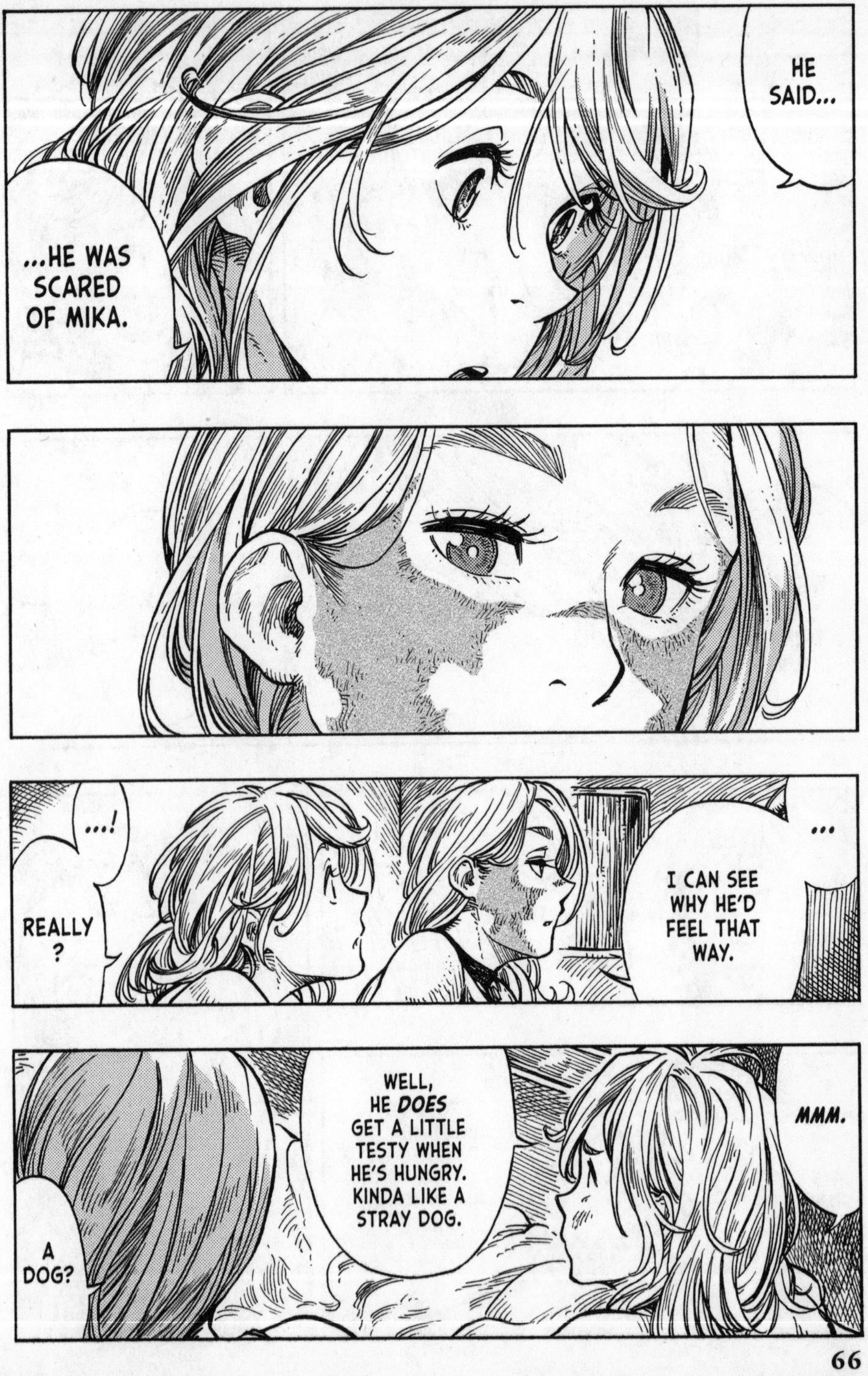
HE SAID...
...HE WAS SCARED OF MIKA.
... I CAN SEE WHY HE'D FEEL THAT WAY.
...! REALLY?
MMM.
WELL, HE *DOES* GET A LITTLE TESTY WHEN HE'S HUNGRY. KINDA LIKE A STRAY DOG.
A DOG?

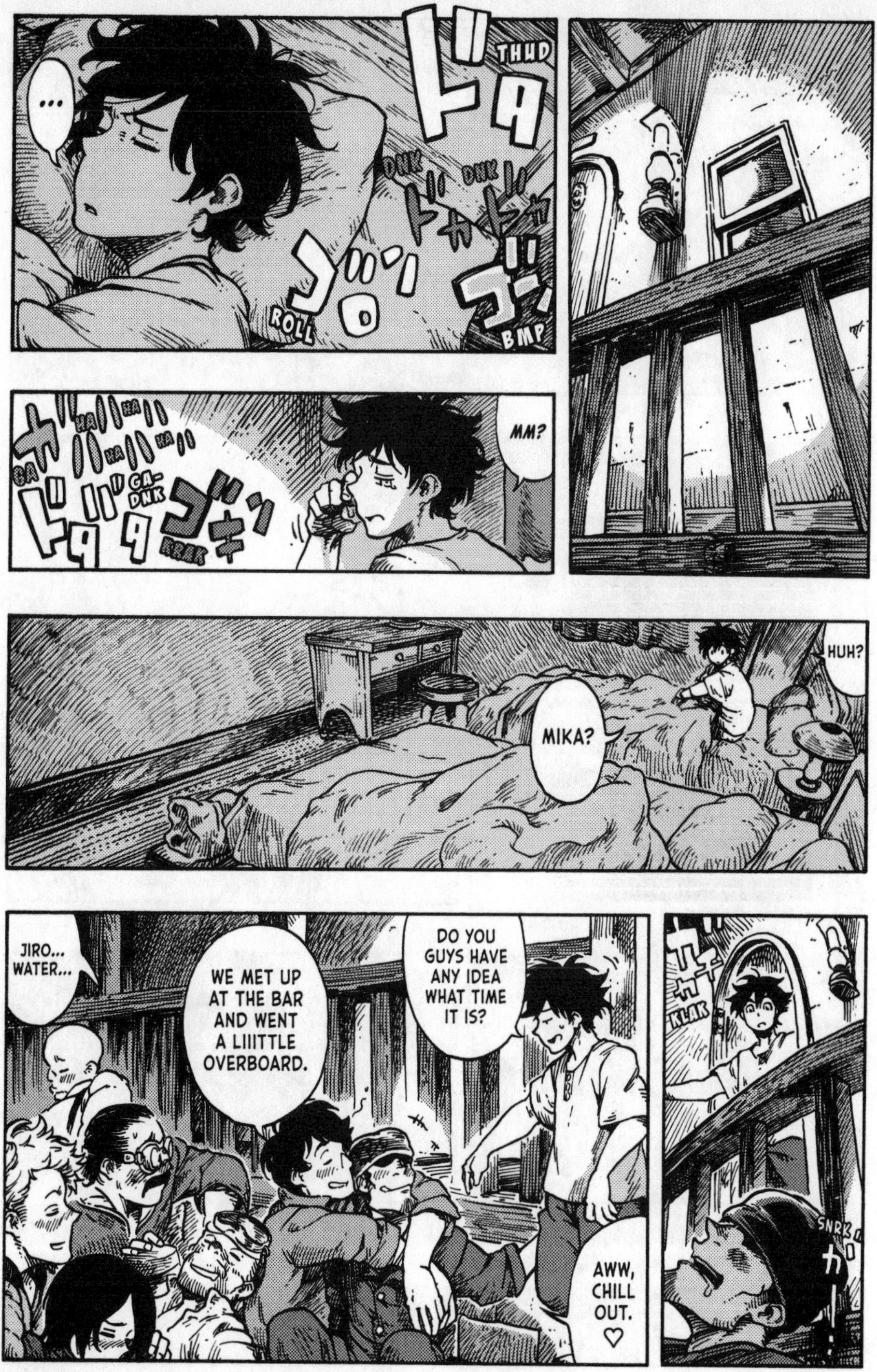
...
THUD
DNK
DNK
ROLL
BMP
MM?
HA HA HA HA
GA-DNK
KRAK
HUH?
MIKA?
KLAK
SNRK
DO YOU GUYS HAVE ANY IDEA WHAT TIME IT IS?
WE MET UP AT THE BAR AND WENT A LIIITTLE OVERBOARD.
JIRO... WATER...
AWW, CHILL OUT. ♡

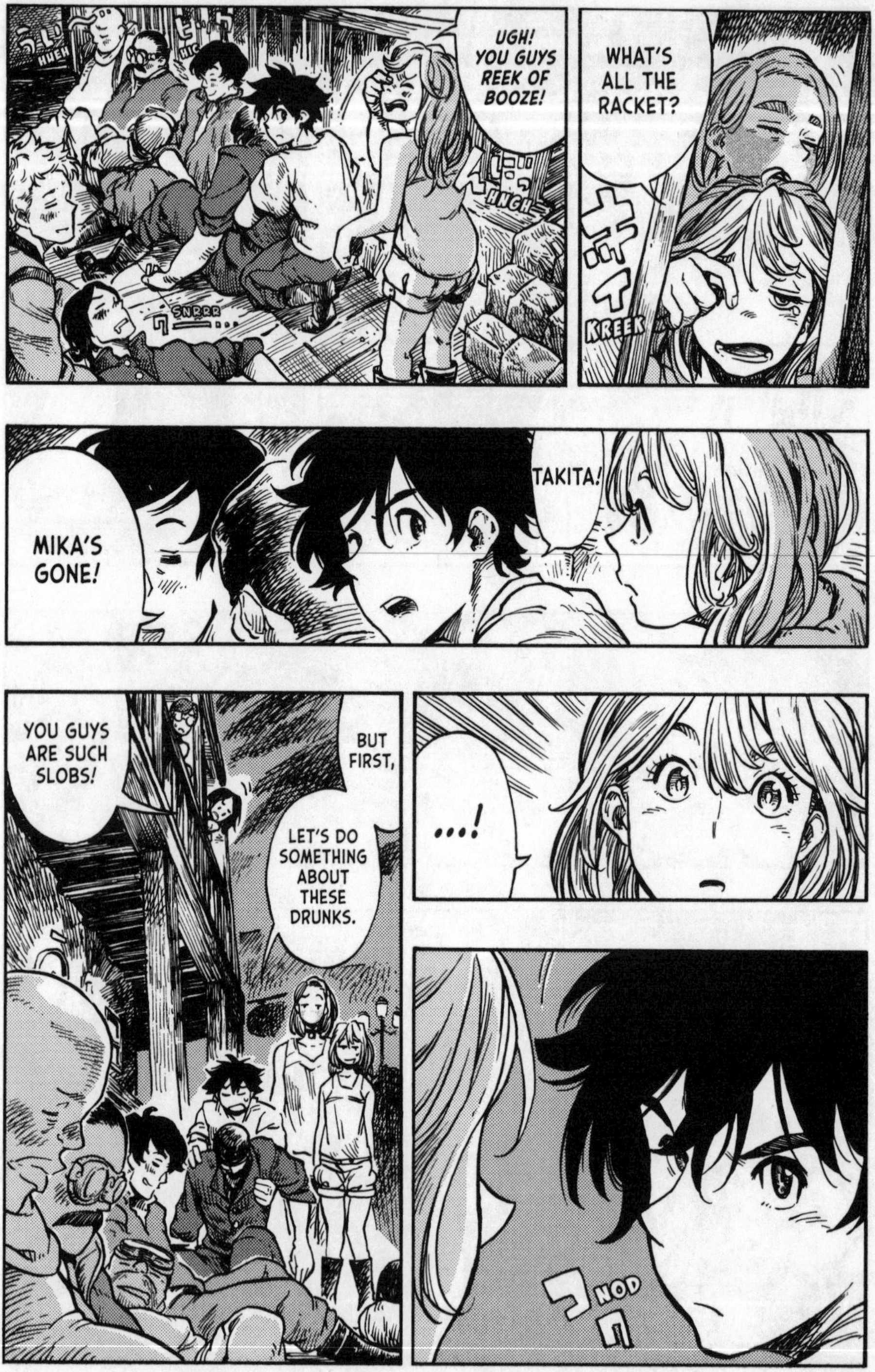
WHAT'S ALL THE RACKET?
KREEK
UGH! YOU GUYS REEK OF BOOZE!
HIC
HUEH
ANGH
SNRRR
TAKITA!
MIKA'S GONE!
...!
NOD
BUT FIRST,
LET'S DO SOMETHING ABOUT THESE DRUNKS.
YOU GUYS ARE SUCH SLOBS!

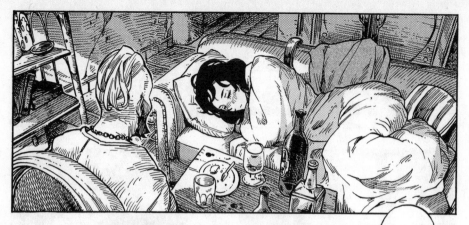

I KNOW I'M ALWAYS CAUSIN' YA GRIEF.

SFFF...

SORRY, KIDDO.

...I PROMISE THIS'LL BE THE LAST TIME.

BUT...

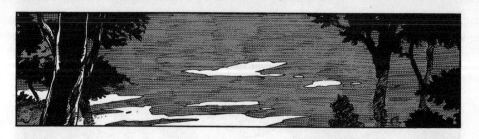

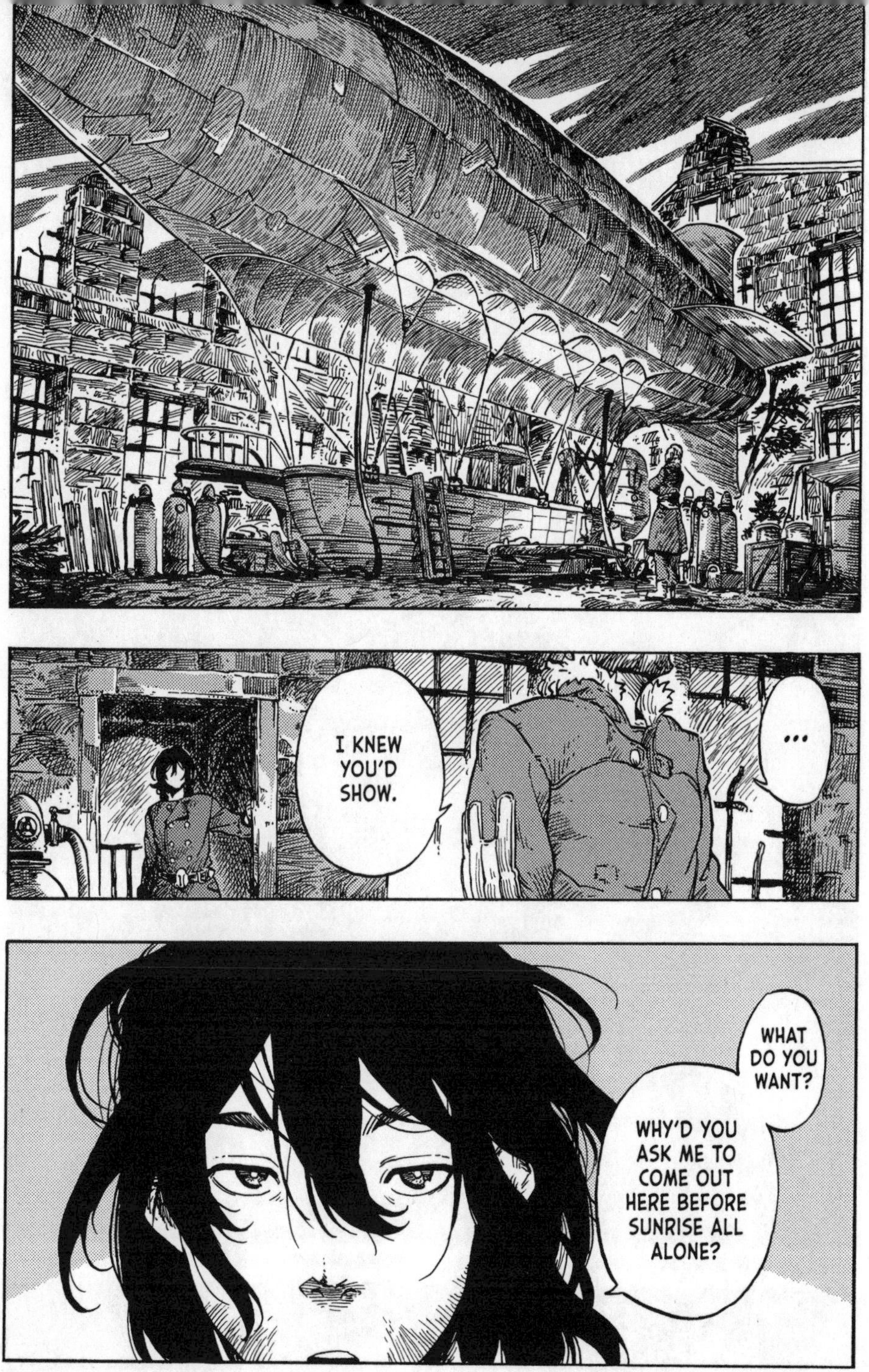
...
I KNEW YOU'D SHOW.
WHAT DO YOU WANT?
WHY'D YOU ASK ME TO COME OUT HERE BEFORE SUNRISE ALL ALONE?

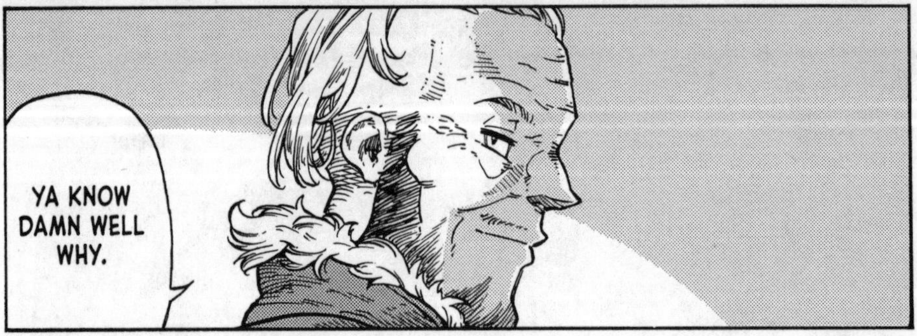
YA KNOW DAMN WELL WHY.

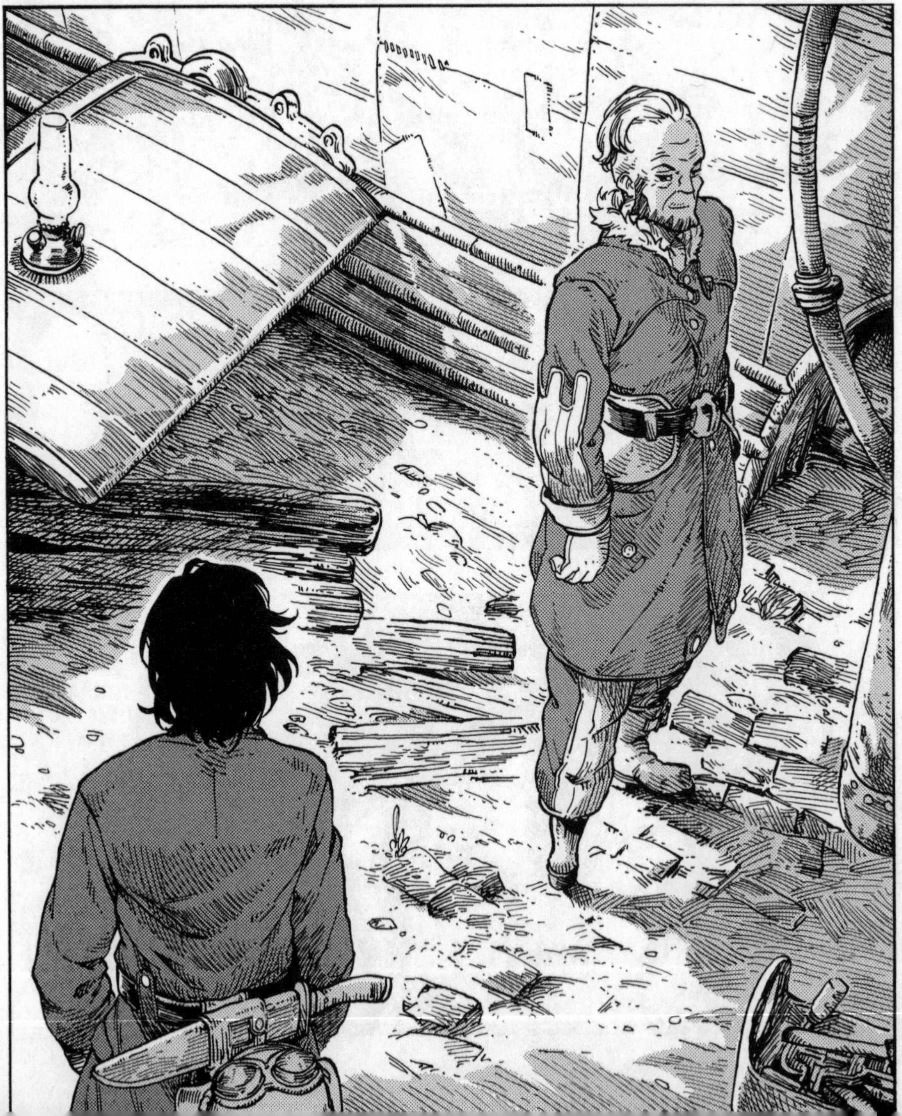

Flight 32 What it Takes to Drake

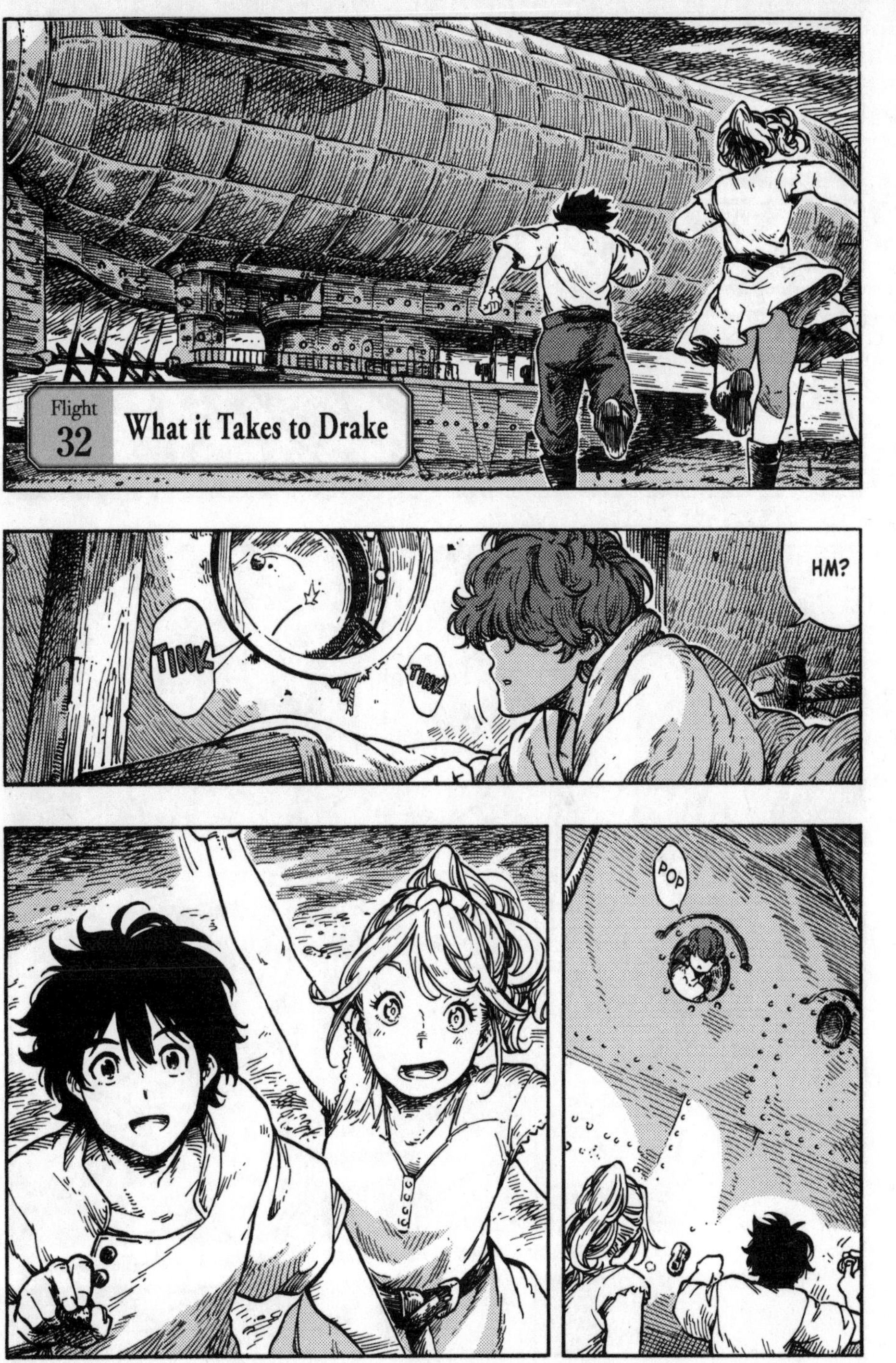
HM?
TINK
TINK
POP

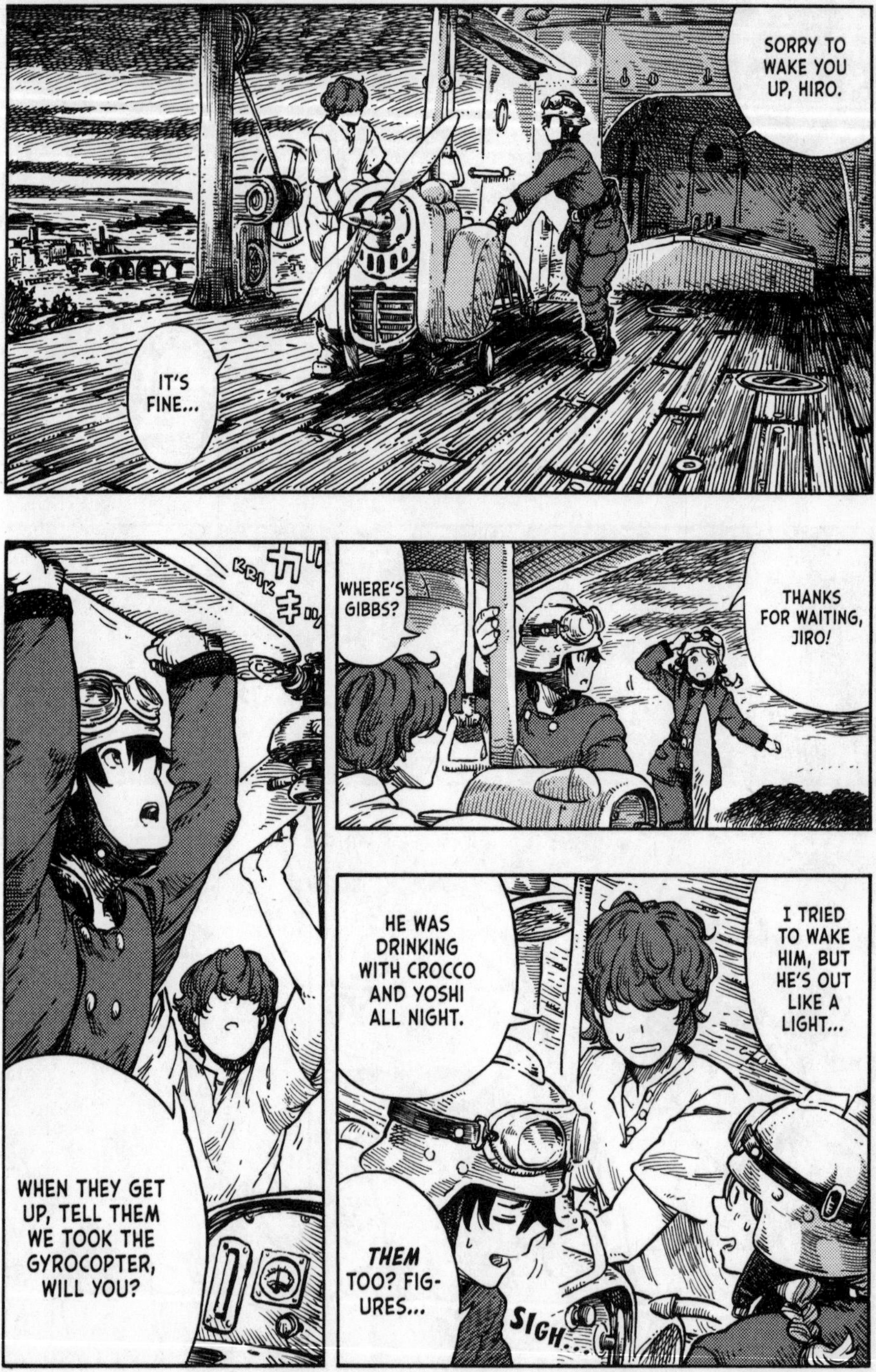
SORRY TO WAKE YOU UP, HIRO.
IT'S FINE...
THANKS FOR WAITING, JIRO!
WHERE'S GIBBS?
I TRIED TO WAKE HIM, BUT HE'S OUT LIKE A LIGHT...
HE WAS DRINKING WITH CROCCO AND YOSHI ALL NIGHT.
THEM TOO? FIG-URES...
SIGH...
KRIK
WHEN THEY GET UP, TELL THEM WE TOOK THE GYROCOPTER, WILL YOU?

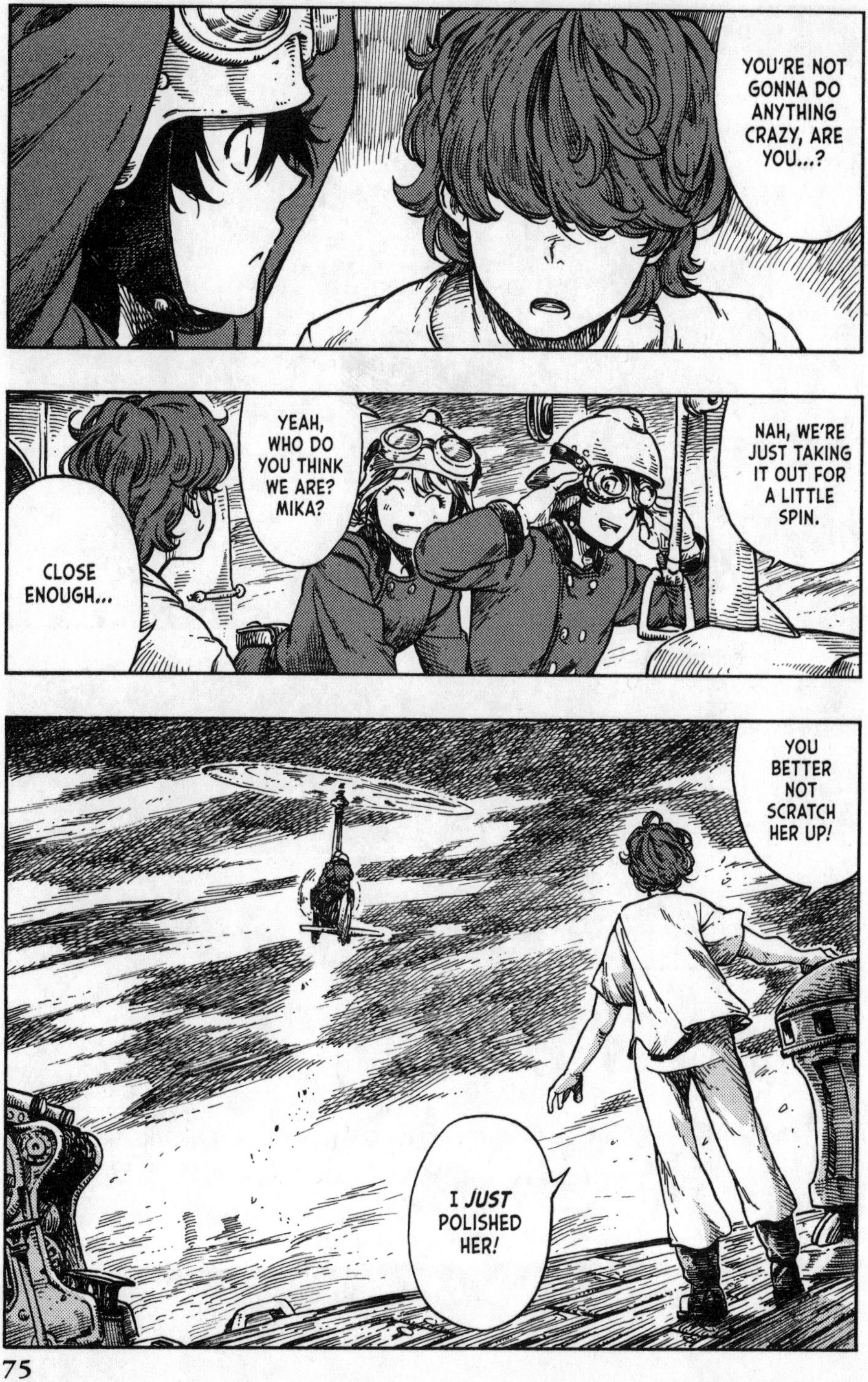
YOU'RE NOT GONNA DO ANYTHING CRAZY, ARE YOU...?
NAH, WE'RE JUST TAKING IT OUT FOR A LITTLE SPIN.
YEAH, WHO DO YOU THINK WE ARE? MIKA?
CLOSE ENOUGH...
YOU BETTER NOT SCRATCH HER UP!
I *JUST* POLISHED HER!

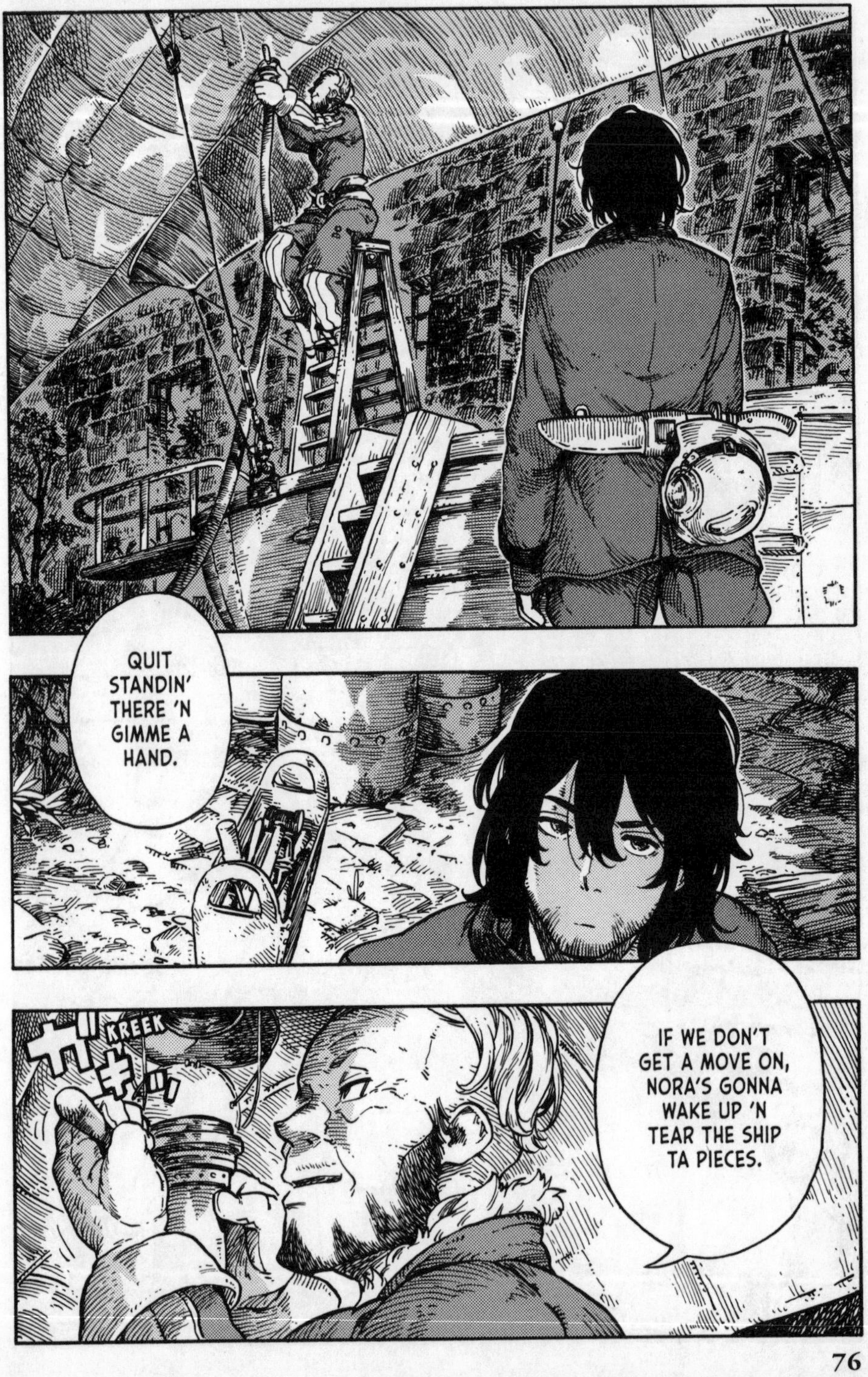
QUIT STANDIN' THERE 'N GIMME A HAND.
IF WE DON'T GET A MOVE ON, NORA'S GONNA WAKE UP 'N TEAR THE SHIP TA PIECES.
KREEK

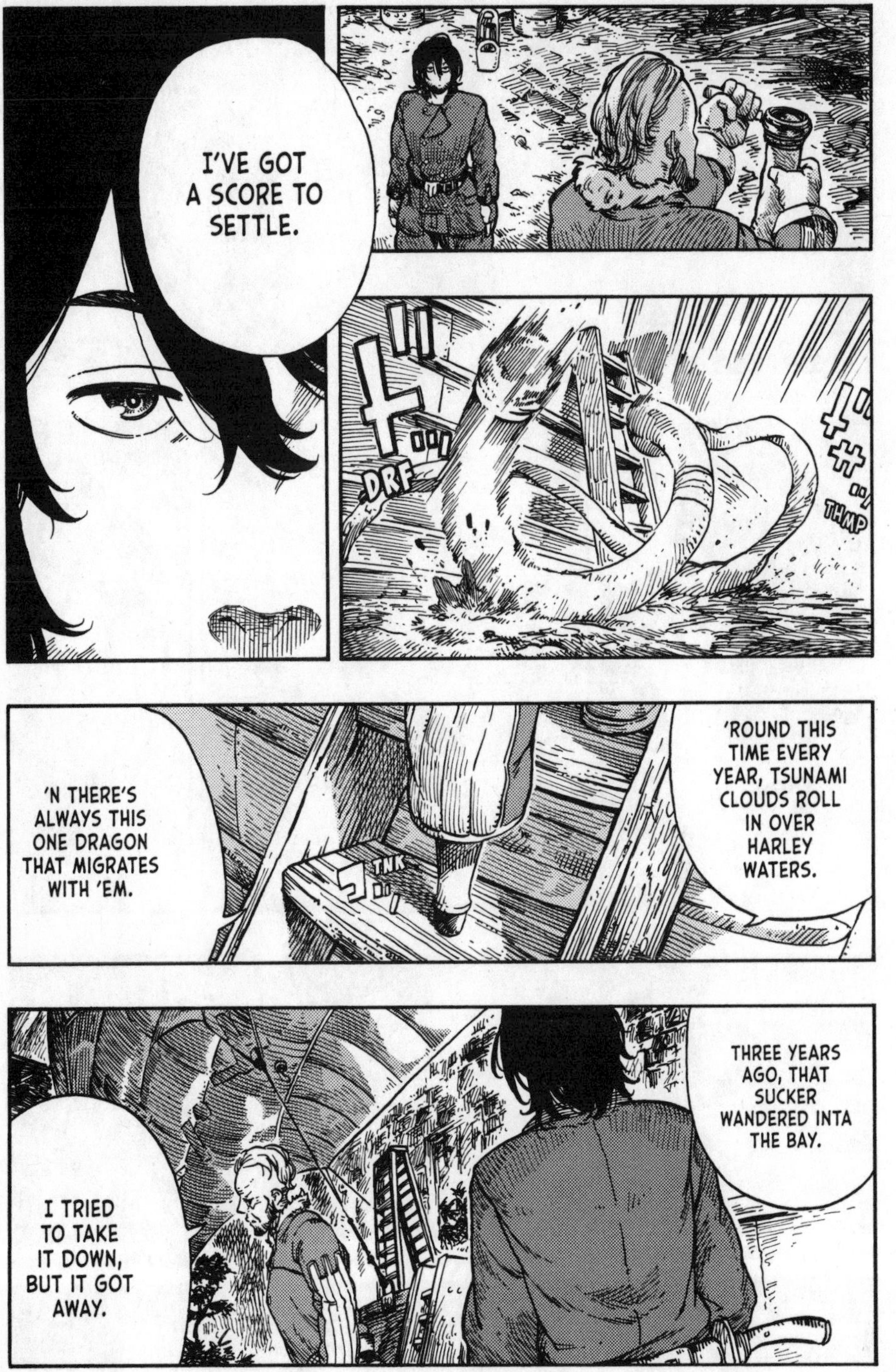
THMP
DRF
I'VE GOT A SCORE TO SETTLE.
'ROUND THIS TIME EVERY YEAR, TSUNAMI CLOUDS ROLL IN OVER HARLEY WATERS.
TNK
'N THERE'S ALWAYS THIS ONE DRAGON THAT MIGRATES WITH 'EM.
THREE YEARS AGO, THAT SUCKER WANDERED INTA THE BAY.
I TRIED TO TAKE IT DOWN, BUT IT GOT AWAY.

MY HARPOON...

...IS STILL STUCK IN THAT THING'S BACK.

THAT ONE?

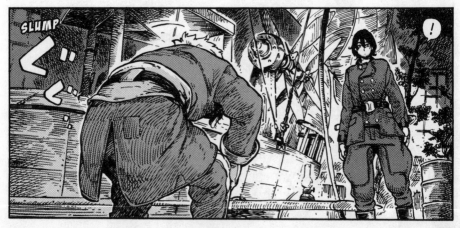

SLUMP

!

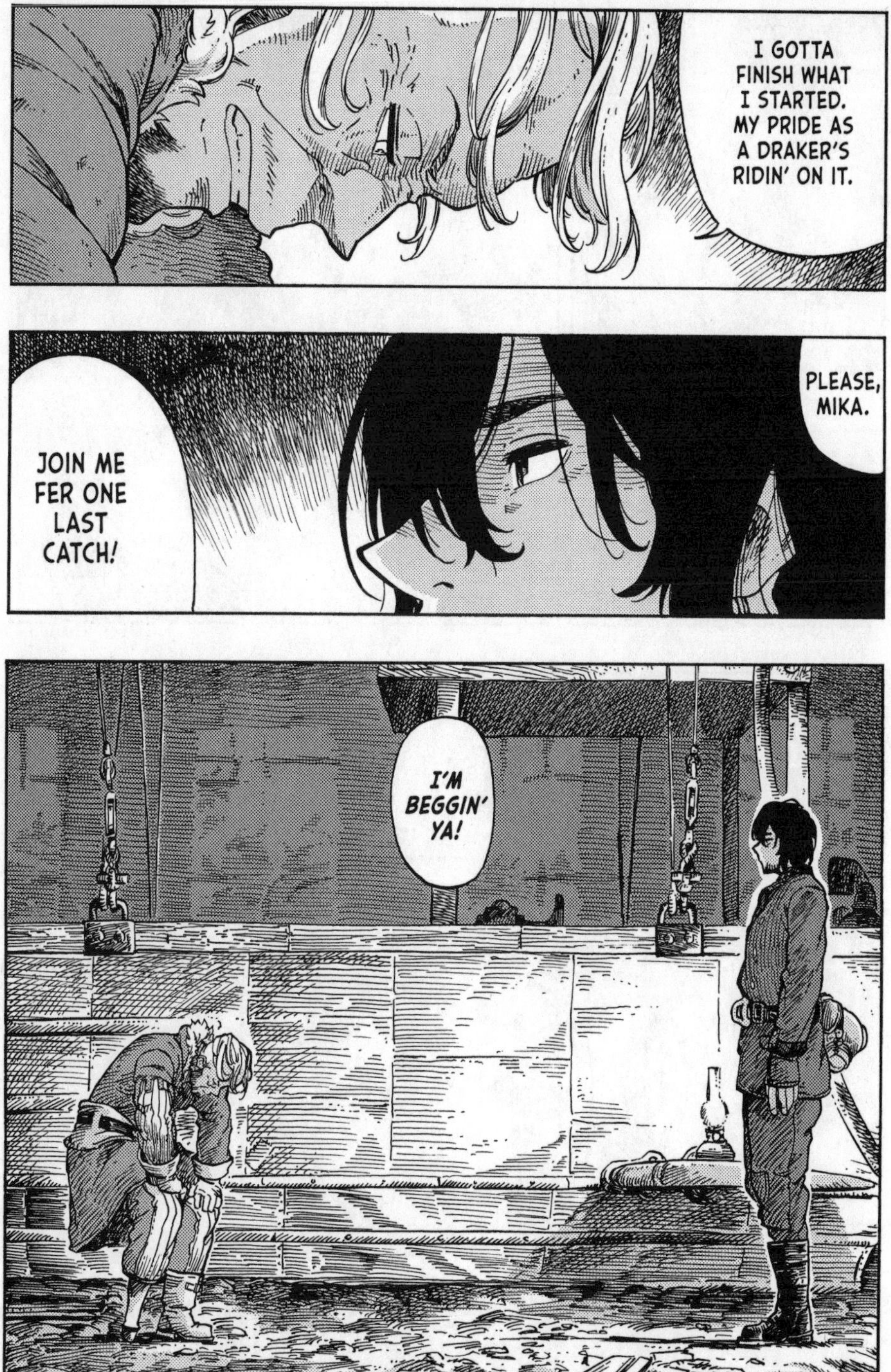
I GOTTA FINISH WHAT I STARTED. MY PRIDE AS A DRAKER'S RIDIN' ON IT.
PLEASE, MIKA.
JOIN ME FER ONE LAST CATCH!
I'M BEGGIN' YA!

WITH THAT LEG? NOT HAPPENING.
SKRF
...THE HELL'RE YOU TALKIN' ABOUT?
I AIN'T DONE YET!
I CAN STILL FIGHT, DAMN IT!
LOOK!
HWHP
TO PREPARE FER THIS...
I HAD THE BLACKSMITH FORGE THIS SPECIAL PROSTHETIC FER ME!

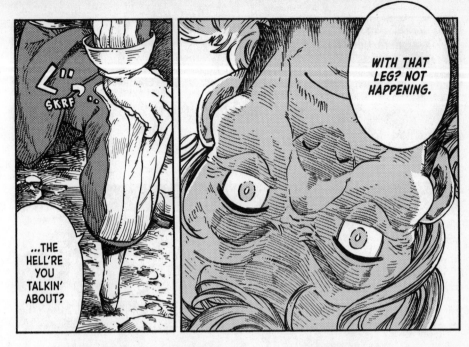

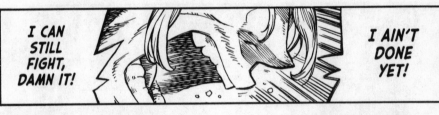

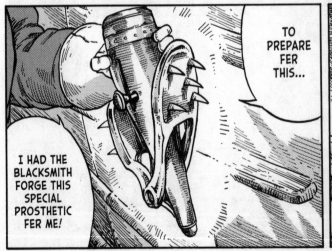

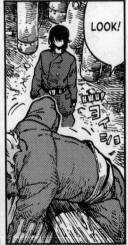

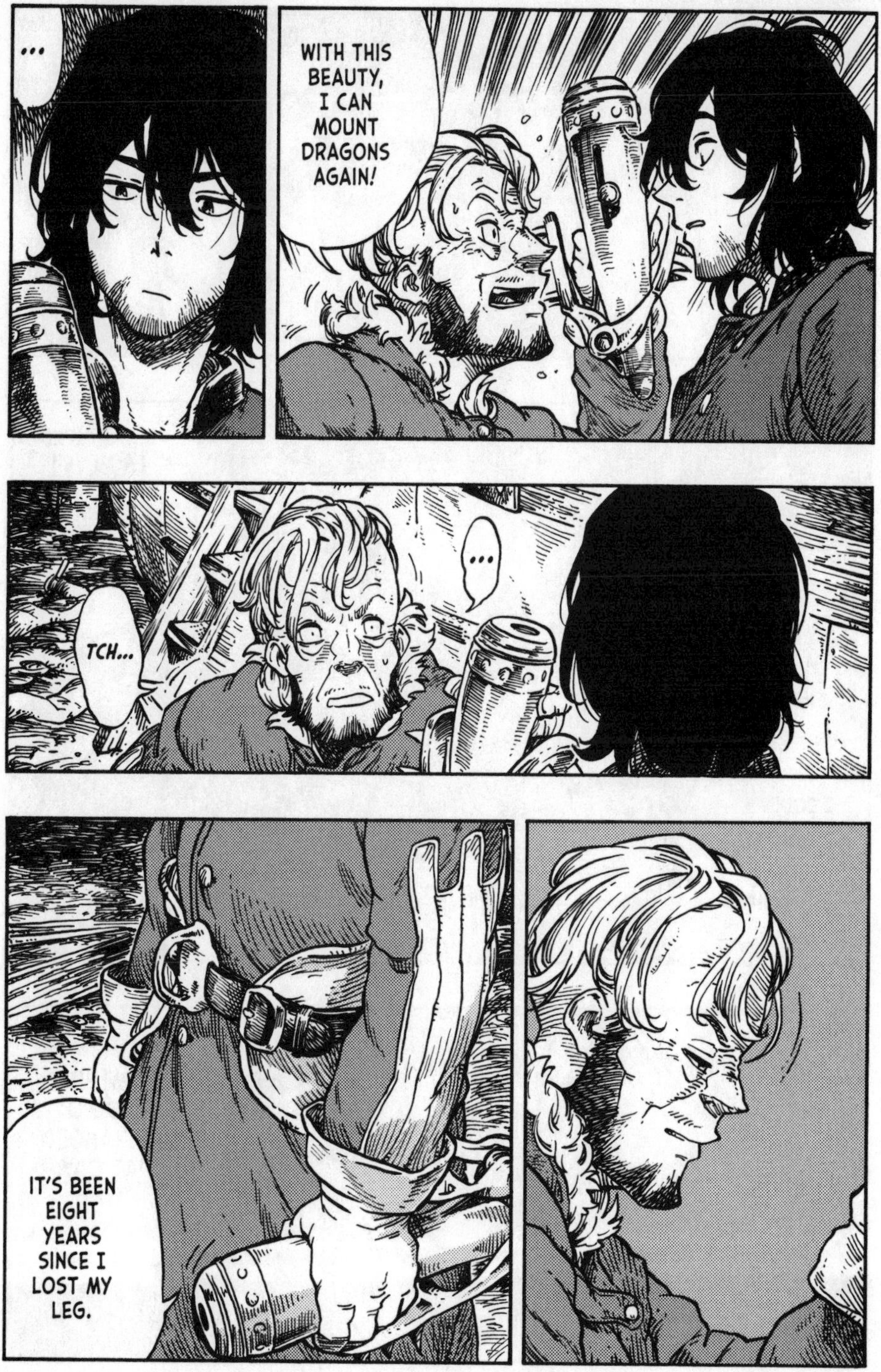
WITH THIS BEAUTY, I CAN MOUNT DRAGONS AGAIN!
...
...
TCH...
IT'S BEEN EIGHT YEARS SINCE I LOST MY LEG.

AFTER WE SPLIT UP...

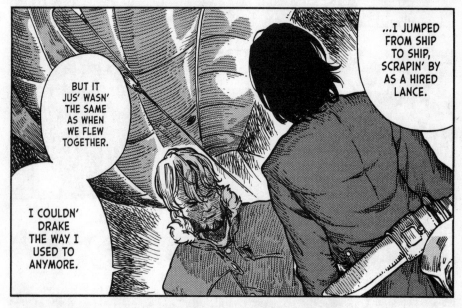

...I JUMPED FROM SHIP TO SHIP, SCRAPIN' BY AS A HIRED LANCE.

BUT IT JUS' WASN' THE SAME AS WHEN WE FLEW TOGETHER.

I COULDN' DRAKE THE WAY I USED TO ANYMORE.

SUMTHIN INSIDE O' ME CHANGED THAT DAY.

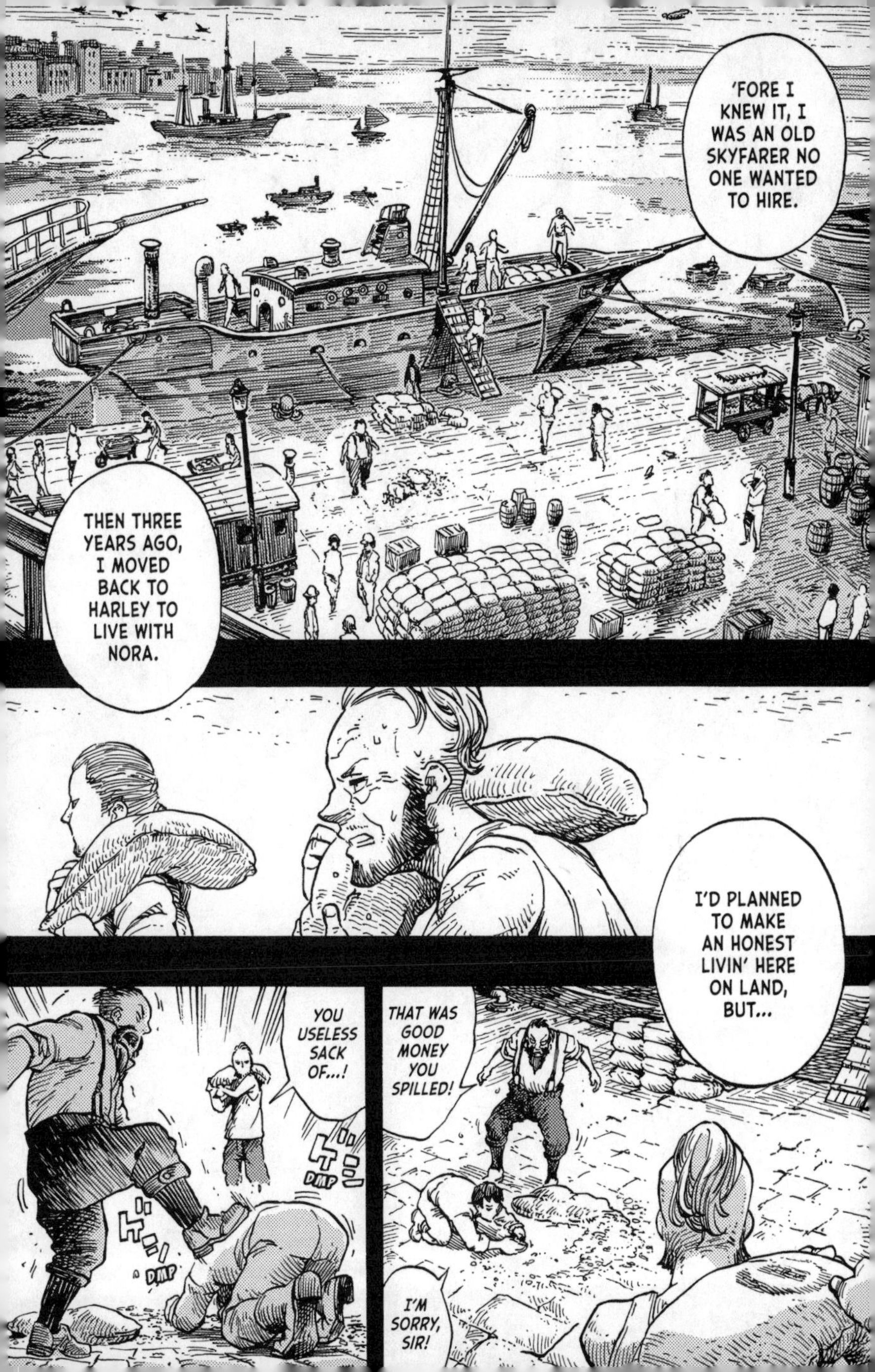
'FORE I KNEW IT, I WAS AN OLD SKYFARER NO ONE WANTED TO HIRE.
THEN THREE YEARS AGO, I MOVED BACK TO HARLEY TO LIVE WITH NORA.
I'D PLANNED TO MAKE AN HONEST LIVIN' HERE ON LAND, BUT...
THAT WAS GOOD MONEY YOU SPILLED!
I'M SORRY, SIR!
YOU USELESS SACK OF...!
DMP
DMP

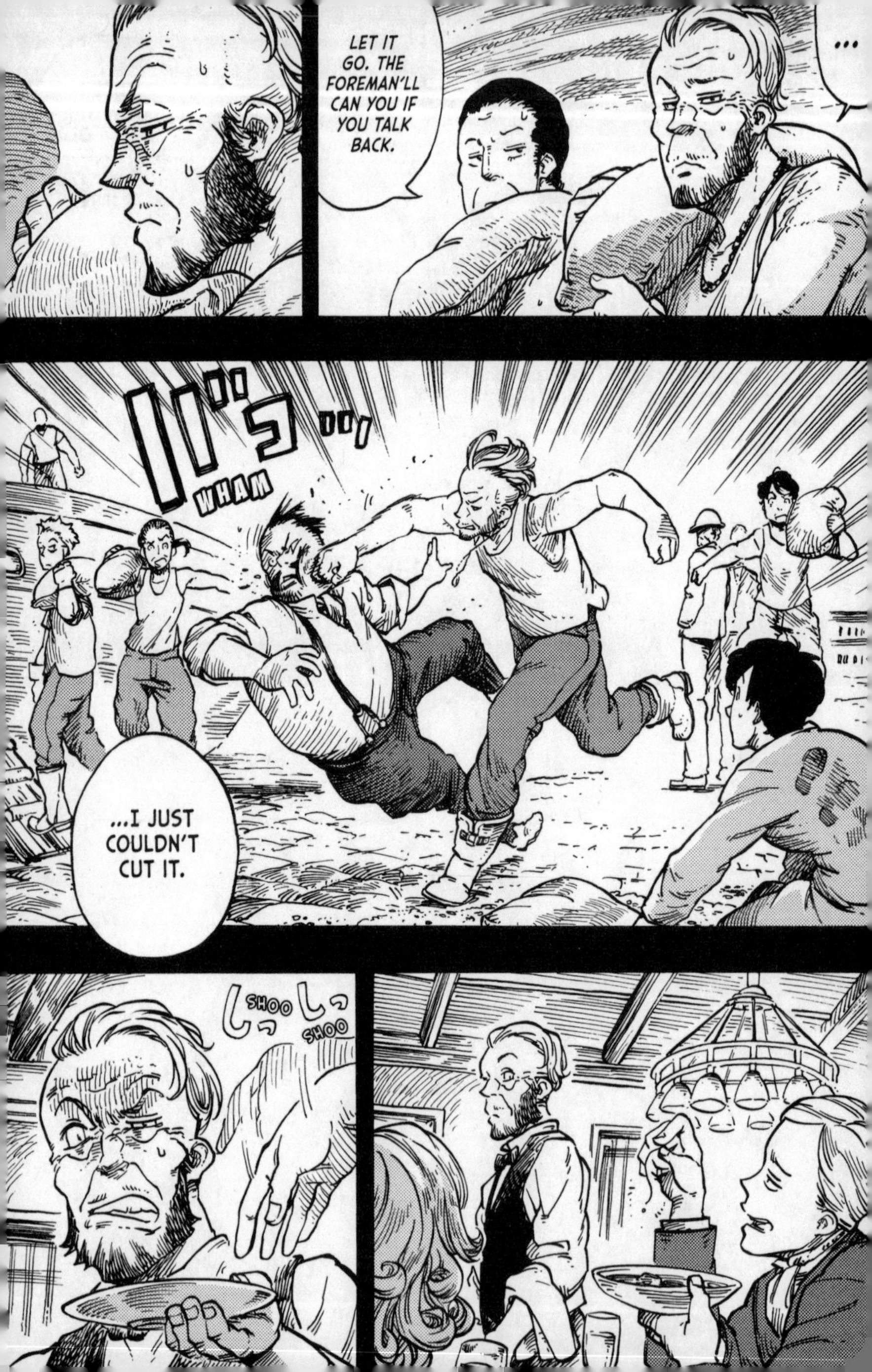
...
LET IT GO. THE FOREMAN'LL CAN YOU IF YOU TALK BACK.
WHAM
...I JUST COULDN'T CUT IT.
しっ SHOO しっ SHOO

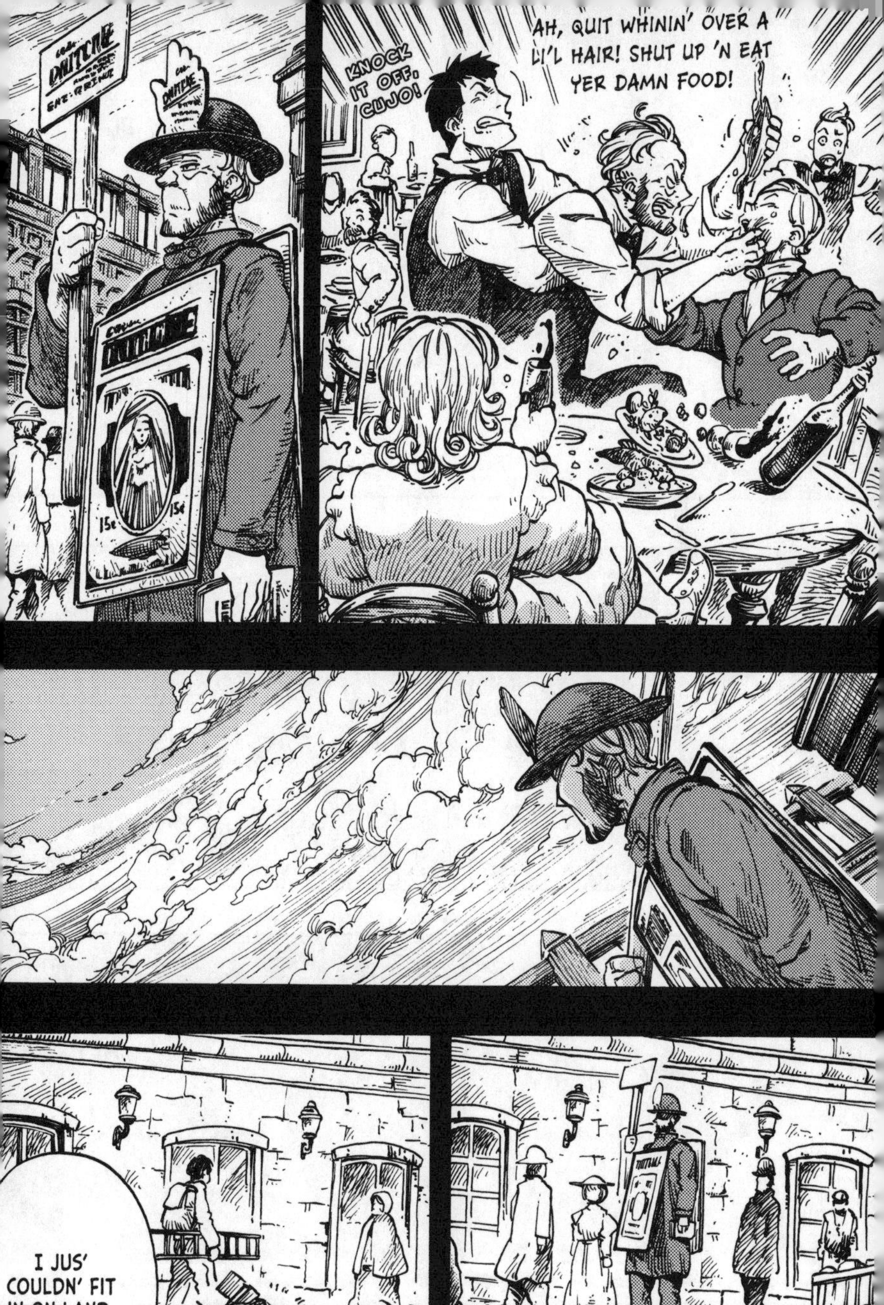
AH, QUIT WHININ' OVER A LI'L HAIR! SHUT UP 'N EAT YER DAMN FOOD!
KNOCK IT OFF, CUJO!
I JUS' COULDN' FIT IN ON LAND.

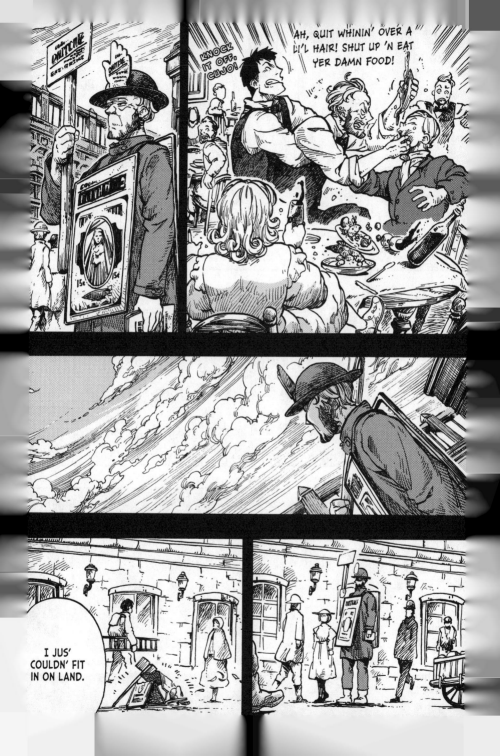

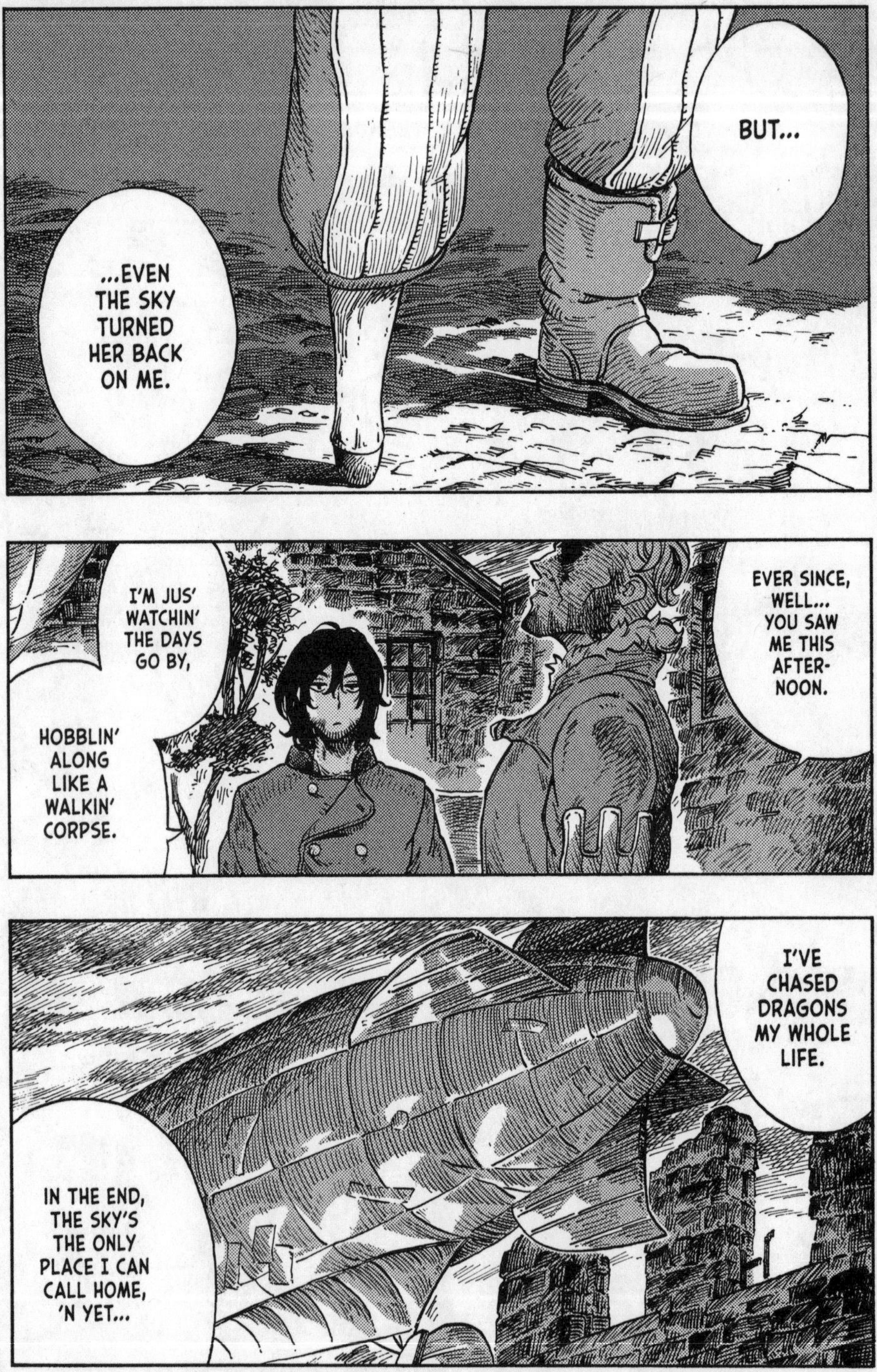
BUT...
...EVEN THE SKY TURNED HER BACK ON ME.
EVER SINCE, WELL... YOU SAW ME THIS AFTERNOON.
I'M JUS' WATCHIN' THE DAYS GO BY,
HOBBLIN' ALONG LIKE A WALKIN' CORPSE.
I'VE CHASED DRAGONS MY WHOLE LIFE.
IN THE END, THE SKY'S THE ONLY PLACE I CAN CALL HOME, 'N YET...

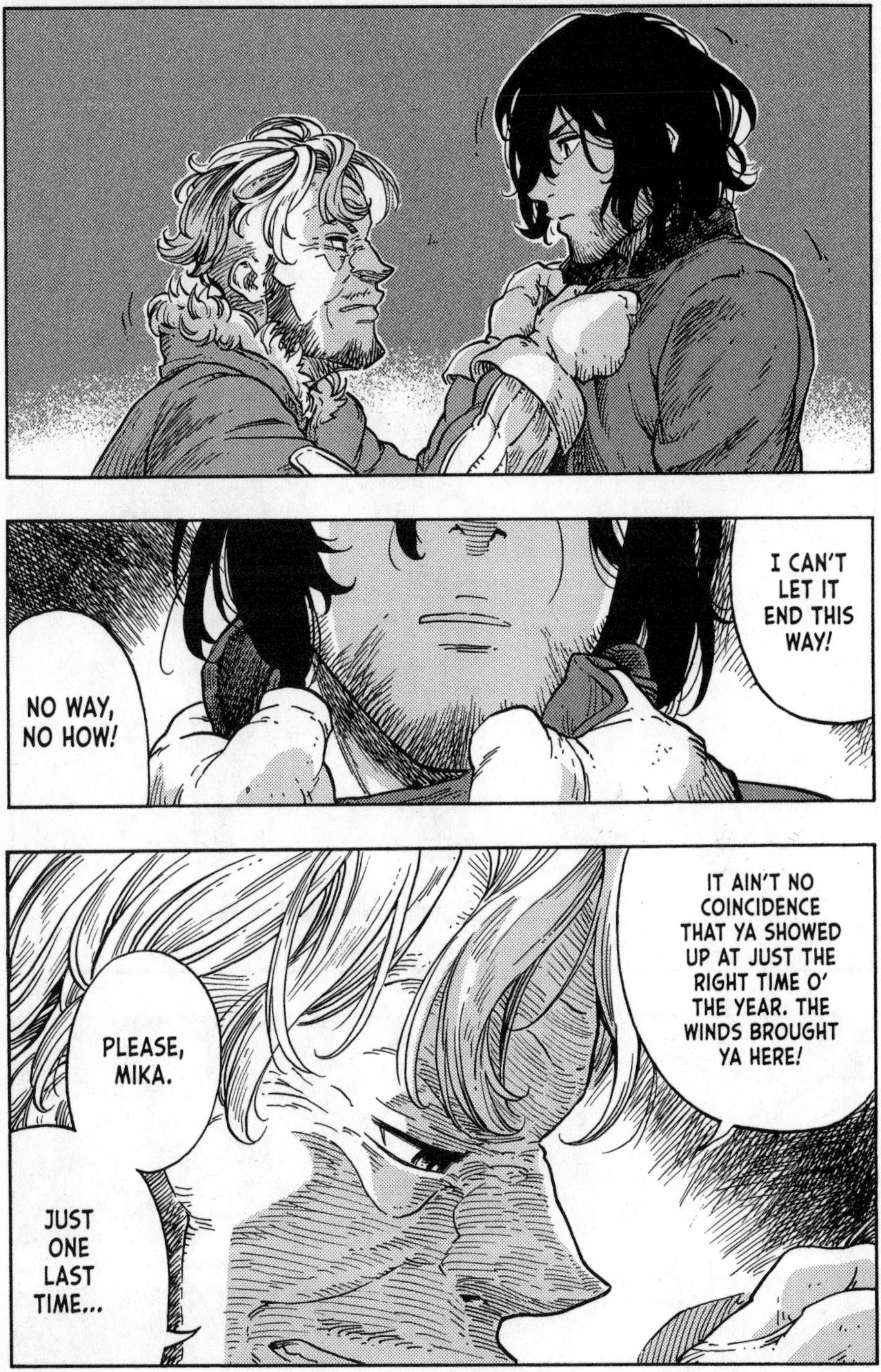
I CAN'T LET IT END THIS WAY!
NO WAY, NO HOW!
IT AIN'T NO COINCIDENCE THAT YA SHOWED UP AT JUST THE RIGHT TIME O' THE YEAR. THE WINDS BROUGHT YA HERE!
PLEASE, MIKA.
JUST ONE LAST TIME...

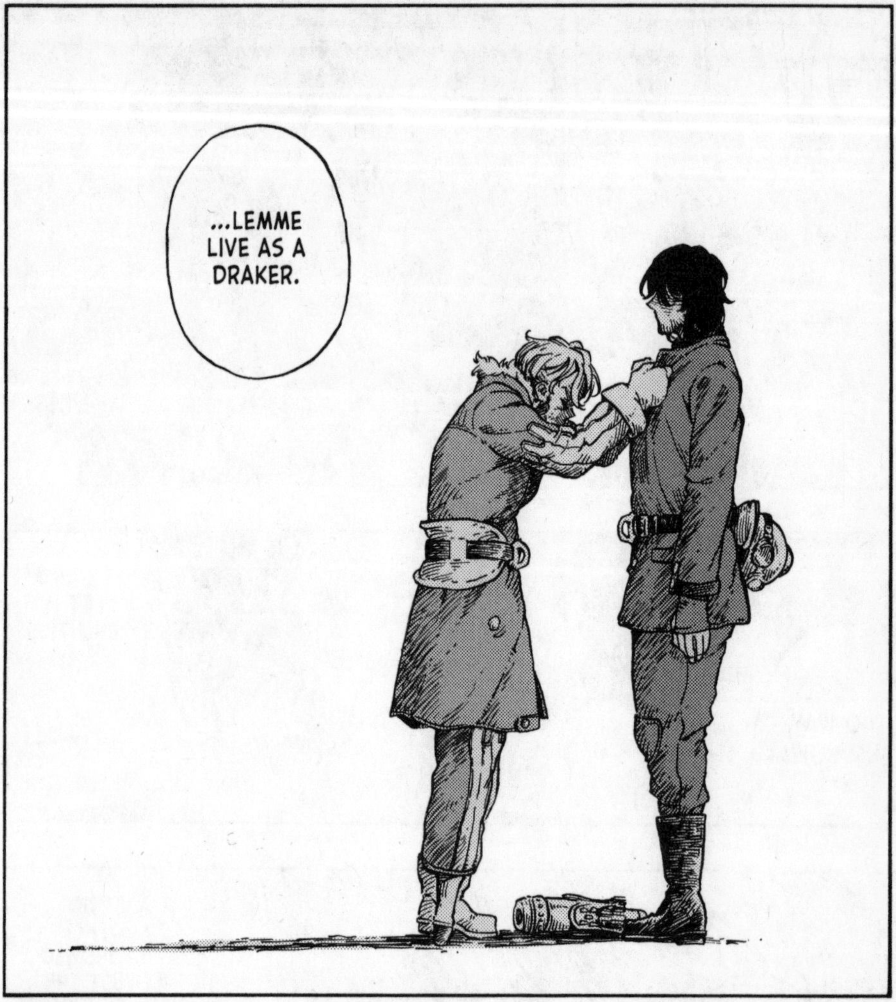
...LEMME LIVE AS A DRAKER.

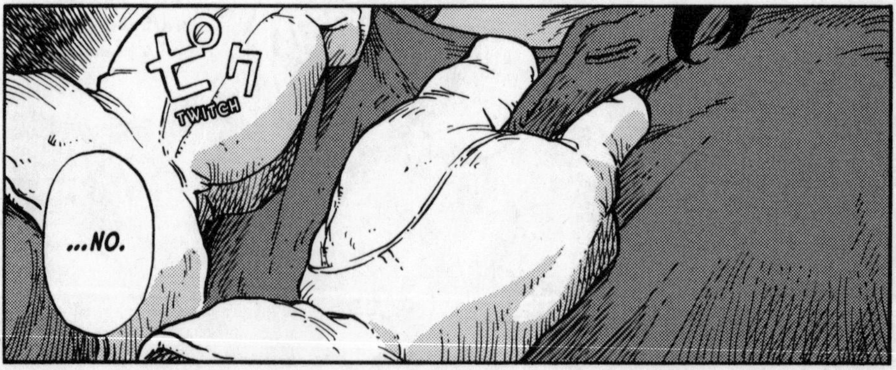
ピク
TWITCH
...NO.

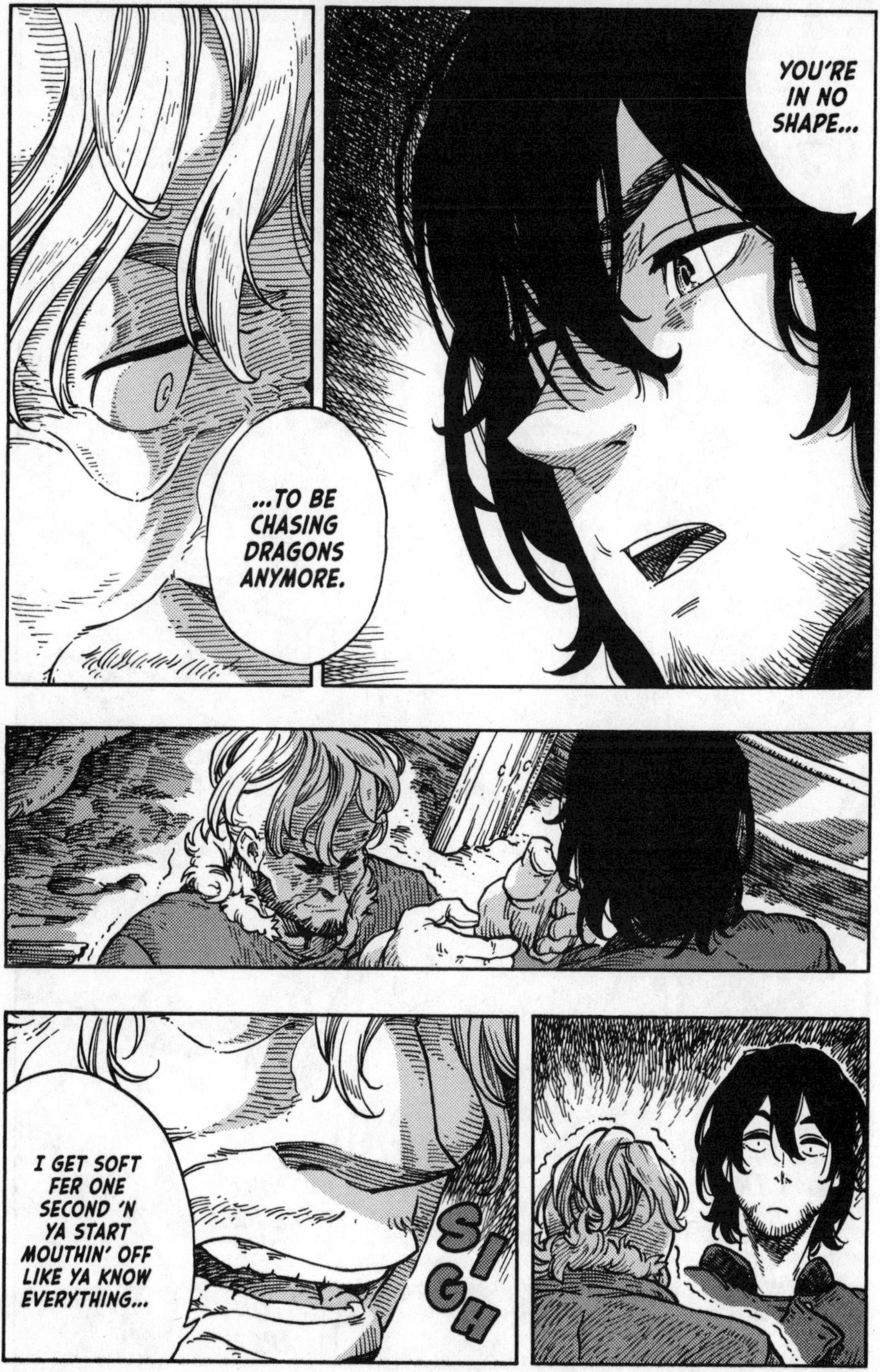
YOU'RE IN NO SHAPE...
...TO BE CHASING DRAGONS ANYMORE.
I GET SOFT FER ONE SECOND 'N YA START MOUTHIN' OFF LIKE YA KNOW EVERYTHING...
SIGH

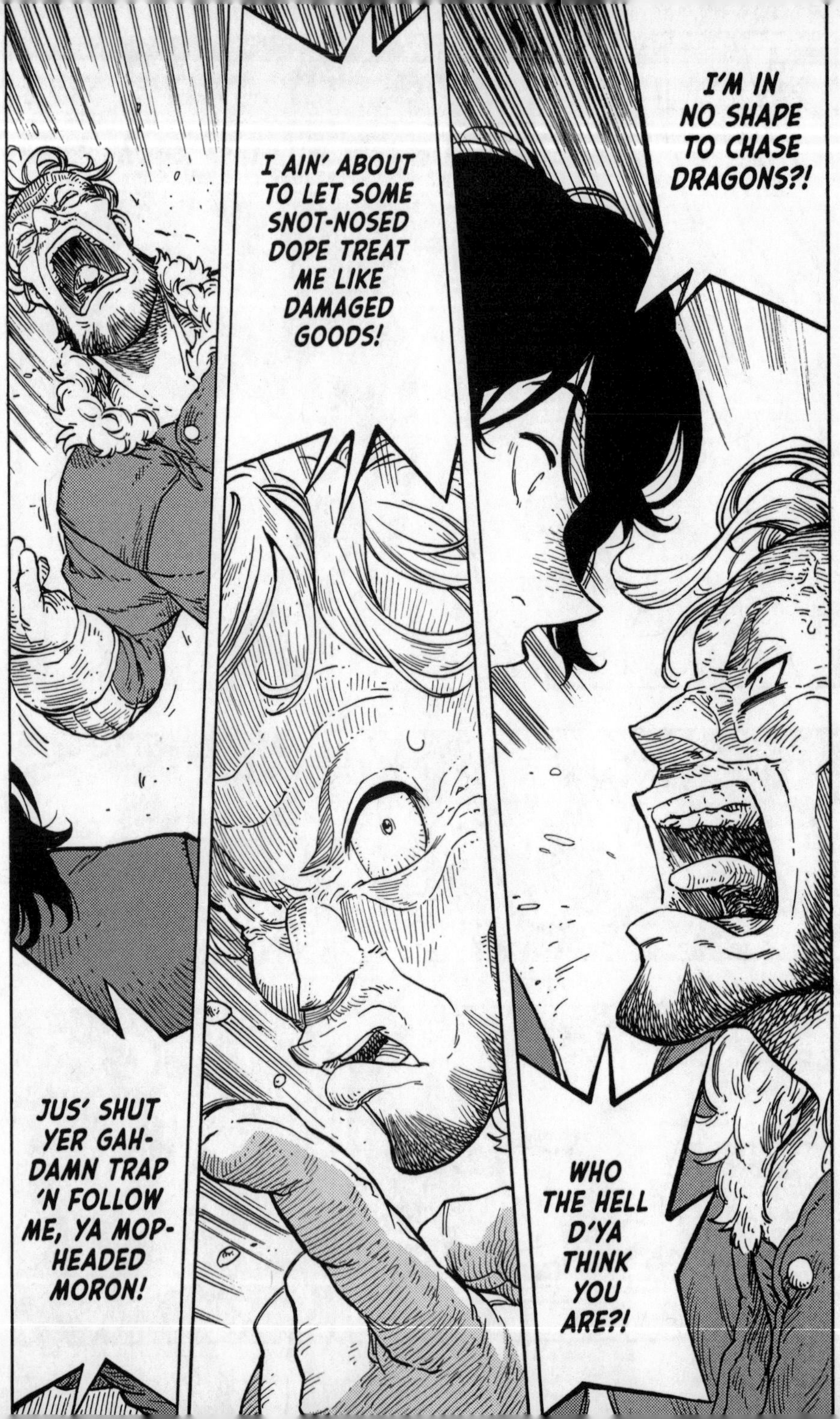
I'M IN NO SHAPE TO CHASE DRAGONS?!
WHO THE HELL D'YA THINK YOU ARE?!
I AIN' ABOUT TO LET SOME SNOT-NOSED DOPE TREAT ME LIKE DAMAGED GOODS!
JUS' SHUT YER GAH-DAMN TRAP 'N FOLLOW ME, YA MOP-HEADED MORON!

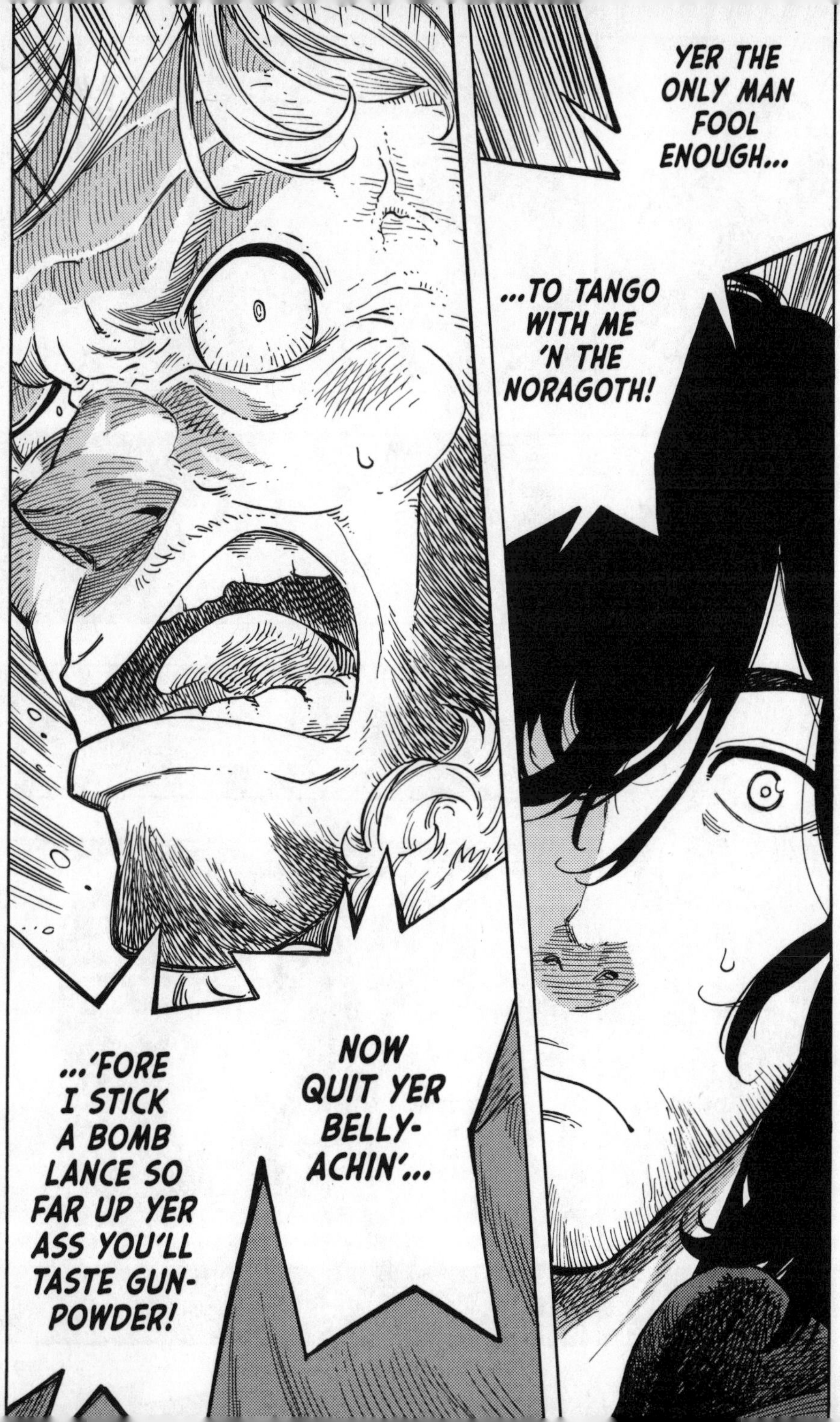
YER THE ONLY MAN FOOL ENOUGH...
...TO TANGO WITH ME 'N THE NORAGOTH!
NOW QUIT YER BELLY-ACHIN'...
...'FORE I STICK A BOMB LANCE SO FAR UP YER ASS YOU'LL TASTE GUN-POWDER!

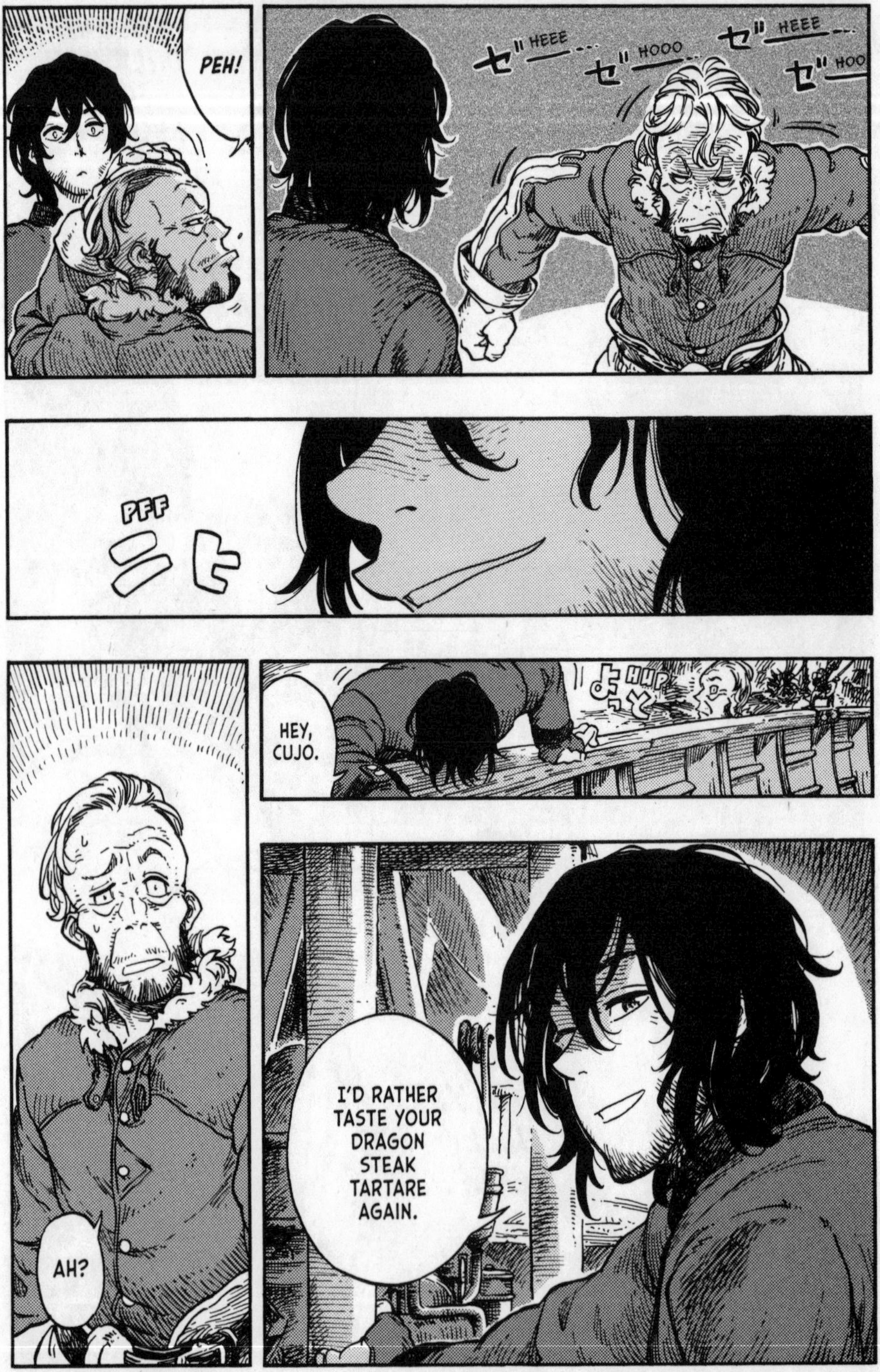
ゼー HEEE...
ゼー HOOO...
ゼー HEEE...
ゼー HOO
PEH!
PFF
ニヒ
よっと HUP
HEY, CUJO.
I'D RATHER TASTE YOUR DRAGON STEAK TARTARE AGAIN.
AH?

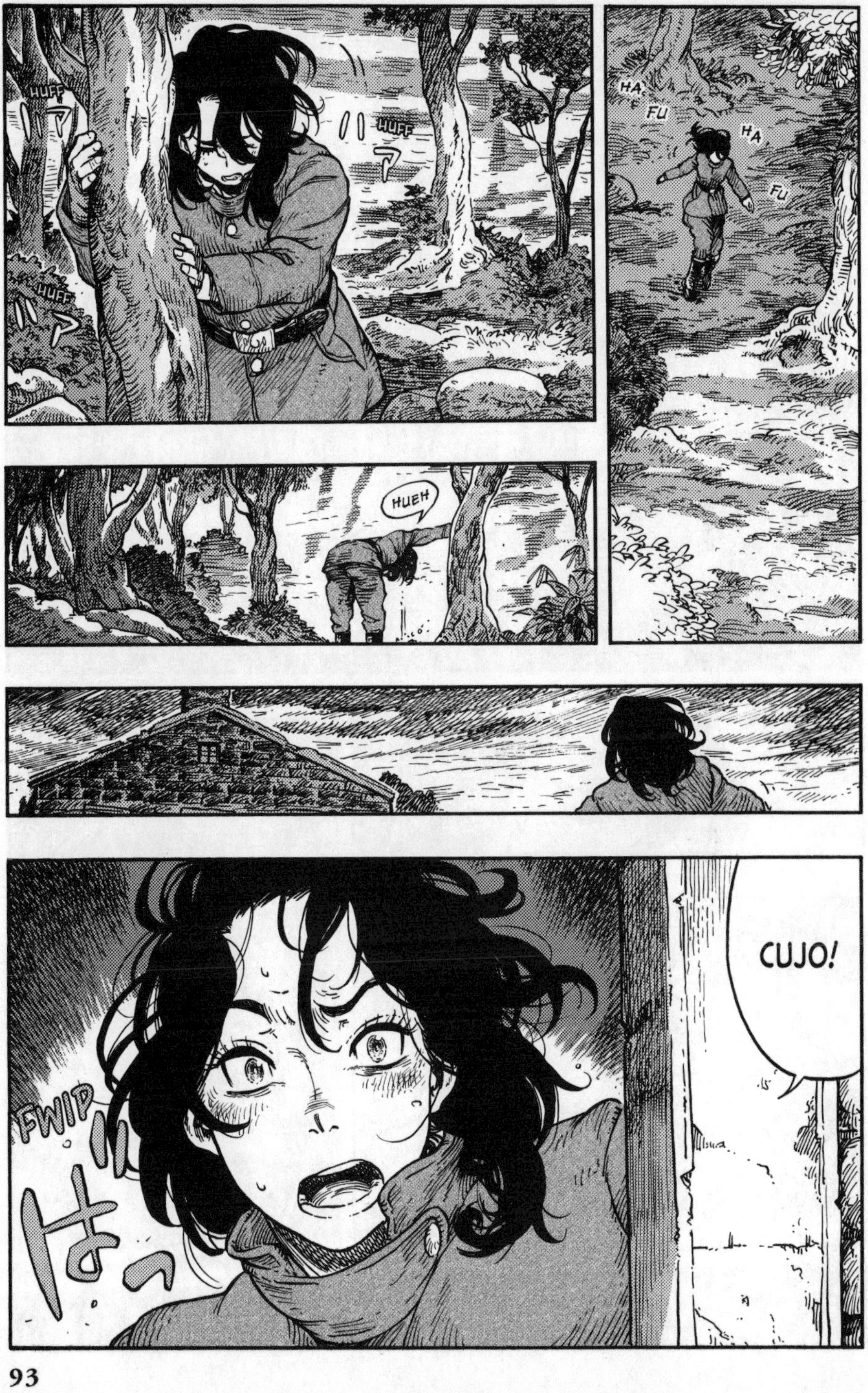

HA
FU
HA
FU
HUFF
HUFF
HUFF
HUEH
CUJO!
FWIP
はっ

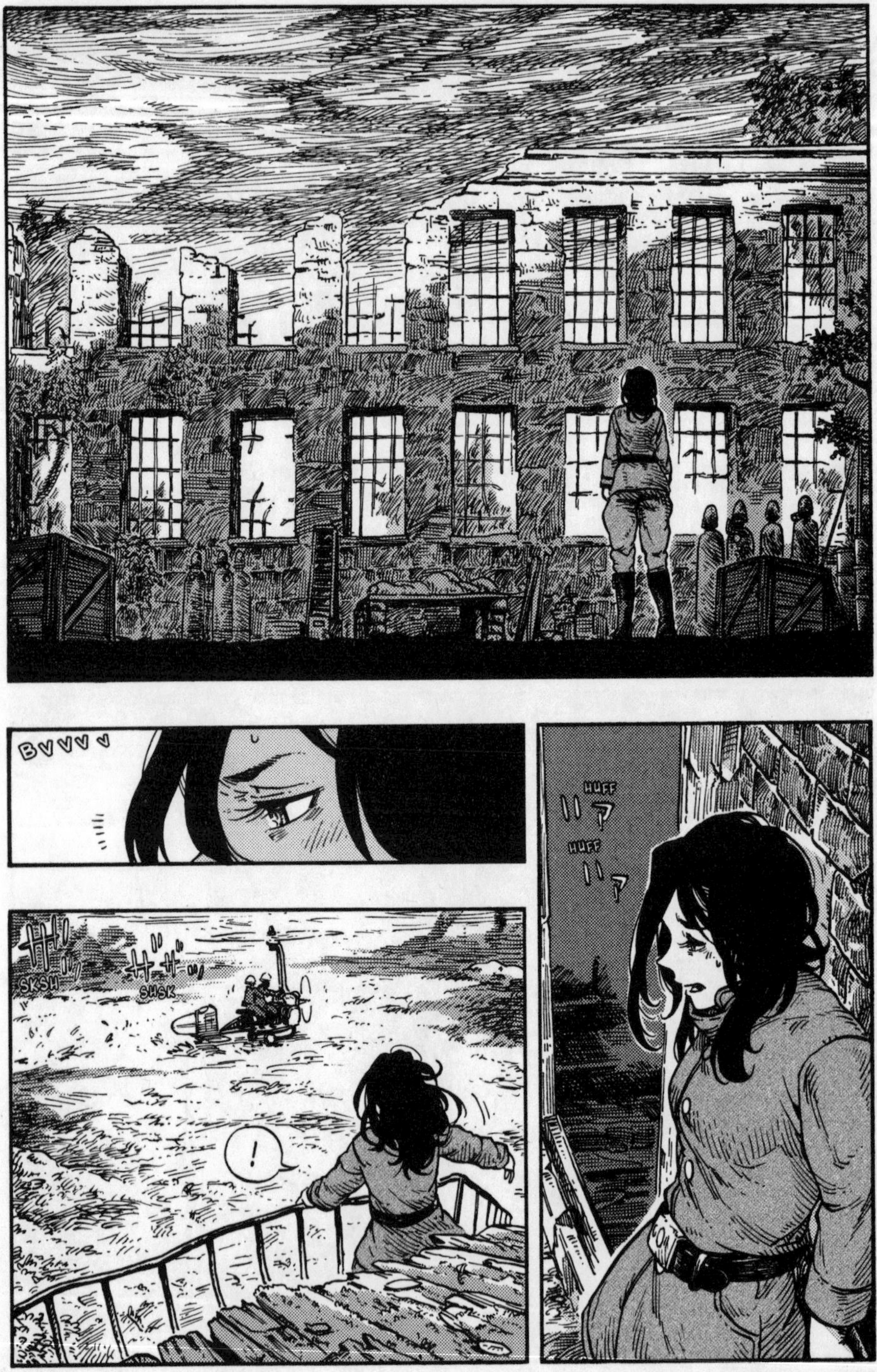
HUFF
HUFF
BVVVV
SKSH
SHSK
!

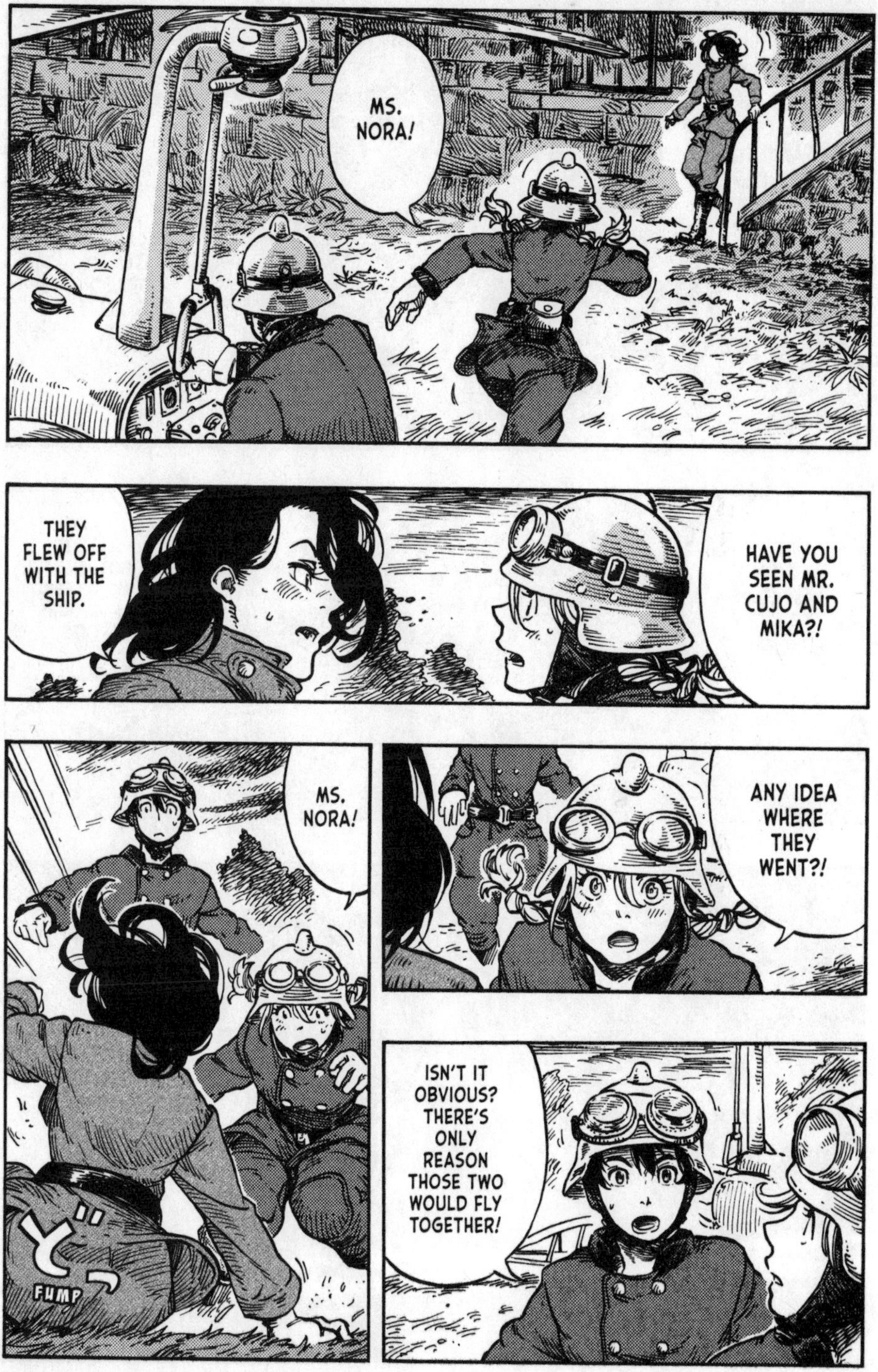
MS. NORA!
HAVE YOU SEEN MR. CUJO AND MIKA?!
THEY FLEW OFF WITH THE SHIP.
ANY IDEA WHERE THEY WENT?!
ISN'T IT OBVIOUS? THERE'S ONLY REASON THOSE TWO WOULD FLY TOGETHER!
MS. NORA!
FUMP

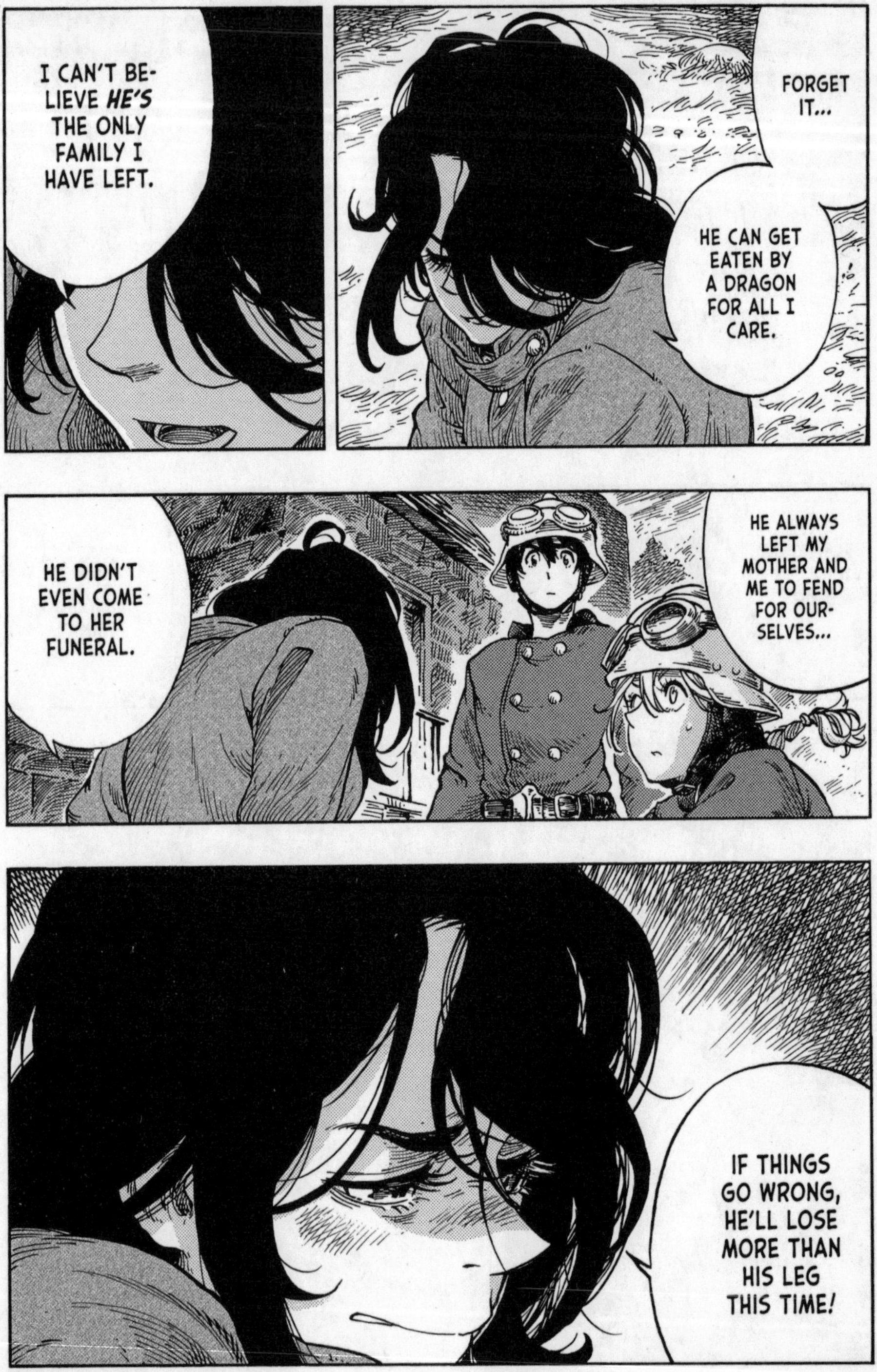
FORGET IT...
HE CAN GET EATEN BY A DRAGON FOR ALL I CARE.
I CAN'T BE-LIEVE *HE'S* THE ONLY FAMILY I HAVE LEFT.
HE ALWAYS LEFT MY MOTHER AND ME TO FEND FOR OUR-SELVES...
HE DIDN'T EVEN COME TO HER FUNERAL.
IF THINGS GO WRONG, HE'LL LOSE MORE THAN HIS LEG THIS TIME!

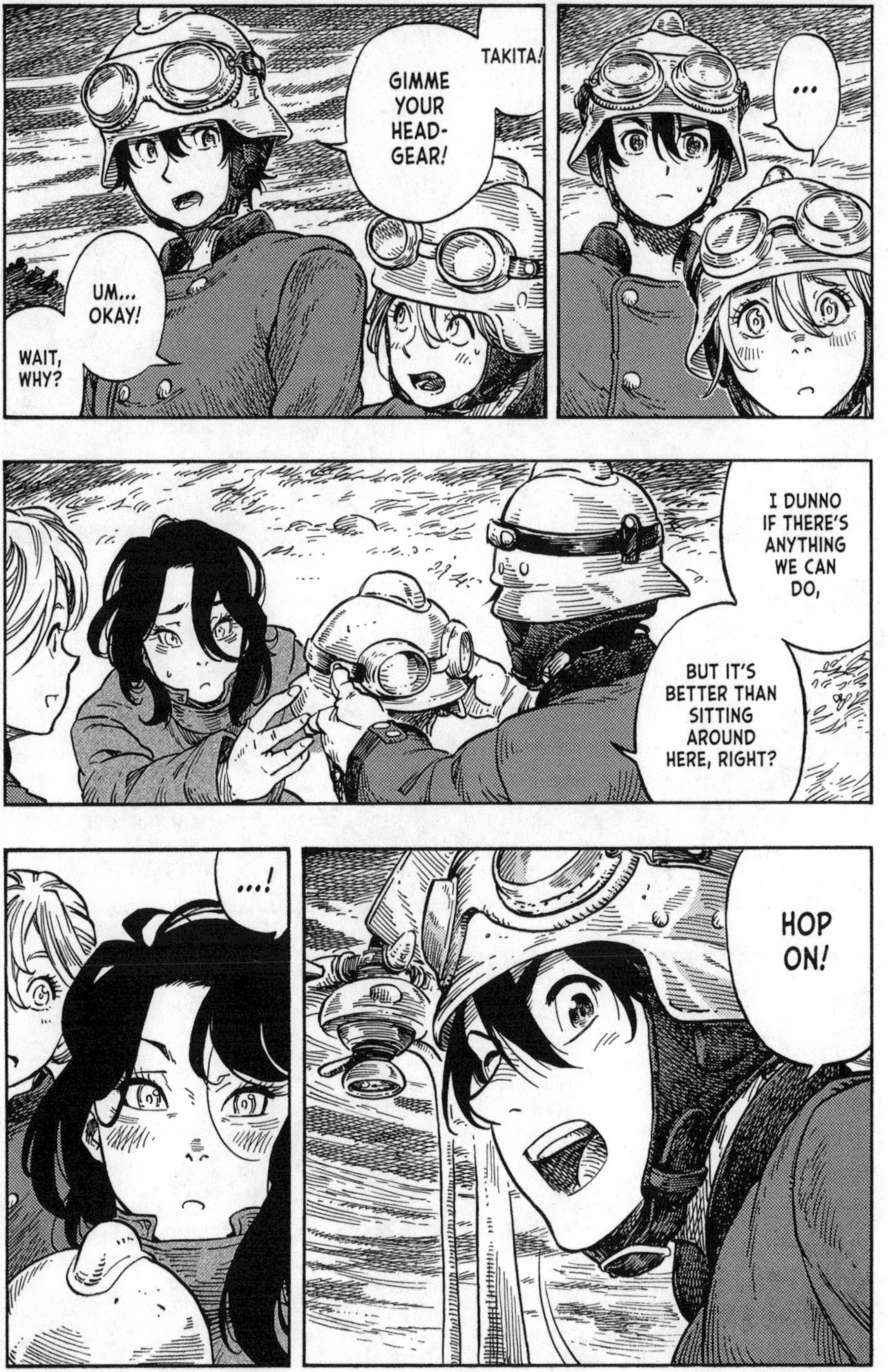
...
TAKITA!
GIMME YOUR HEAD-GEAR!
UM... OKAY!
WAIT, WHY?
I DUNNO IF THERE'S ANYTHING WE CAN DO,
BUT IT'S BETTER THAN SITTING AROUND HERE, RIGHT?
HOP ON!
...!

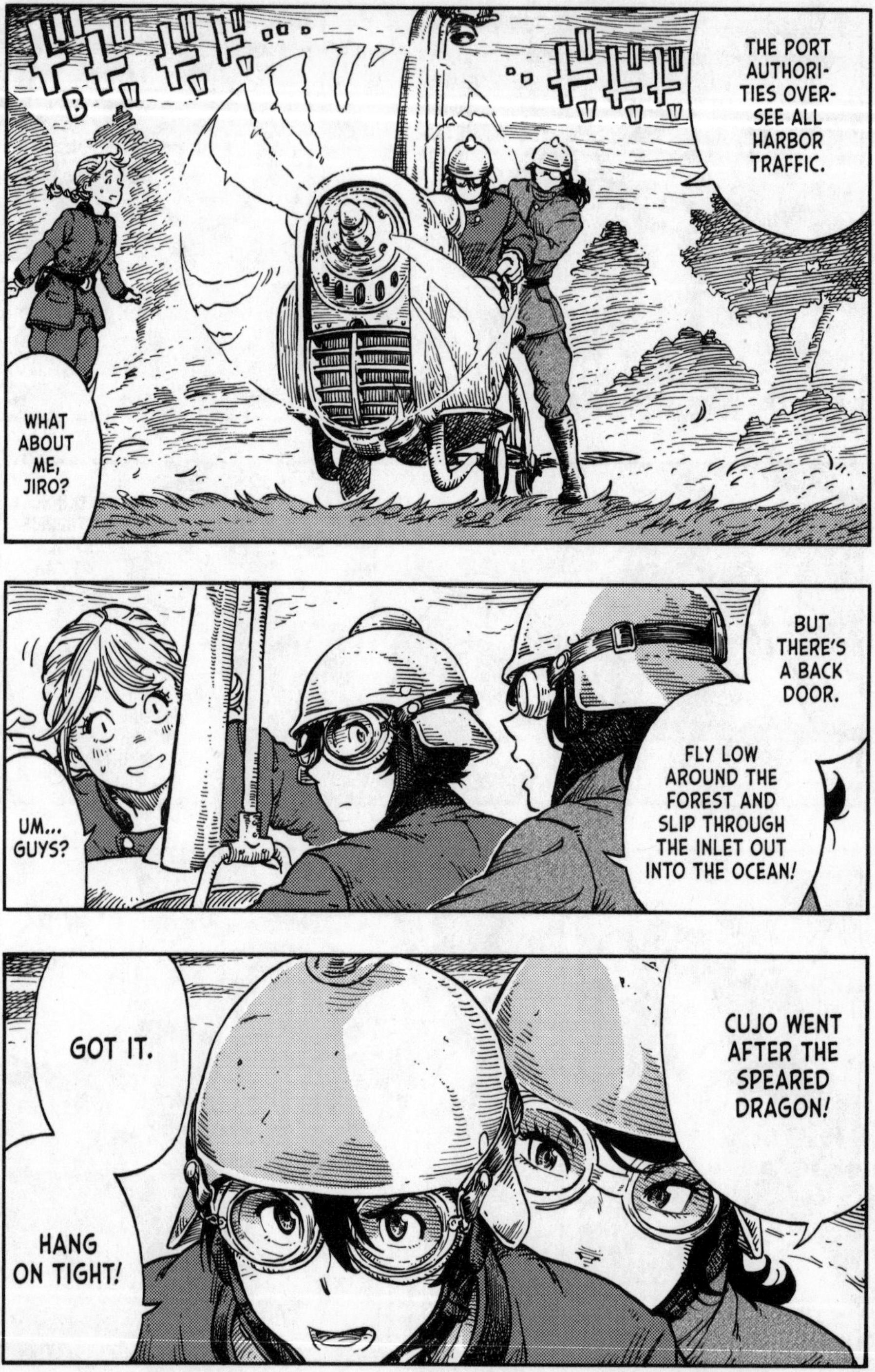
THE PORT AUTHORITIES OVERSEE ALL HARBOR TRAFFIC.
WHAT ABOUT ME, JIRO?
BUT THERE'S A BACK DOOR.
FLY LOW AROUND THE FOREST AND SLIP THROUGH THE INLET OUT INTO THE OCEAN!
UM... GUYS?
CUJO WENT AFTER THE SPEARED DRAGON!
GOT IT.
HANG ON TIGHT!

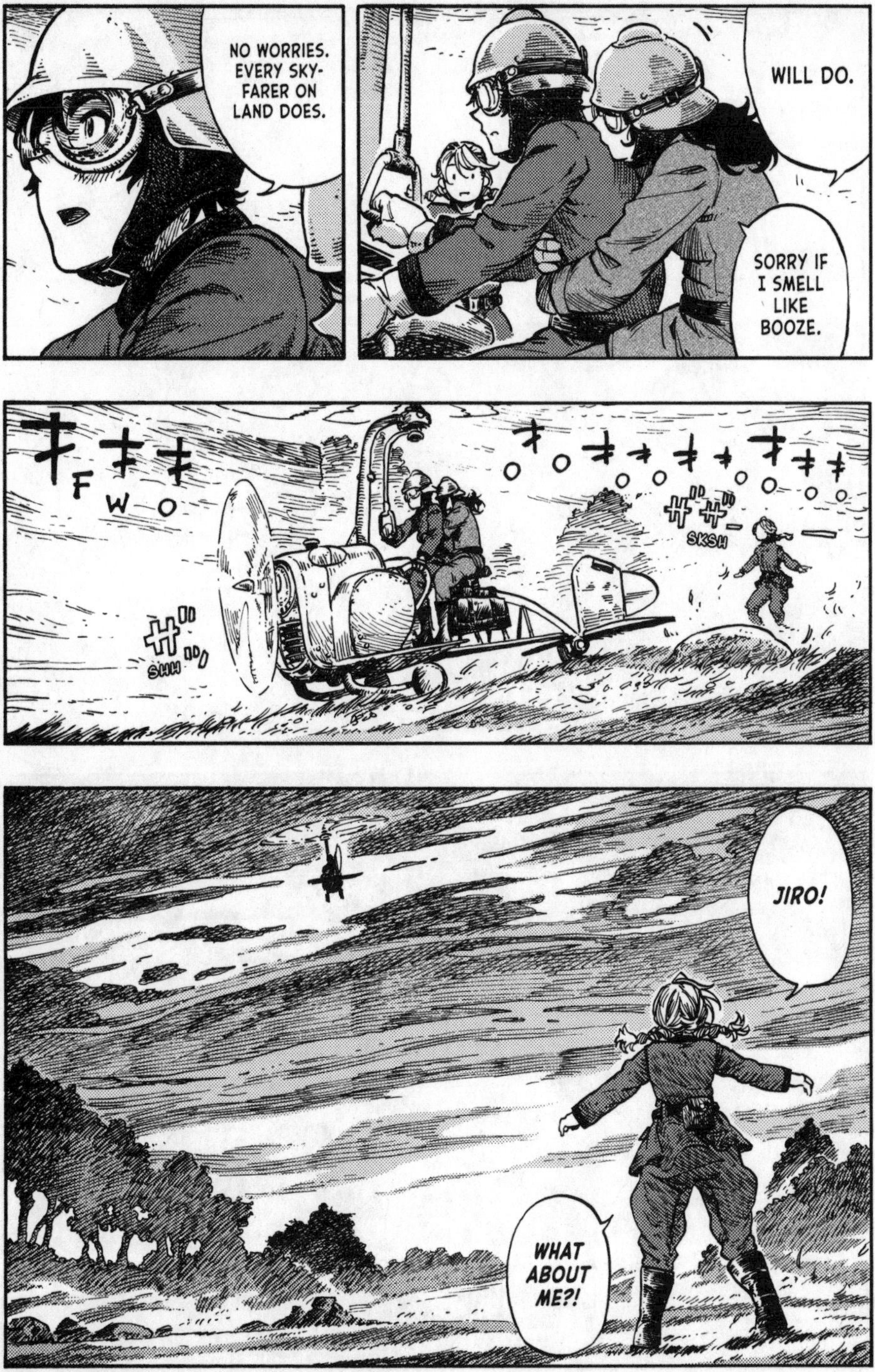
WILL DO.
SORRY IF I SMELL LIKE BOOZE.
NO WORRIES. EVERY SKY-FARER ON LAND DOES.
SKSH
FWO
SHH
JIRO!
WHAT ABOUT ME?!

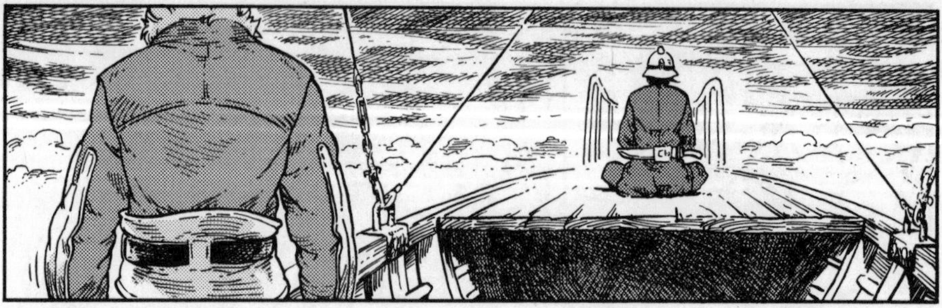

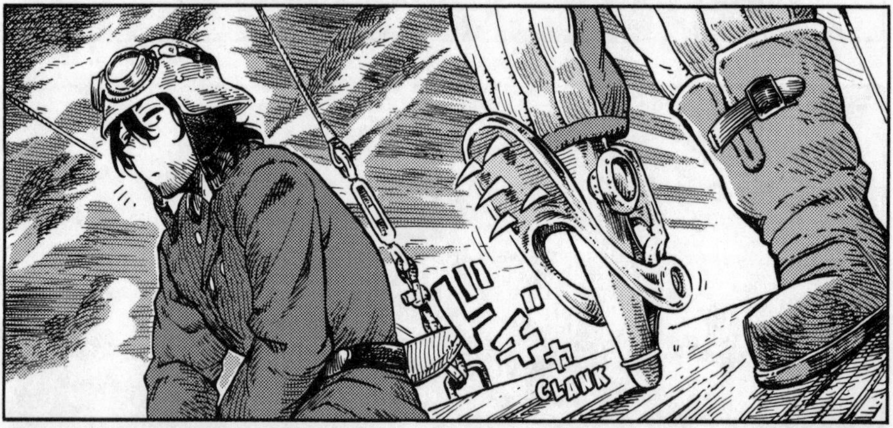
CLANK

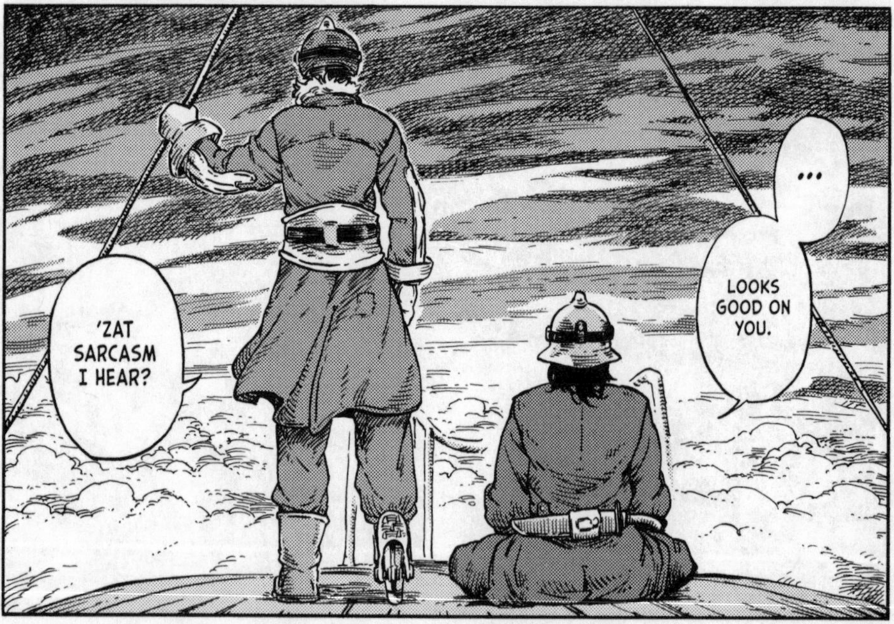
...
LOOKS GOOD ON YOU.
'ZAT SARCASM I HEAR?

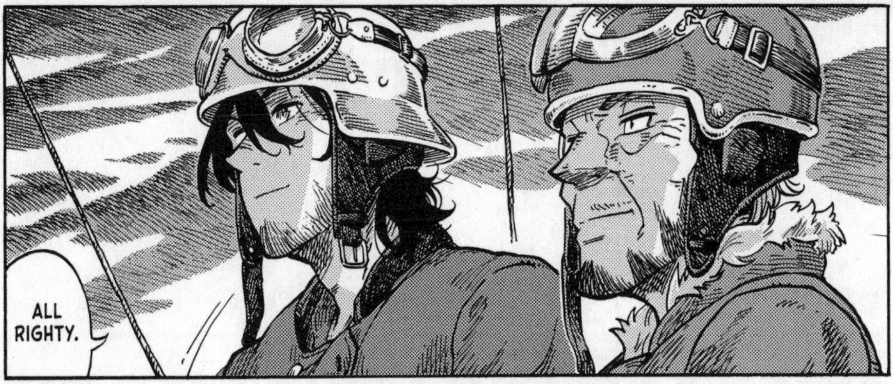
ALL RIGHTY.
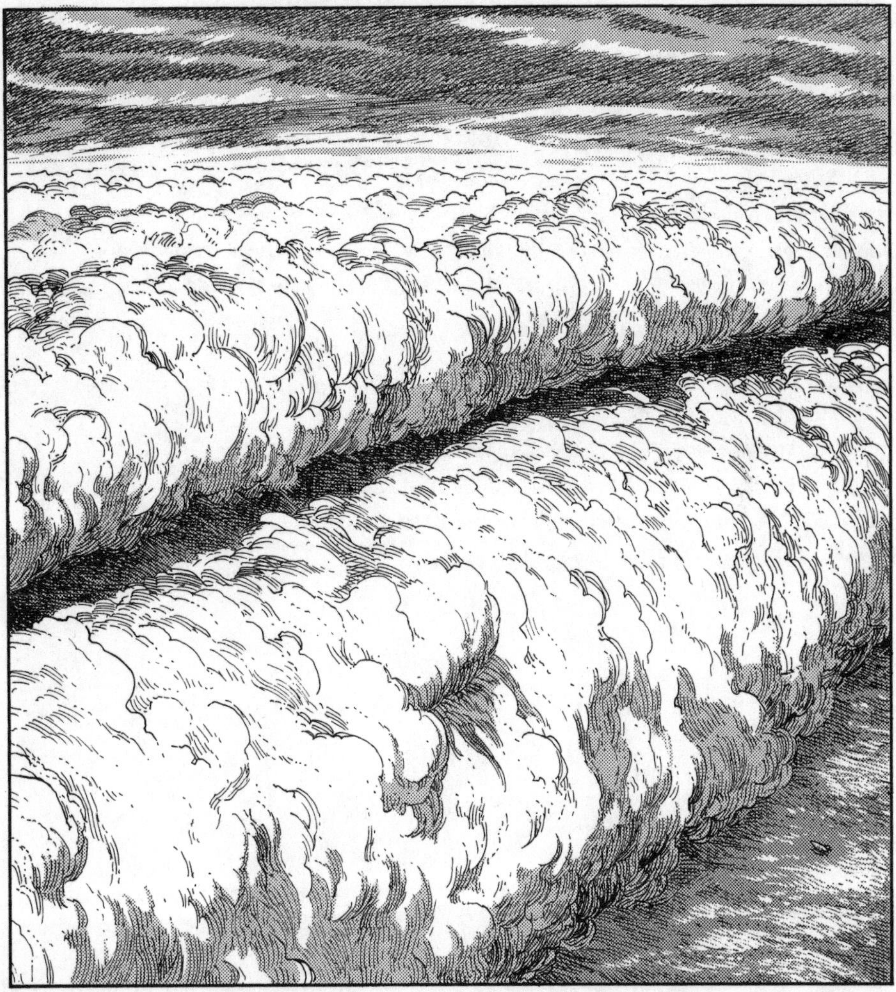

Kraken Tentacle Carpaccio

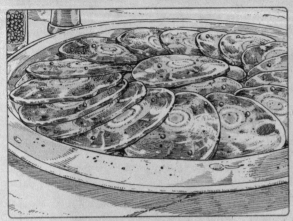

Ingredients (Serves 1)

✦ 150–200 g kraken tentacle

✦ 1 Tbsp capers

✦ 2-3 Tbsp olive oil

✦ Salt

✦ Freshly ground black pepper (optional)

✦ Parmesan cheese (optional)

✦ 60g arugula (optional)

✦ Juice from ½ a lemon (optional)

✦ 1 clove grated garlic (optional)

01
Make a shallow cut lengthwise in the tentacle and, while gripping firmly with a towel or other in one hand, peel the skin off.

02
Skewer skinned tentacle, lightly roast over an open flame, then thinly slice crosswise.

03
If using large capers, roughly chop them. Wash arugula in cold water, remove and shake off excess moisture.

04
Arrange sliced tentacle on a plate. Scatter capers on top, as well as garlic and cheese if using.

05
Drizzle with lemon juice and olive oil, top with arugula. Sprinkle salt and pepper and serve.

I COULD GO FER SOME WINE.

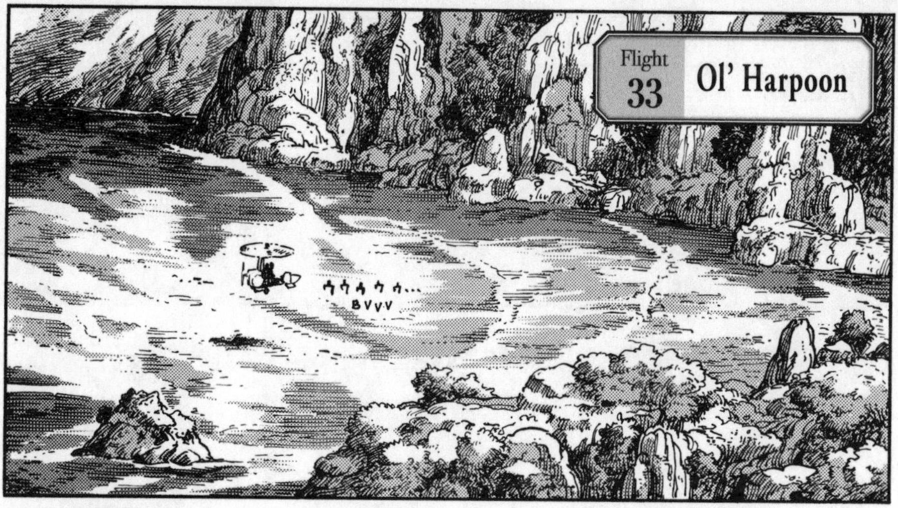
Flight 33 Ol' Harpoon
ウウウウウ...
BVVV
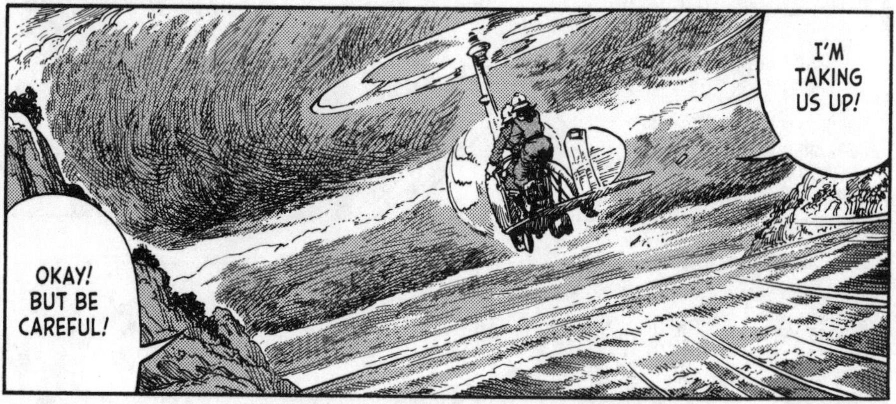
I'M TAKING US UP!
OKAY! BUT BE CAREFUL!
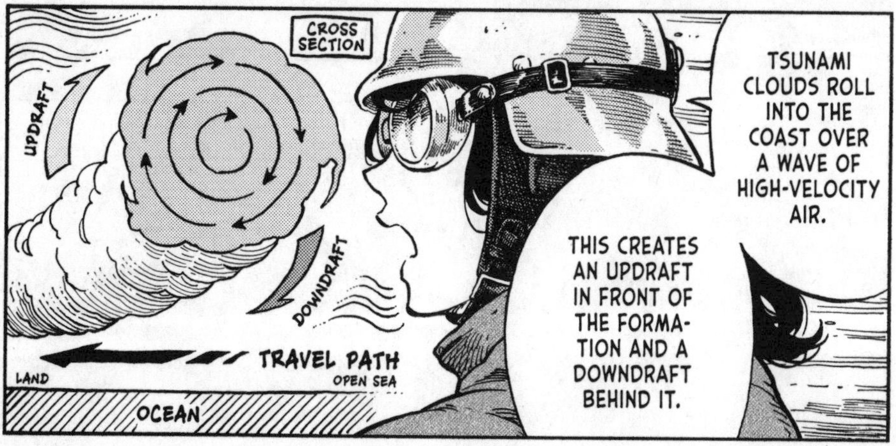
TSUNAMI CLOUDS ROLL INTO THE COAST OVER A WAVE OF HIGH-VELOCITY AIR.
THIS CREATES AN UPDRAFT IN FRONT OF THE FORMA-TION AND A DOWNDRAFT BEHIND IT.
CROSS SECTION
UPDRAFT
DOWNDRAFT
TRAVEL PATH
LAND
OPEN SEA
OCEAN

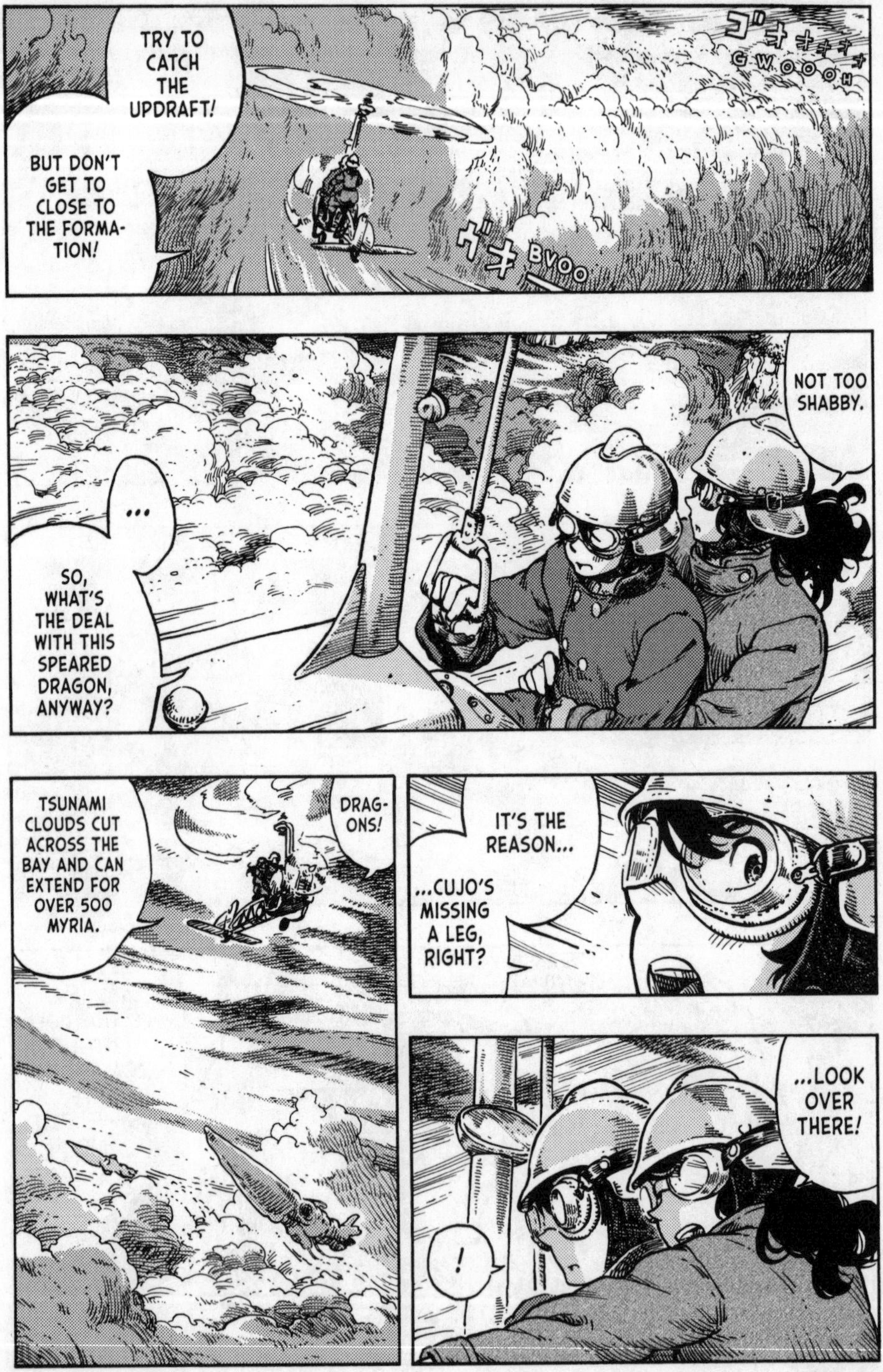
ゴオォォォォ
GWOOOOH
TRY TO CATCH THE UPDRAFT!
BUT DON'T GET TO CLOSE TO THE FORMATION!
ヴオ
BVOO
NOT TOO SHABBY.
...
SO, WHAT'S THE DEAL WITH THIS SPEARED DRAGON, ANYWAY?
IT'S THE REASON...
...CUJO'S MISSING A LEG, RIGHT?
...LOOK OVER THERE!
!
DRAGONS!
TSUNAMI CLOUDS CUT ACROSS THE BAY AND CAN EXTEND FOR OVER 500 MYRIA.

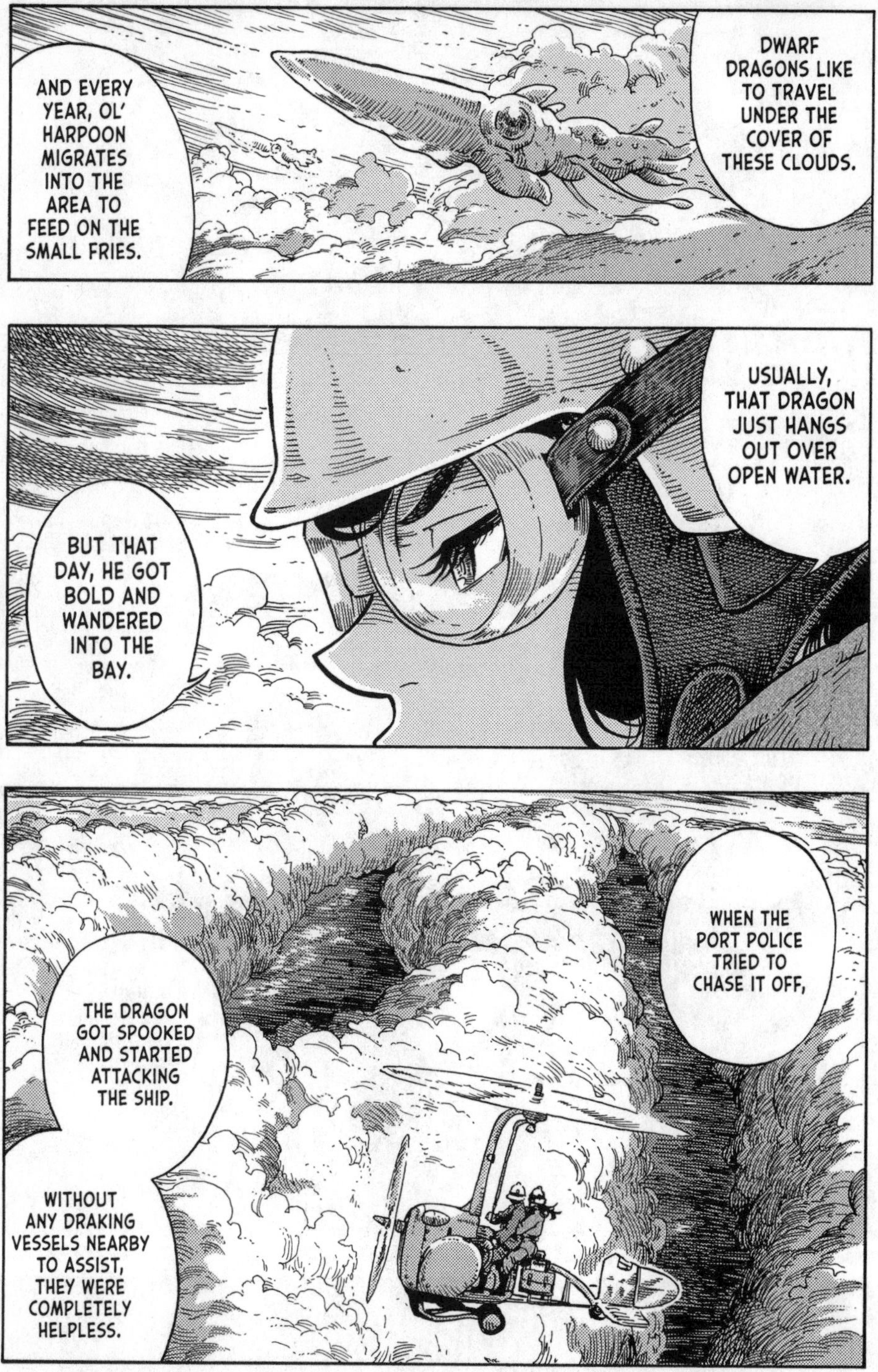
DWARF DRAGONS LIKE TO TRAVEL UNDER THE COVER OF THESE CLOUDS.
AND EVERY YEAR, OL' HARPOON MIGRATES INTO THE AREA TO FEED ON THE SMALL FRIES.
USUALLY, THAT DRAGON JUST HANGS OUT OVER OPEN WATER.
BUT THAT DAY, HE GOT BOLD AND WANDERED INTO THE BAY.
WHEN THE PORT POLICE TRIED TO CHASE IT OFF,
THE DRAGON GOT SPOOKED AND STARTED ATTACKING THE SHIP.
WITHOUT ANY DRAKING VESSELS NEARBY TO ASSIST, THEY WERE COMPLETELY HELPLESS.

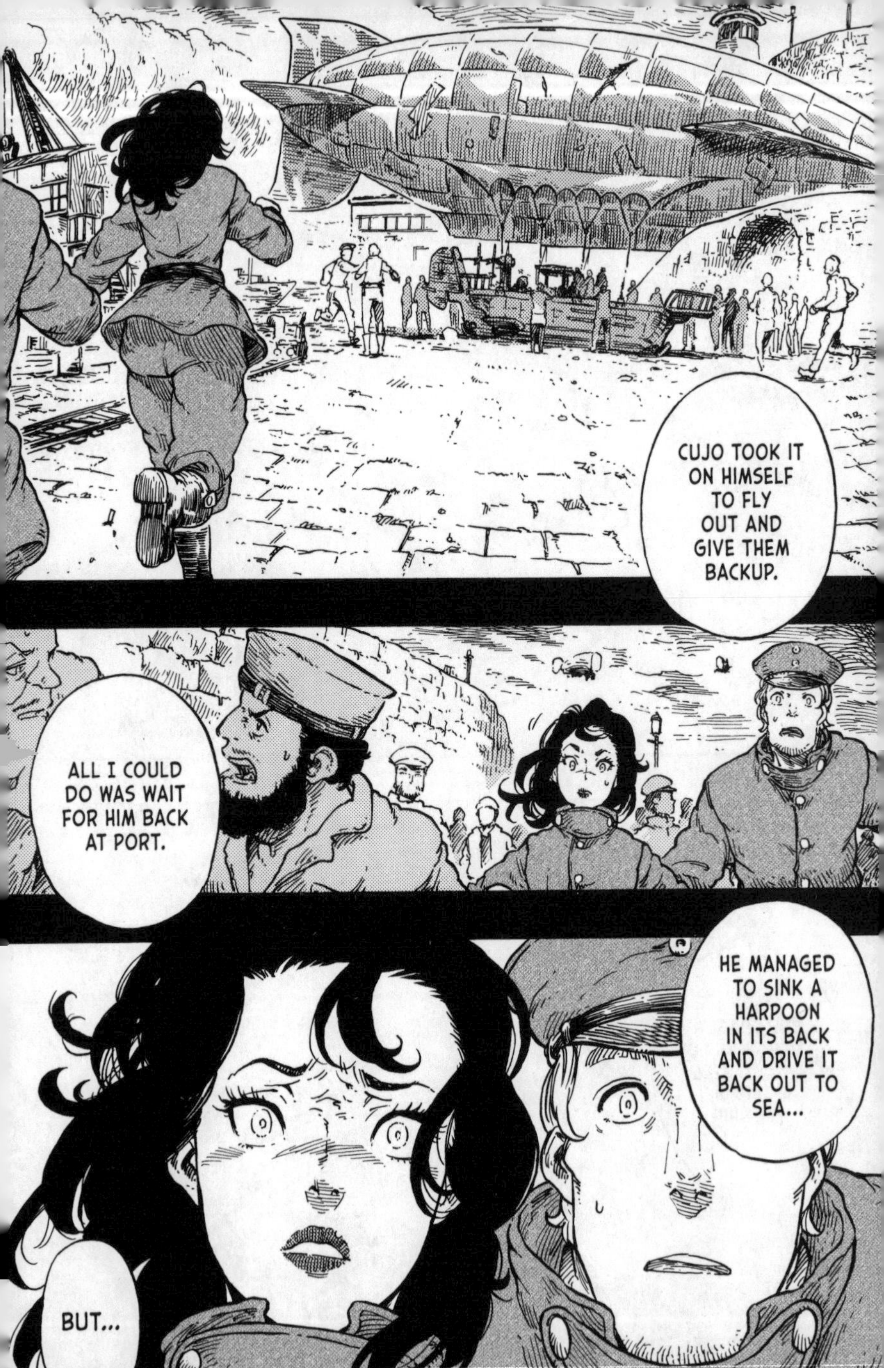
CUJO TOOK IT ON HIMSELF TO FLY OUT AND GIVE THEM BACKUP.
ALL I COULD DO WAS WAIT FOR HIM BACK AT PORT.
HE MANAGED TO SINK A HARPOON IN ITS BACK AND DRIVE IT BACK OUT TO SEA...
BUT...

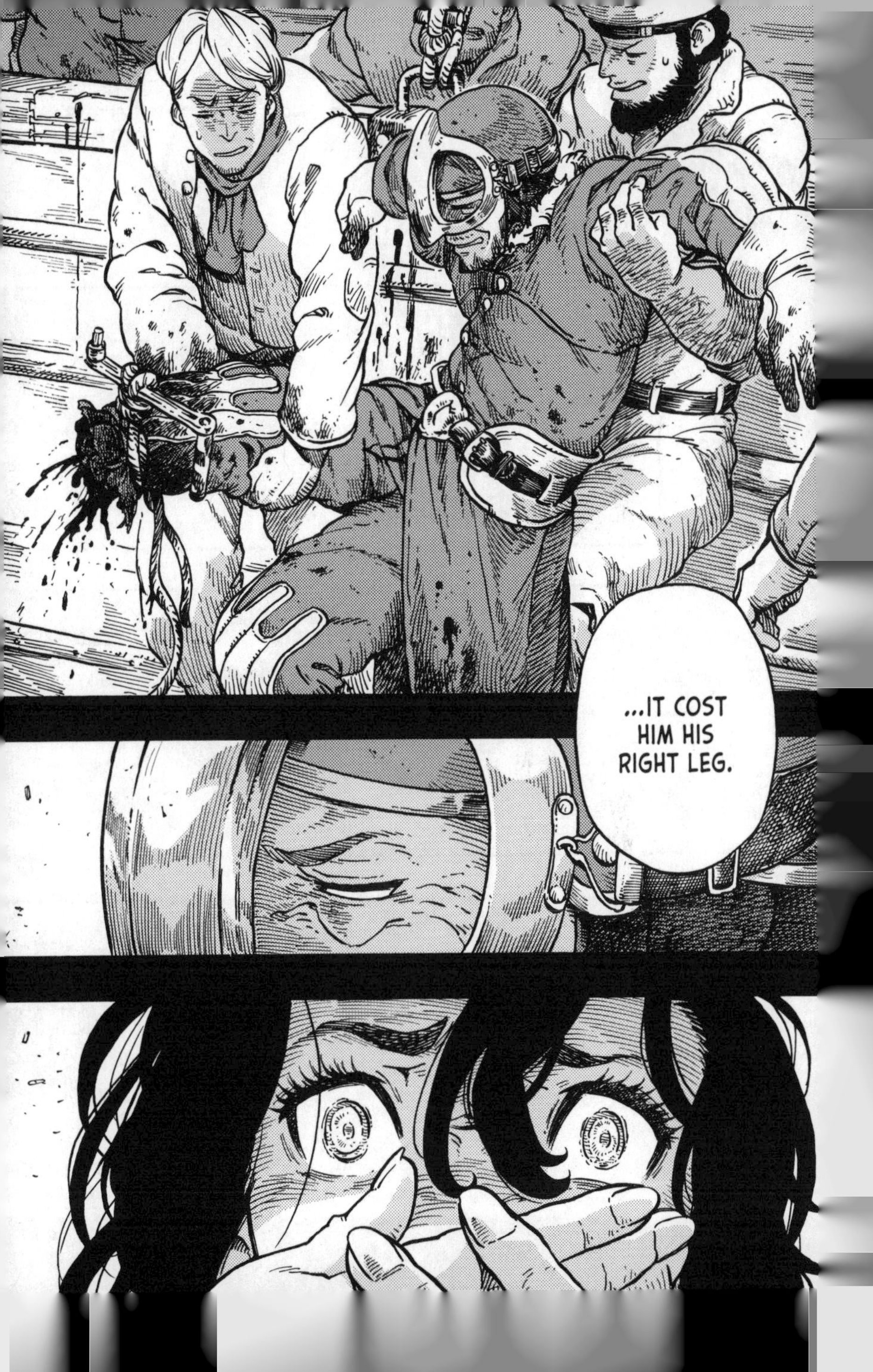
...IT COST HIM HIS RIGHT LEG.

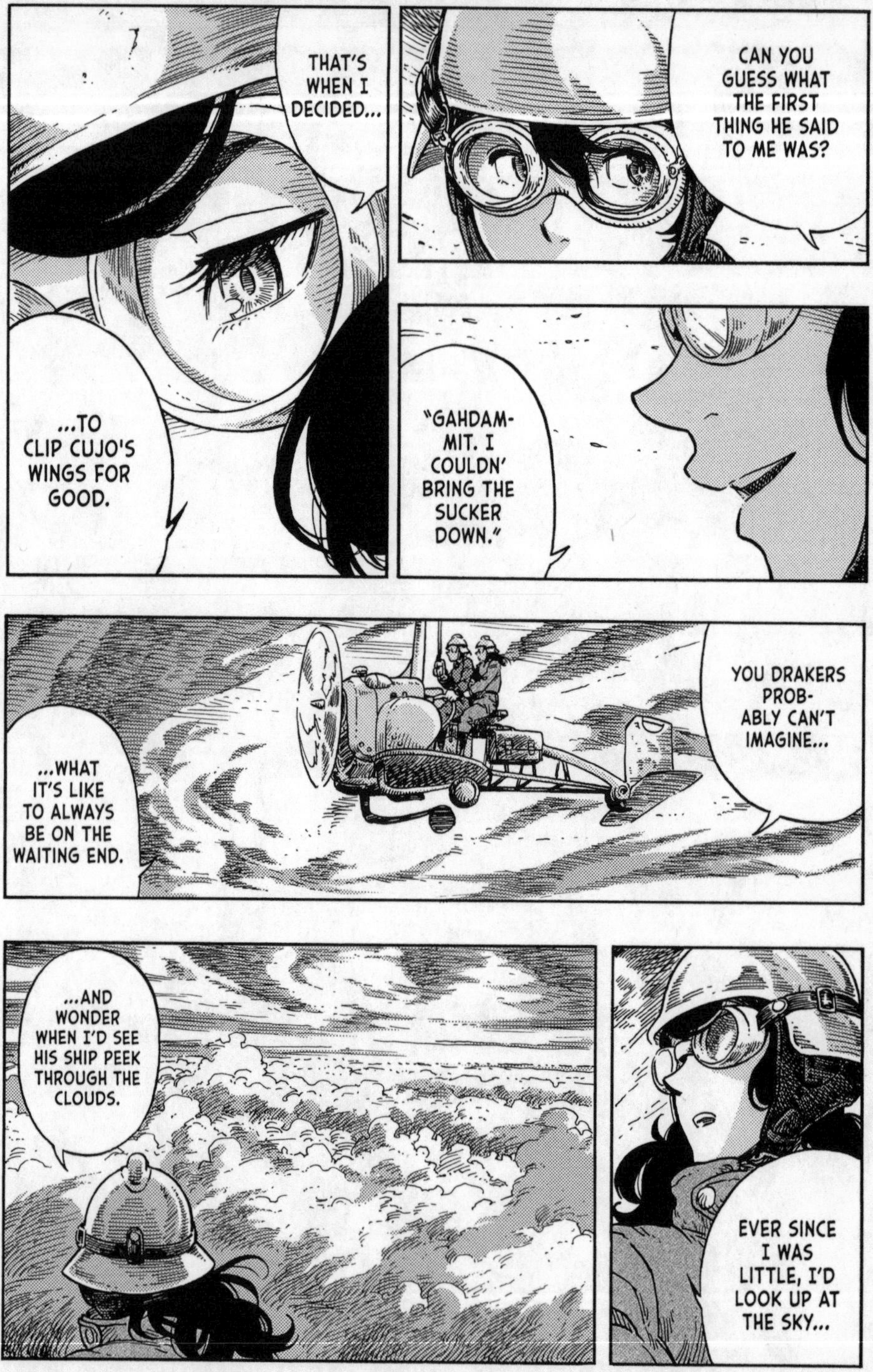
CAN YOU GUESS WHAT THE FIRST THING HE SAID TO ME WAS?
"GAHDAM-MIT. I COULDN' BRING THE SUCKER DOWN."
THAT'S WHEN I DECIDED...
...TO CLIP CUJO'S WINGS FOR GOOD.
YOU DRAKERS PROB-ABLY CAN'T IMAGINE...
...WHAT IT'S LIKE TO ALWAYS BE ON THE WAITING END.
EVER SINCE I WAS LITTLE, I'D LOOK UP AT THE SKY...
...AND WONDER WHEN I'D SEE HIS SHIP PEEK THROUGH THE CLOUDS.

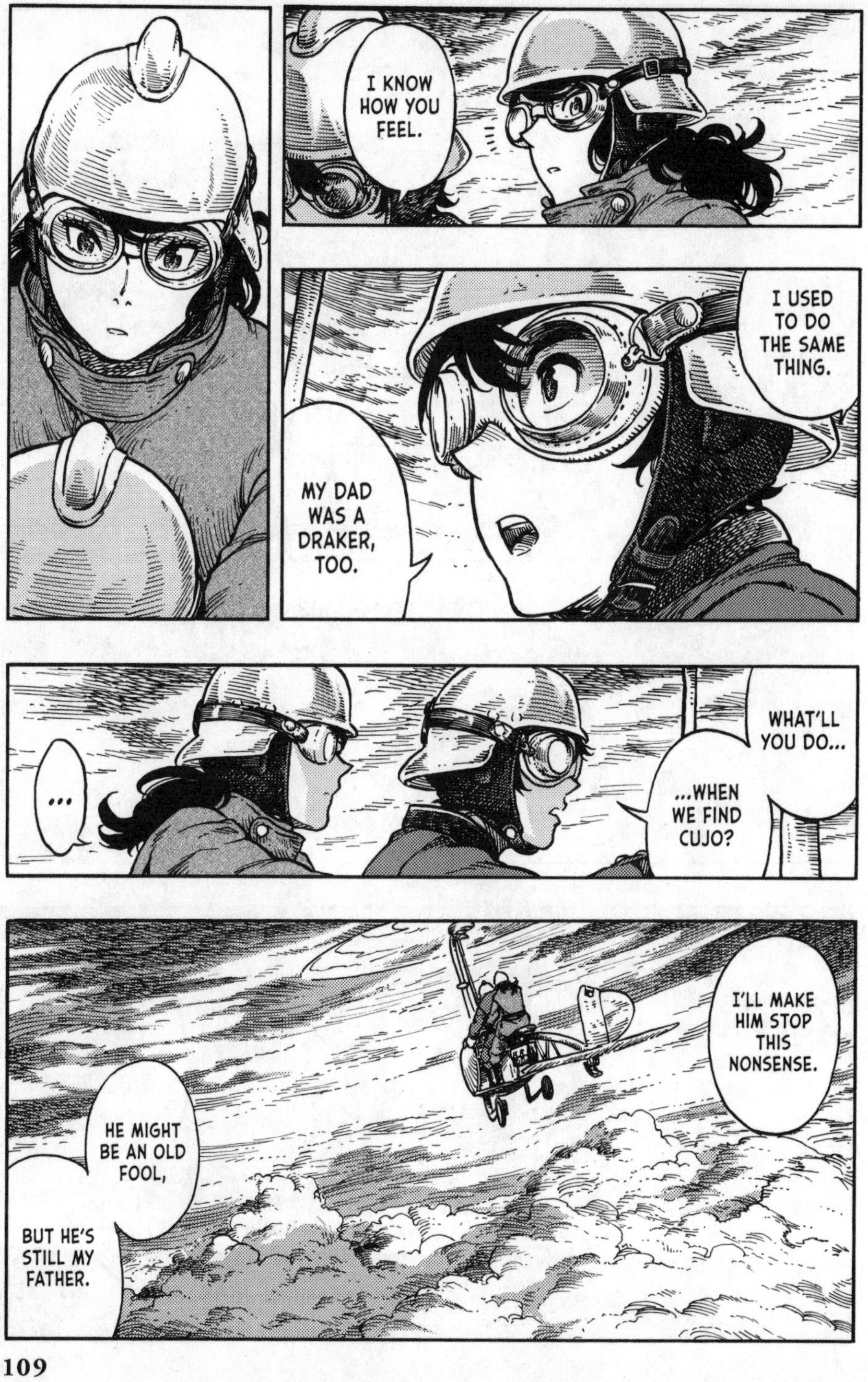
I KNOW HOW YOU FEEL.
I USED TO DO THE SAME THING.
MY DAD WAS A DRAKER, TOO.
WHAT'LL YOU DO...
...WHEN WE FIND CUJO?
...
I'LL MAKE HIM STOP THIS NONSENSE.
HE MIGHT BE AN OLD FOOL,
BUT HE'S STILL MY FATHER.

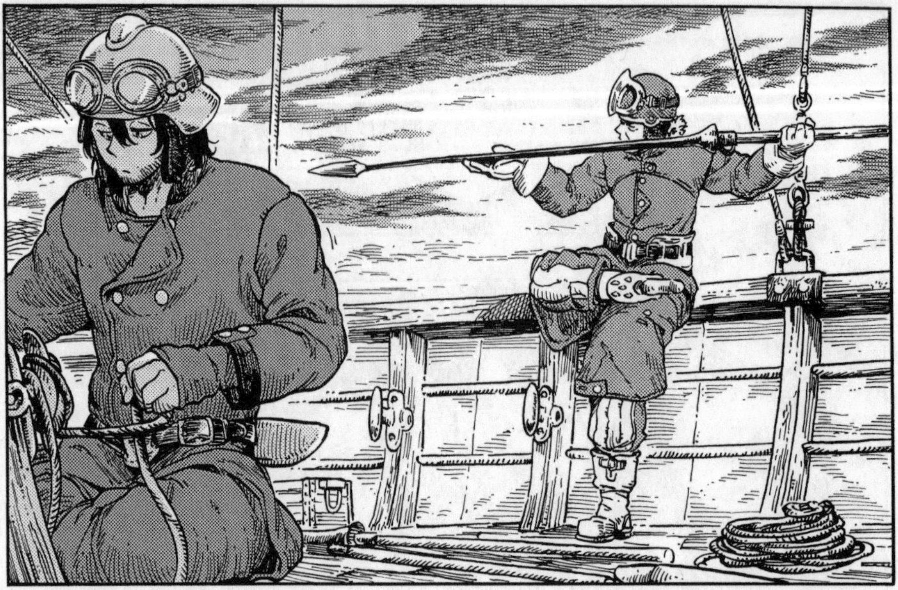

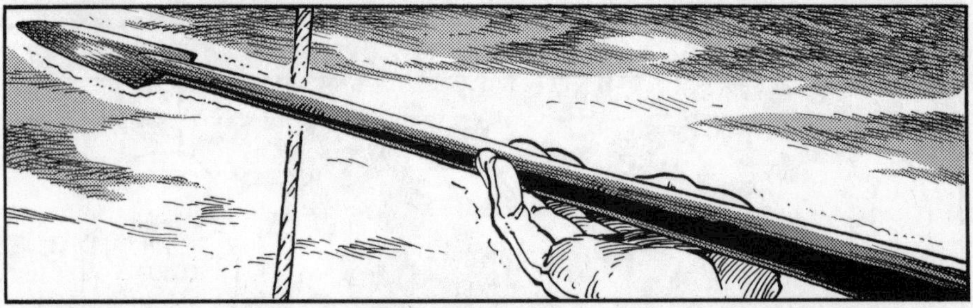

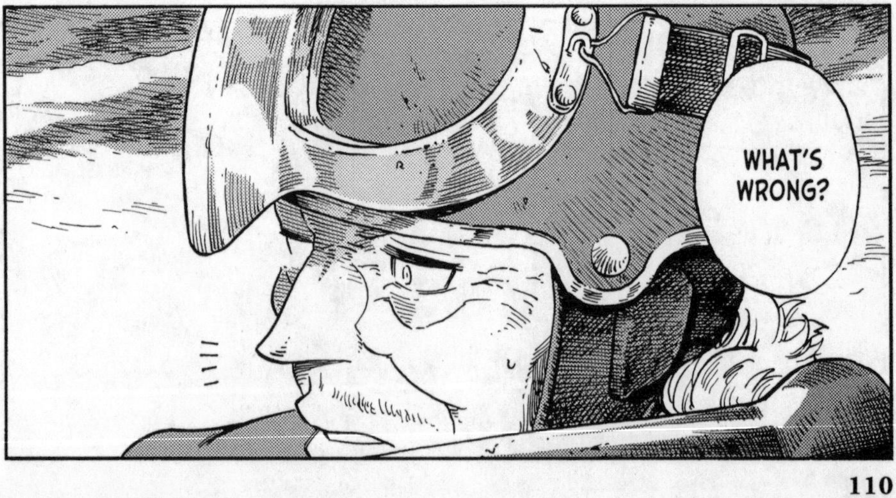
WHAT'S WRONG?

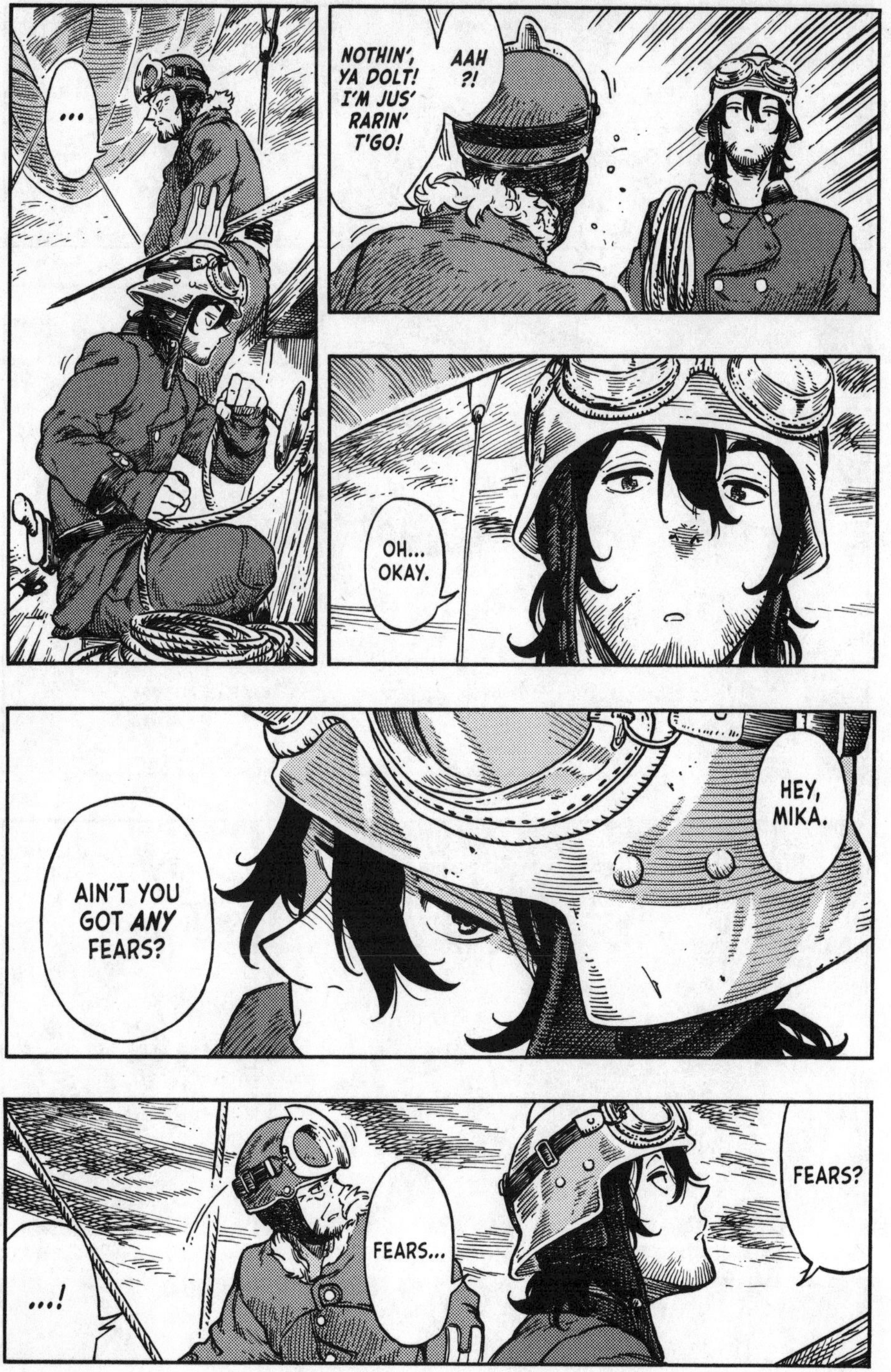
AAH ?!
NOTHIN', YA DOLT! I'M JUS' RARIN' T'GO!
OH... OKAY.
...
HEY, MIKA.
AIN'T YOU GOT *ANY* FEARS?
FEARS?
FEARS...
...!

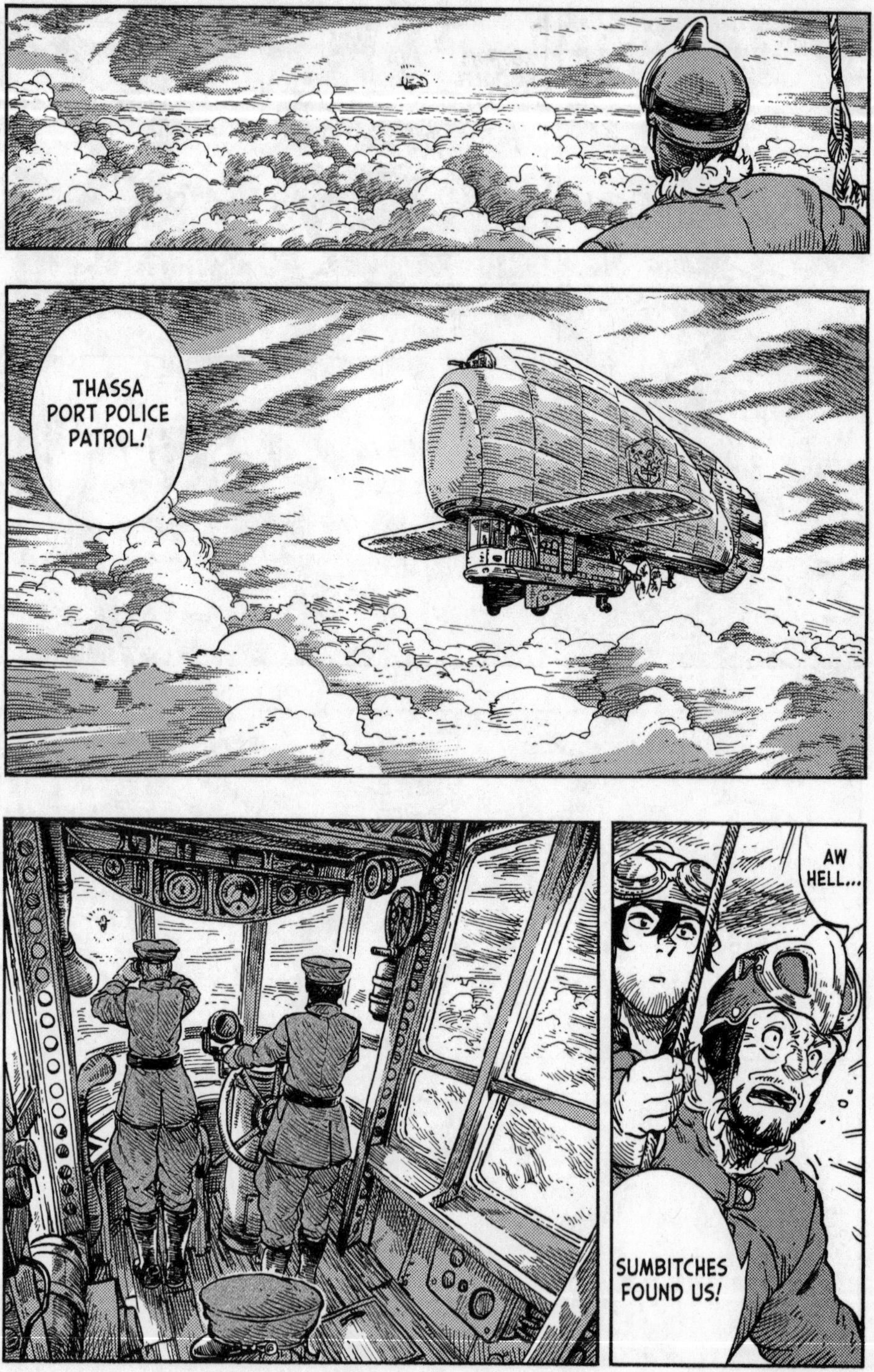
THASSA PORT POLICE PATROL!
AW HELL...
SUMBITCHES FOUND US!

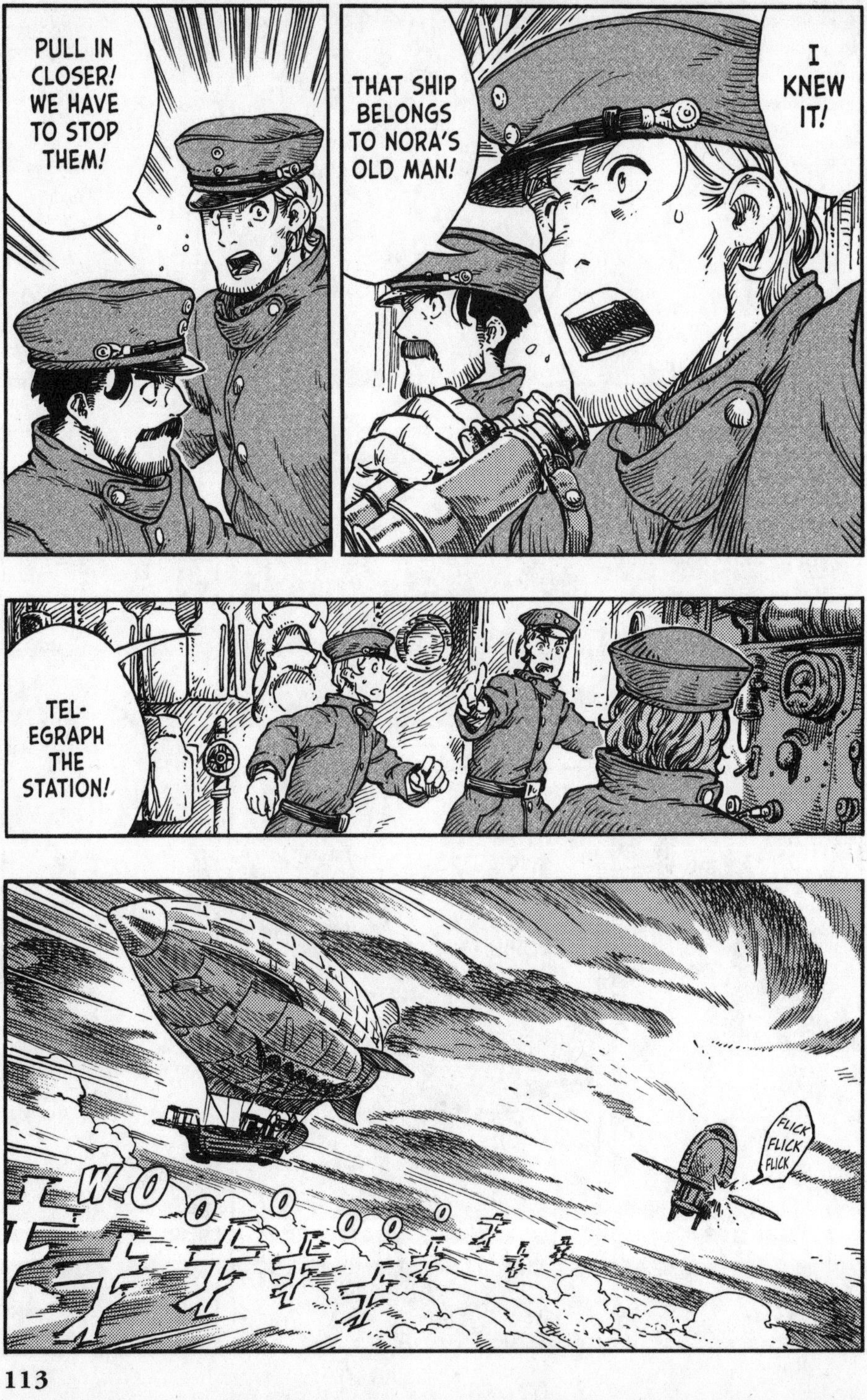
I KNEW IT!
THAT SHIP BELONGS TO NORA'S OLD MAN!
PULL IN CLOSER! WE HAVE TO STOP THEM!
TEL-EGRAPH THE STATION!
WOOOOOOO
FLICK FLICK FLICK

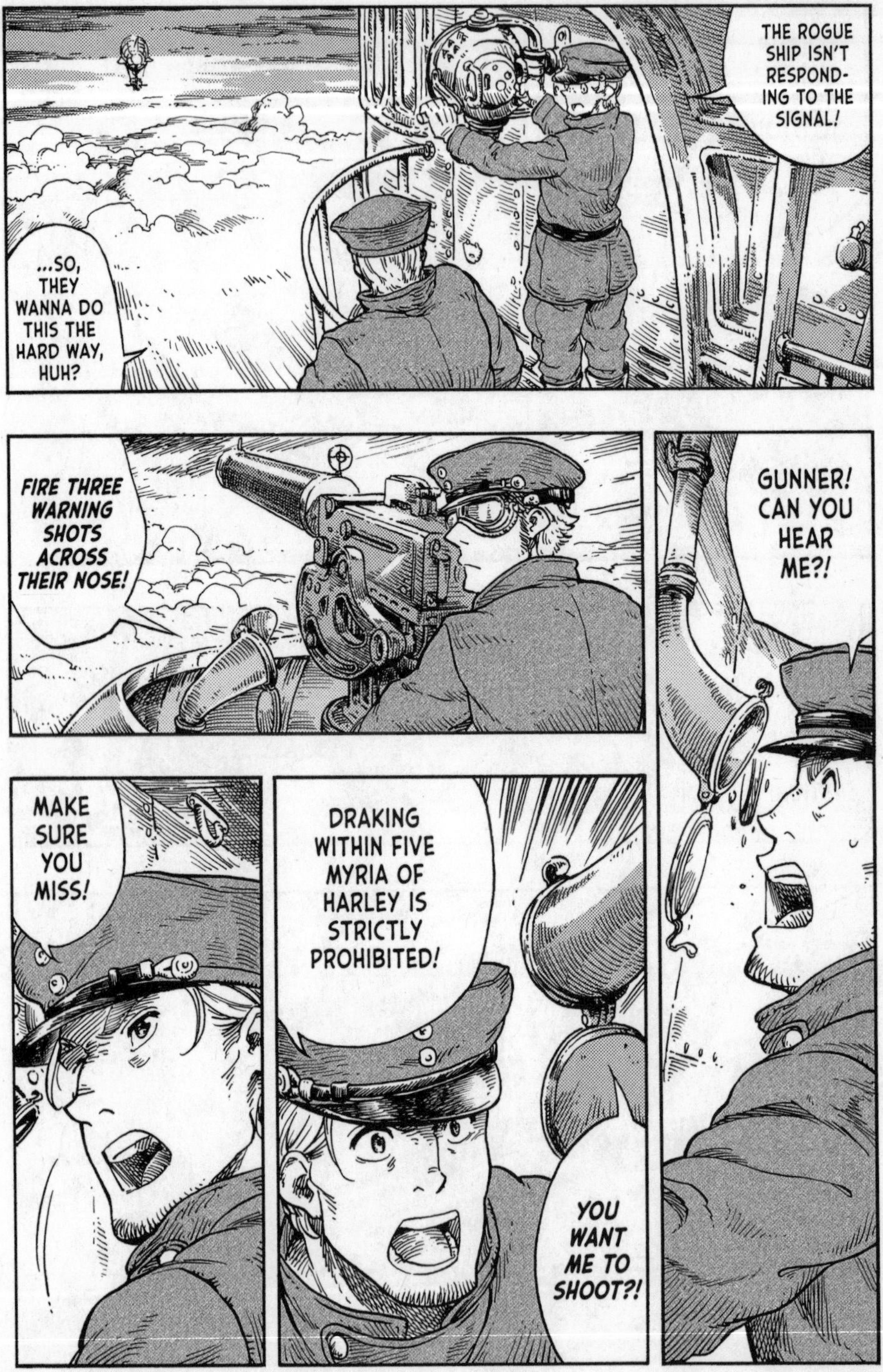
THE ROGUE SHIP ISN'T RESPONDING TO THE SIGNAL!
...SO, THEY WANNA DO THIS THE HARD WAY, HUH?
GUNNER! CAN YOU HEAR ME?!
FIRE THREE WARNING SHOTS ACROSS THEIR NOSE!
YOU WANT ME TO SHOOT?!
DRAKING WITHIN FIVE MYRIA OF HARLEY IS STRICTLY PROHIBITED!
MAKE SURE YOU MISS!

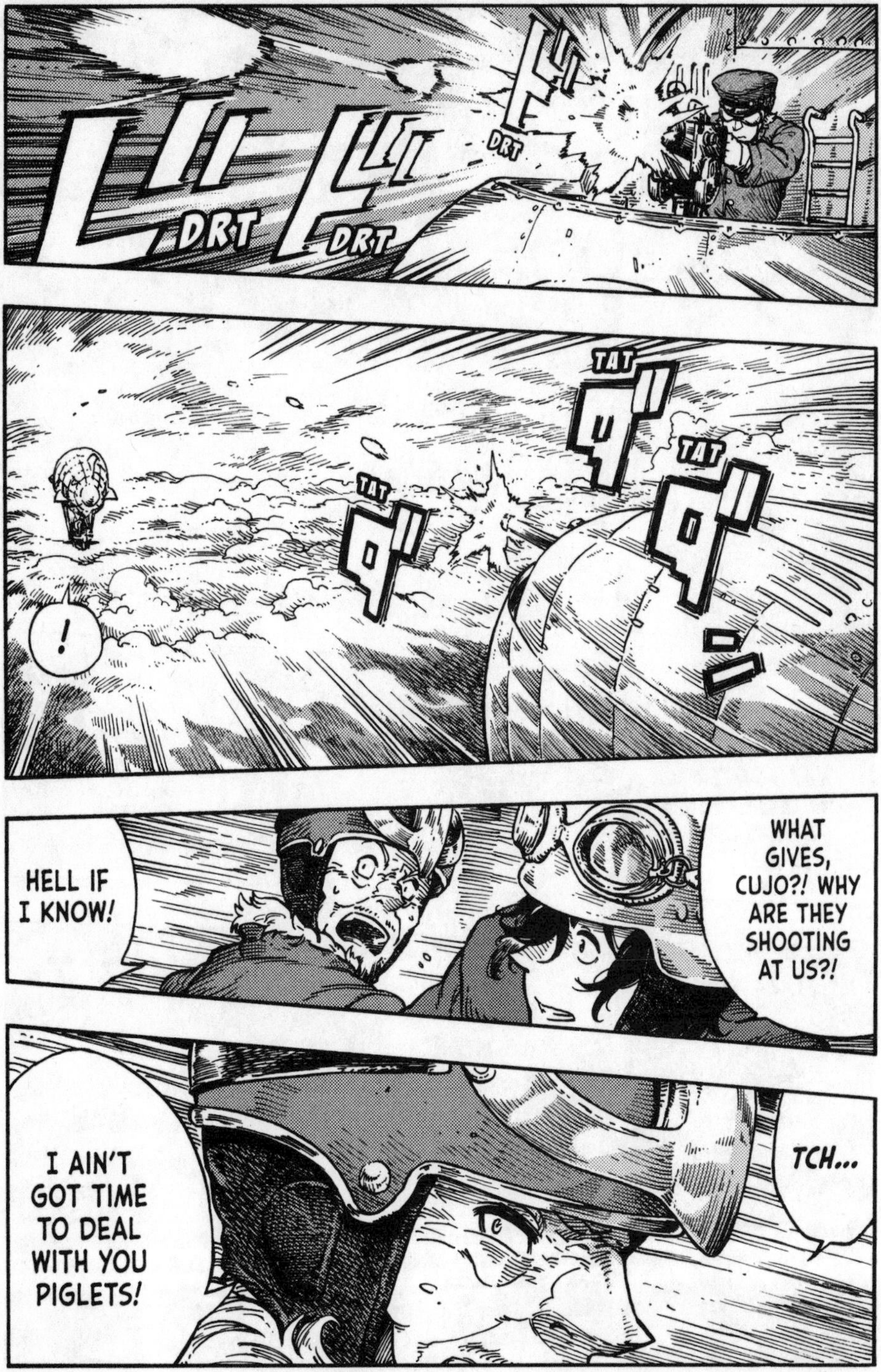
DRT
DRT
DRT
TAT
TAT
TAT
!
WHAT GIVES, CUJO?! WHY ARE THEY SHOOTING AT US?!
HELL IF I KNOW!
TCH...
I AIN'T GOT TIME TO DEAL WITH YOU PIGLETS!

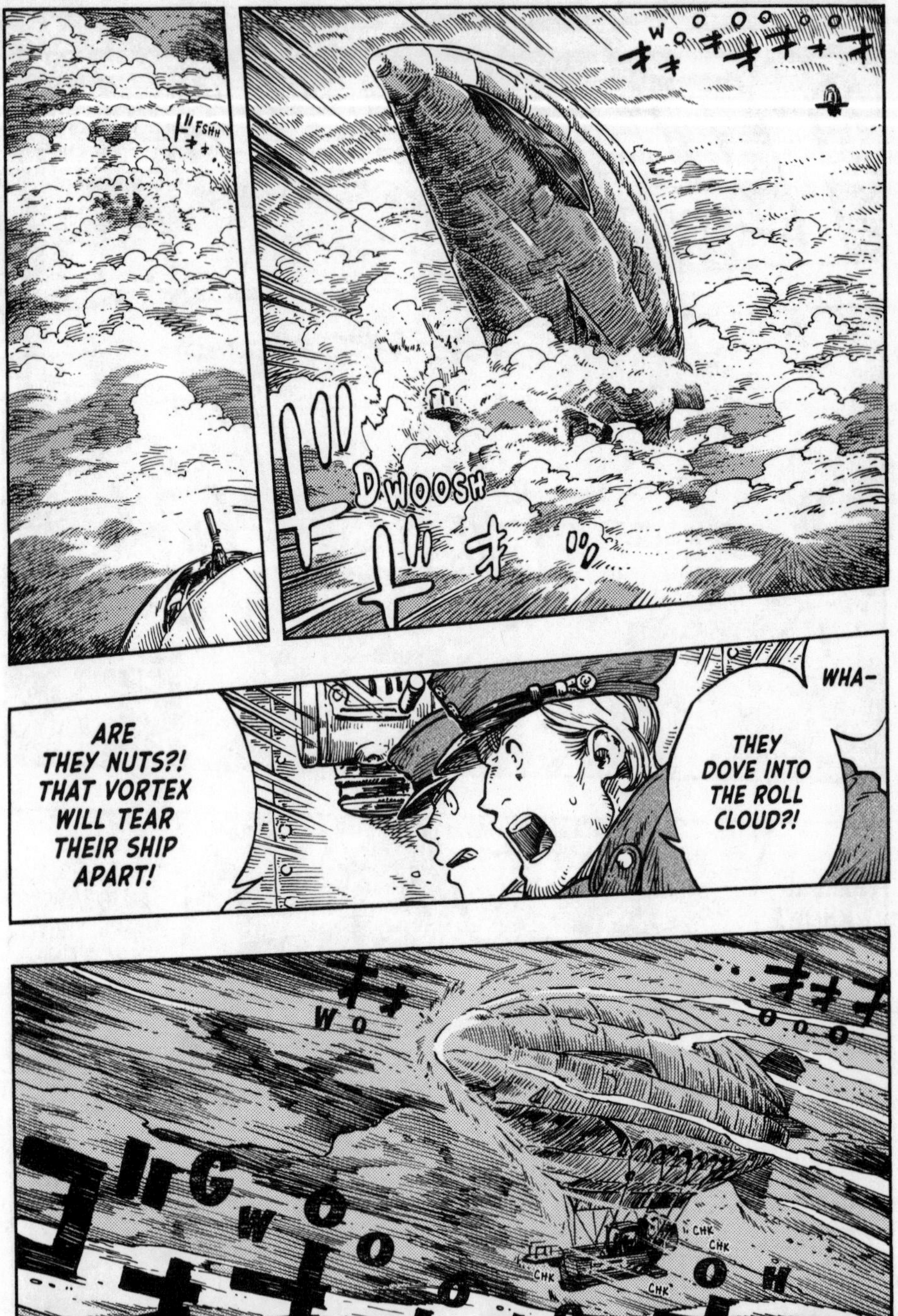

WOOOOOO
DWOOSH
FSHH
WHA-
THEY DOVE INTO THE ROLL CLOUD?!
ARE THEY NUTS?! THAT VORTEX WILL TEAR THEIR SHIP APART!
WOOOO
GWOOOOOOH
CHK
CHK
CHK
CHK

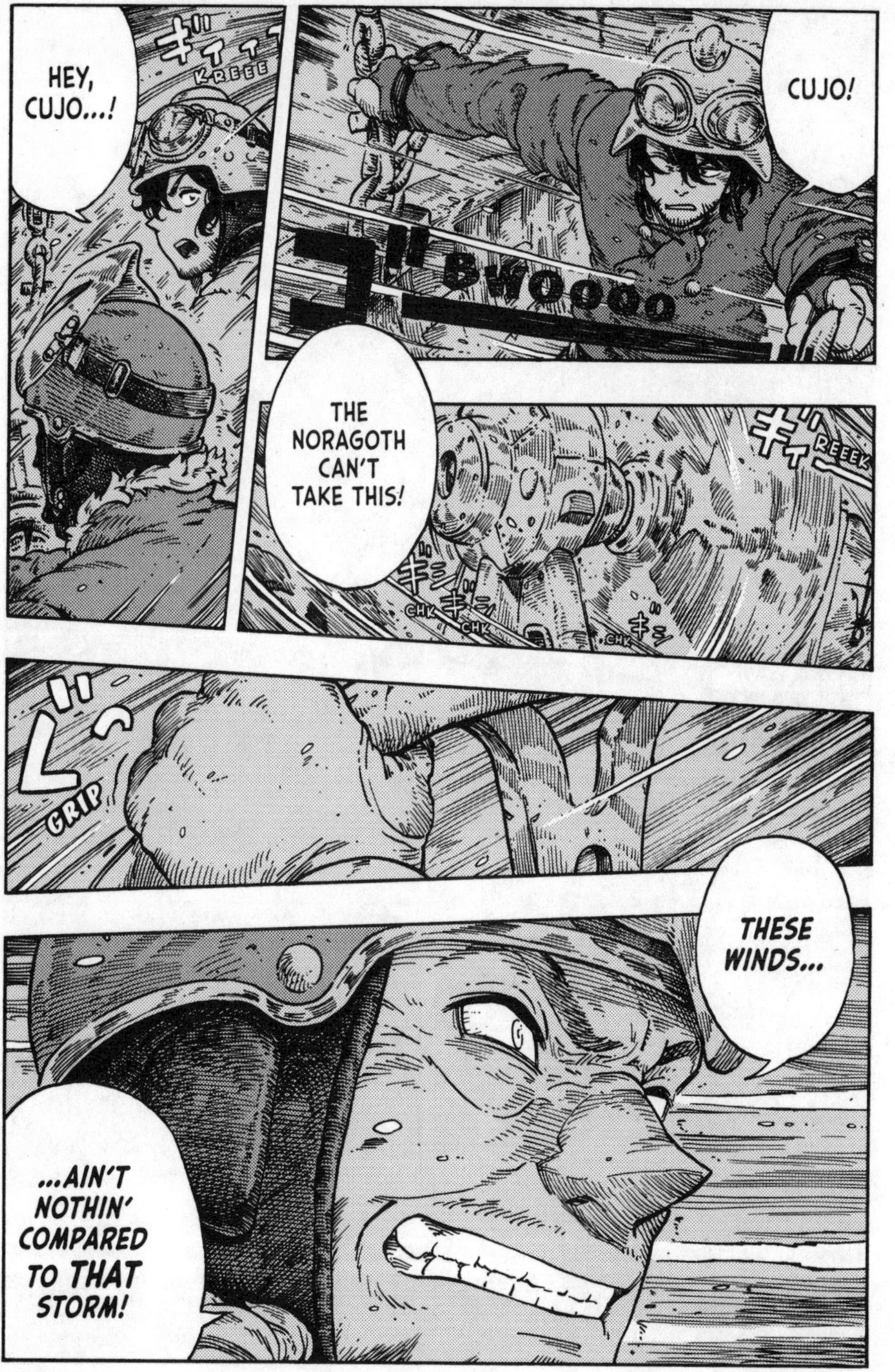
CUJO!
BWOOOO
THE NORAGOTH CAN'T TAKE THIS!
REEEK
CHK
CHK
CHK
HEY, CUJO...!
KREEE
GRIP
THESE WINDS...
...AIN'T NOTHIN' COMPARED TO THAT STORM!

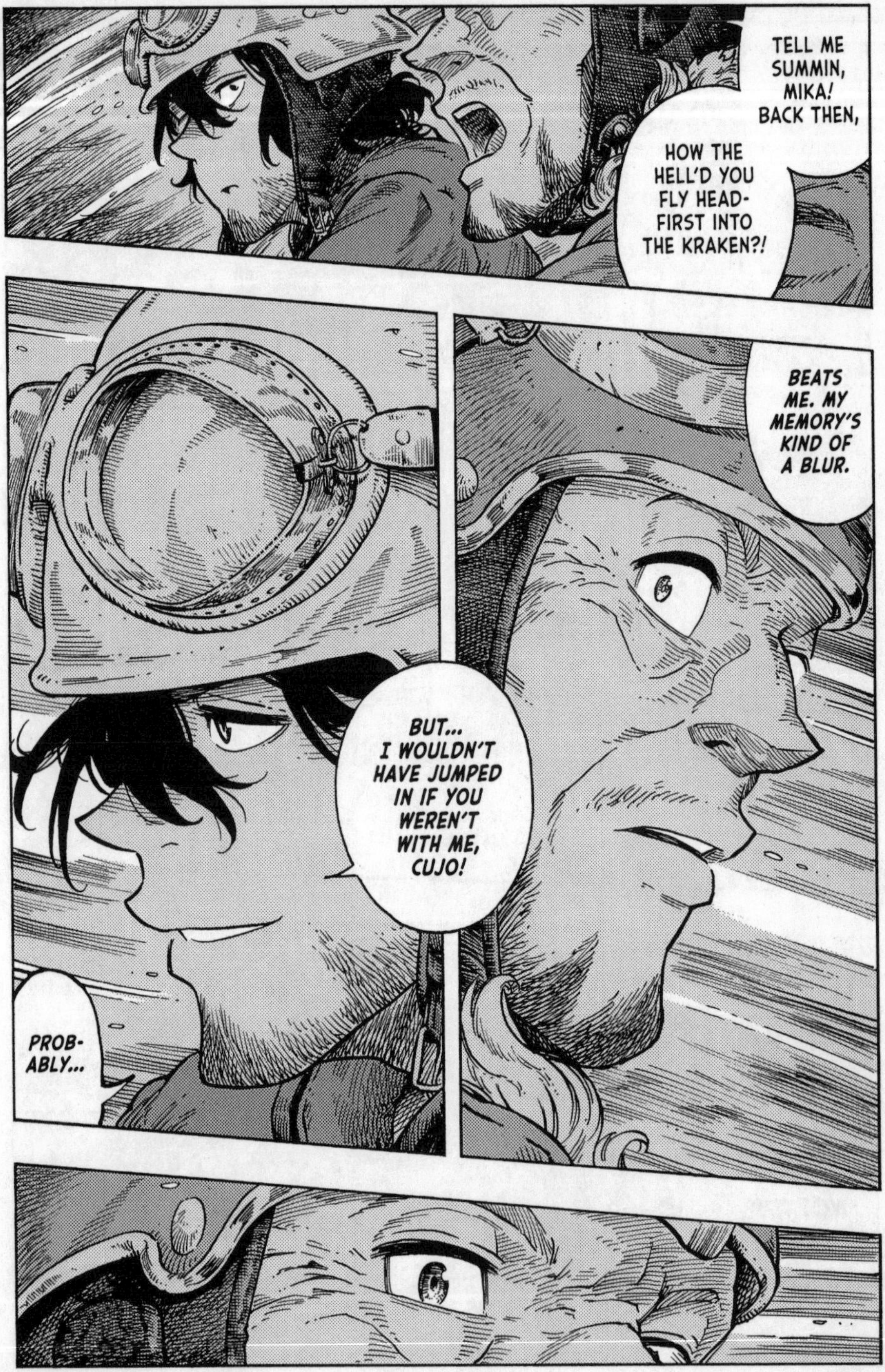
TELL ME SUMMIN, MIKA! BACK THEN,
HOW THE HELL'D YOU FLY HEAD-FIRST INTO THE KRAKEN?!
BEATS ME. MY MEMORY'S KIND OF A BLUR.
BUT... I WOULDN'T HAVE JUMPED IN IF YOU WEREN'T WITH ME, CUJO!
PROB-ABLY...

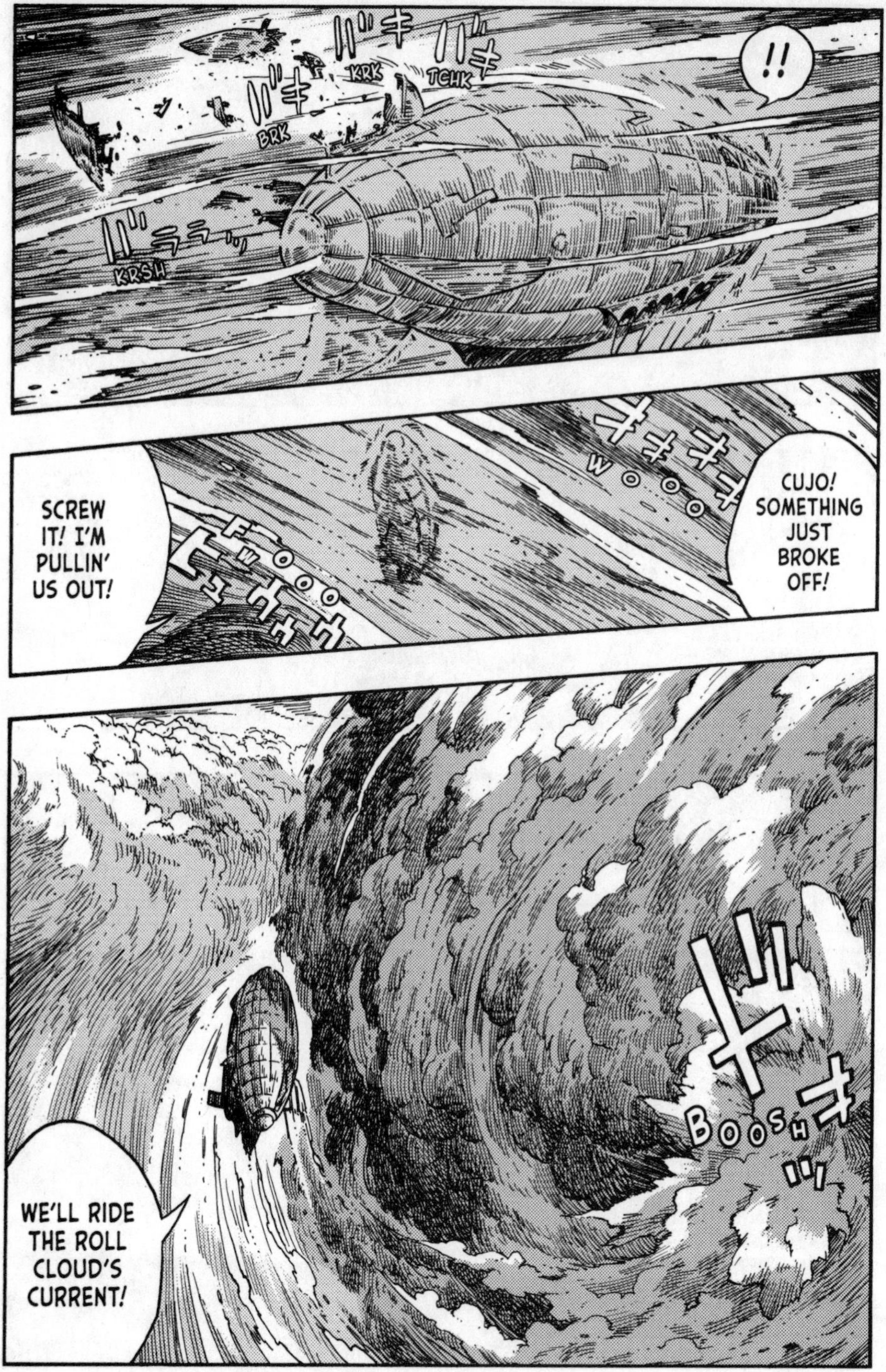
!!
TCHK
KRK
BRK
KRSH
WOOOO
CUJO! SOMETHING JUST BROKE OFF!
SCREW IT! I'M PULLIN' US OUT!
FWOOOO
BOOSH
WE'LL RIDE THE ROLL CLOUD'S CURRENT!

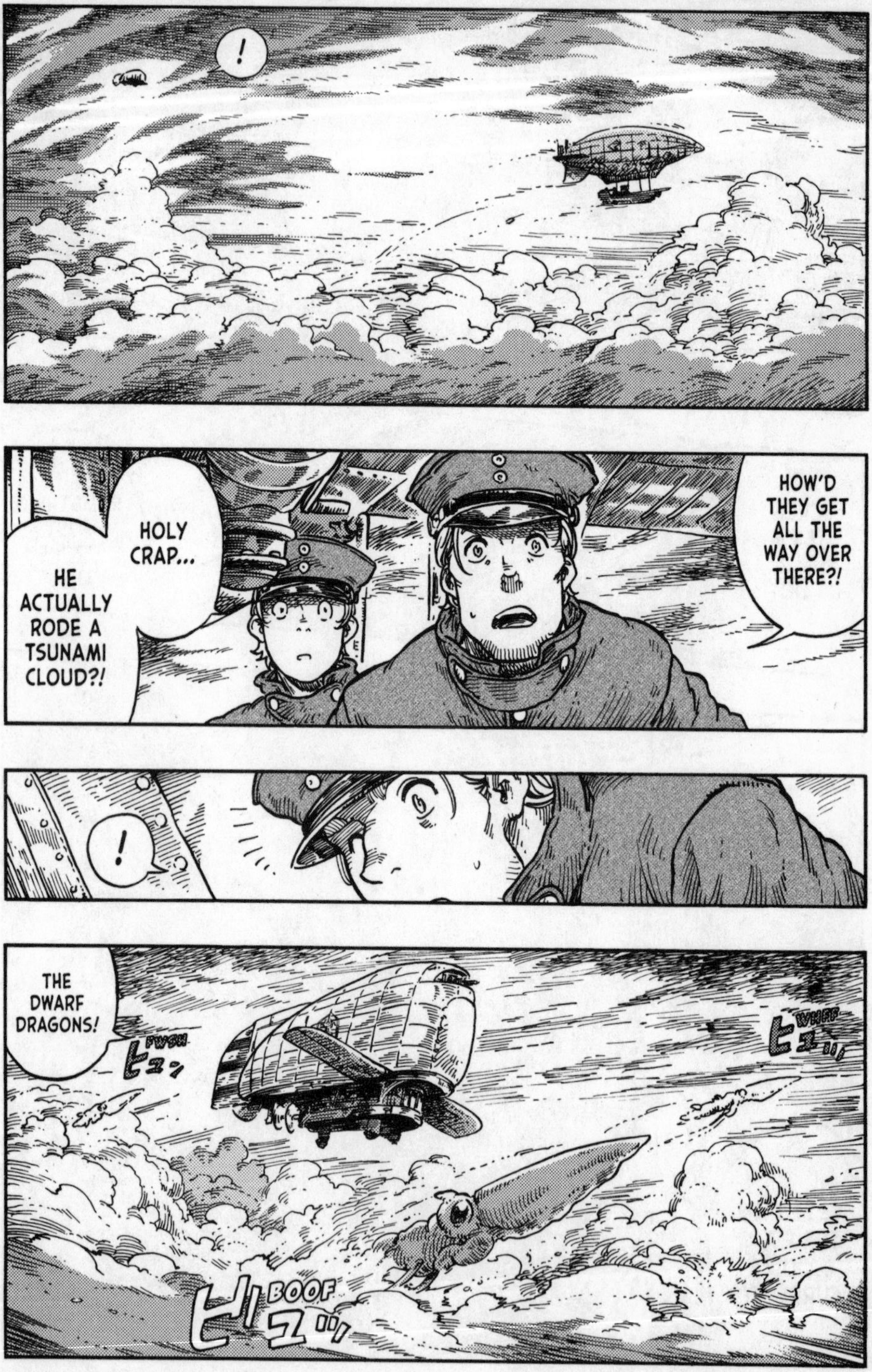
!
HOW'D THEY GET ALL THE WAY OVER THERE?!
HOLY CRAP...
HE ACTUALLY RODE A TSUNAMI CLOUD?!
!
WHFF
THE DWARF DRAGONS!
PWSH
BOOF

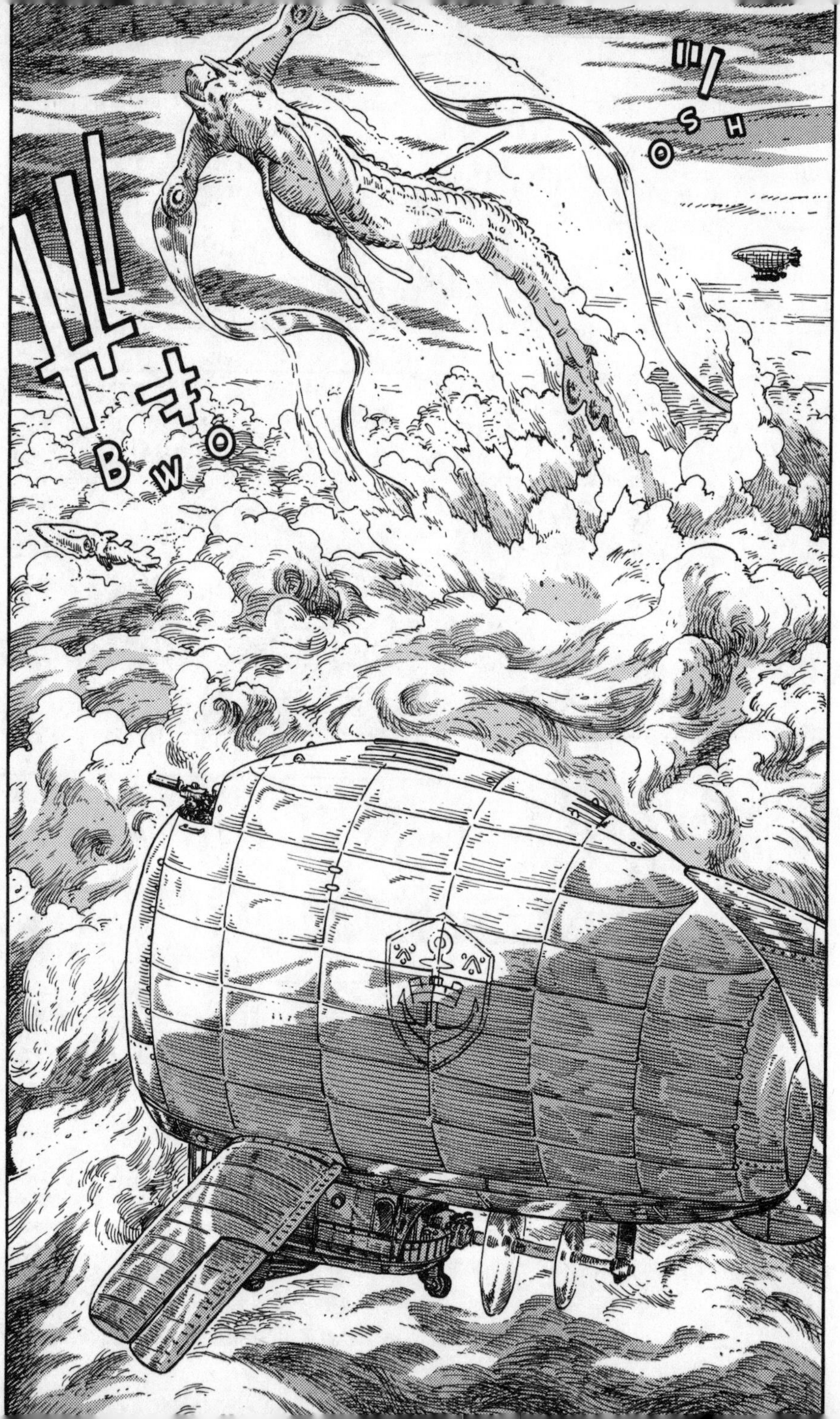
WOOSH
BWOO

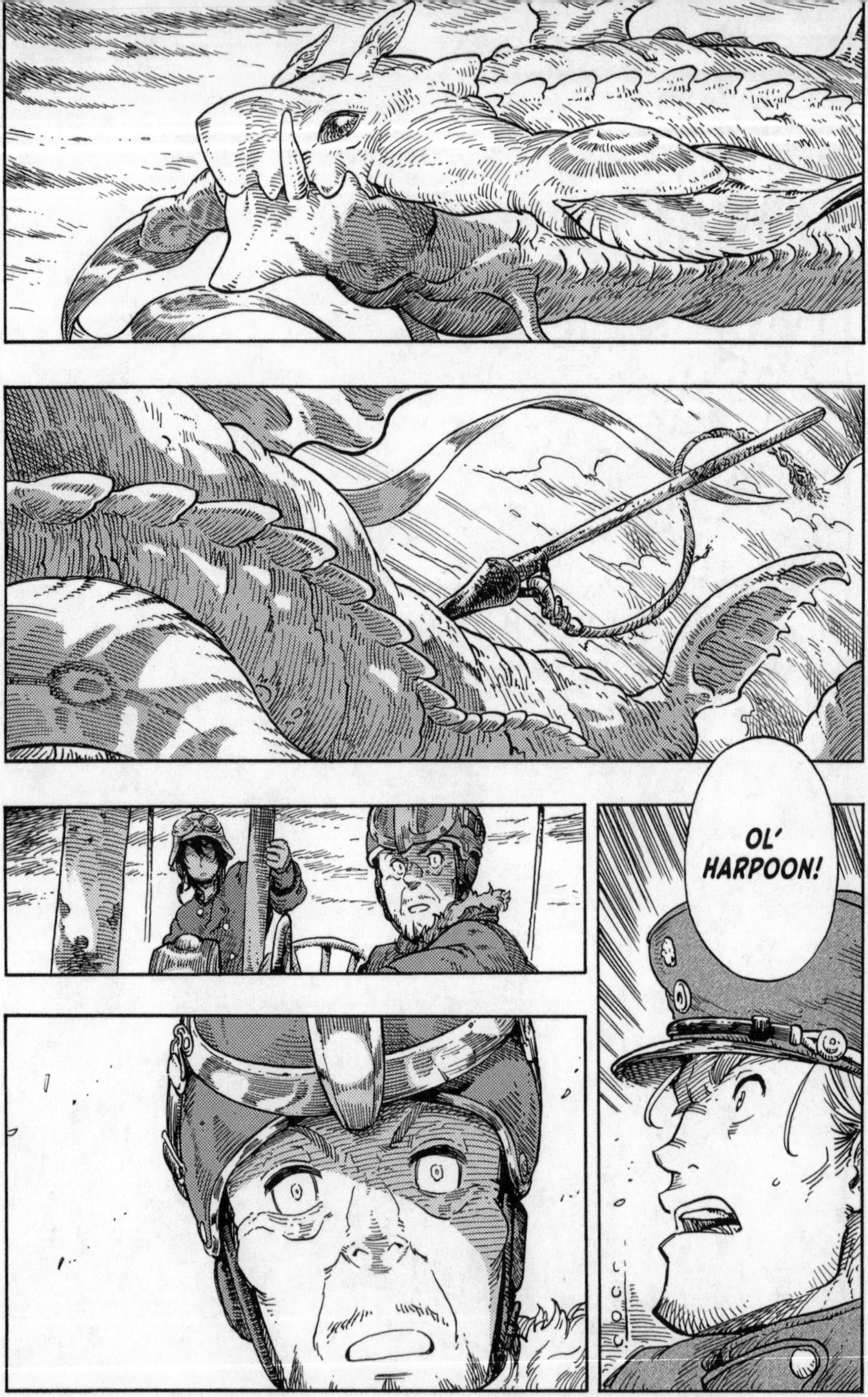
OL' HARPOON!

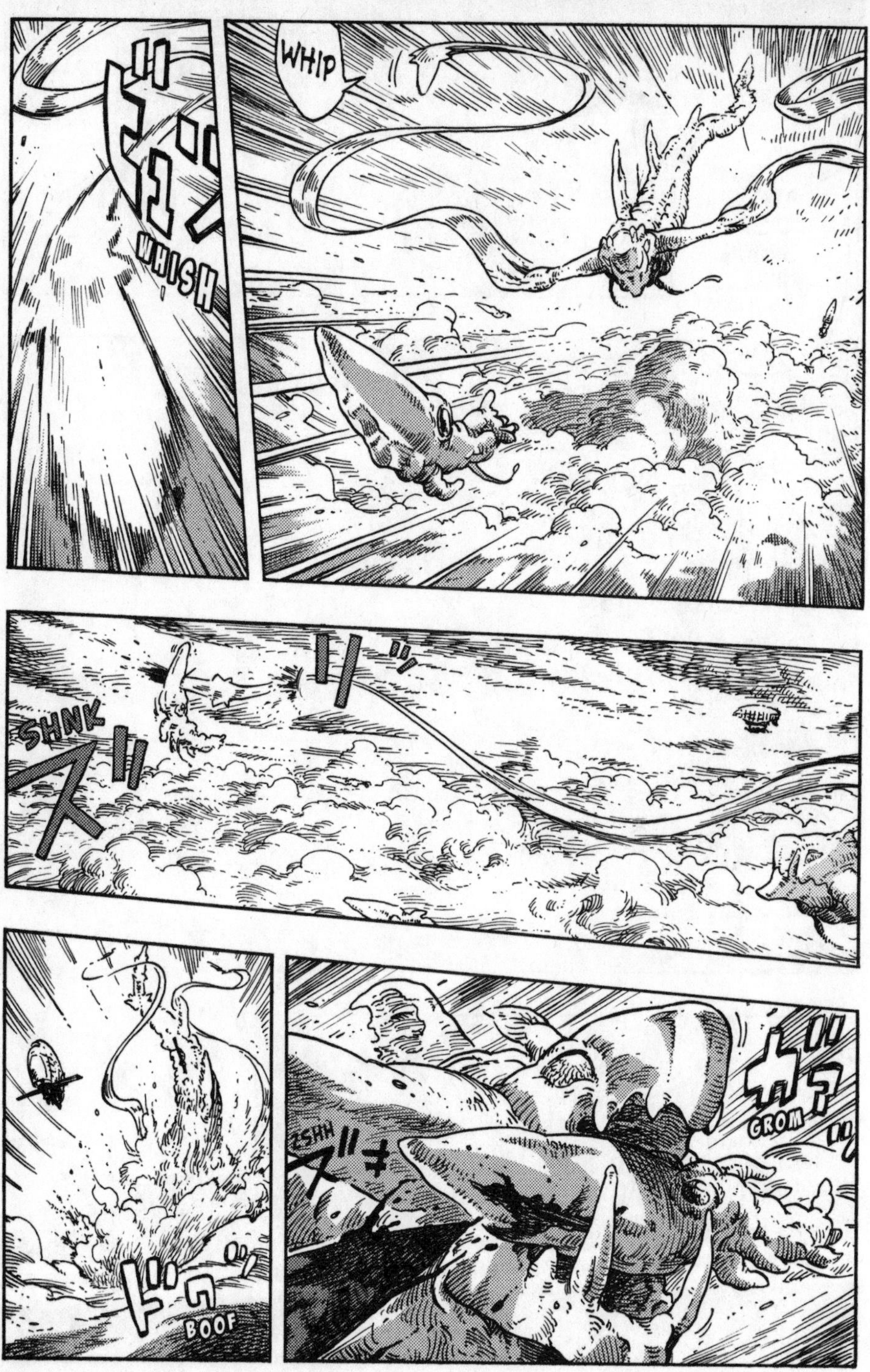
WHIP
WHISH
SHNK
GROM
ZSHH
BOOF

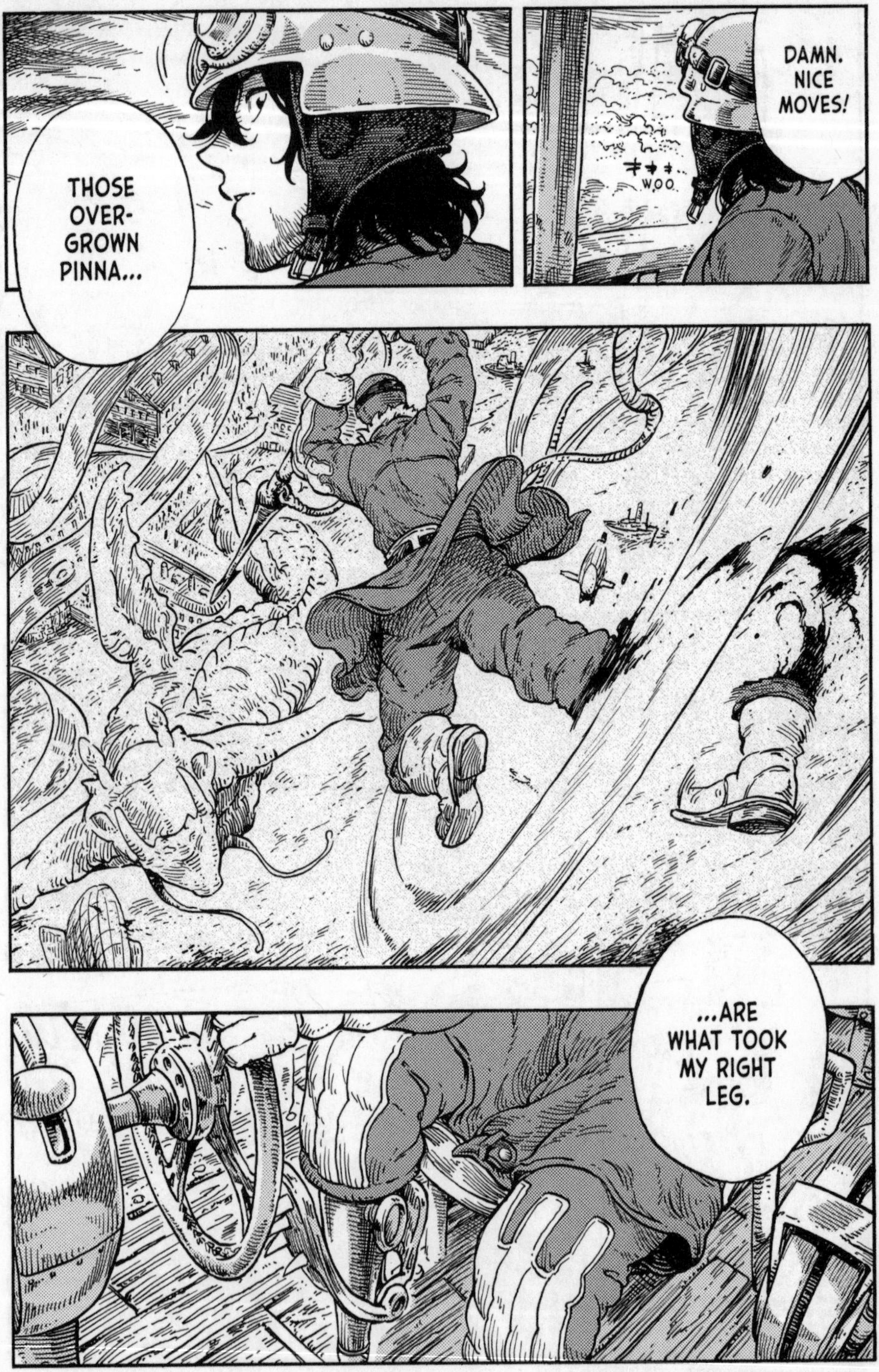
DAMN. NICE MOVES!
WOO
THOSE OVER-GROWN PINNA...
...ARE WHAT TOOK MY RIGHT LEG.

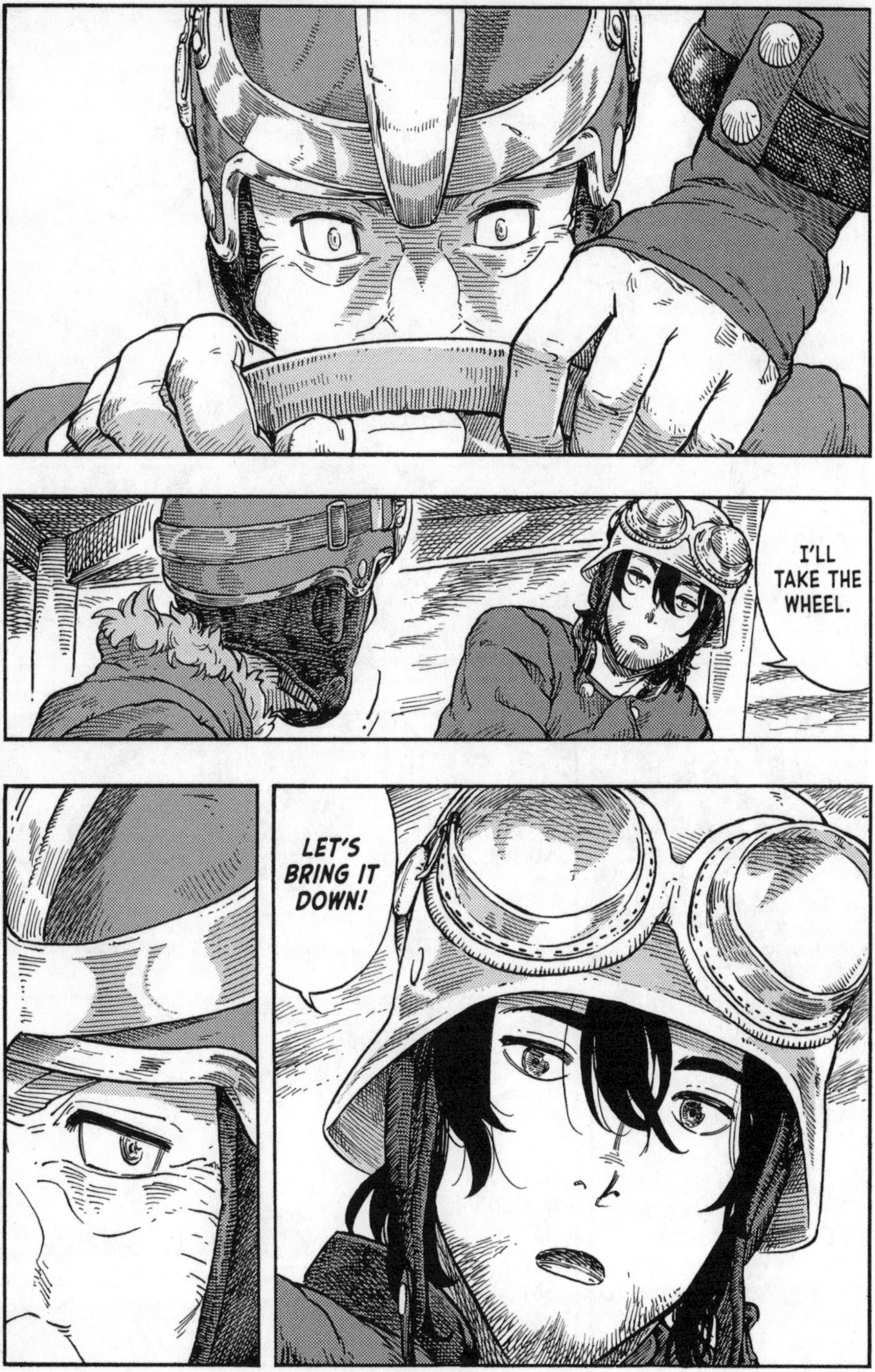
I'LL TAKE THE WHEEL.
LET'S BRING IT DOWN!

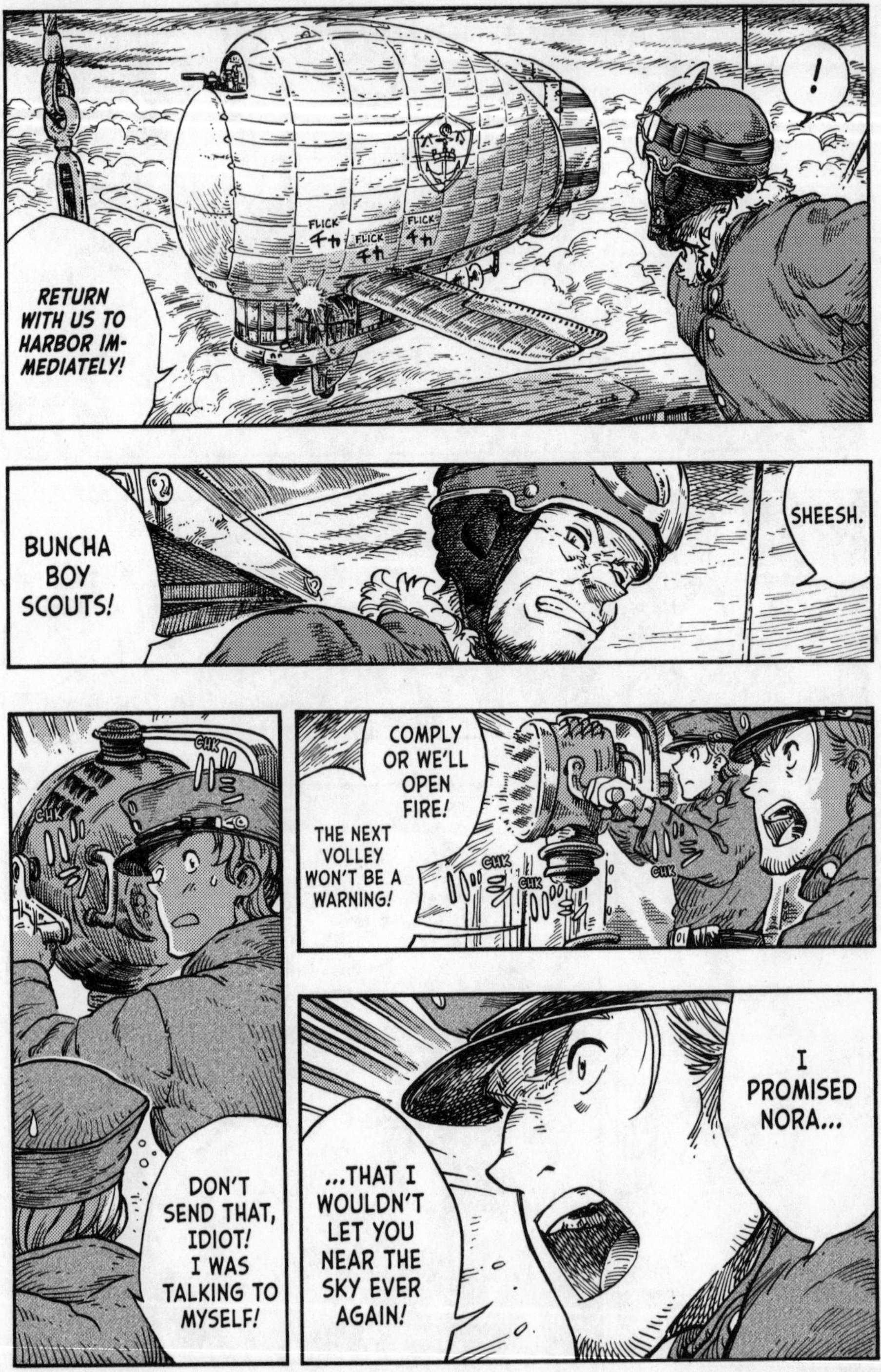
!
FLICK
チカ
FLICK
チカ
FLICK
チカ
RETURN WITH US TO HARBOR IM-MEDIATELY!
SHEESH.
BUNCHA BOY SCOUTS!
COMPLY OR WE'LL OPEN FIRE!
THE NEXT VOLLEY WON'T BE A WARNING!
CHK
CHK
CHK
I PROMISED NORA...
...THAT I WOULDN'T LET YOU NEAR THE SKY EVER AGAIN!
CHK
CHK
DON'T SEND THAT, IDIOT! I WAS TALKING TO MYSELF!

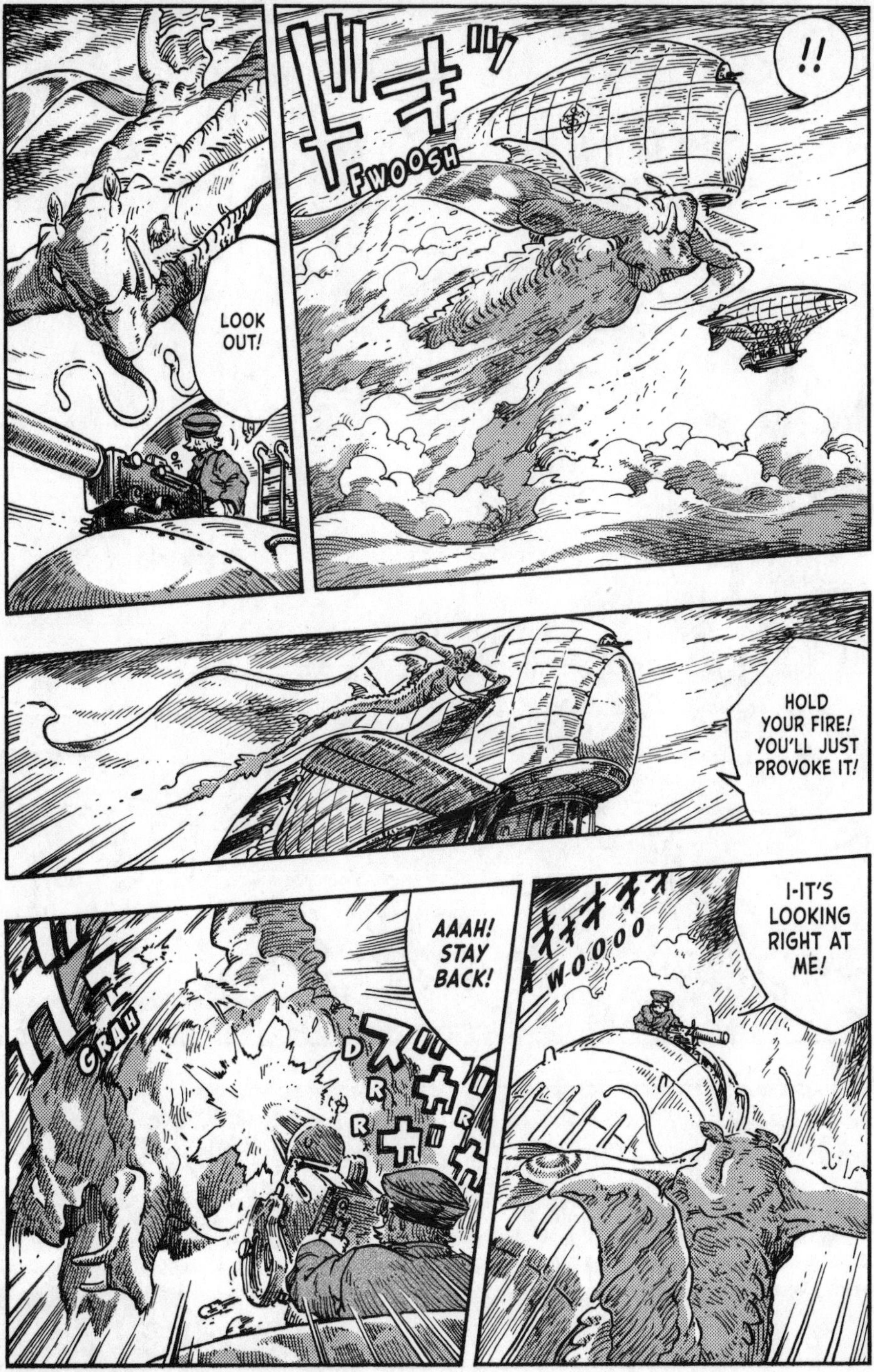

!!
ドギッ
FWOOSH
LOOK OUT!
HOLD YOUR FIRE! YOU'LL JUST PROVOKE IT!
I-IT'S LOOKING RIGHT AT ME!
WOOOO
AAAH! STAY BACK!
DRRR
GRAH

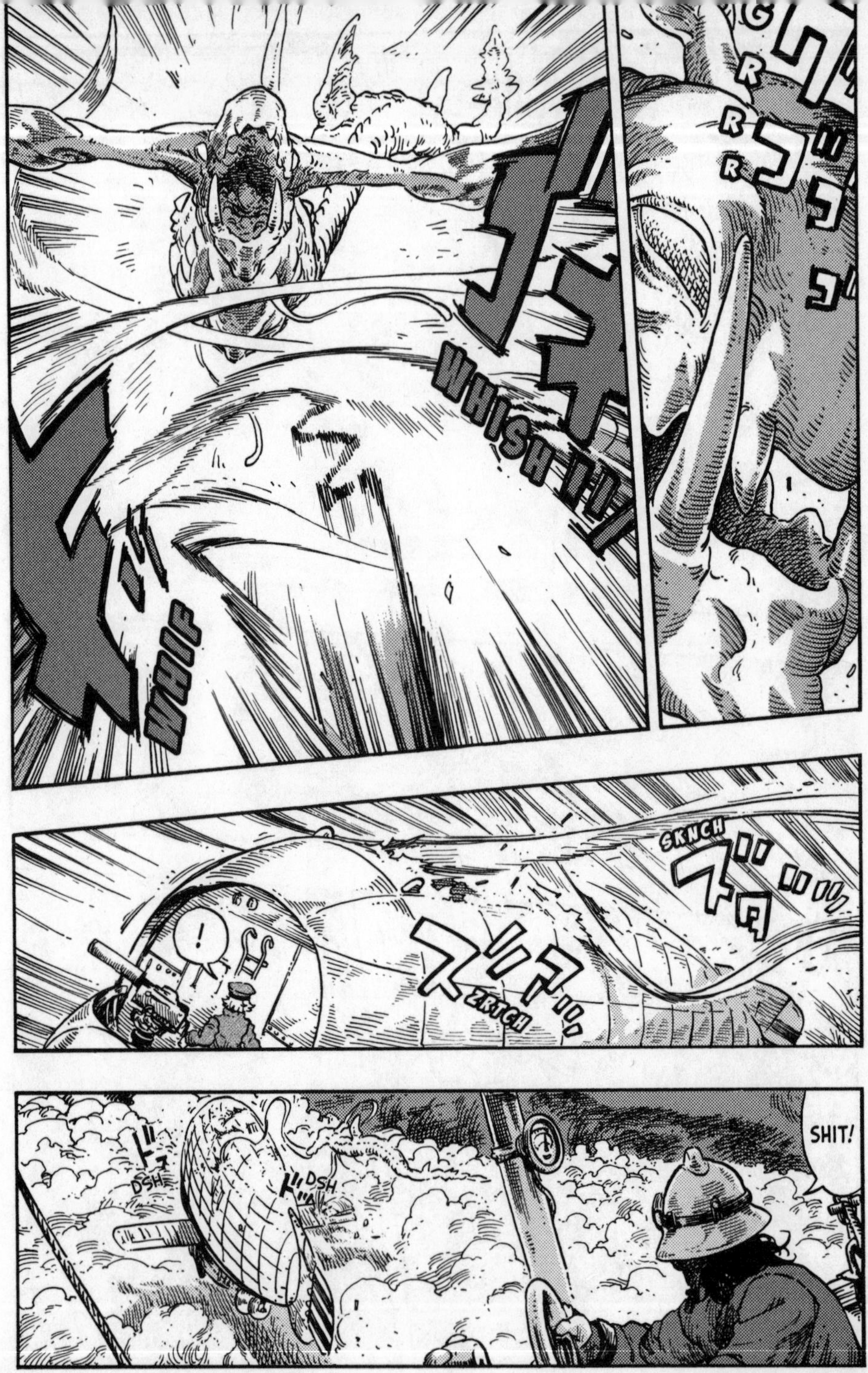
GRRR
WHISH
WHIF
SKNCH
ZRTCH
!
DSH
DSH
SHIT!

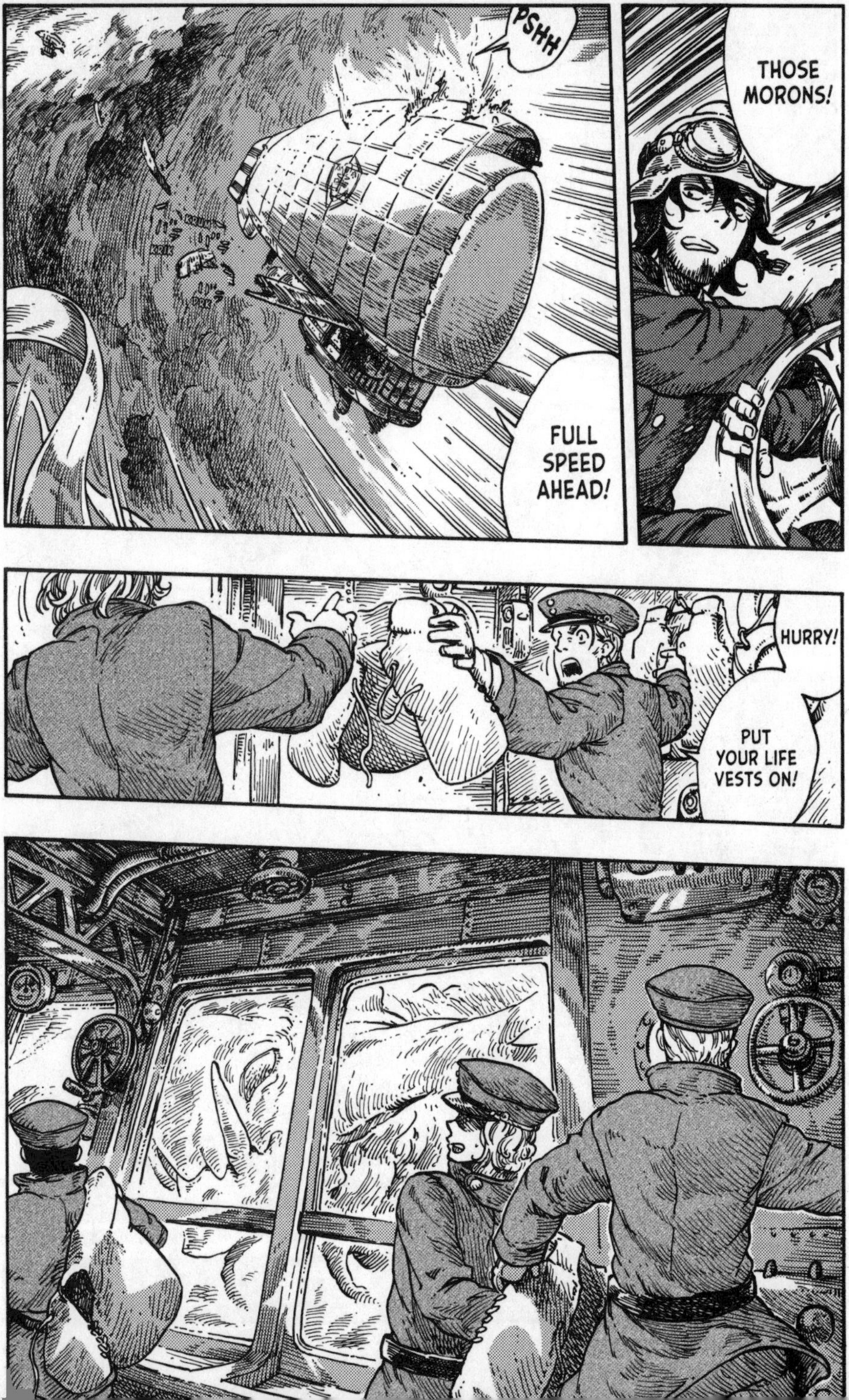
THOSE MORONS!
PSHH
FULL SPEED AHEAD!
HURRY!
PUT YOUR LIFE VESTS ON!

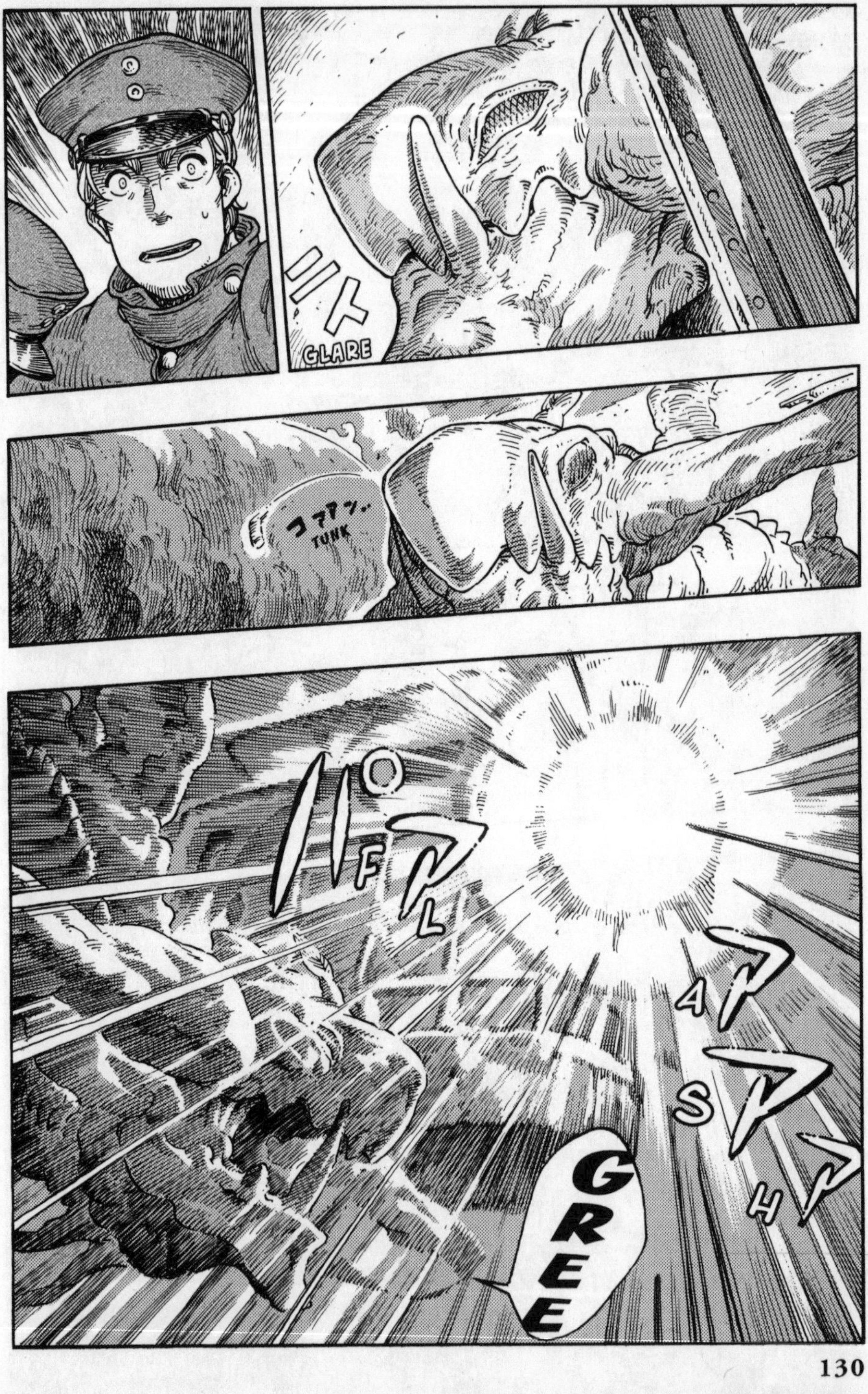
GLARE
TUNK
FLASH
GREE

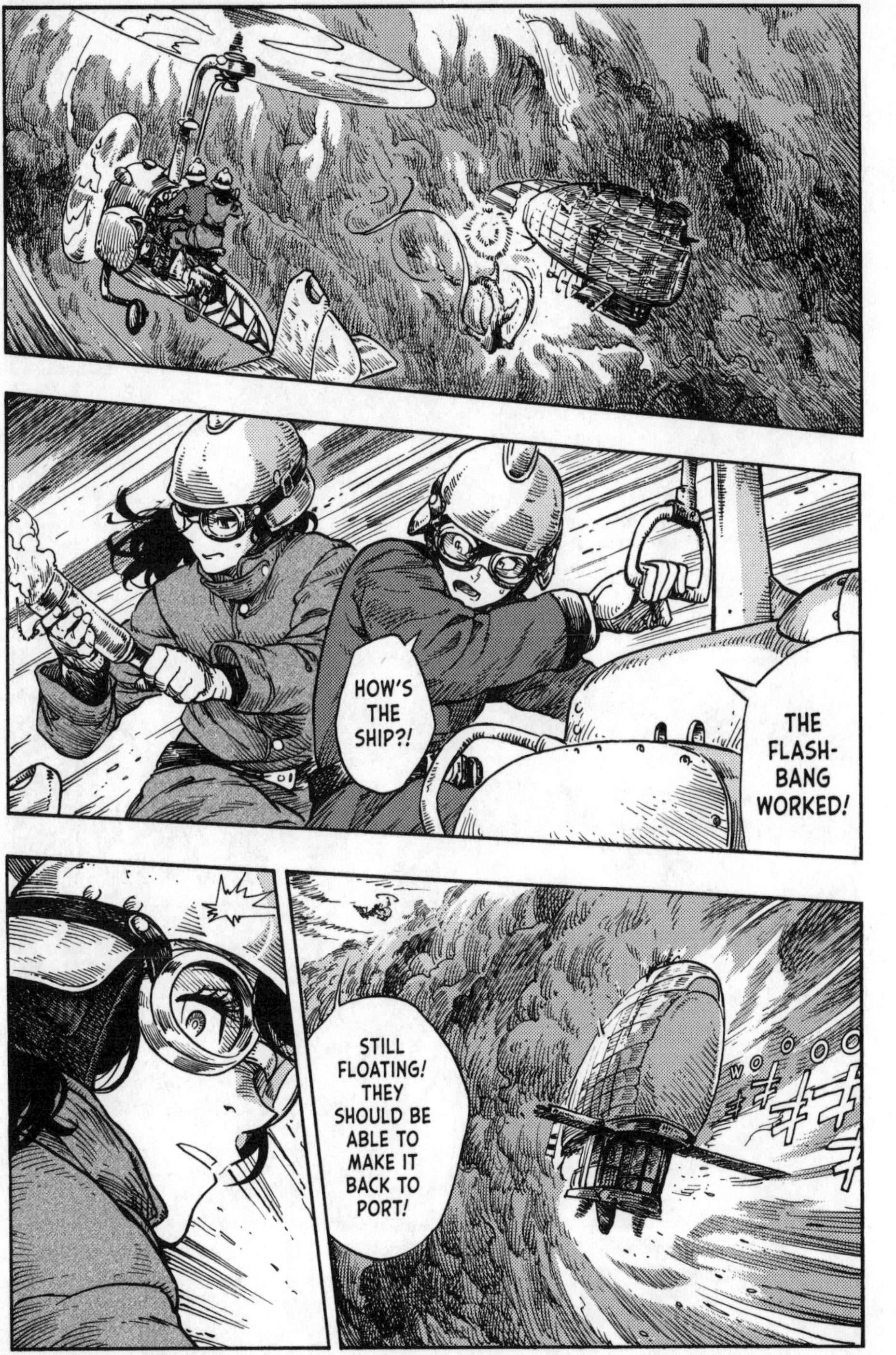
THE FLASH-BANG WORKED!
HOW'S THE SHIP?!
STILL FLOATING! THEY SHOULD BE ABLE TO MAKE IT BACK TO PORT!

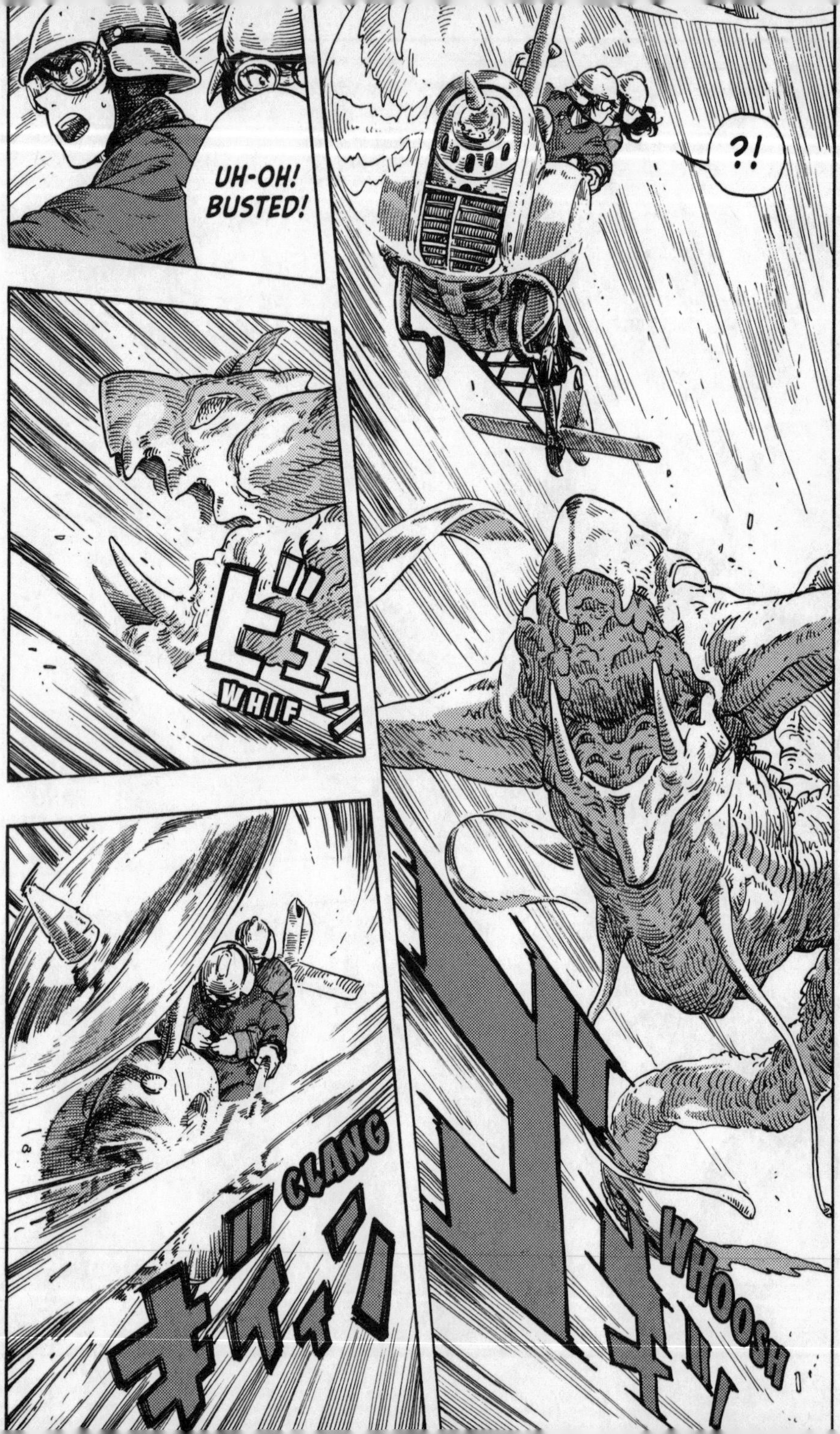
?!
WHOOSH
UH-OH! BUSTED!
WHIF
CLANG

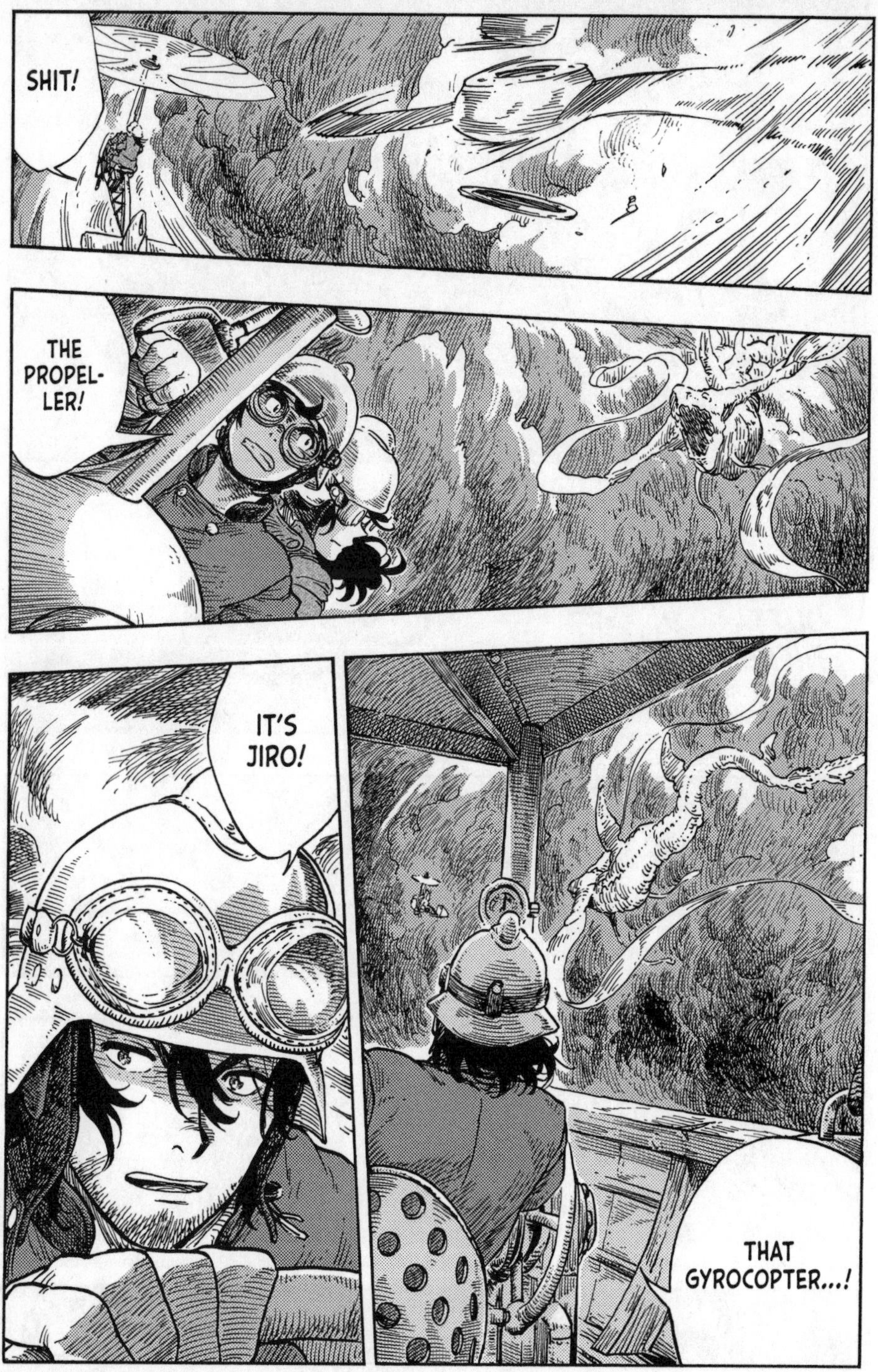
SHIT!
THE PROPEL-LER!
THAT GYROCOPTER...!
IT'S JIRO!

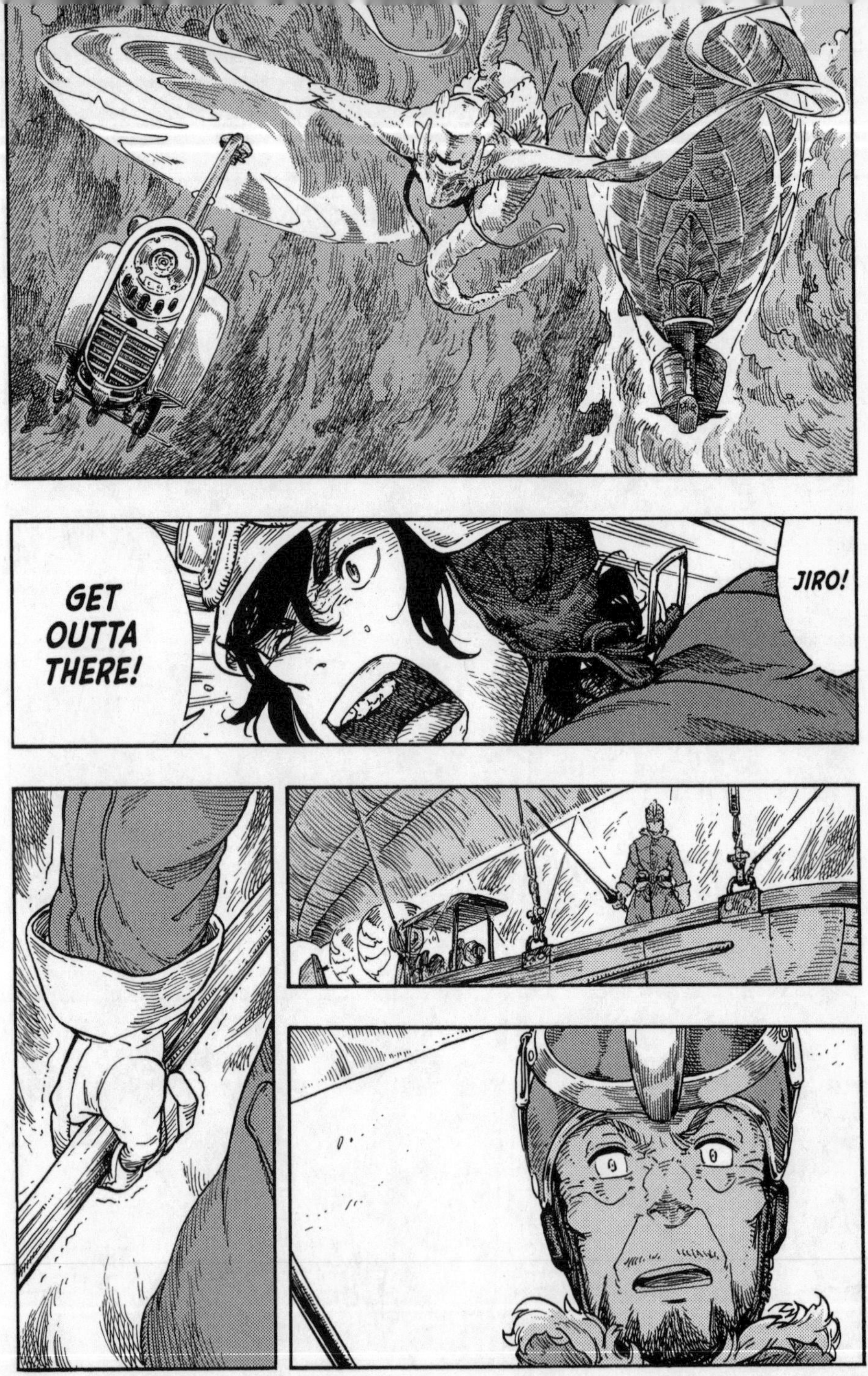
JIRO!
GET OUTTA THERE!

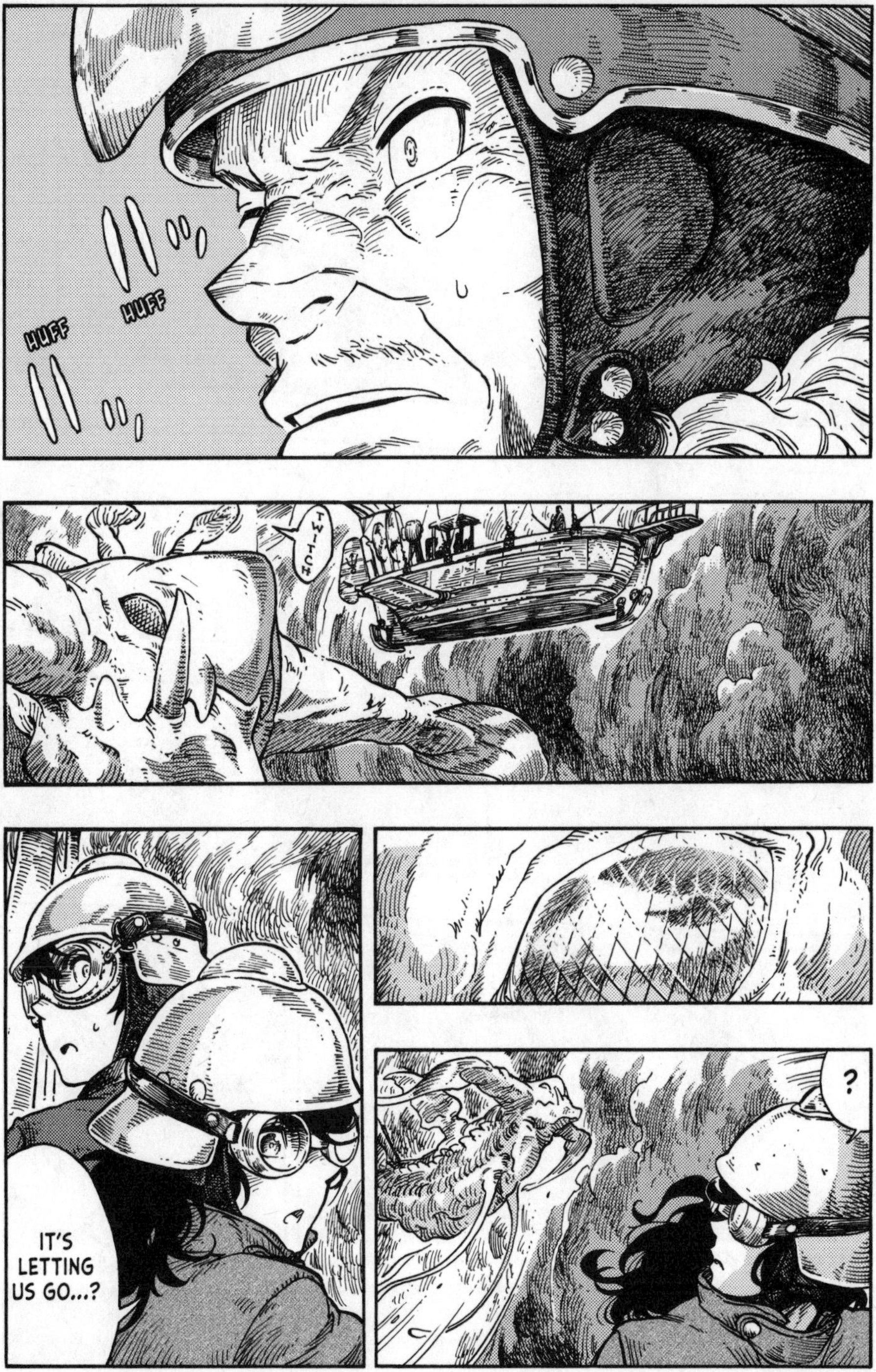
HUFF
HUFF
TWITCH
?
IT'S LETTING US GO...?

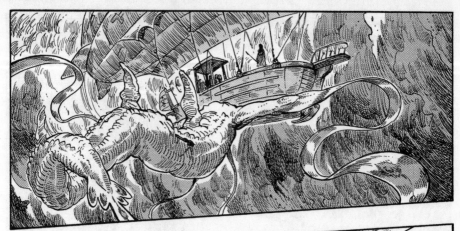

SON OF
A....

...!

YOU
REMEMBER
ME?!

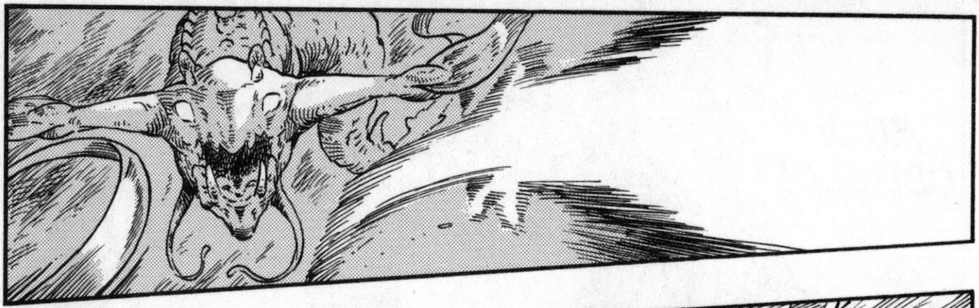
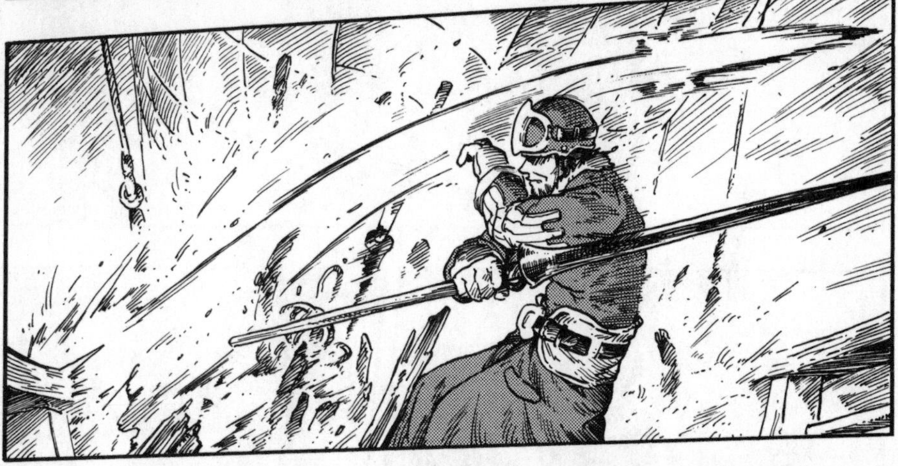
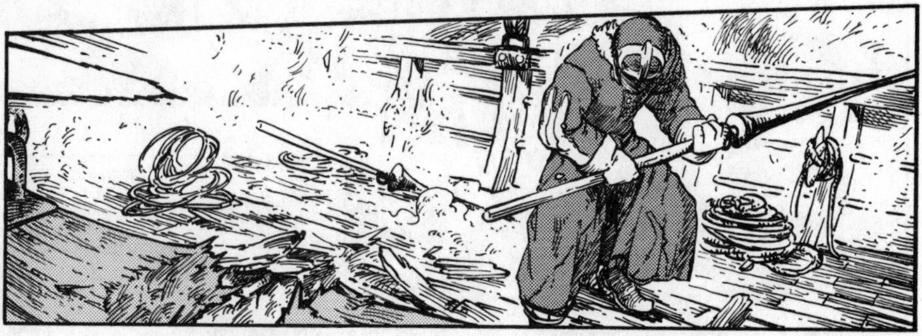
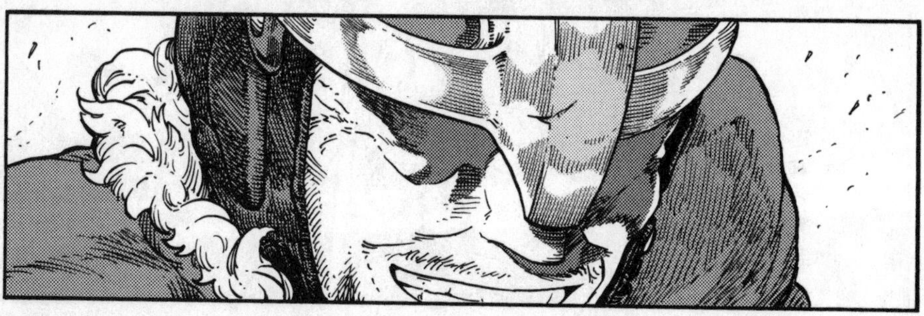

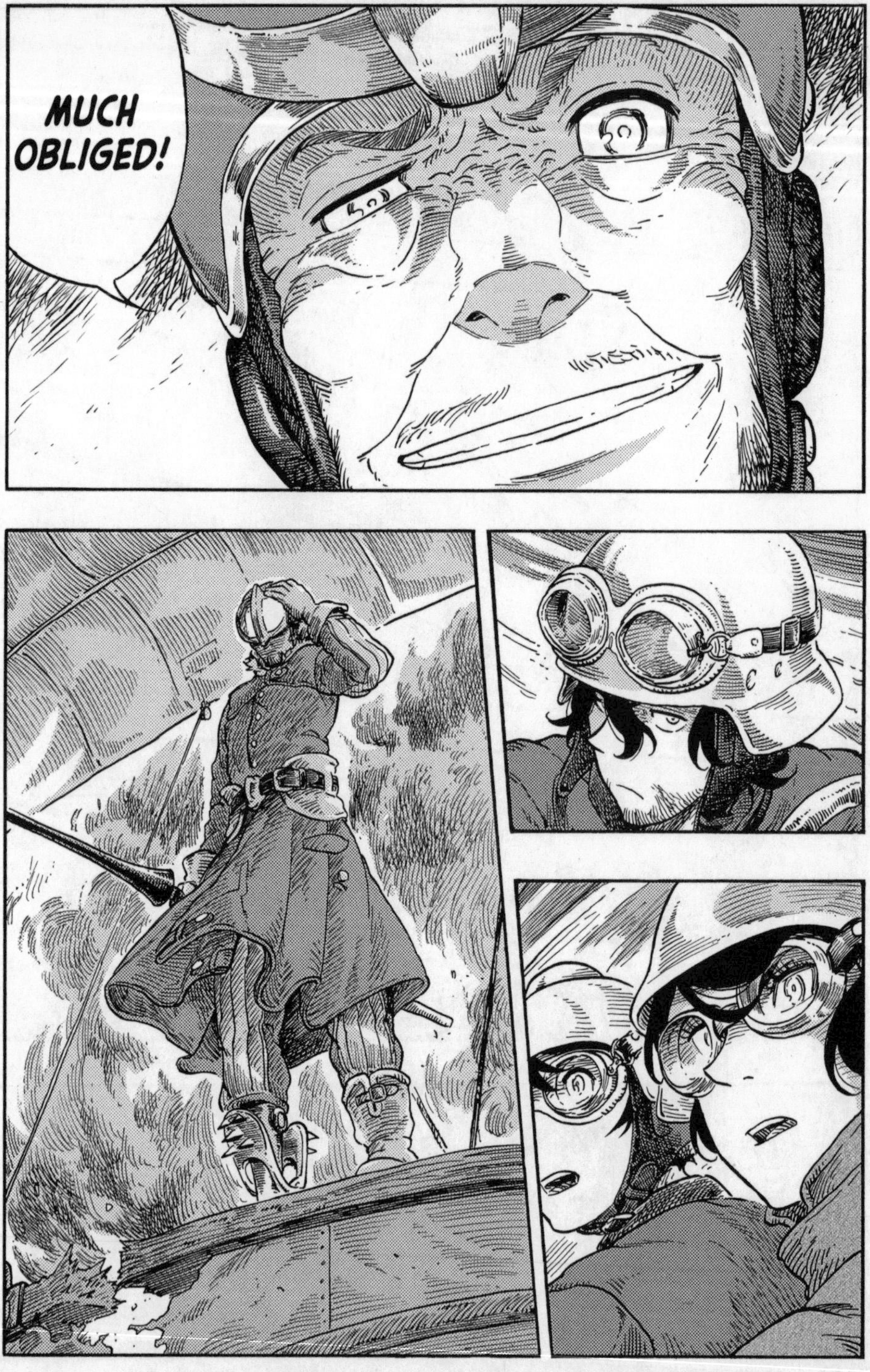
MUCH OBLIGED!

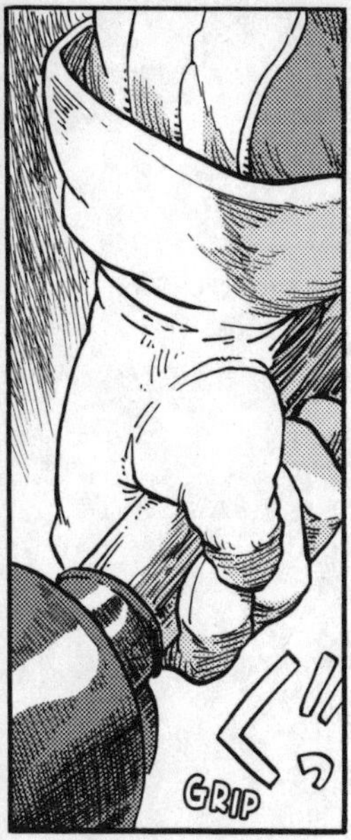
GRIP
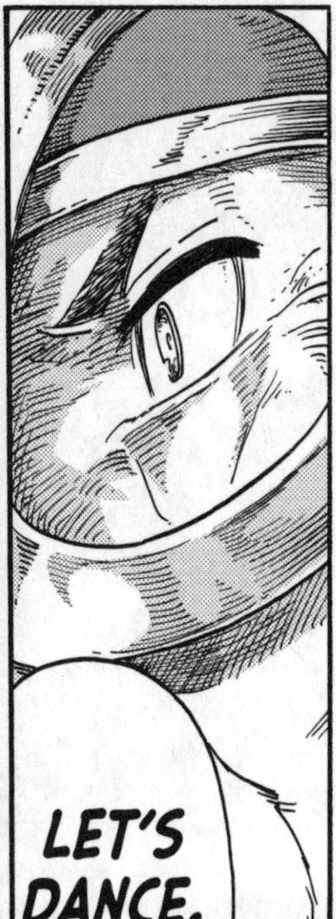
LET'S DANCE.
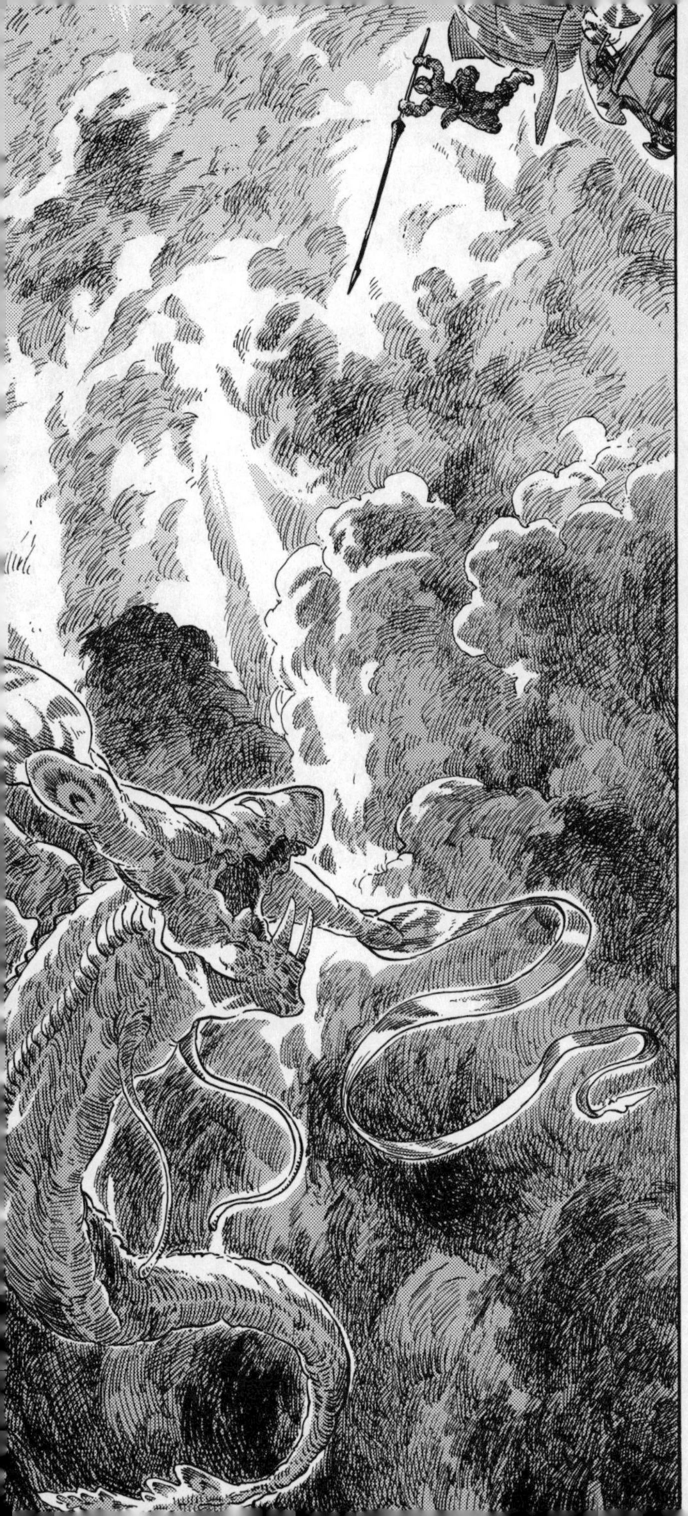

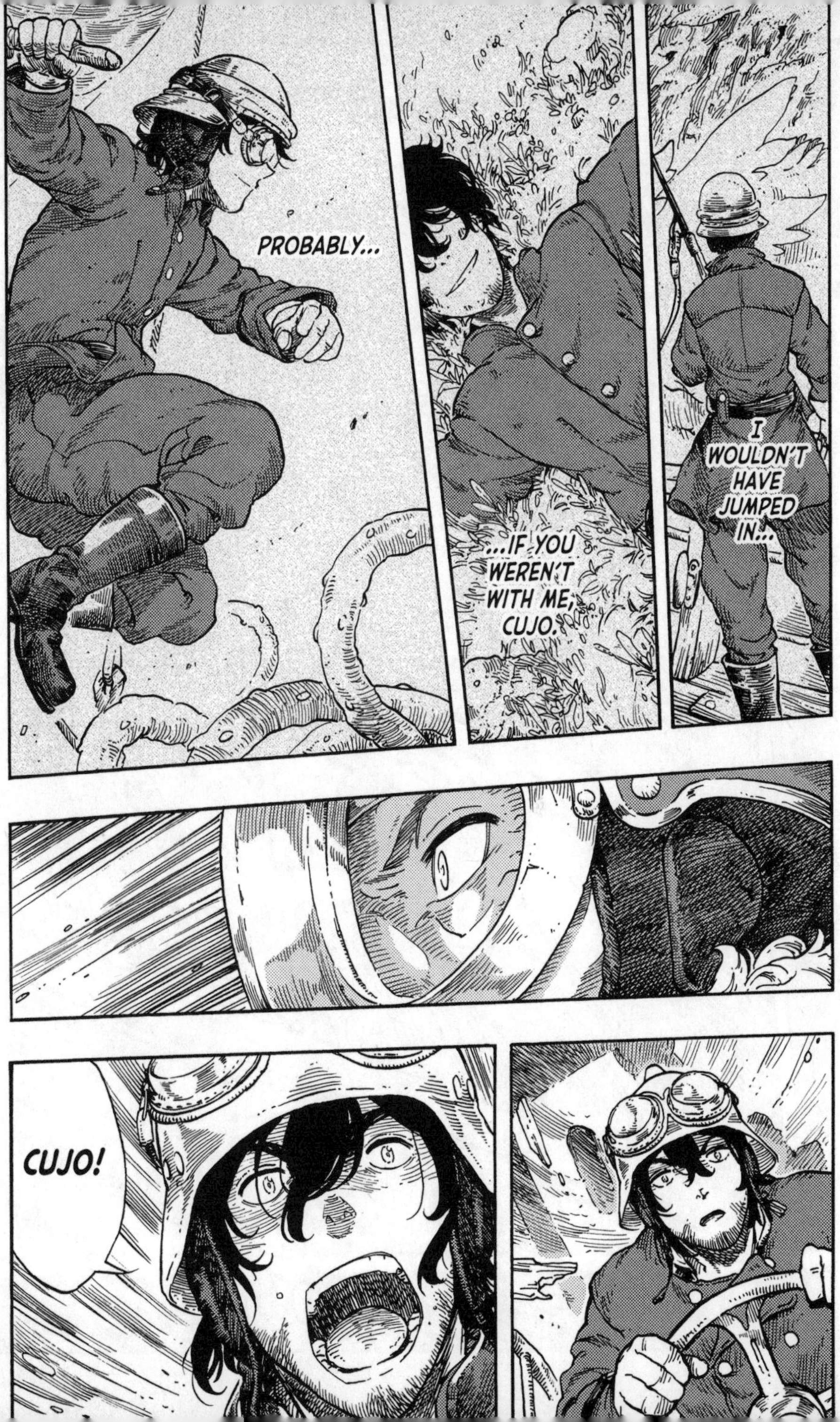
I WOULDN'T HAVE JUMPED IN...
...IF YOU WEREN'T WITH ME, CUJO.
PROBABLY...
CUJO!

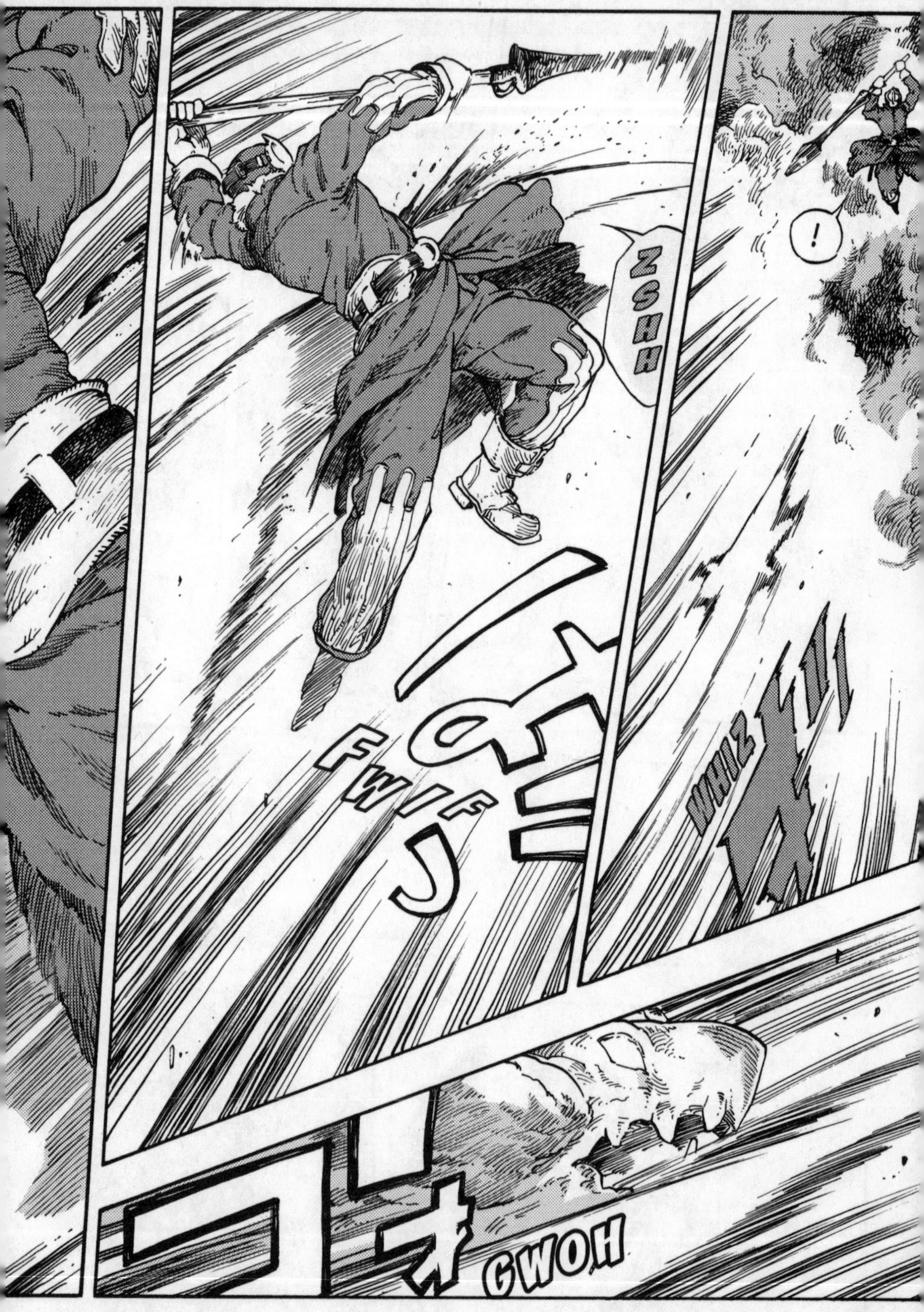
!
WHIZ
ZSHH
FWIF
GWOH

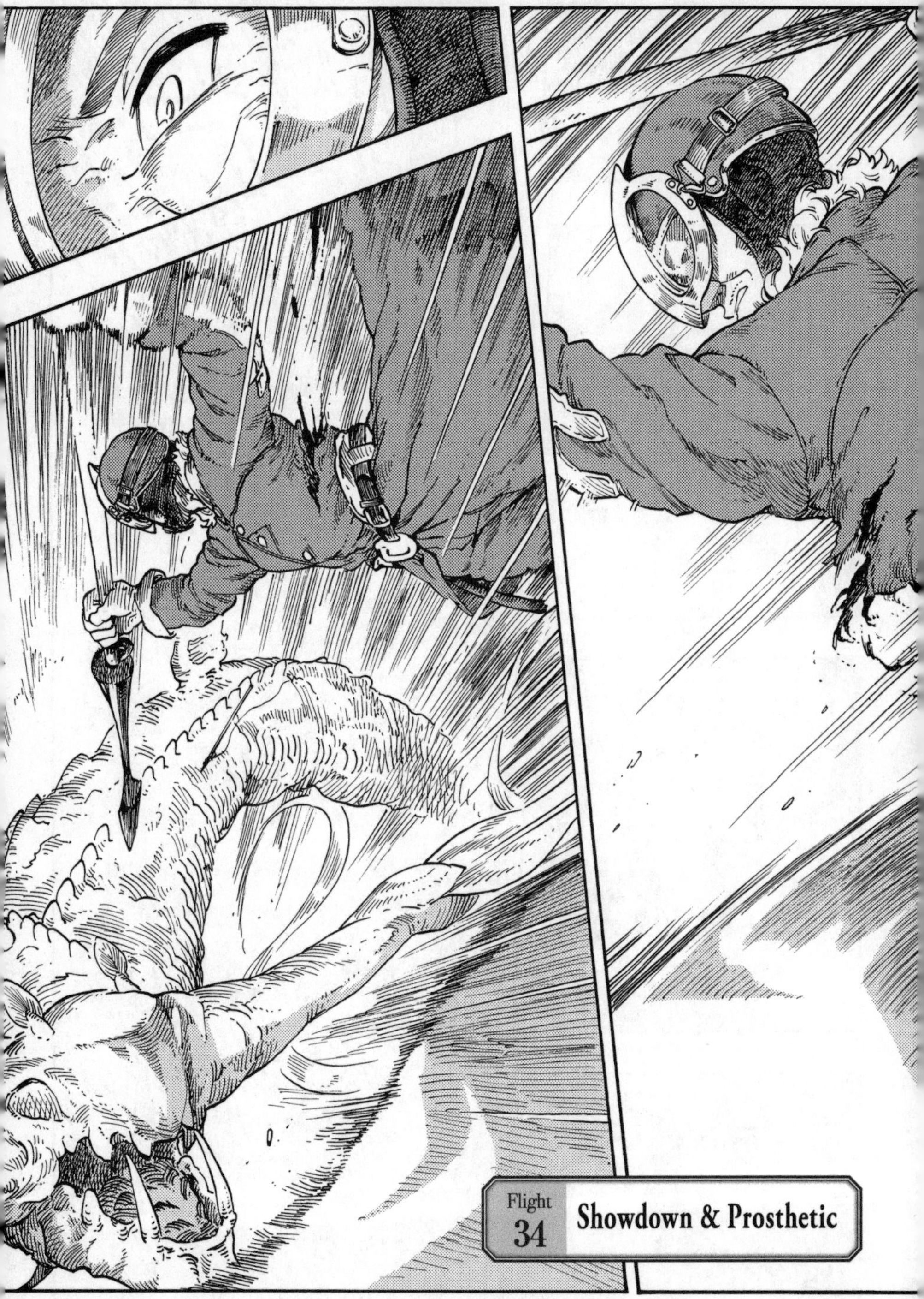
Flight 34
Showdown & Prosthetic

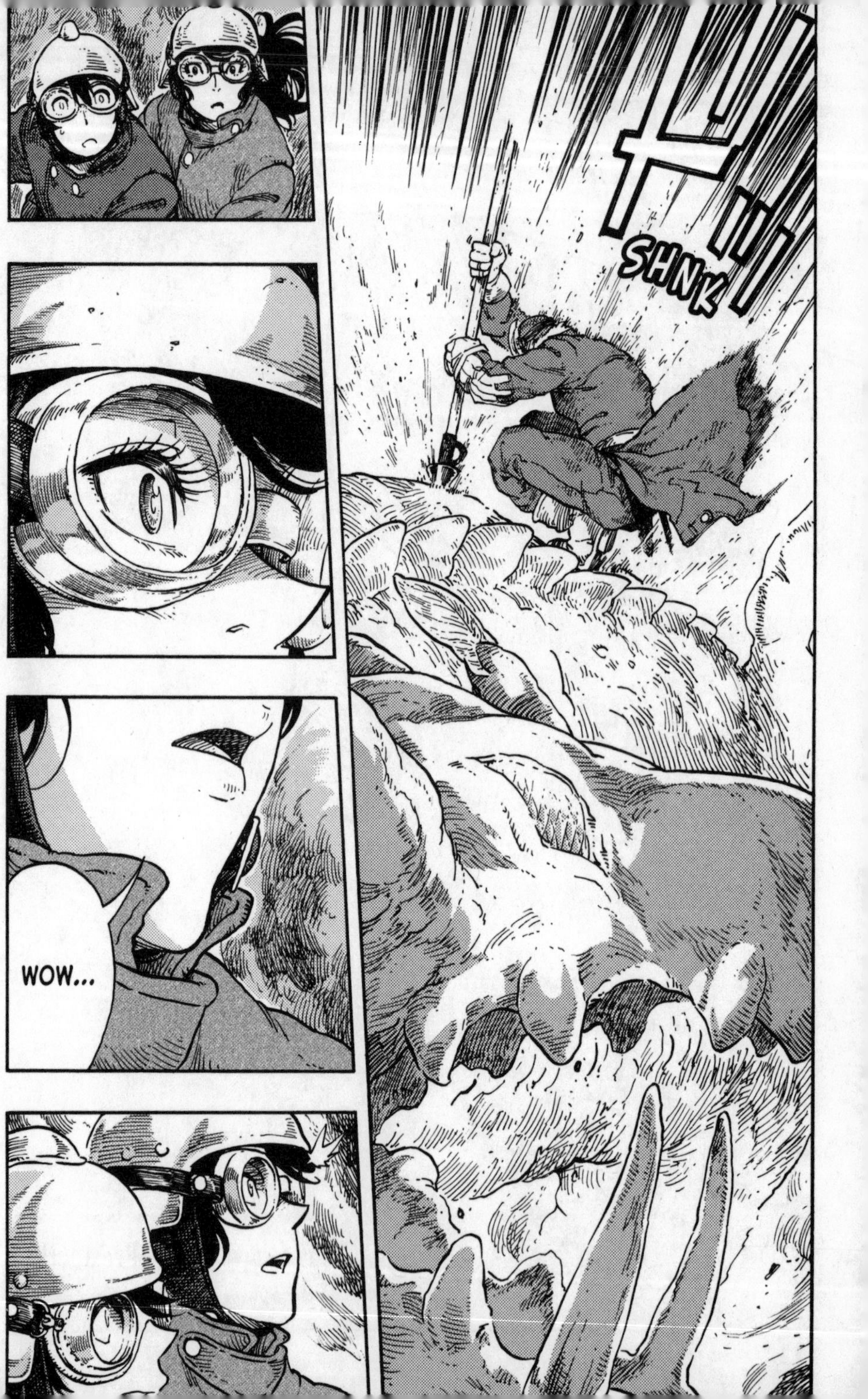
SHNK
WOW...

TCH....

MISSED ITS VITALS....!

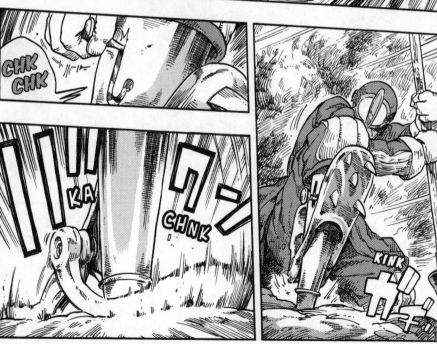

CHK CHK

KA

CHNK

KINK

145

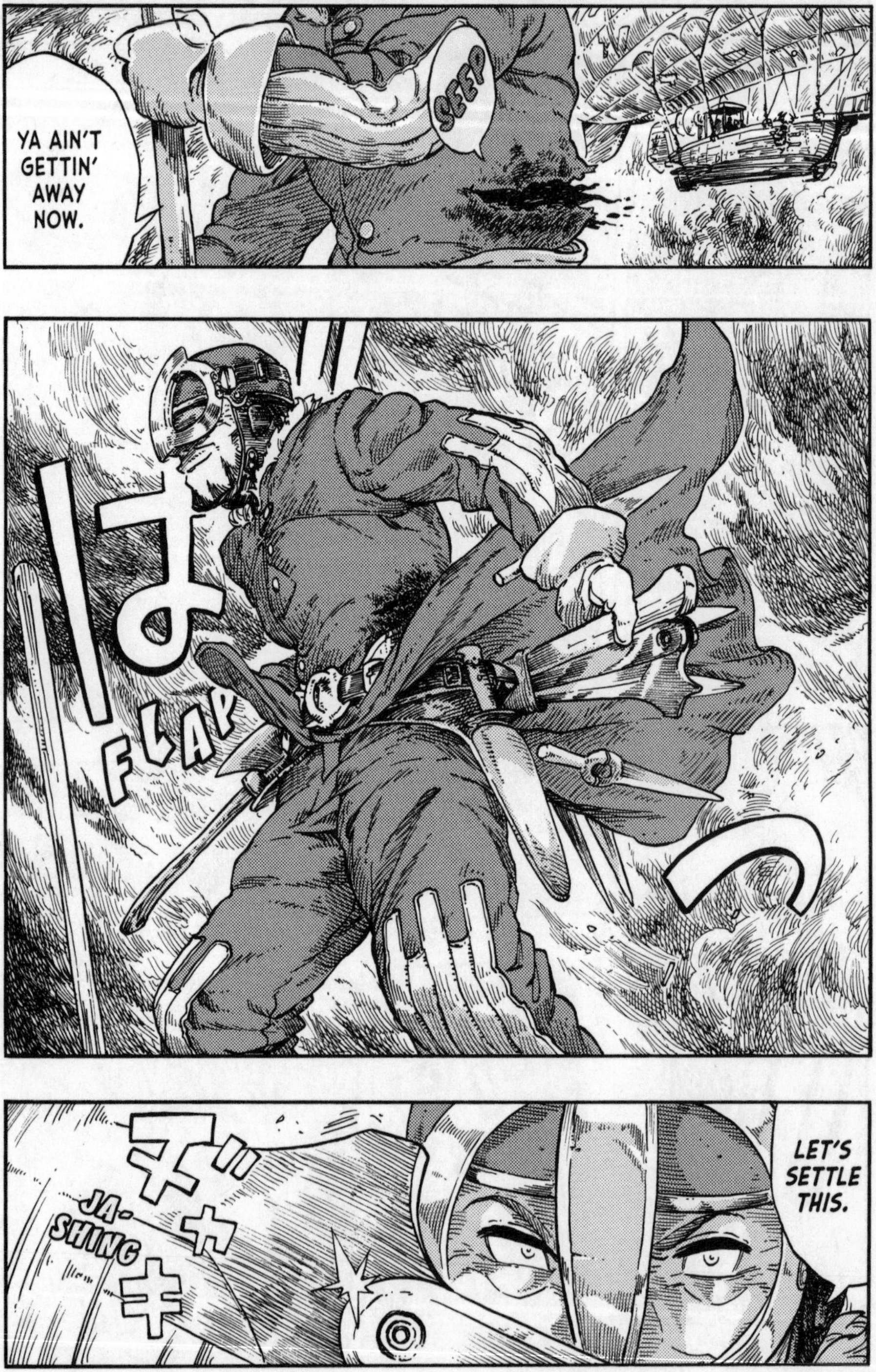
SEEP
YA AIN'T GETTIN' AWAY NOW.
FLAP
LET'S SETTLE THIS.
JA-SHING

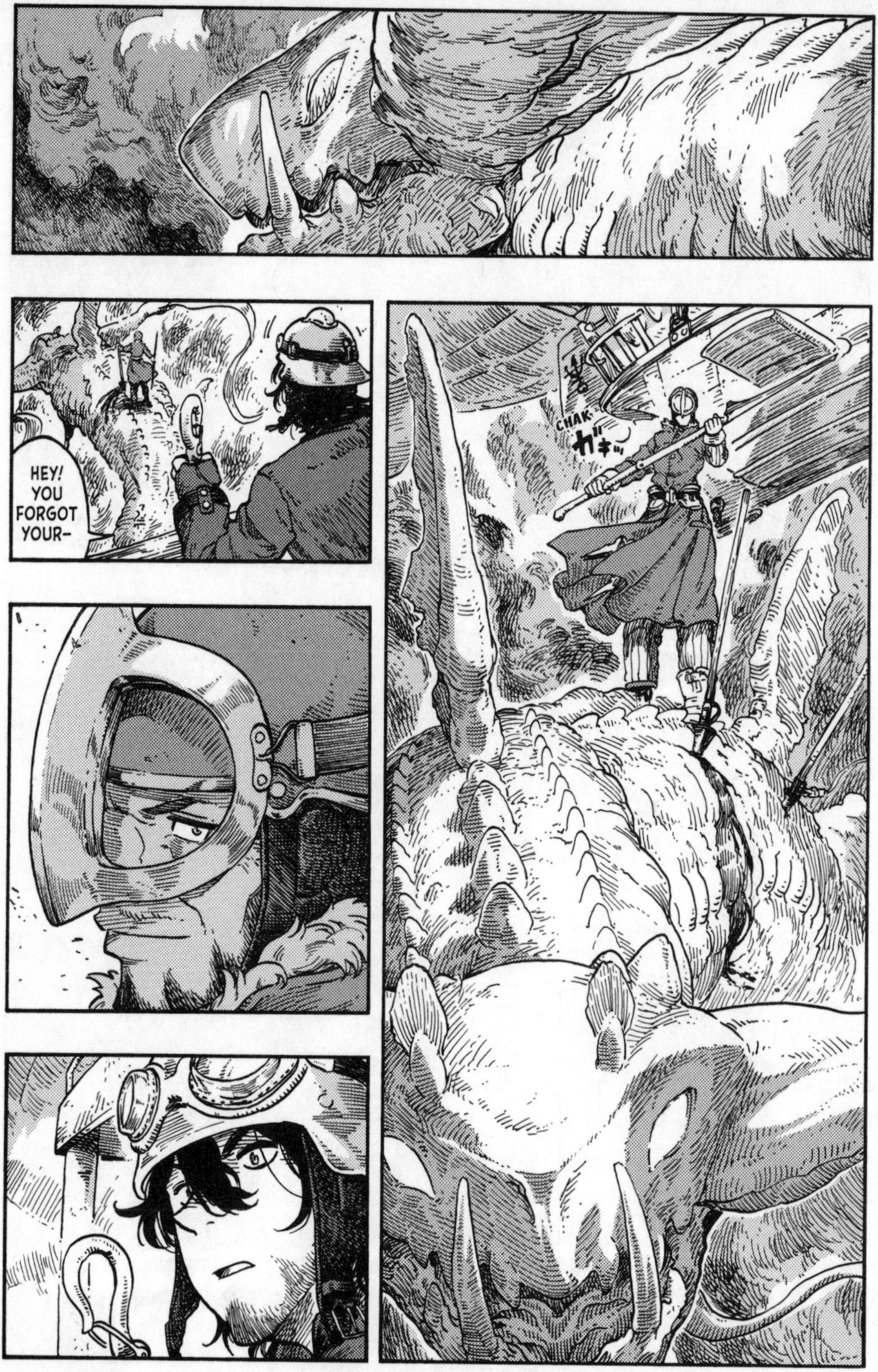
CHAK
ガキッ
HEY! YOU FORGOT YOUR–

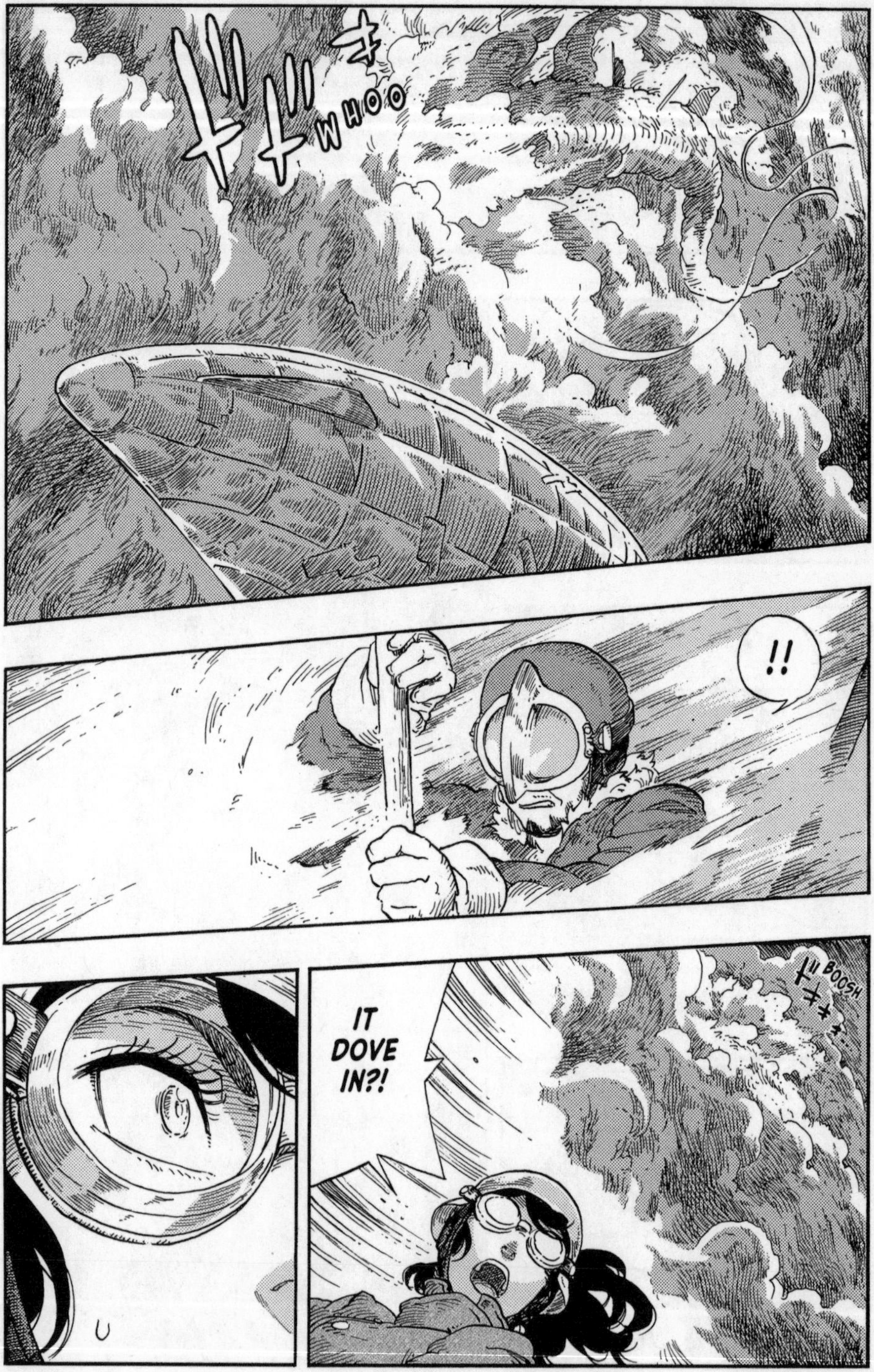
WHOO
!!
BOOSH
IT DOVE IN?!

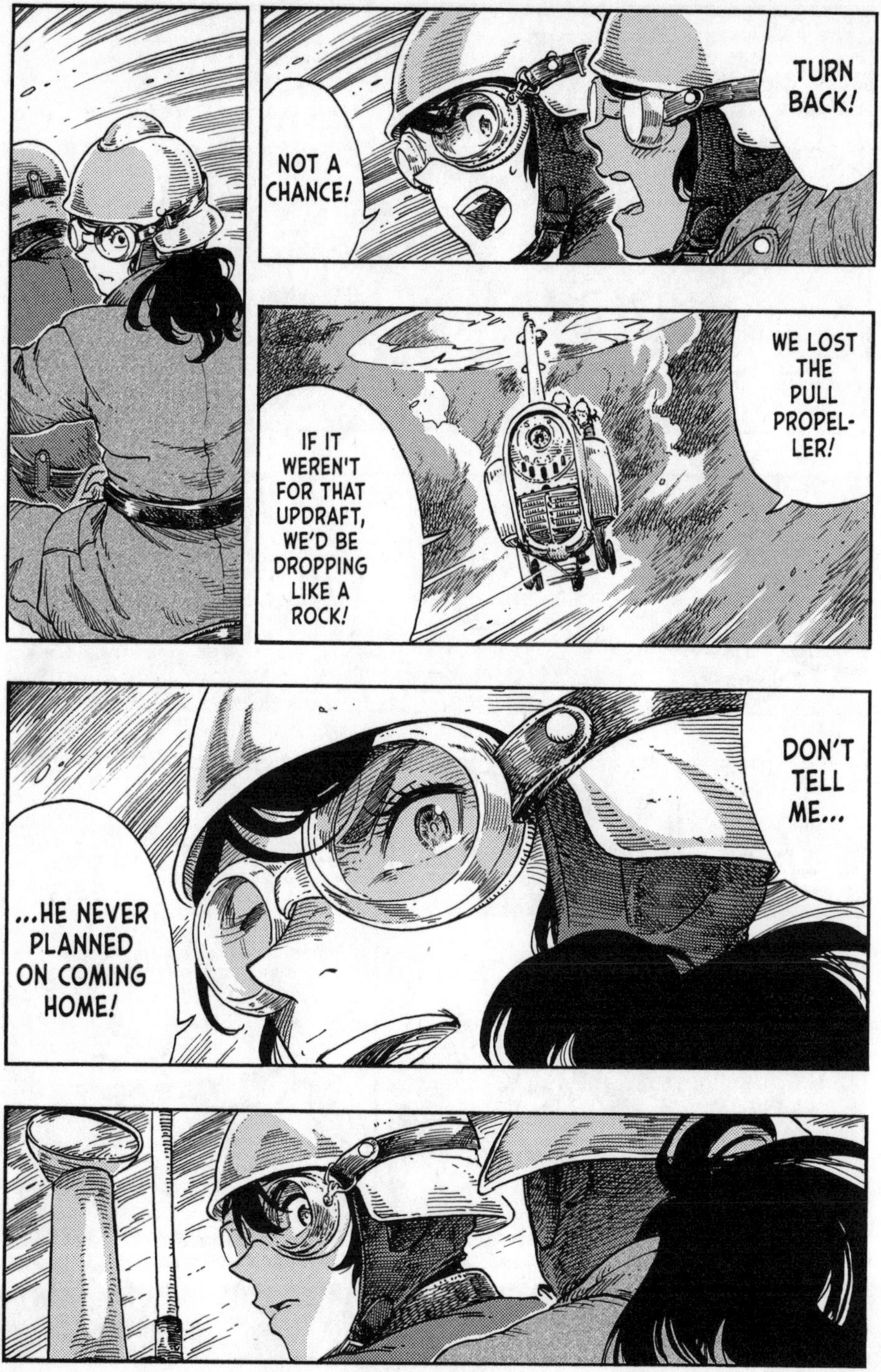
TURN BACK!
NOT A CHANCE!
WE LOST THE PULL PROPEL-LER!
IF IT WEREN'T FOR THAT UPDRAFT, WE'D BE DROPPING LIKE A ROCK!
DON'T TELL ME...
...HE NEVER PLANNED ON COMING HOME!

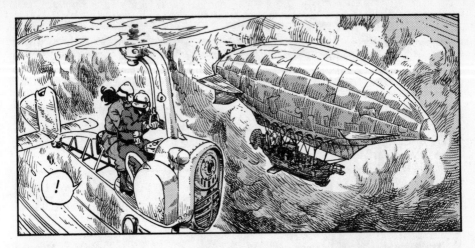

JIRO!

...!

RAM INTO THE NORA-GOTH!

WELL... GUESS IT'S EITHER THAT OR CRASH INTO THE OCEAN!

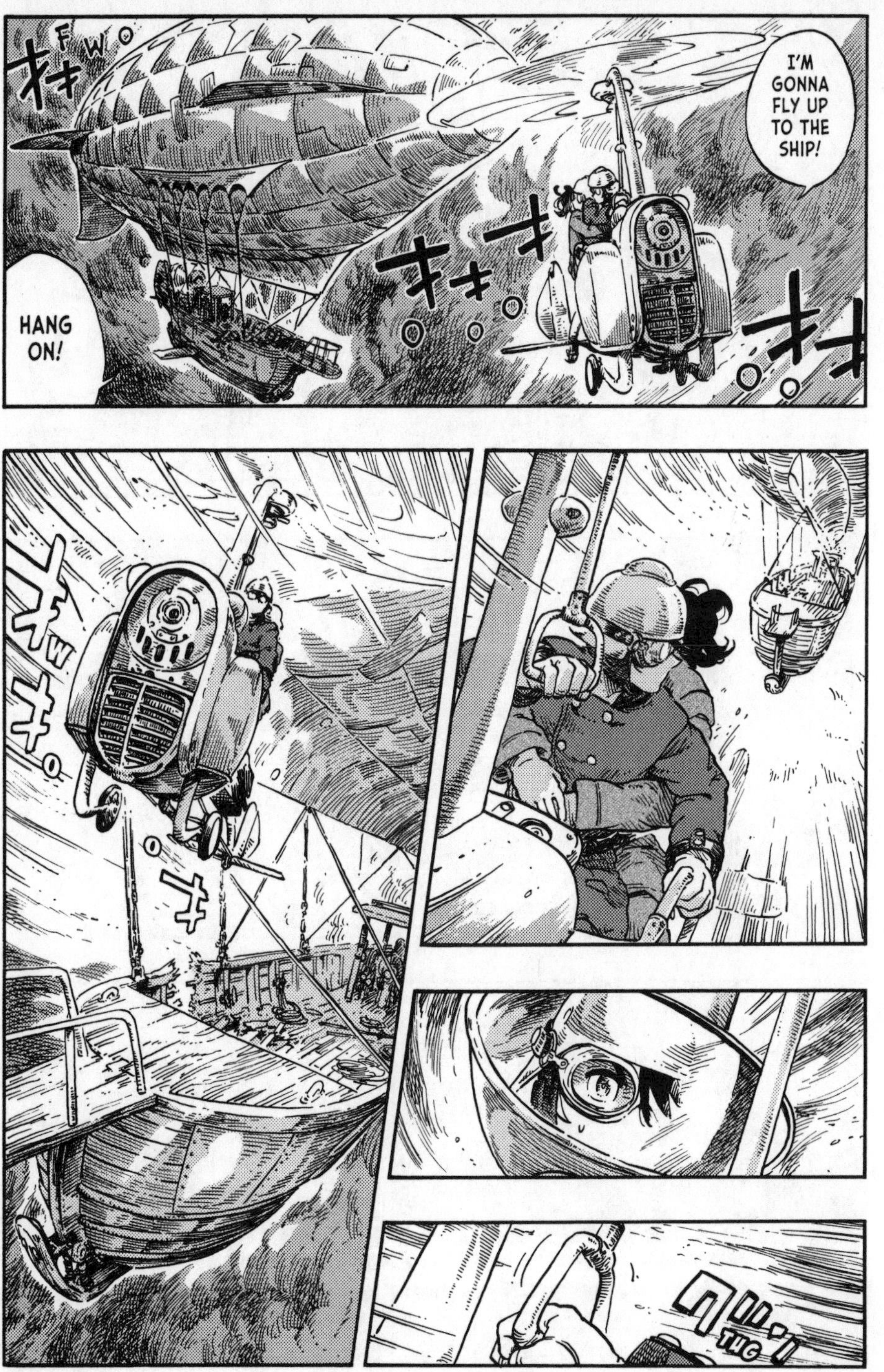
FWO
I'M GONNA FLY UP TO THE SHIP!
HANG ON!
TUG!

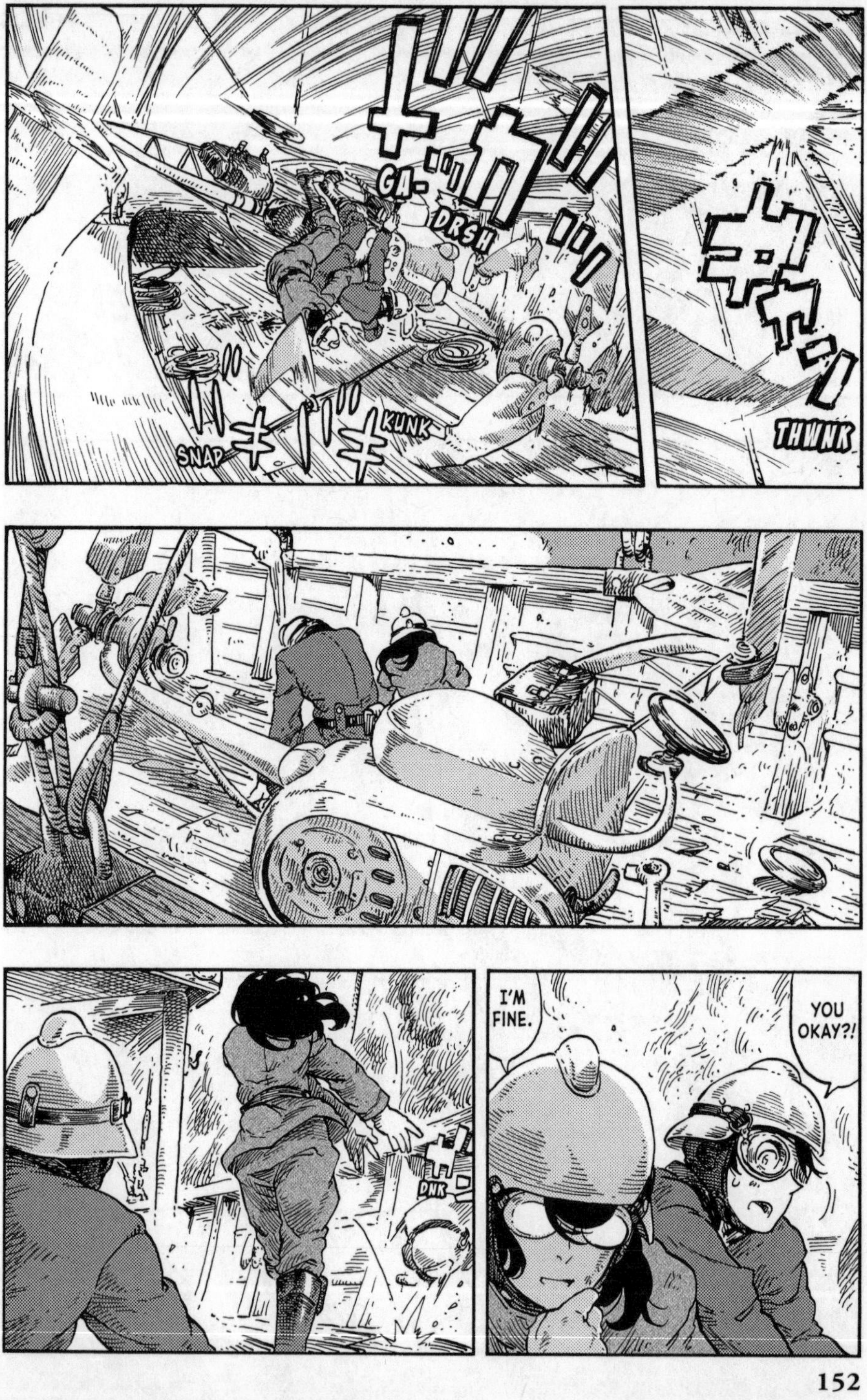
THWNK
GA-DRSH
KUNK
SNAP
YOU OKAY?!
I'M FINE.
DNK

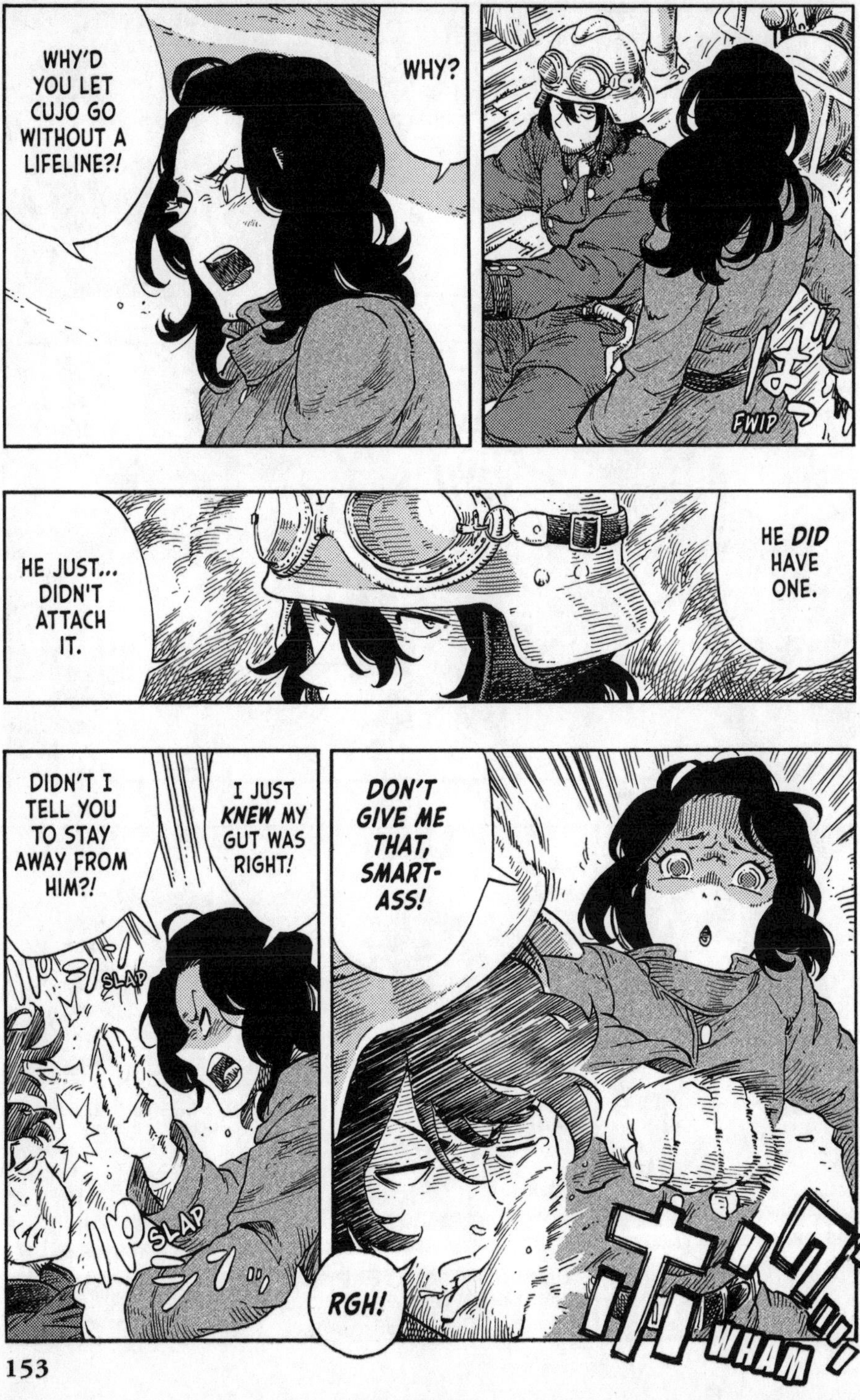
FWIP
WHY?
WHY'D YOU LET CUJO GO WITHOUT A LIFELINE?!
HE *DID* HAVE ONE.
HE JUST... DIDN'T ATTACH IT.
DON'T GIVE ME THAT, SMART-ASS!
RGH!
WHAM
I JUST *KNEW* MY GUT WAS RIGHT!
DIDN'T I TELL YOU TO STAY AWAY FROM HIM?!
SLAP
SLAP

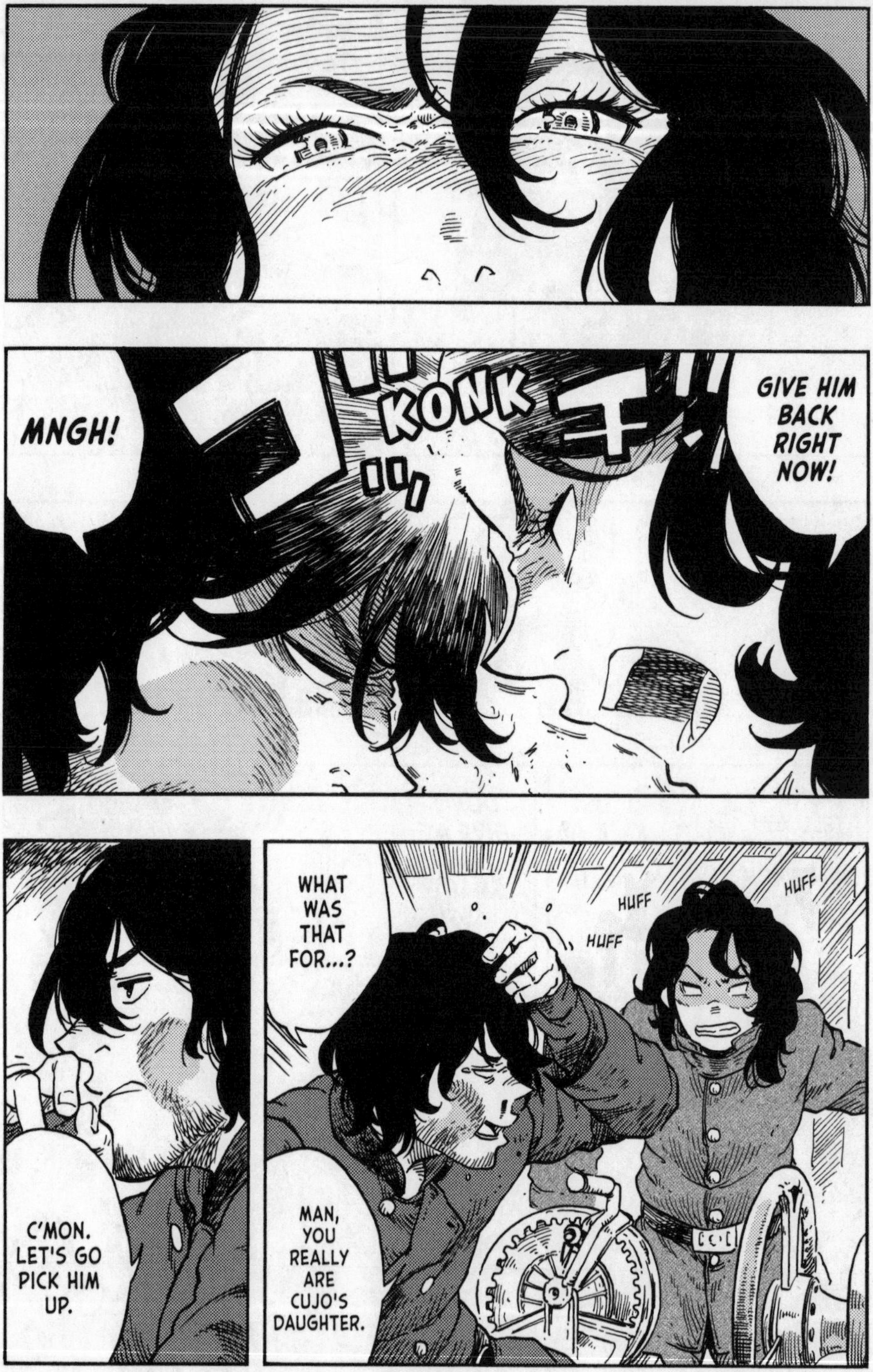
GIVE HIM BACK RIGHT NOW!
KONK
MNGH!
HUFF
HUFF
HUFF
WHAT WAS THAT FOR...?
MAN, YOU REALLY ARE CUJO'S DAUGHTER.
C'MON. LET'S GO PICK HIM UP.

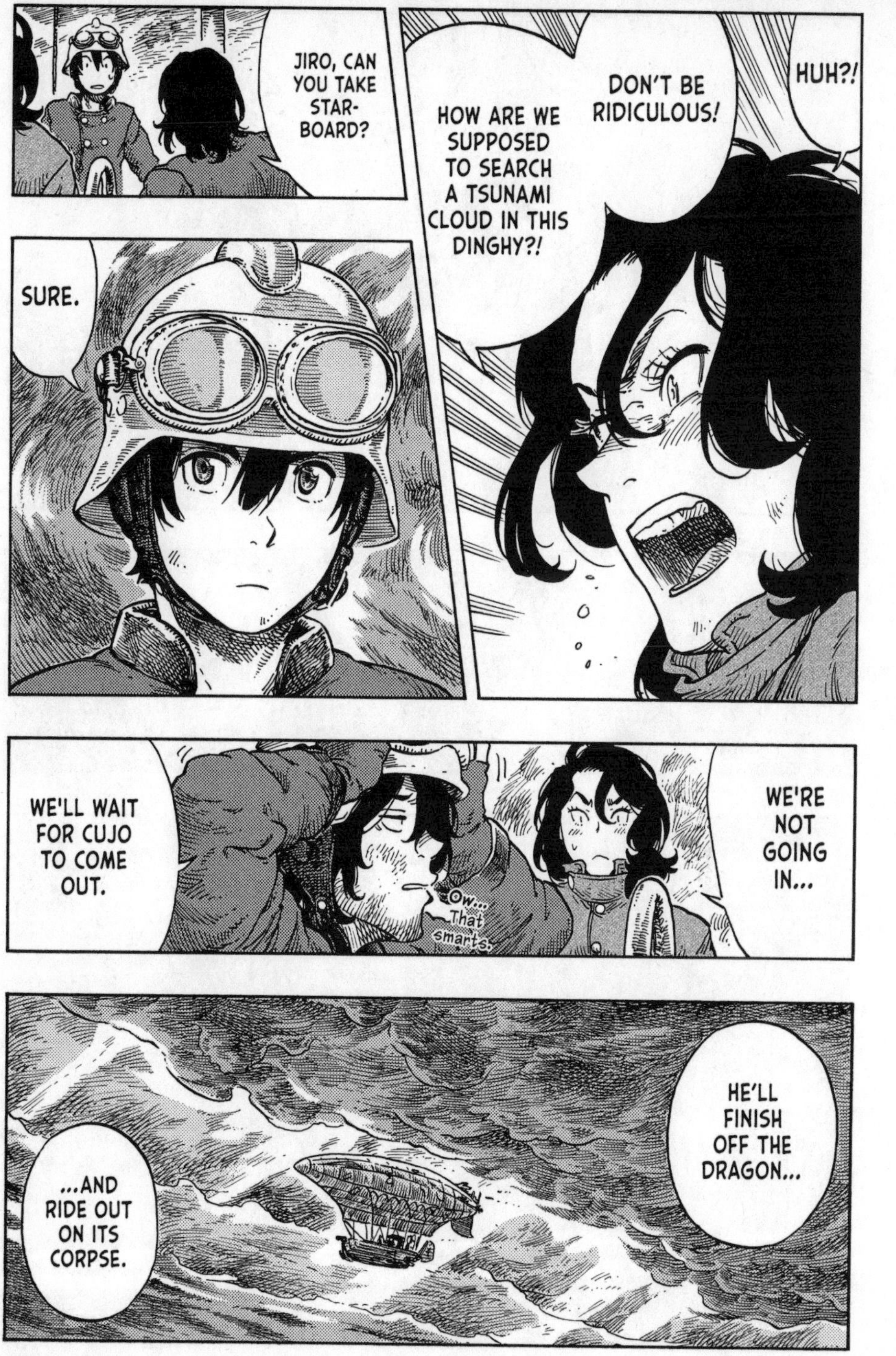
JIRO, CAN YOU TAKE STAR-BOARD?
SURE.
HUH?!
DON'T BE RIDICULOUS!
HOW ARE WE SUPPOSED TO SEARCH A TSUNAMI CLOUD IN THIS DINGHY?!
WE'RE NOT GOING IN...
WE'LL WAIT FOR CUJO TO COME OUT.
Ow... That smarts.
HE'LL FINISH OFF THE DRAGON...
...AND RIDE OUT ON ITS CORPSE.

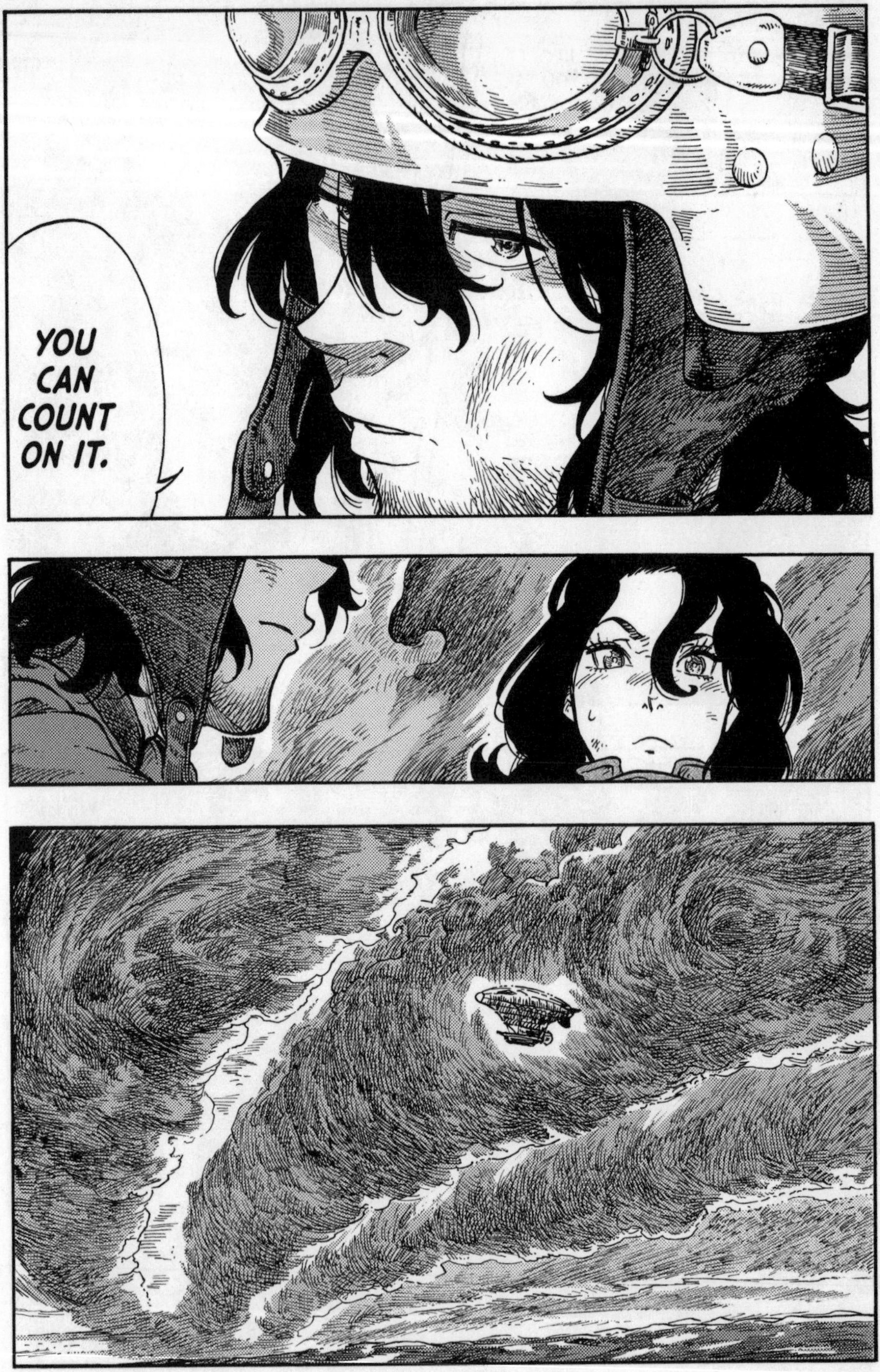
YOU CAN COUNT ON IT.

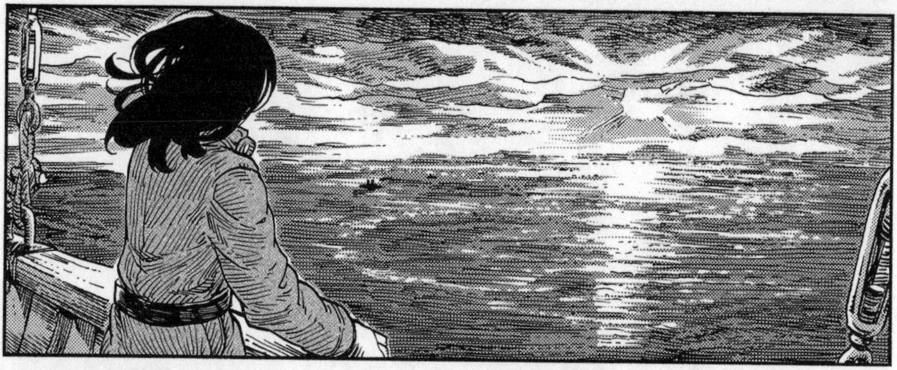
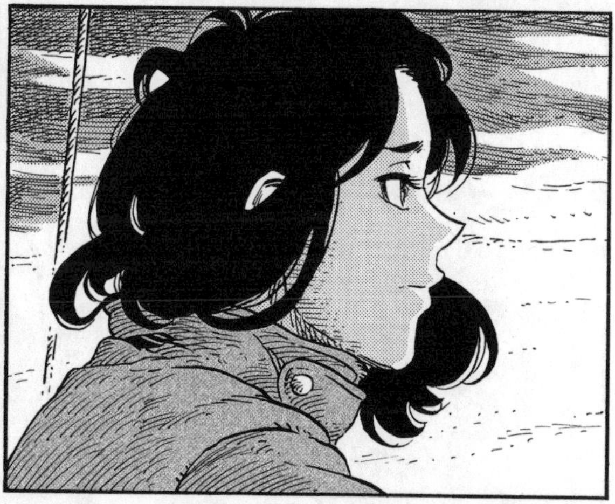
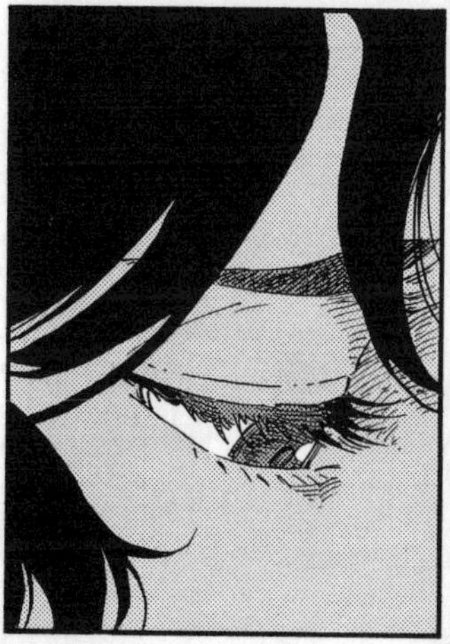
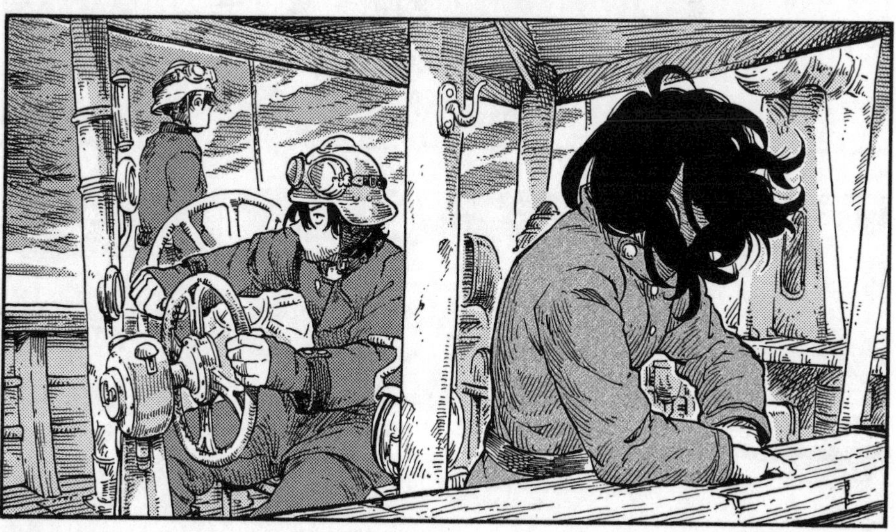

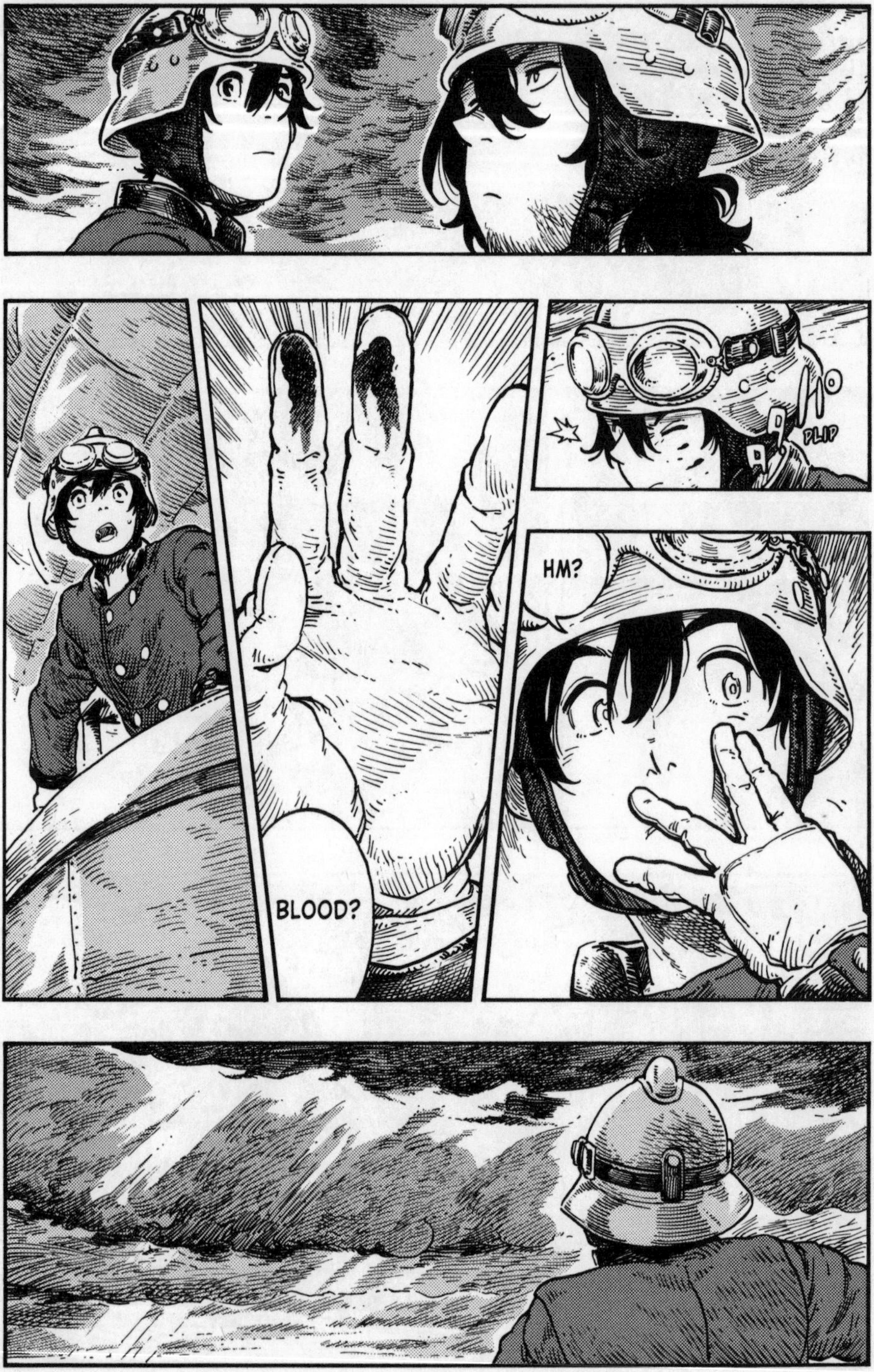
PLIP
HM?
BLOOD?

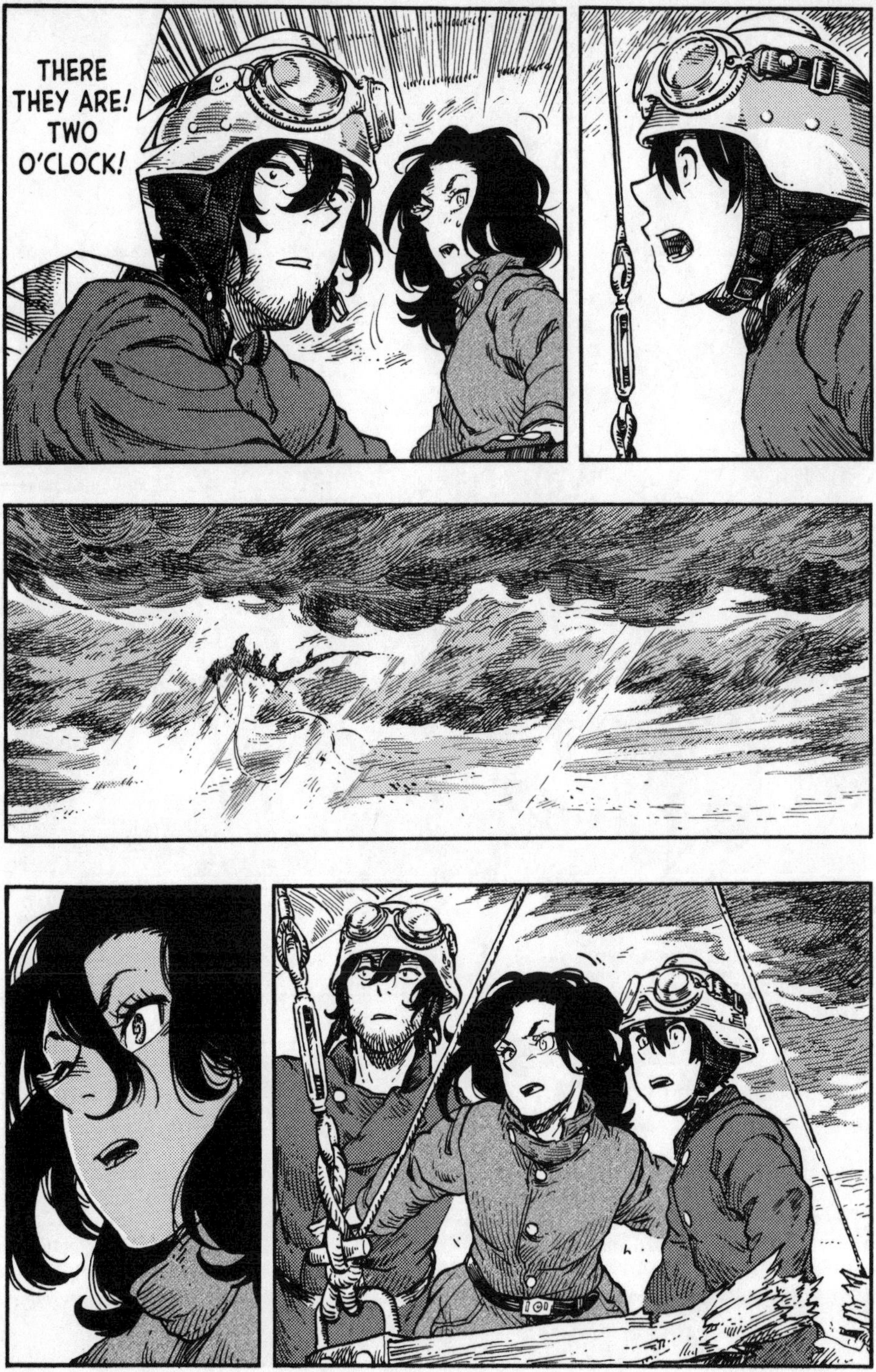
THERE THEY ARE! TWO O'CLOCK!

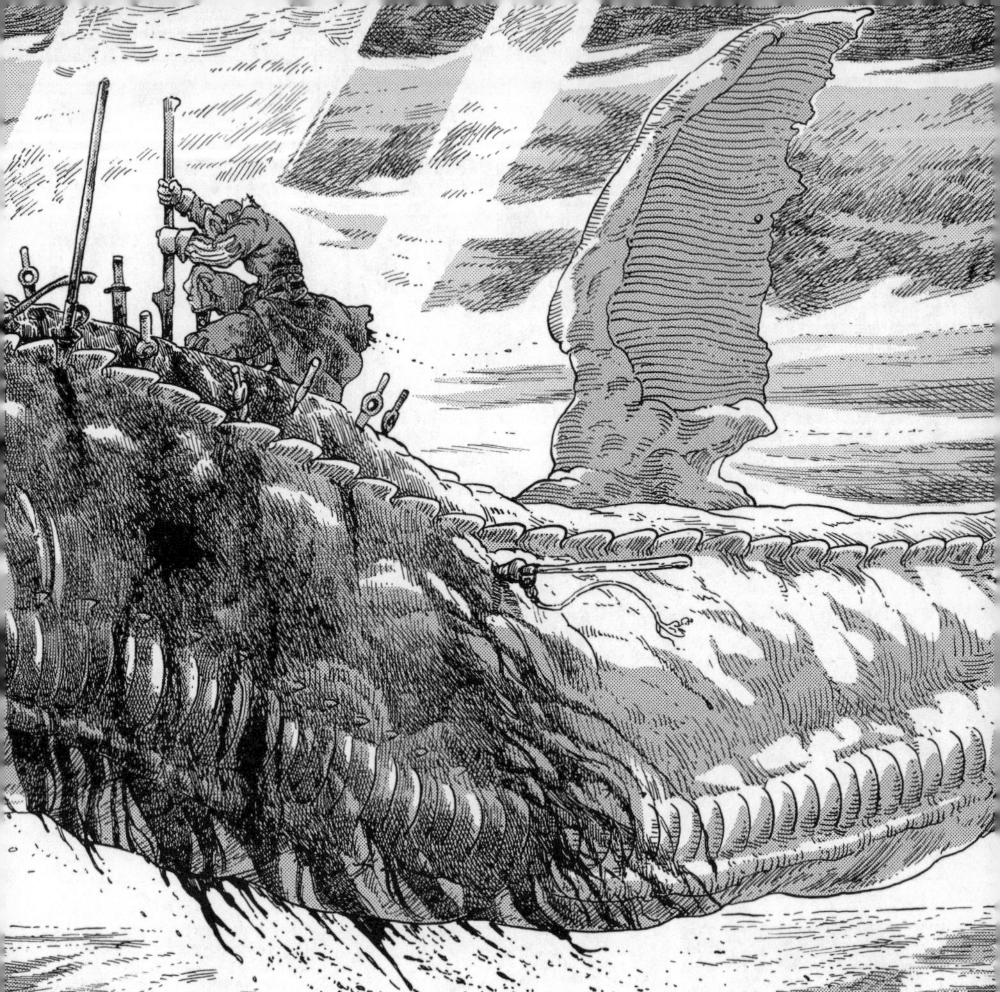
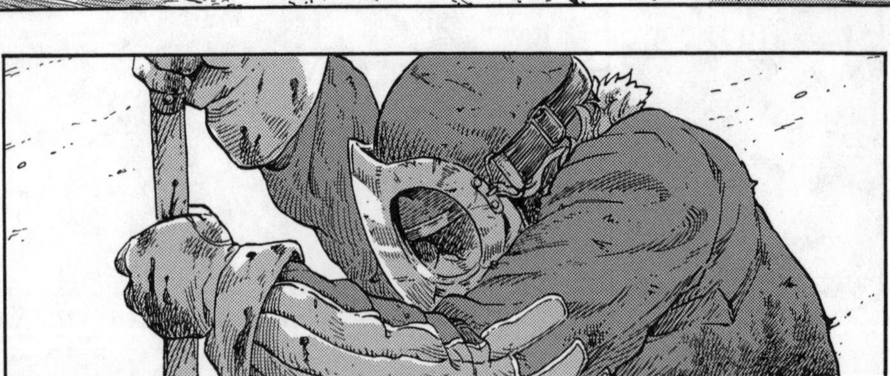

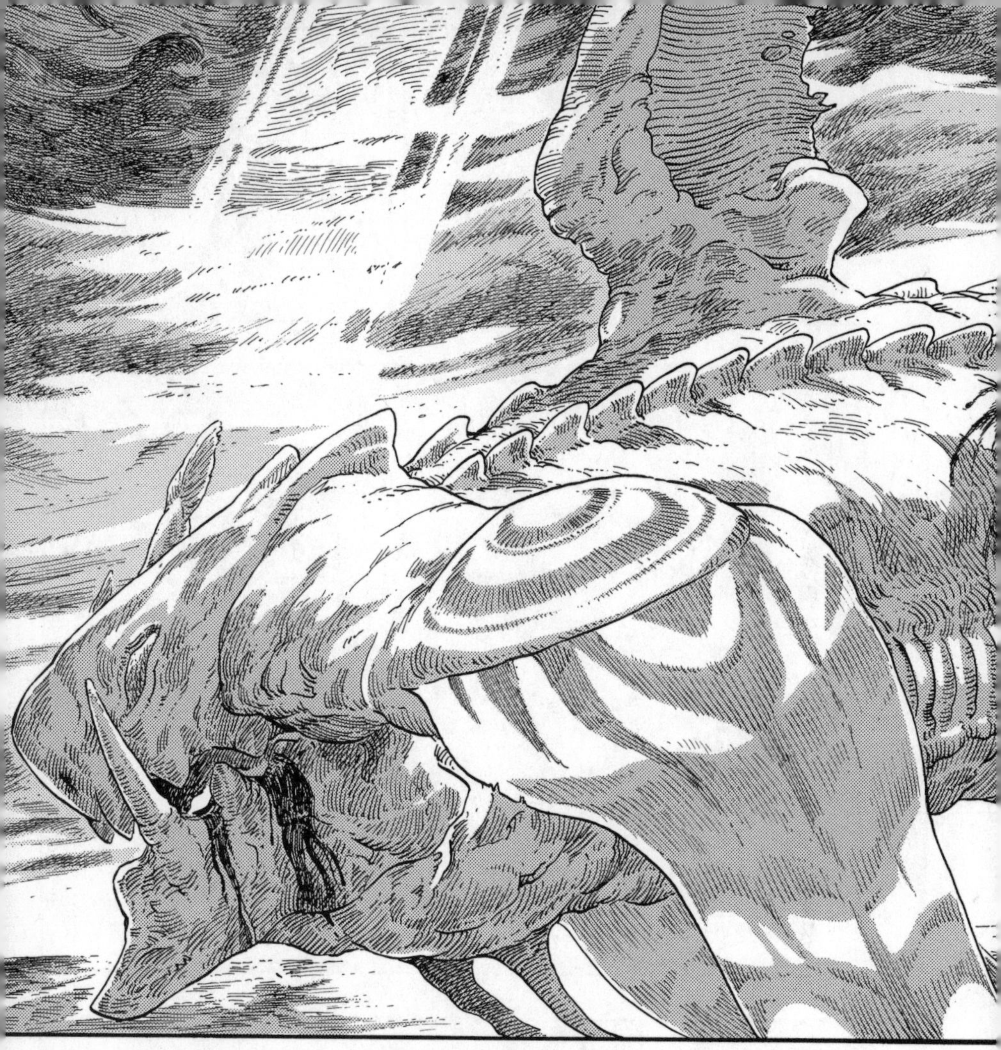
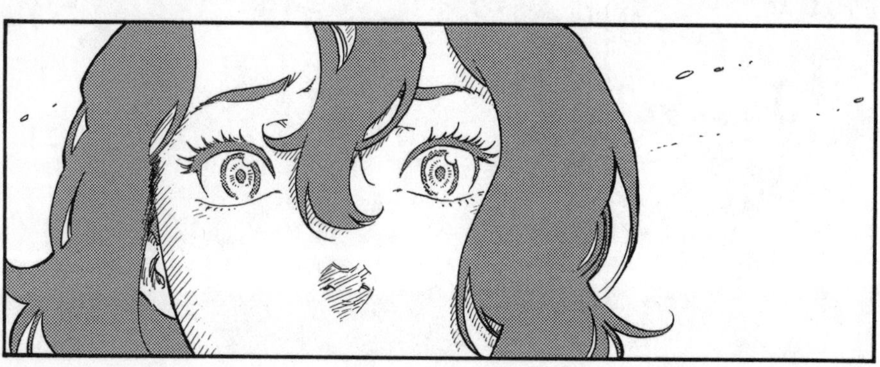

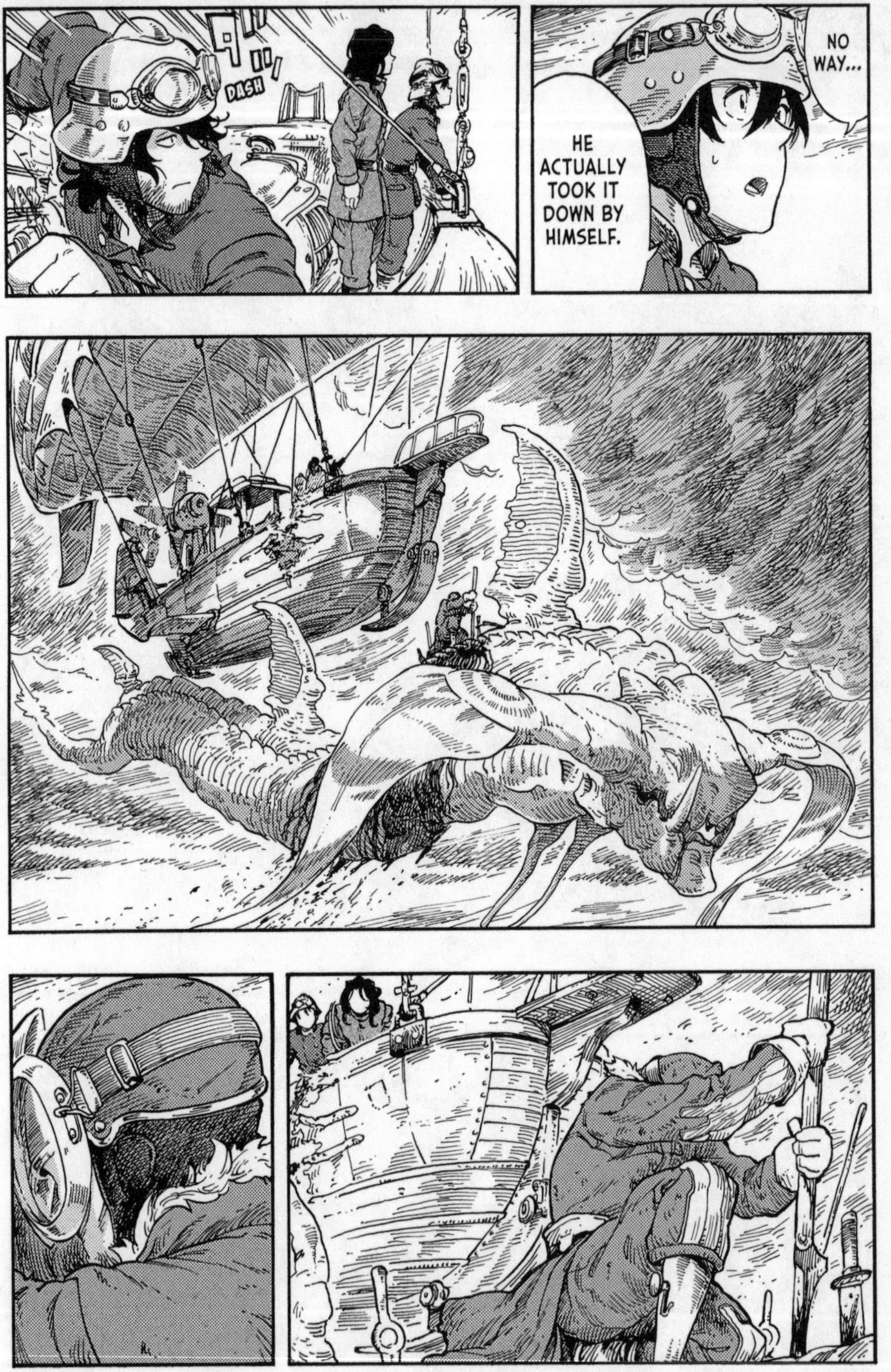
NO WAY...
HE ACTUALLY TOOK IT DOWN BY HIMSELF.
DASH

NO!
CUJOOO!

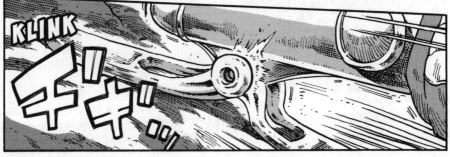

KLINK

ガギン
GA-
KINK

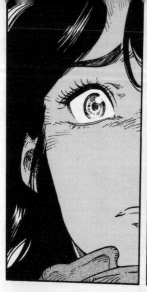

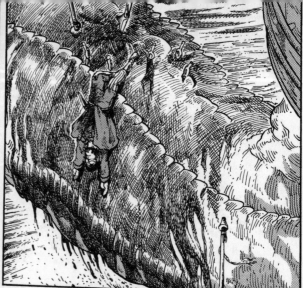

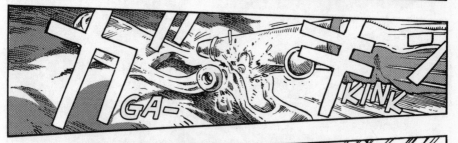

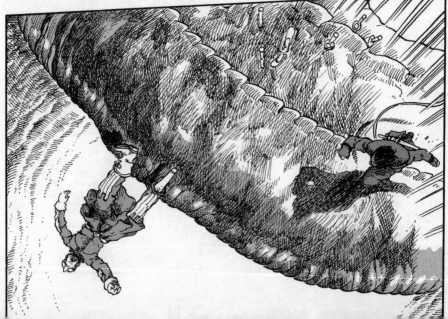

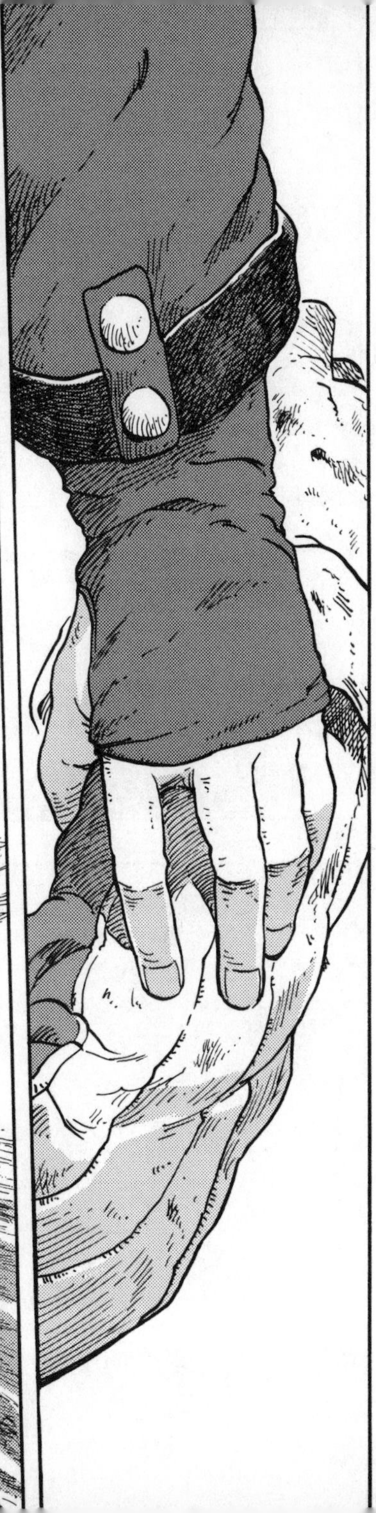

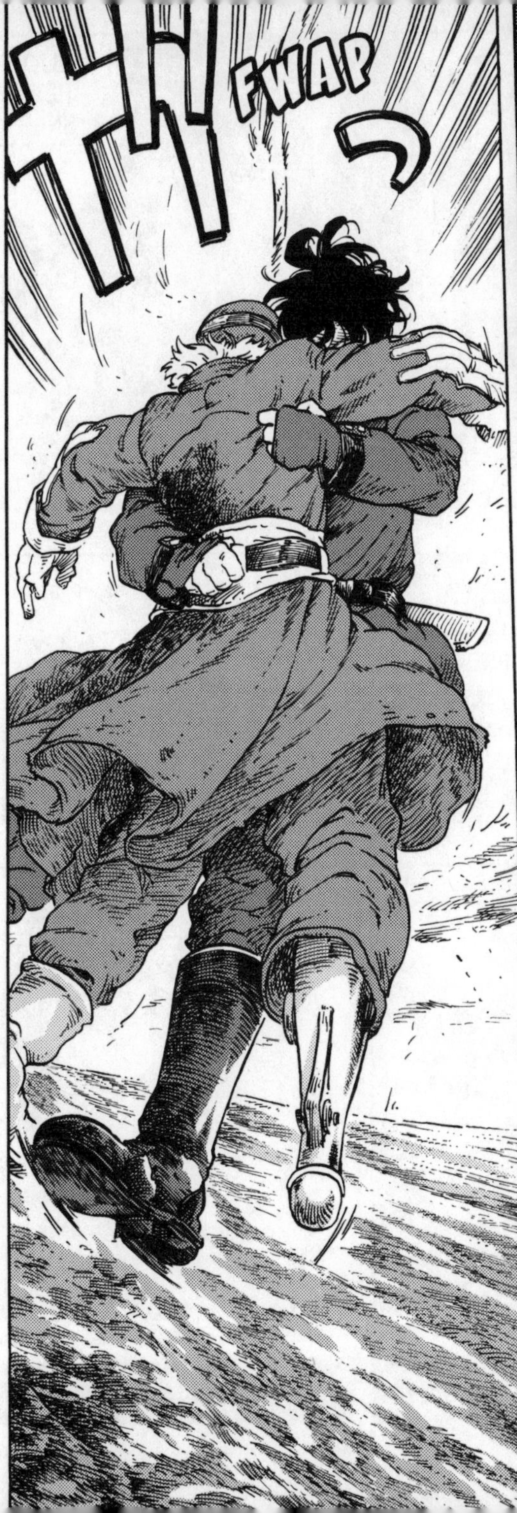
FWAP

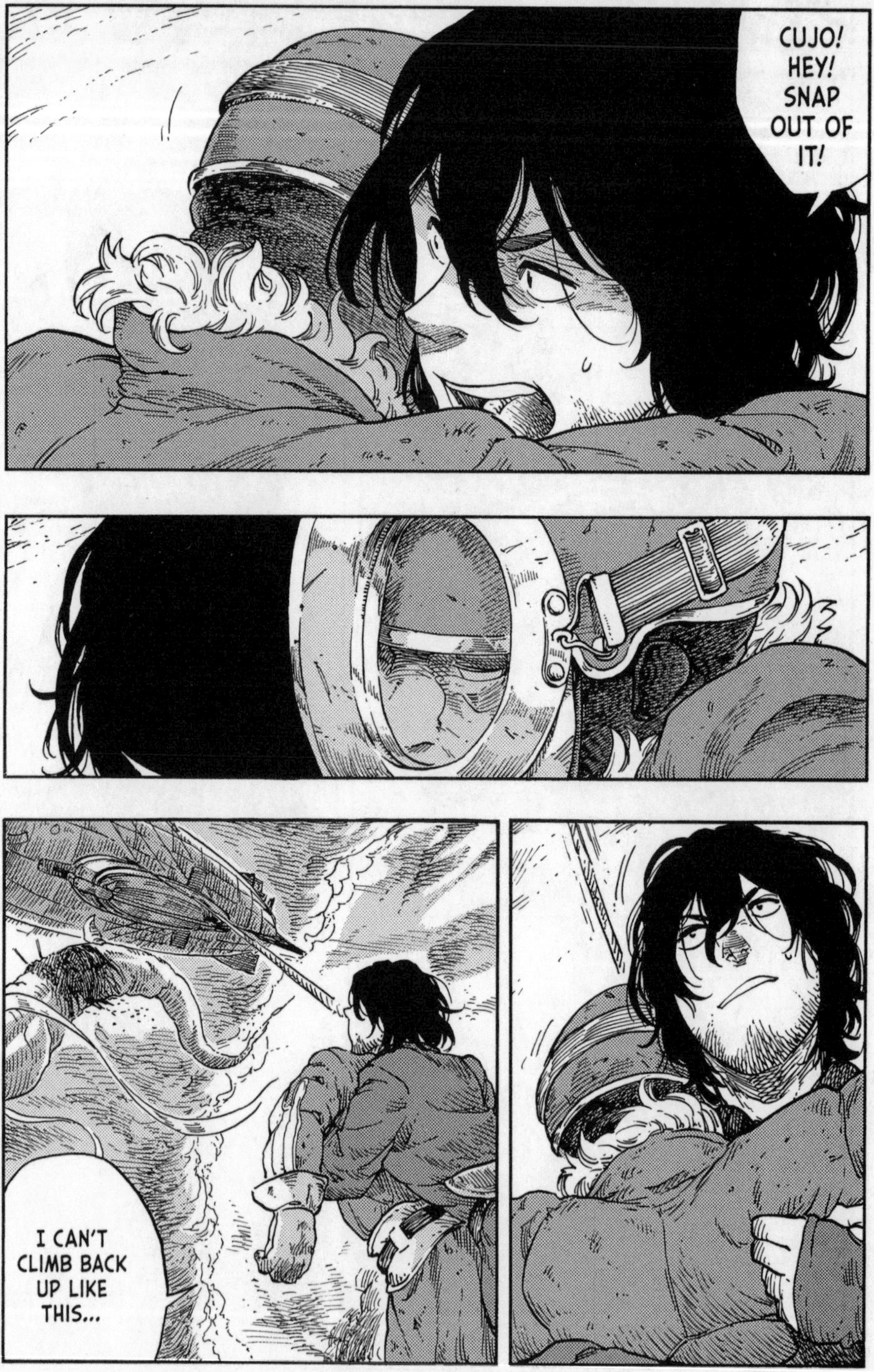
CUJO! HEY! SNAP OUT OF IT!
I CAN'T CLIMB BACK UP LIKE THIS...

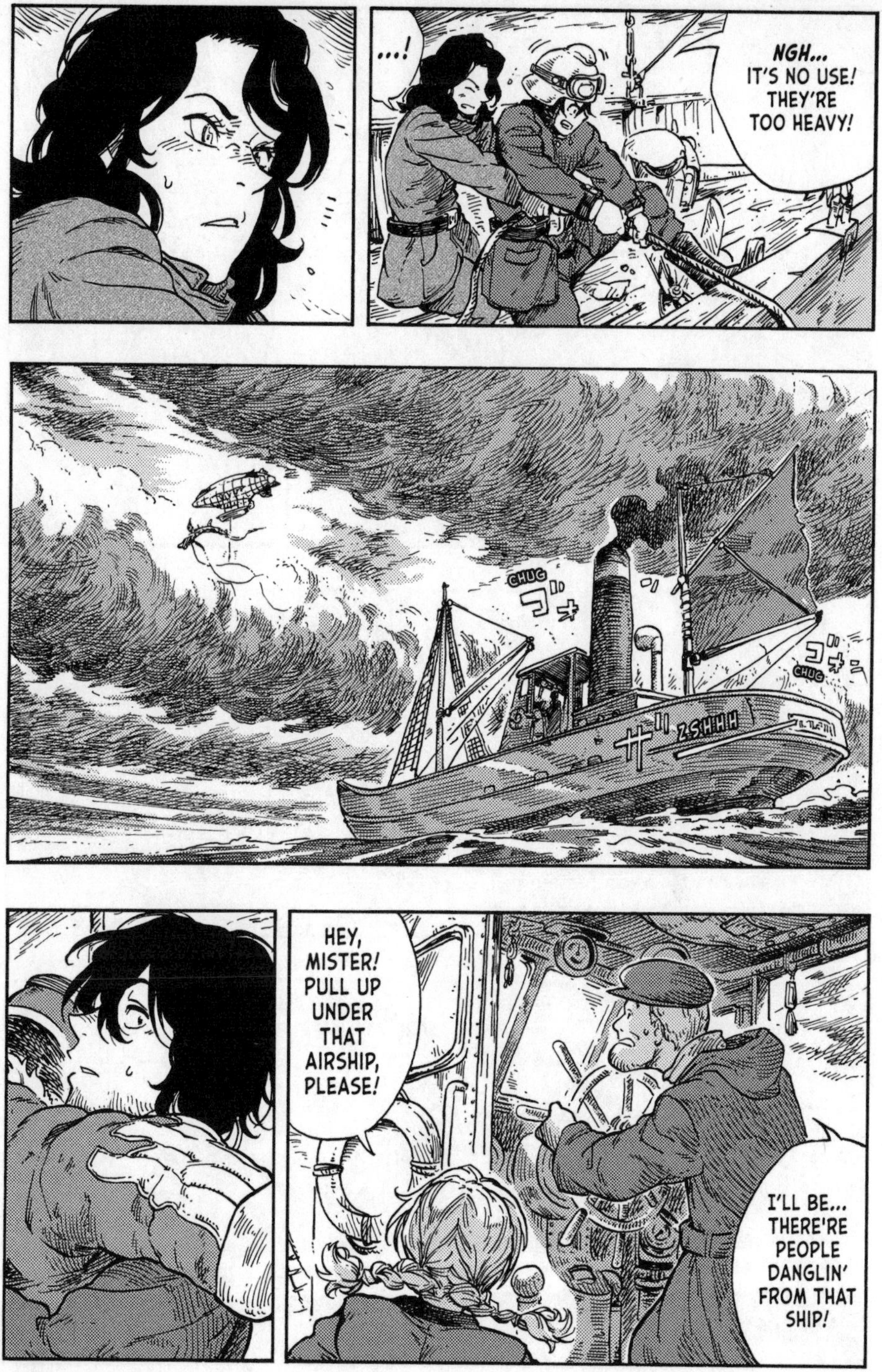
NGH... IT'S NO USE! THEY'RE TOO HEAVY!
...!
CHUG
ZSHHH
CHUG
HEY, MISTER! PULL UP UNDER THAT AIRSHIP, PLEASE!
I'LL BE... THERE'RE PEOPLE DANGLIN' FROM THAT SHIP!

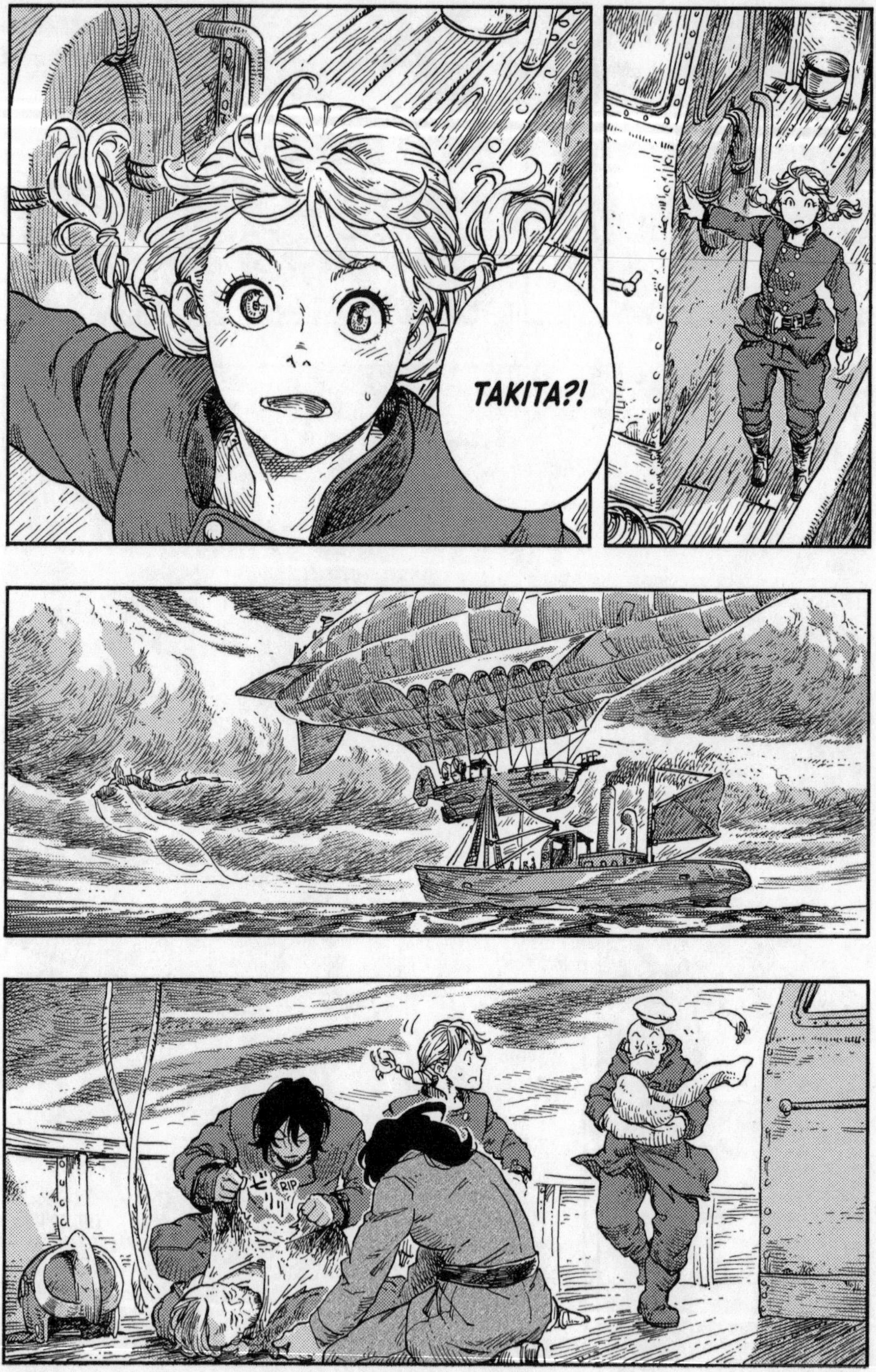
TAKITA?!
RIP

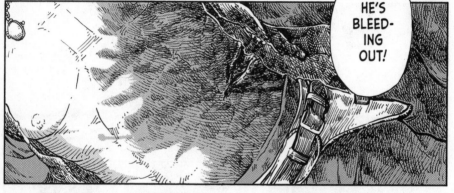

HE'S BLEED- ING OUT!

I'LL GETCHA BACK TO TOWN RIGHT QUICK!

PLEASE HURRY!

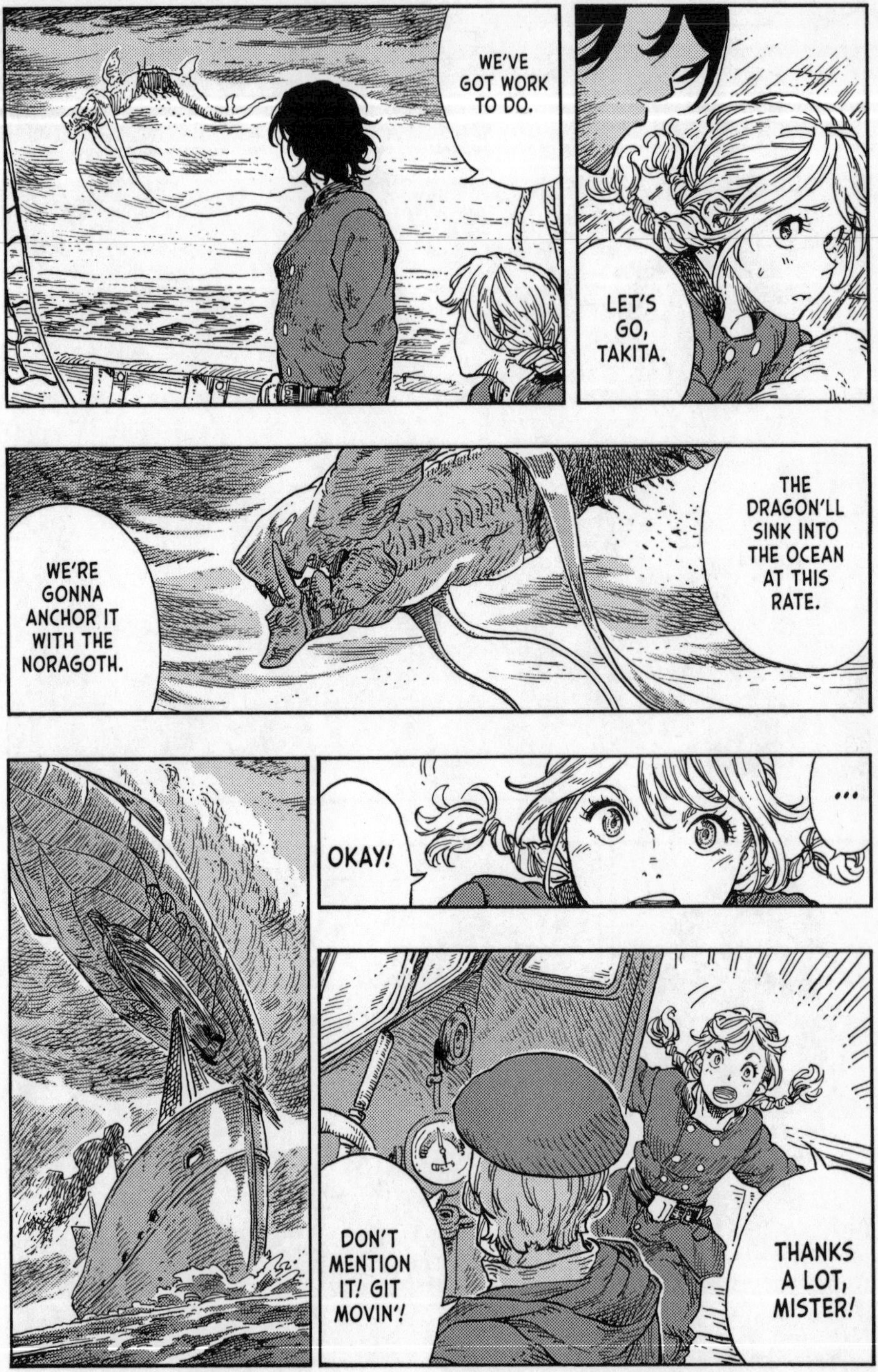
LET'S GO, TAKITA.
WE'VE GOT WORK TO DO.
THE DRAGON'LL SINK INTO THE OCEAN AT THIS RATE.
WE'RE GONNA ANCHOR IT WITH THE NORAGOTH.
...
OKAY!
THANKS A LOT, MISTER!
DON'T MENTION IT! GIT MOVIN'!

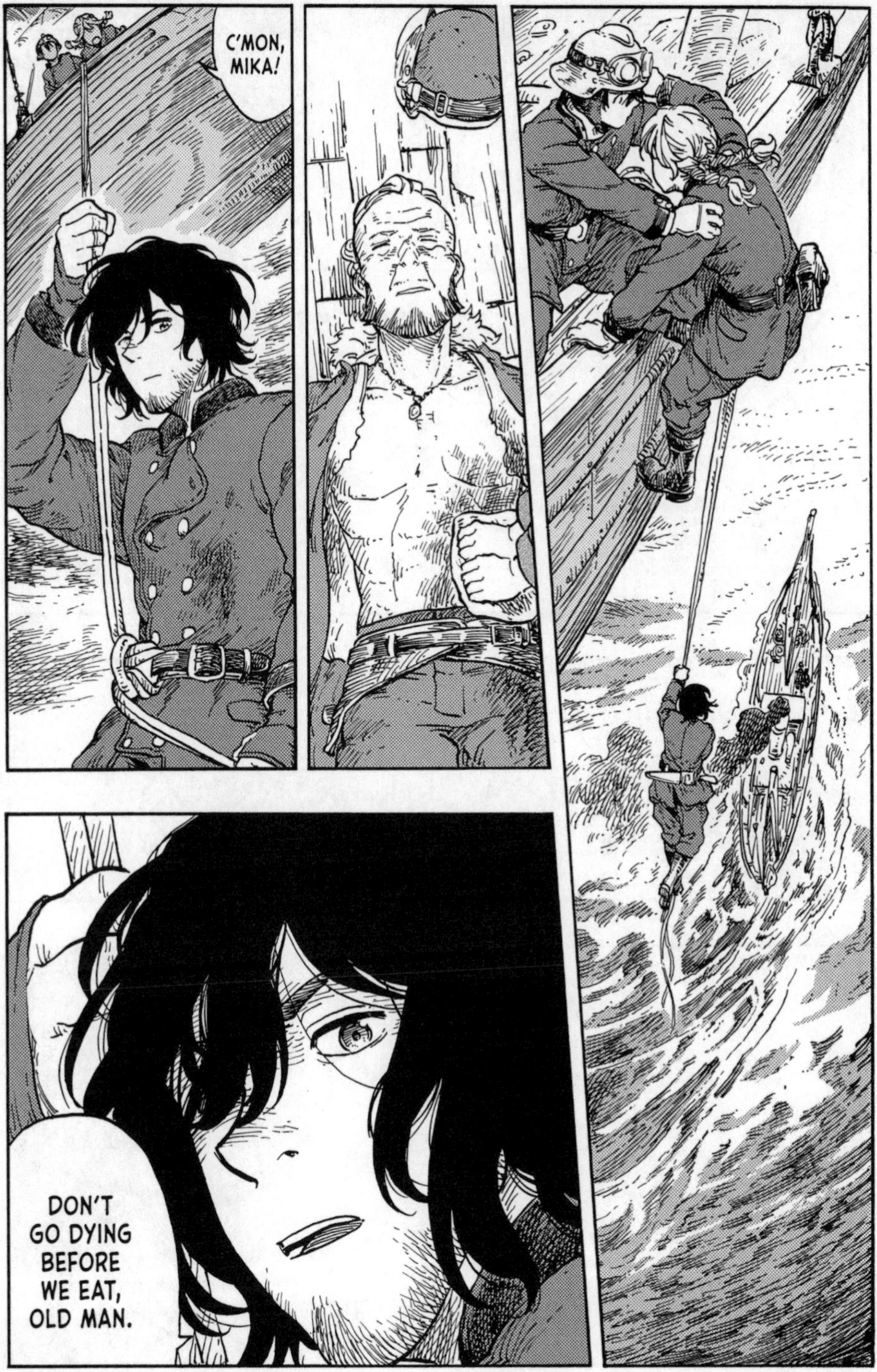
C'MON, MIKA!
DON'T GO DYING BEFORE WE EAT, OLD MAN.

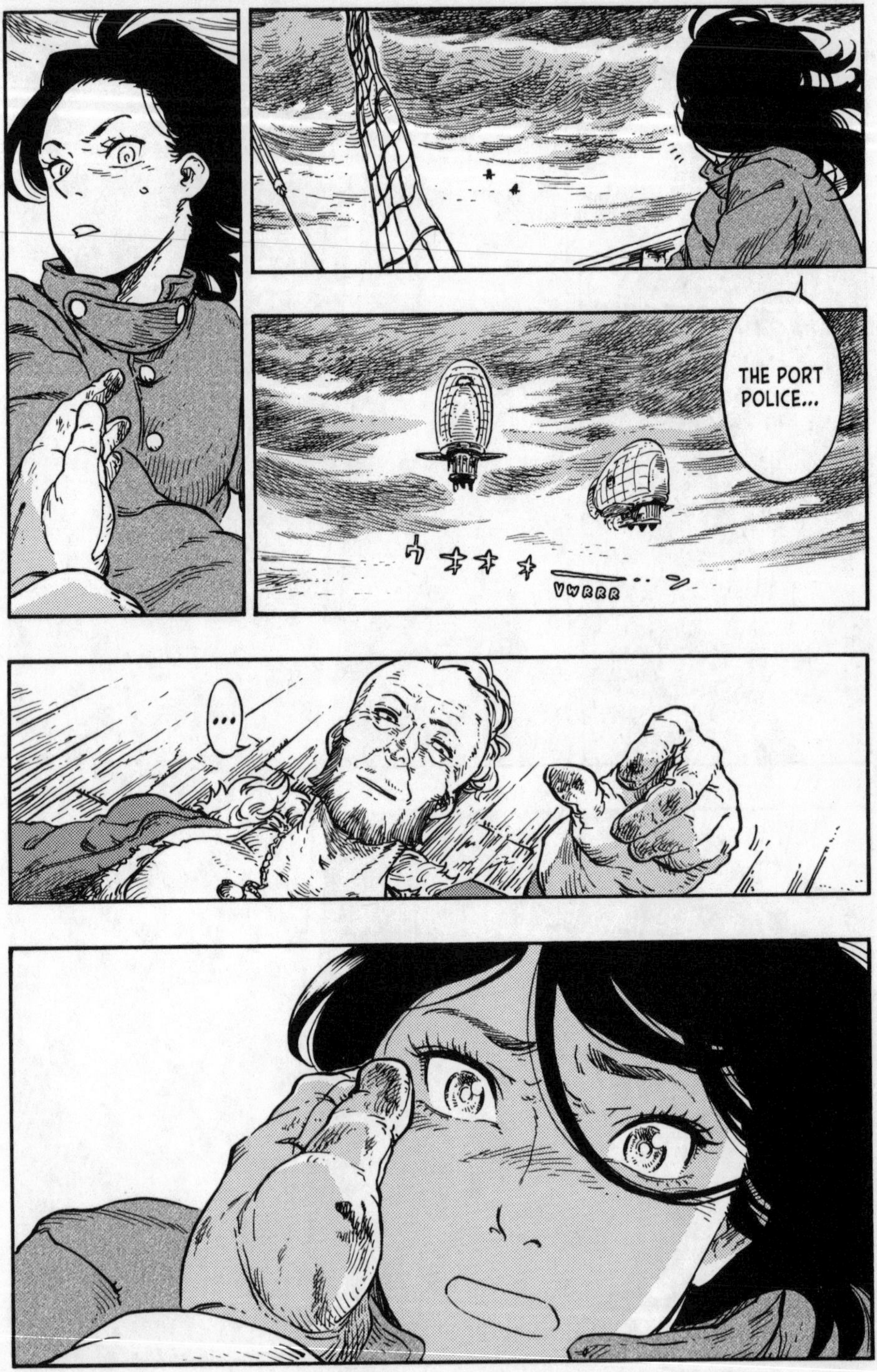
THE PORT POLICE...
ウォォォ――・・ン
VWRRR
...

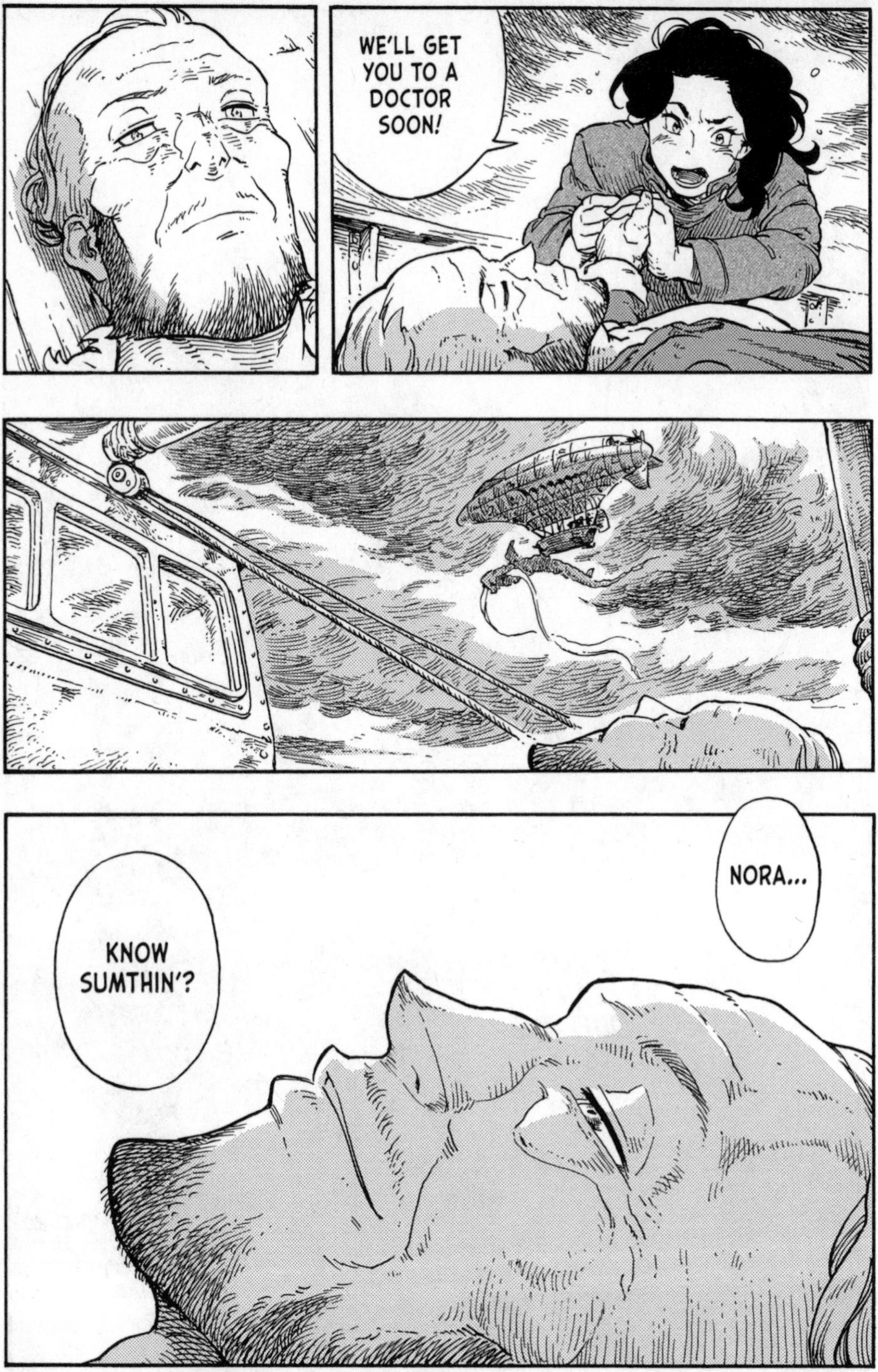
WE'LL GET YOU TO A DOCTOR SOON!
NORA...
KNOW SUMTHIN'?

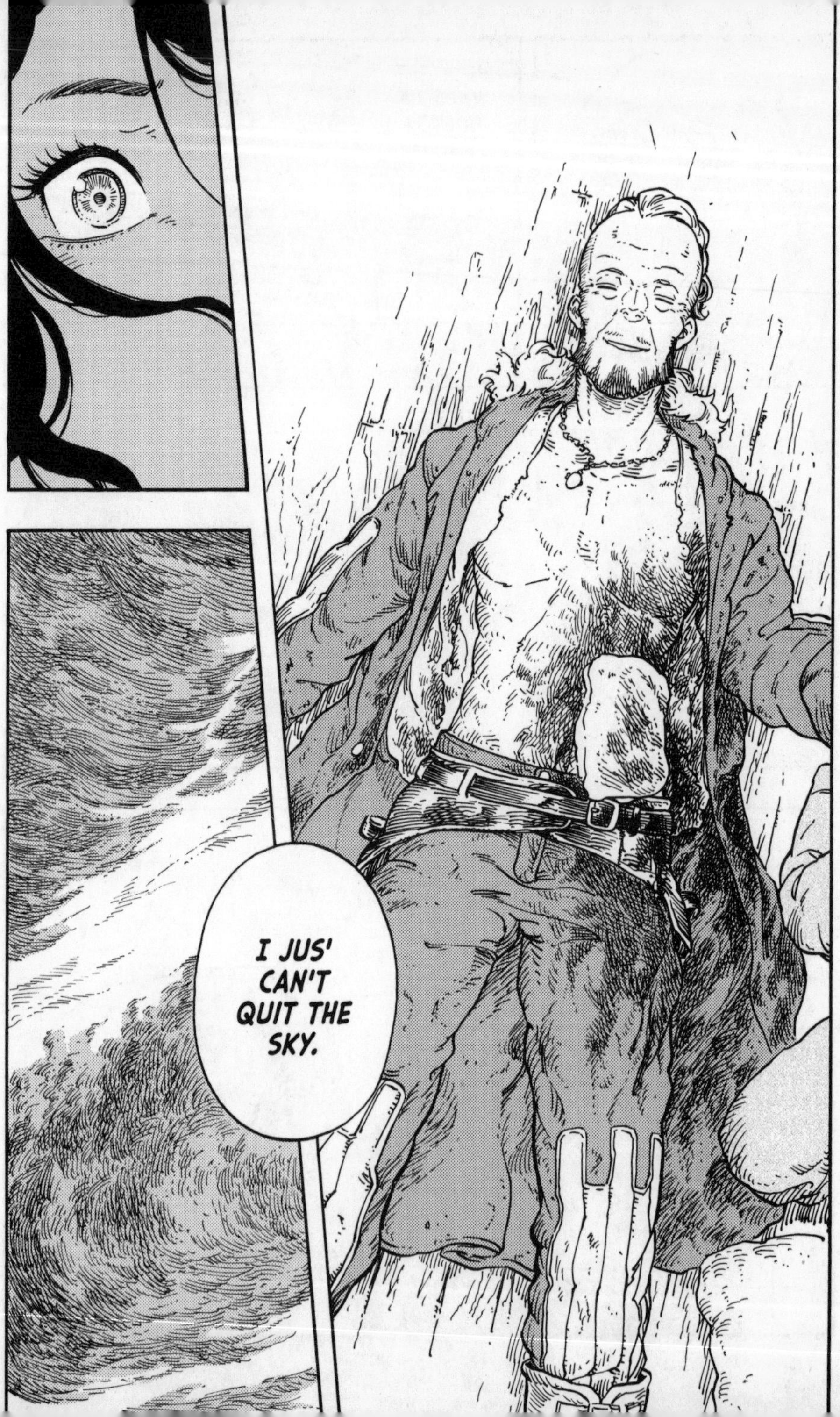
I JUS' CAN'T QUIT THE SKY.

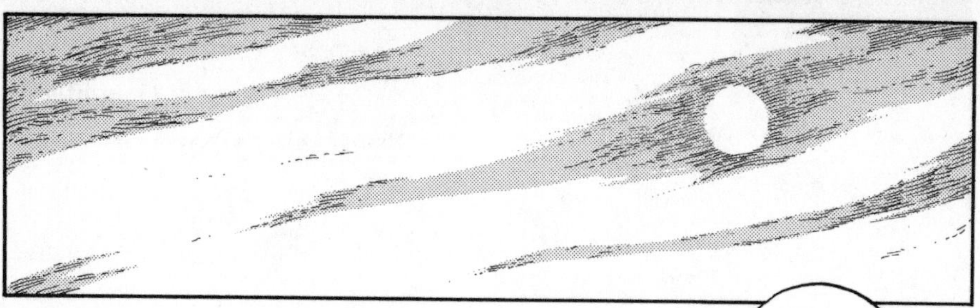

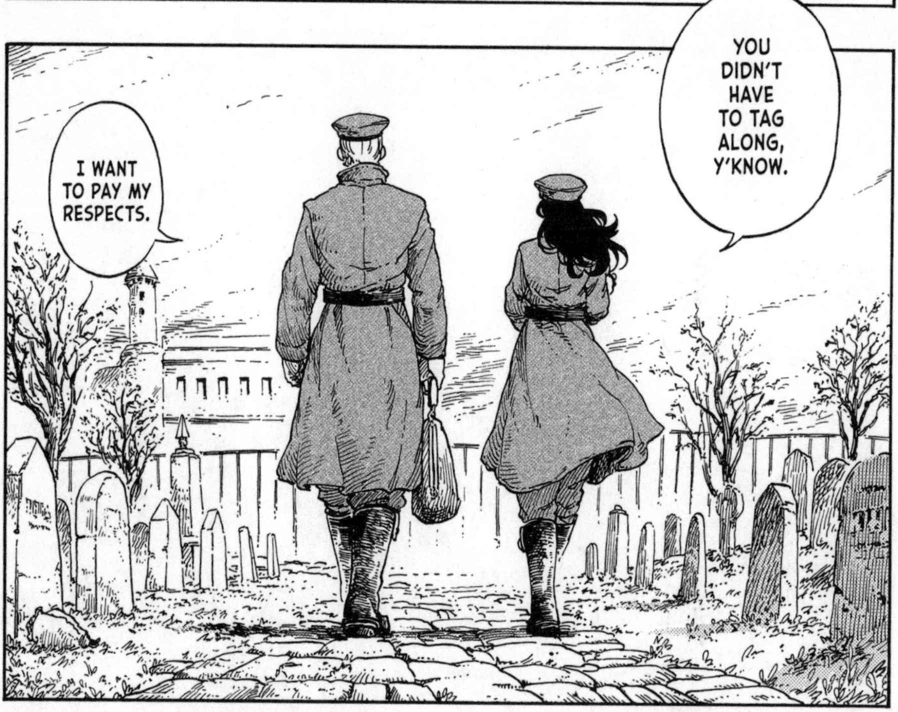
YOU DIDN'T HAVE TO TAG ALONG, Y'KNOW.
I WANT TO PAY MY RESPECTS.

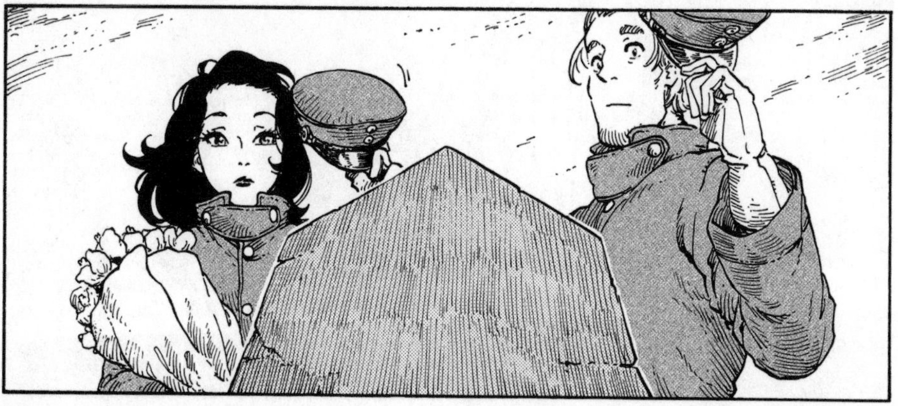

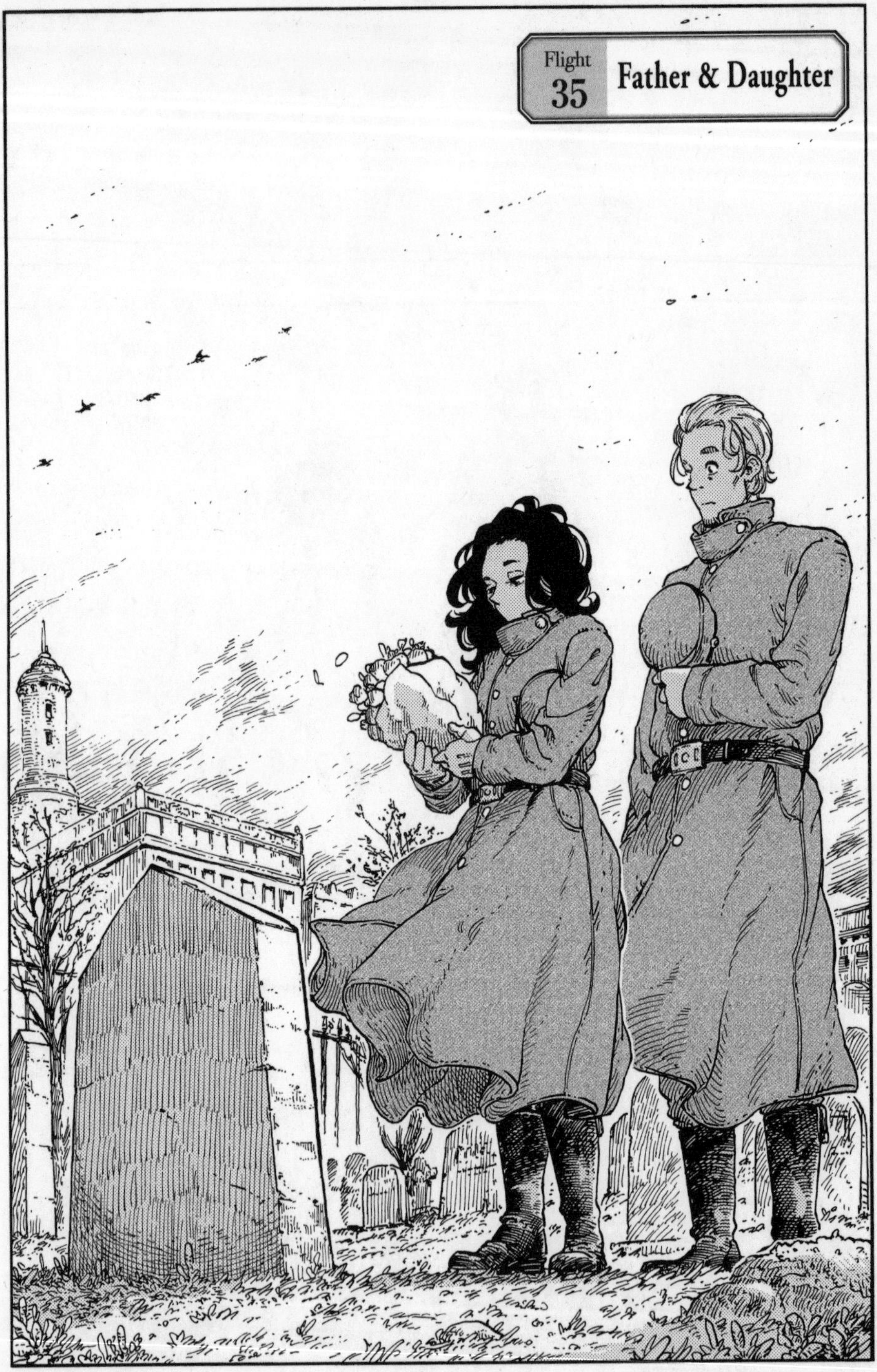
Flight 35
Father & Daughter

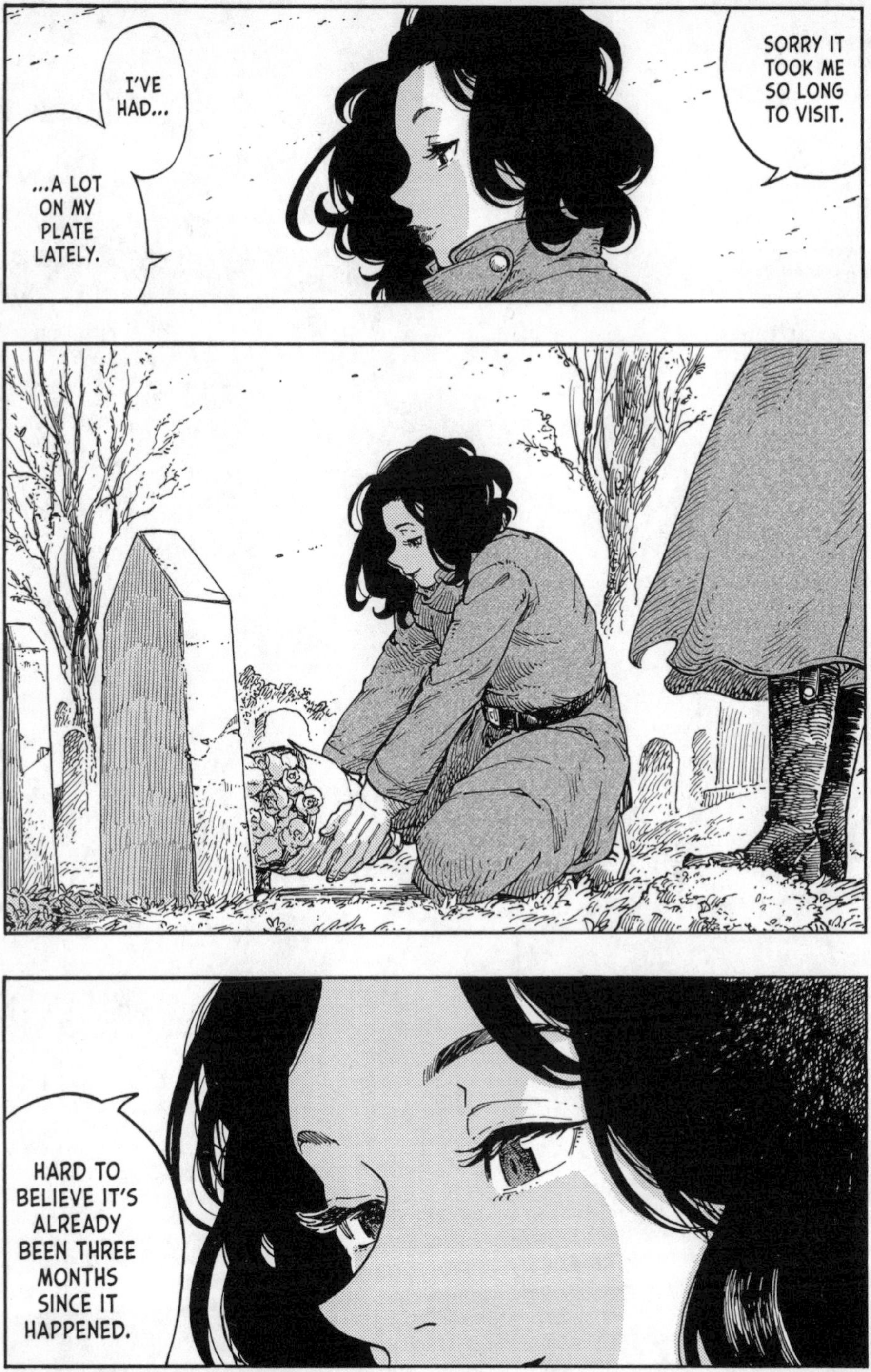
SORRY IT TOOK ME SO LONG TO VISIT.
I'VE HAD...
...A LOT ON MY PLATE LATELY.
HARD TO BELIEVE IT'S ALREADY BEEN THREE MONTHS SINCE IT HAPPENED.

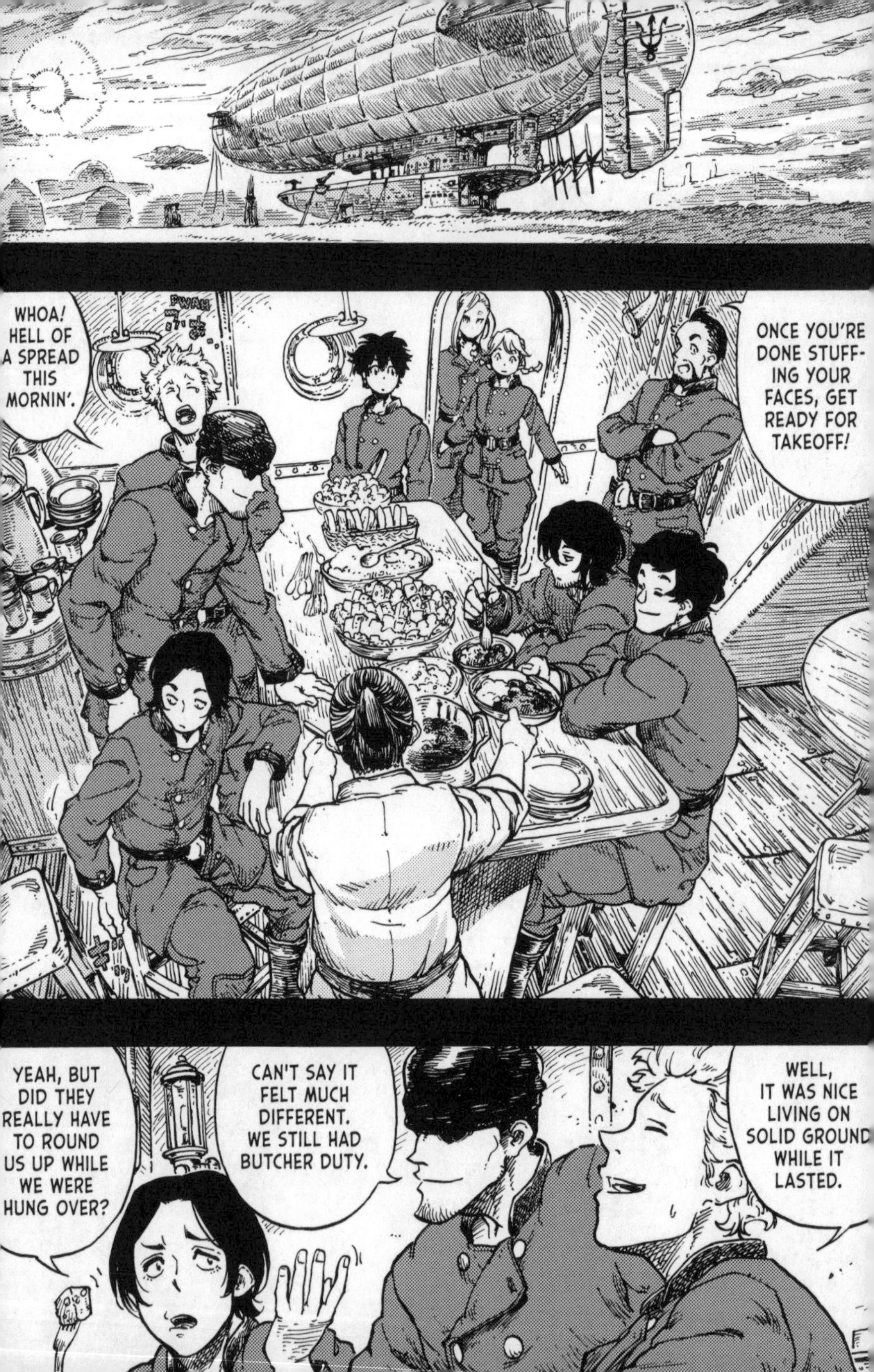
ONCE YOU'RE DONE STUFFING YOUR FACES, GET READY FOR TAKEOFF!
WHOA! HELL OF A SPREAD THIS MORNIN'.
WELL, IT WAS NICE LIVING ON SOLID GROUND WHILE IT LASTED.
CAN'T SAY IT FELT MUCH DIFFERENT. WE STILL HAD BUTCHER DUTY.
YEAH, BUT DID THEY REALLY HAVE TO ROUND US UP WHILE WE WERE HUNG OVER?

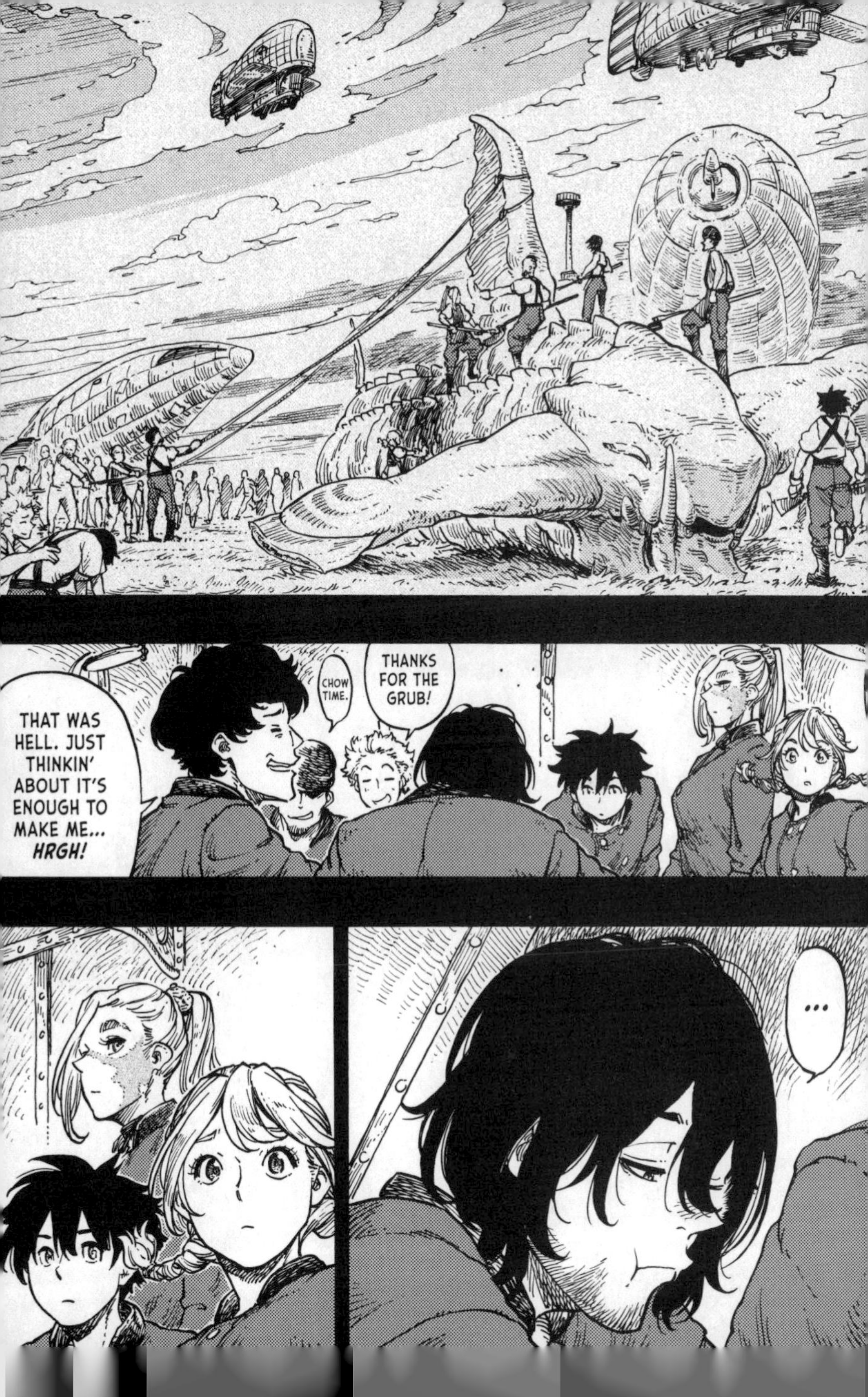
THANKS FOR THE GRUB!
CHOW TIME.
THAT WAS HELL. JUST THINKIN' ABOUT IT'S ENOUGH TO MAKE ME... *HRGH!*
...

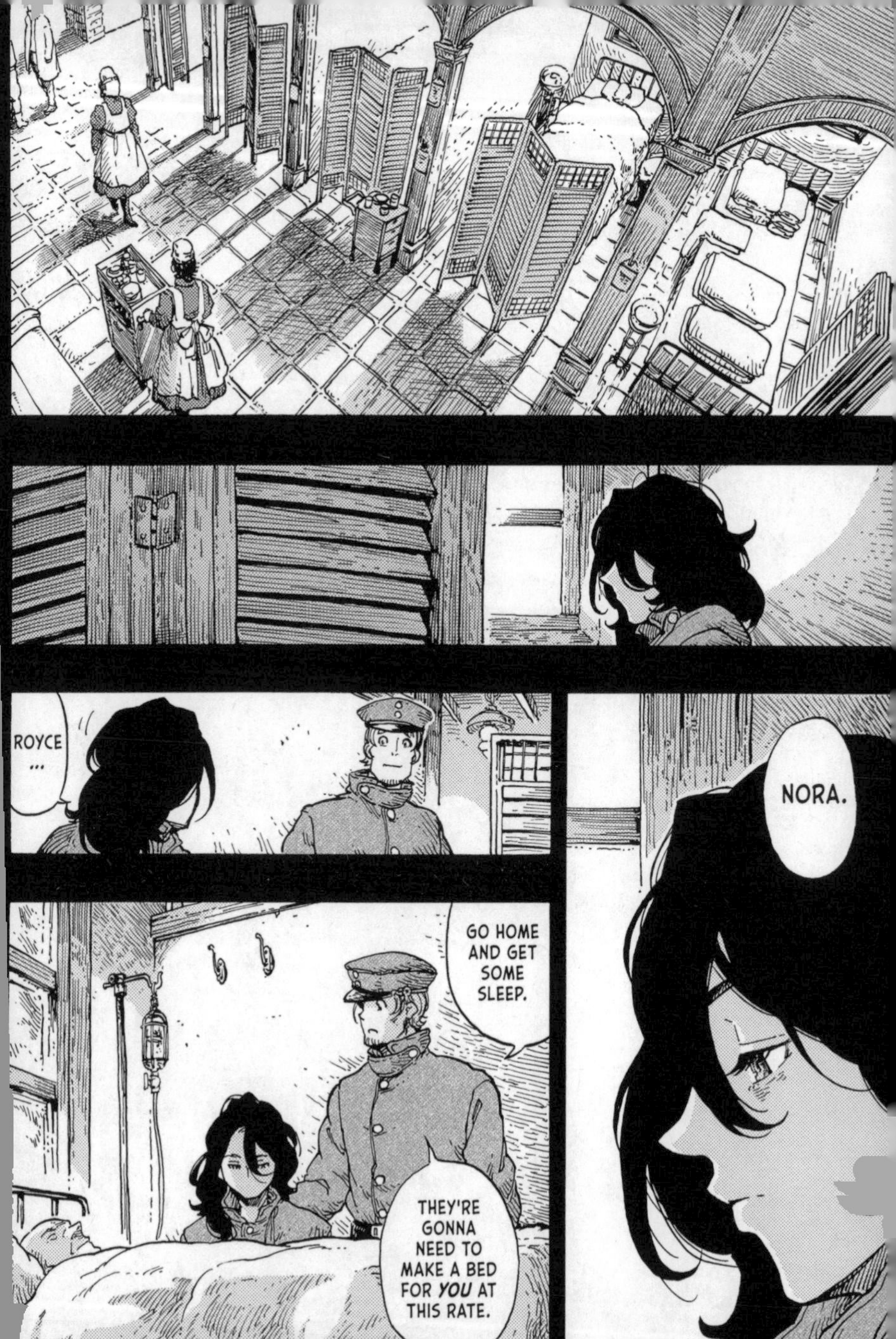
NORA.
ROYCE ...
GO HOME AND GET SOME SLEEP.
THEY'RE GONNA NEED TO MAKE A BED FOR *YOU* AT THIS RATE.

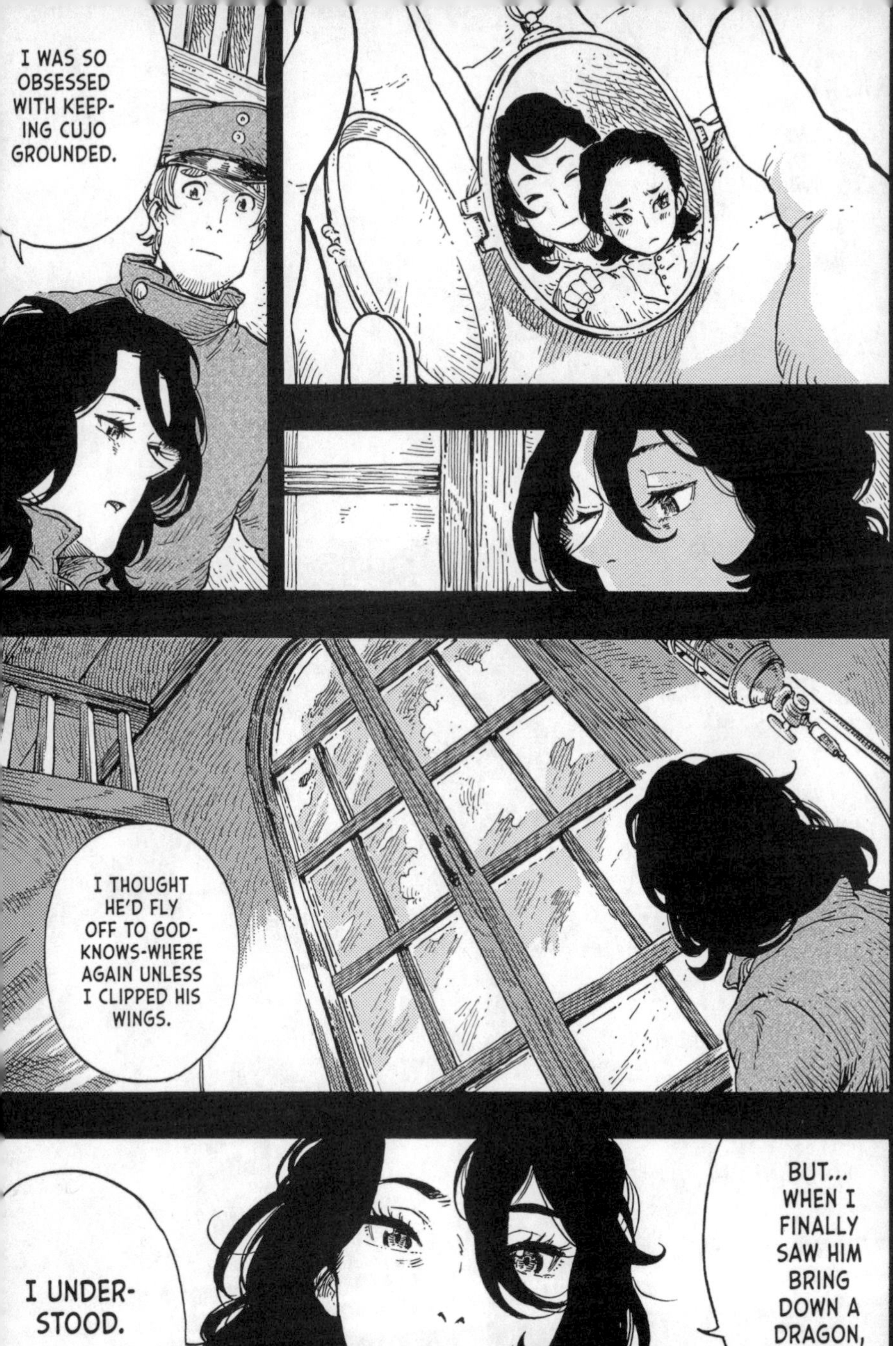
I WAS SO OBSESSED WITH KEEP-ING CUJO GROUNDED.
I THOUGHT HE'D FLY OFF TO GOD-KNOWS-WHERE AGAIN UNLESS I CLIPPED HIS WINGS.
BUT... WHEN I FINALLY SAW HIM BRING DOWN A DRAGON,
I UNDER-STOOD.

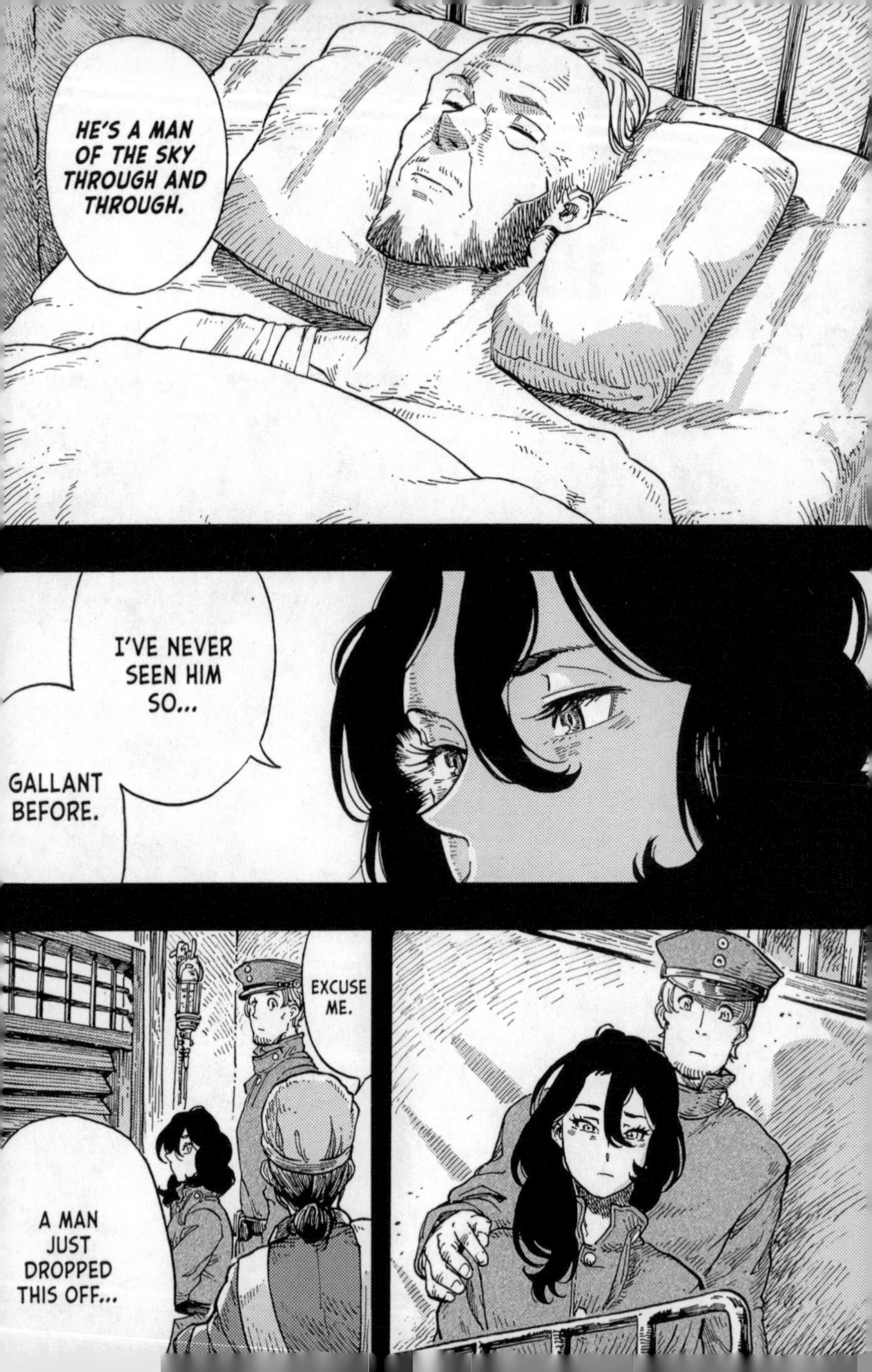
HE'S A MAN OF THE SKY THROUGH AND THROUGH.
I'VE NEVER SEEN HIM SO...
GALLANT BEFORE.
EXCUSE ME.
A MAN JUST DROPPED THIS OFF...

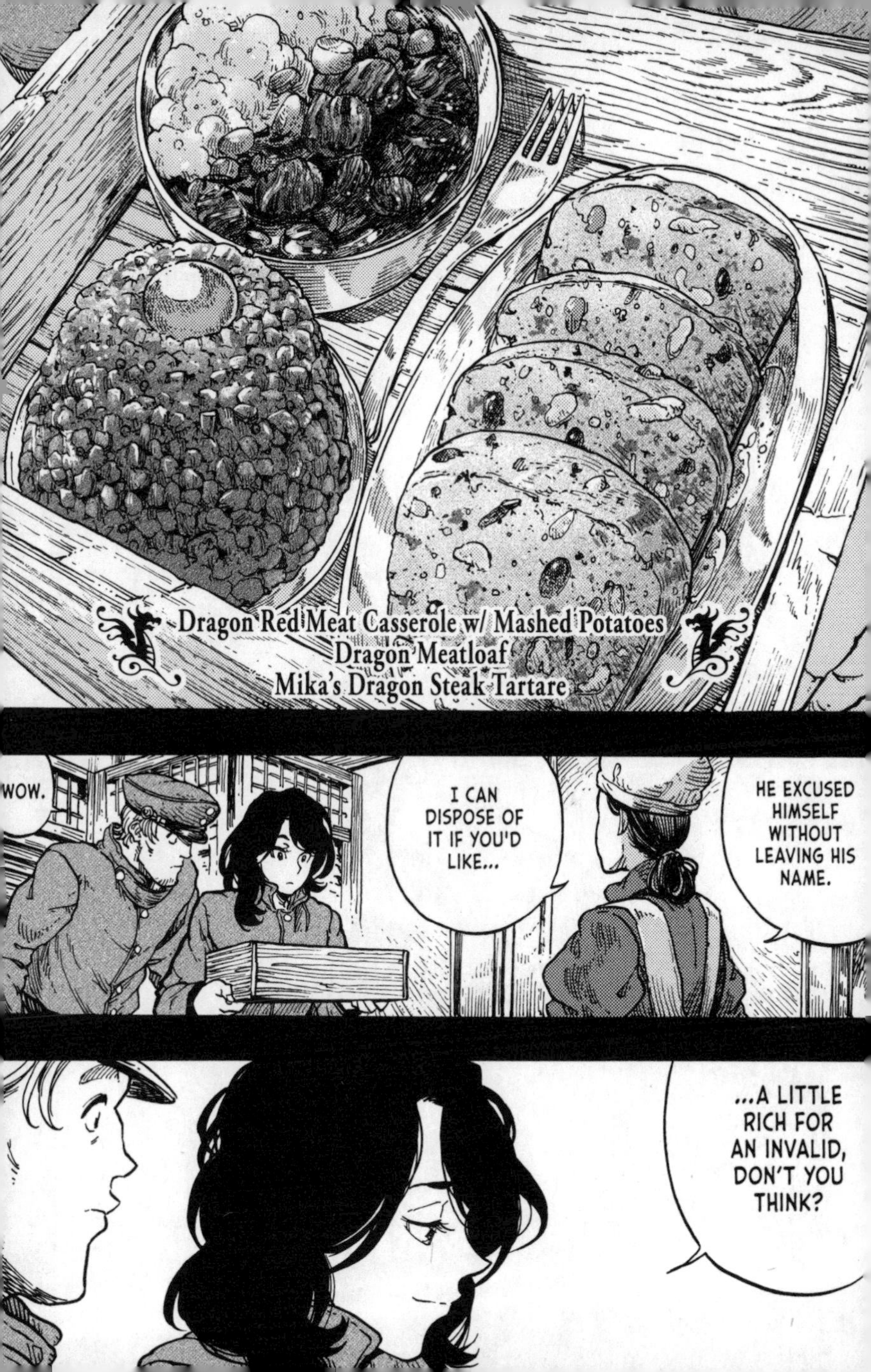
Dragon Red Meat Casserole w/ Mashed Potatoes
Dragon Meatloaf
Mika's Dragon Steak Tartare
HE EXCUSED HIMSELF WITHOUT LEAVING HIS NAME.
I CAN DISPOSE OF IT IF YOU'D LIKE...
WOW.
...A LITTLE RICH FOR AN INVALID, DON'T YOU THINK?

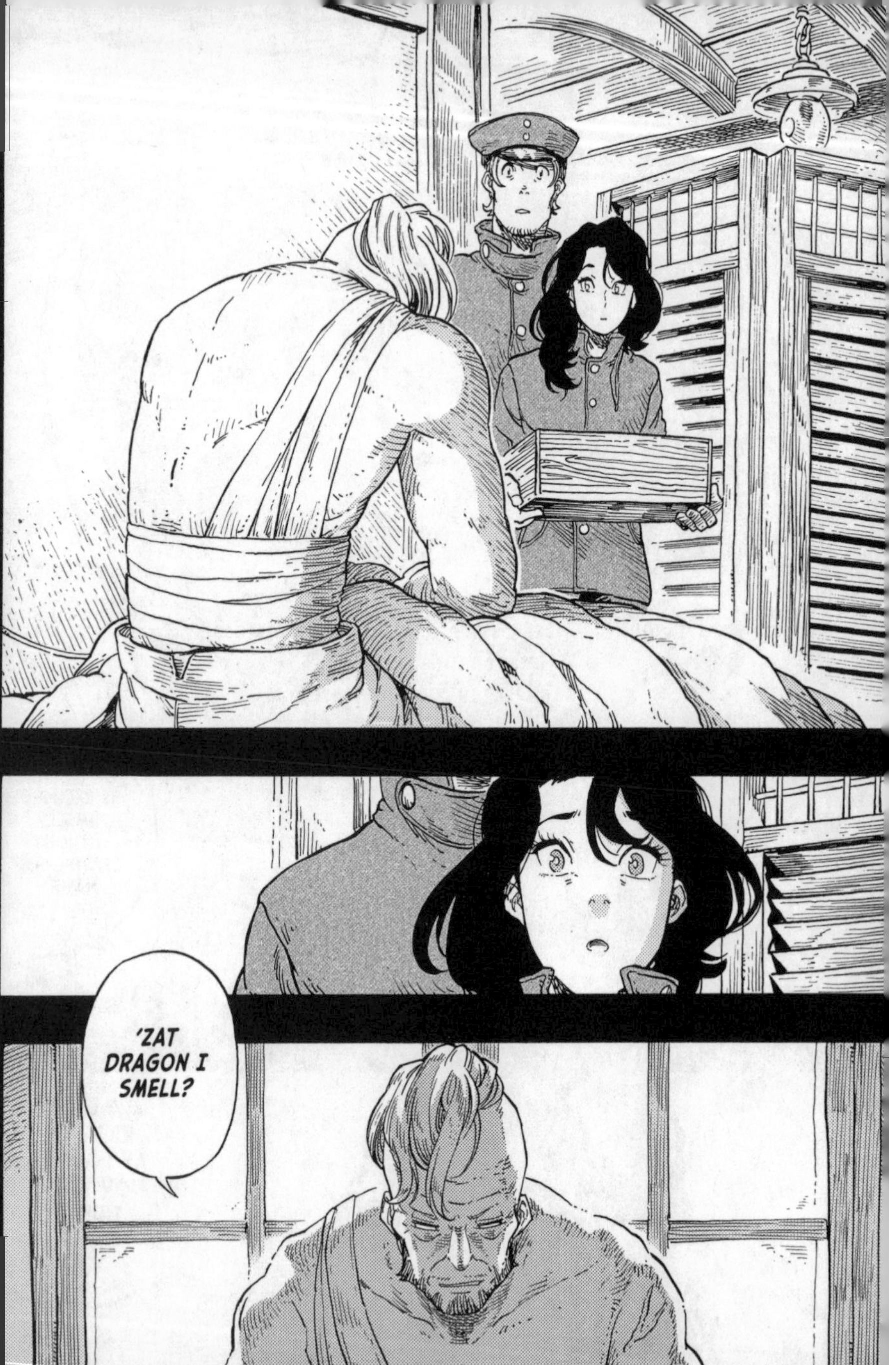
'ZAT DRAGON I SMELL?

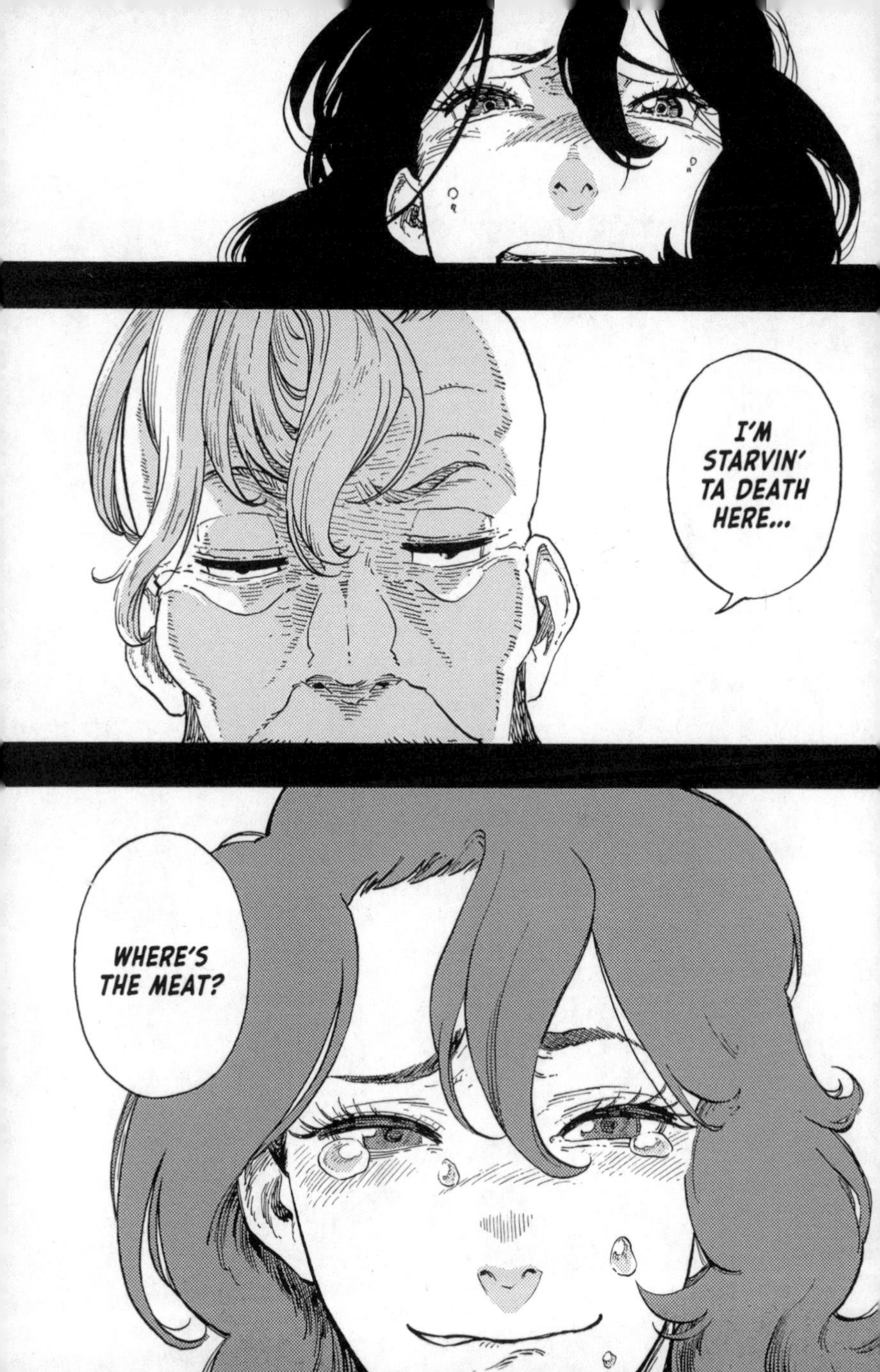
I'M STARVIN' TA DEATH HERE...
WHERE'S THE MEAT?

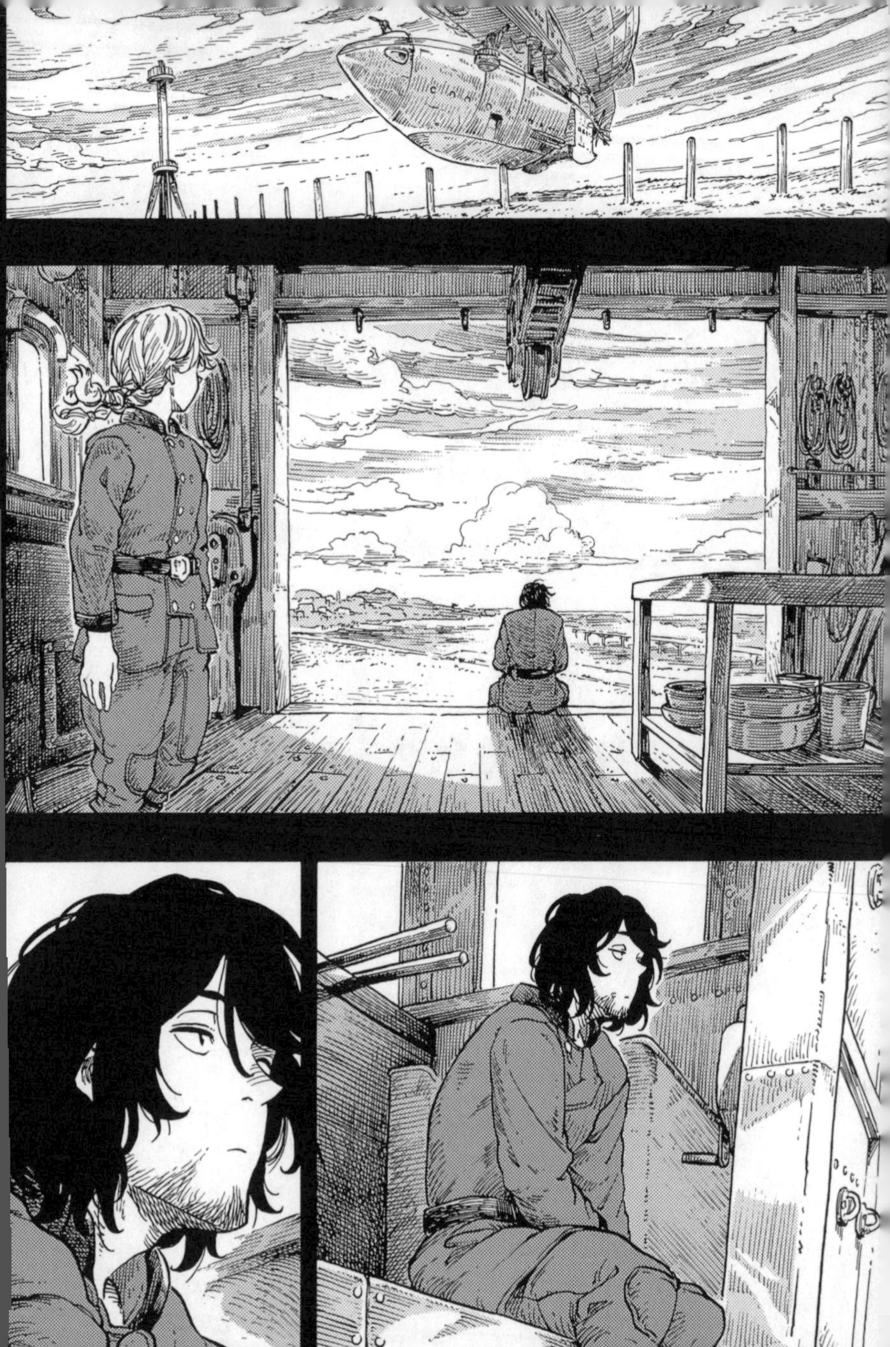

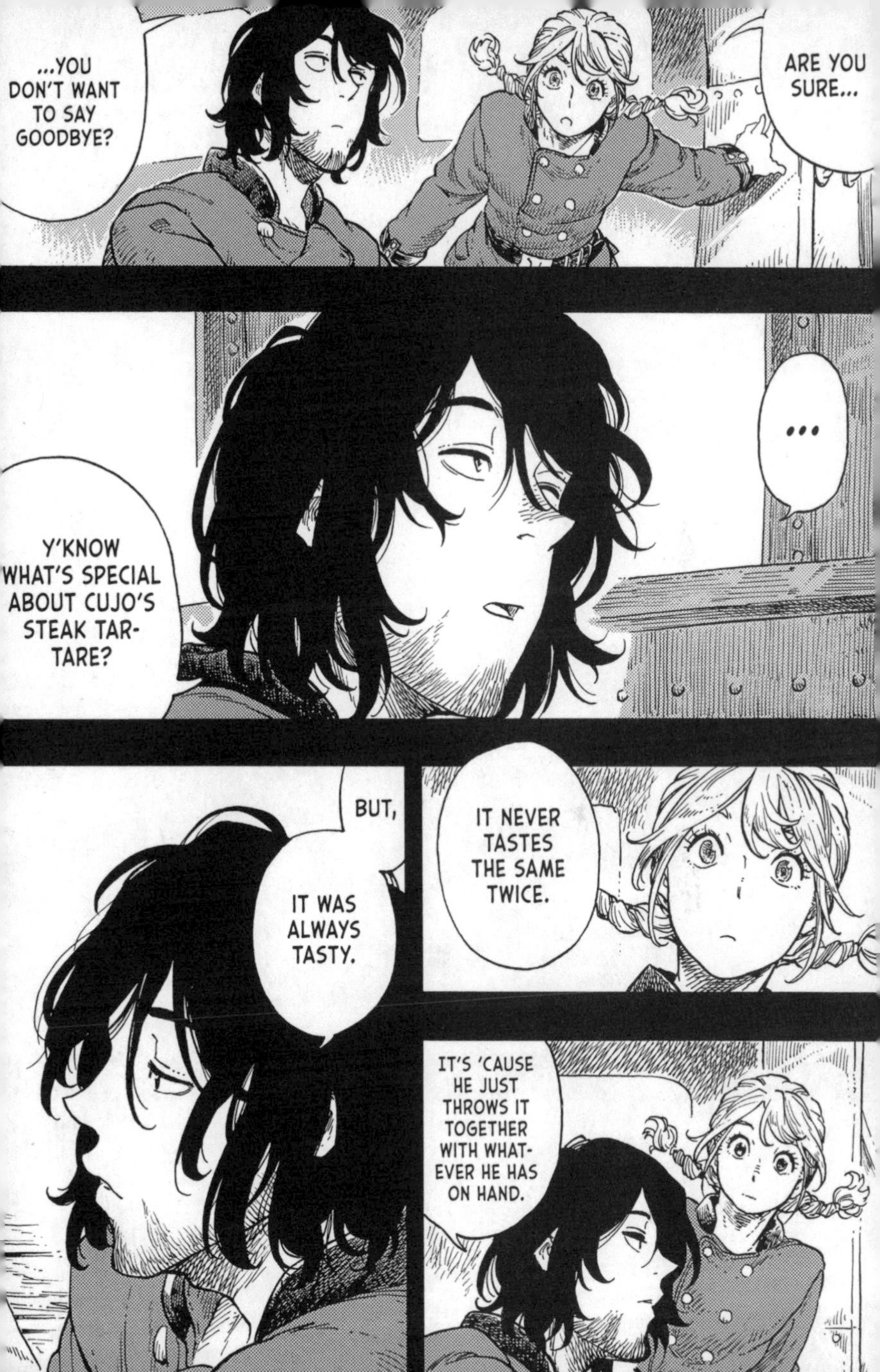
ARE YOU SURE...
...YOU DON'T WANT TO SAY GOODBYE?
...
Y'KNOW WHAT'S SPECIAL ABOUT CUJO'S STEAK TAR-TARE?
IT NEVER TASTES THE SAME TWICE.
IT'S 'CAUSE HE JUST THROWS IT TOGETHER WITH WHAT-EVER HE HAS ON HAND.
BUT,
IT WAS ALWAYS TASTY.

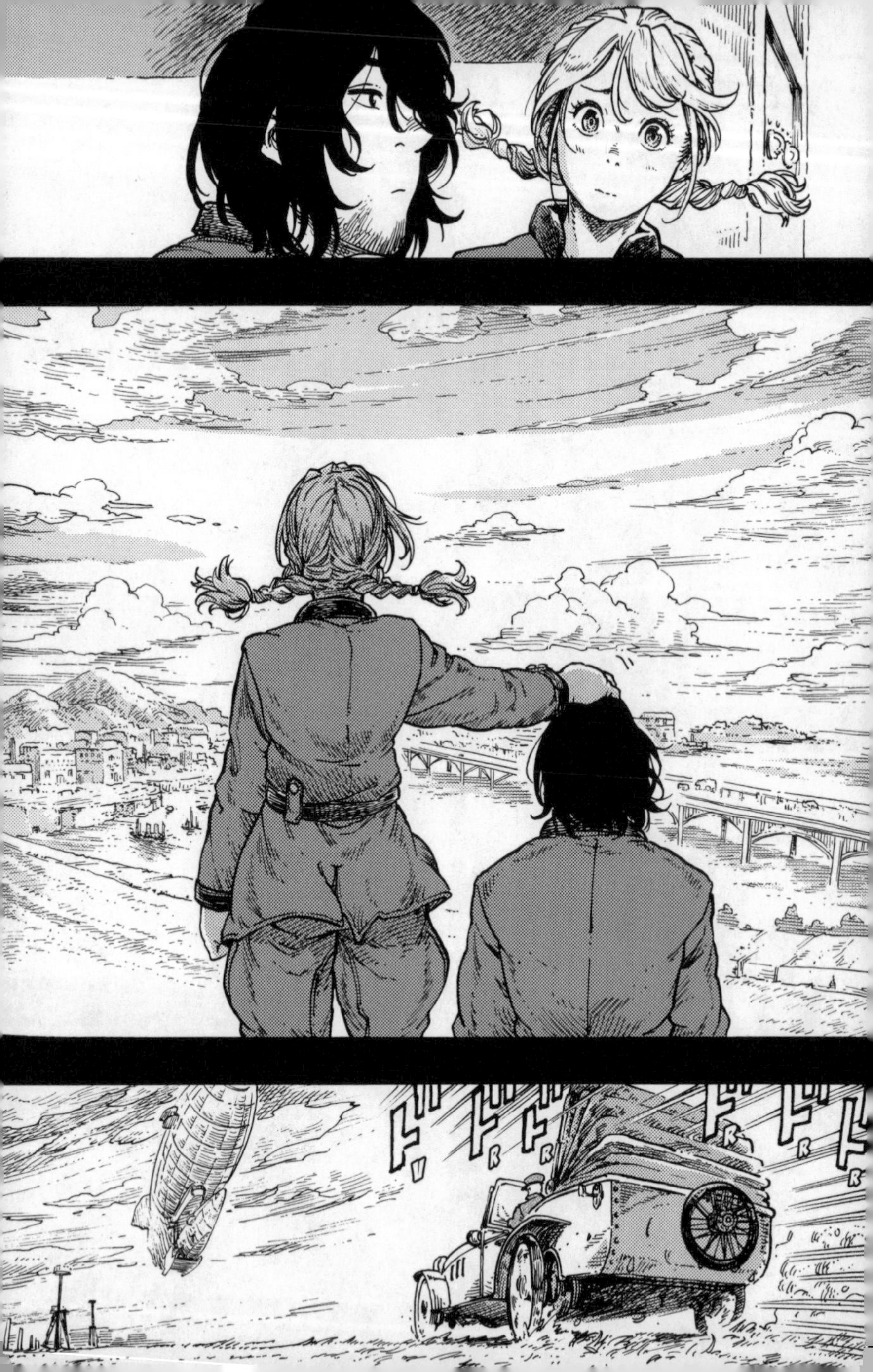

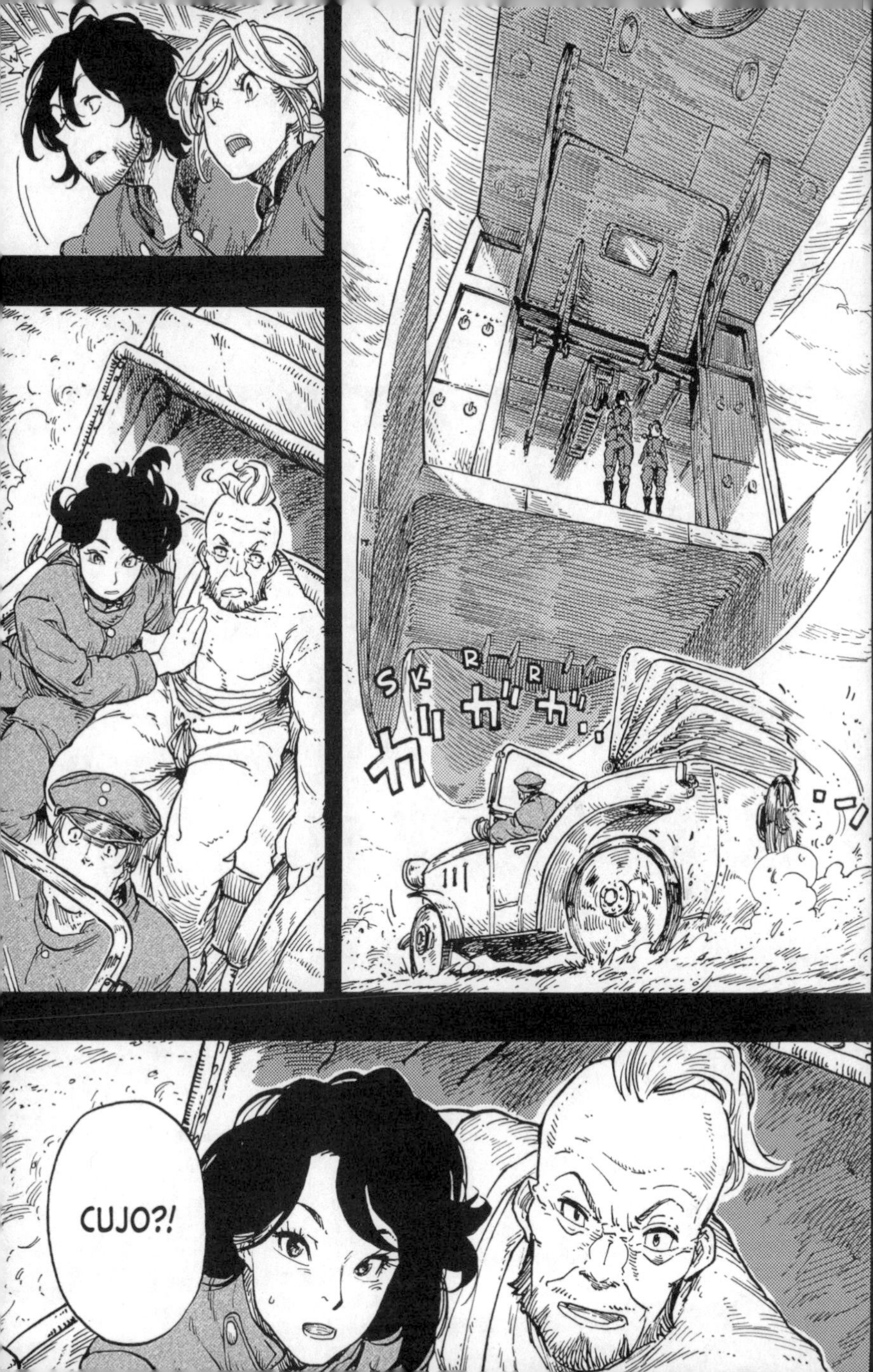
SKRRR
CUJO?!

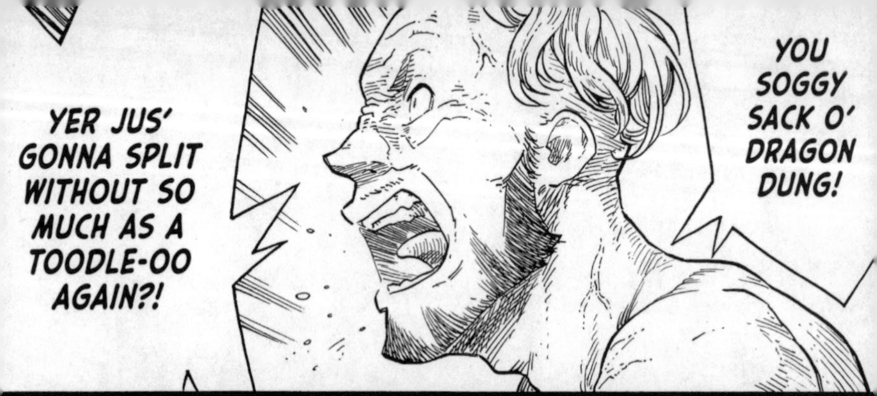
YOU SOGGY SACK O' DRAGON DUNG!
YER JUS' GONNA SPLIT WITHOUT SO MUCH AS A TOODLE-OO AGAIN?!
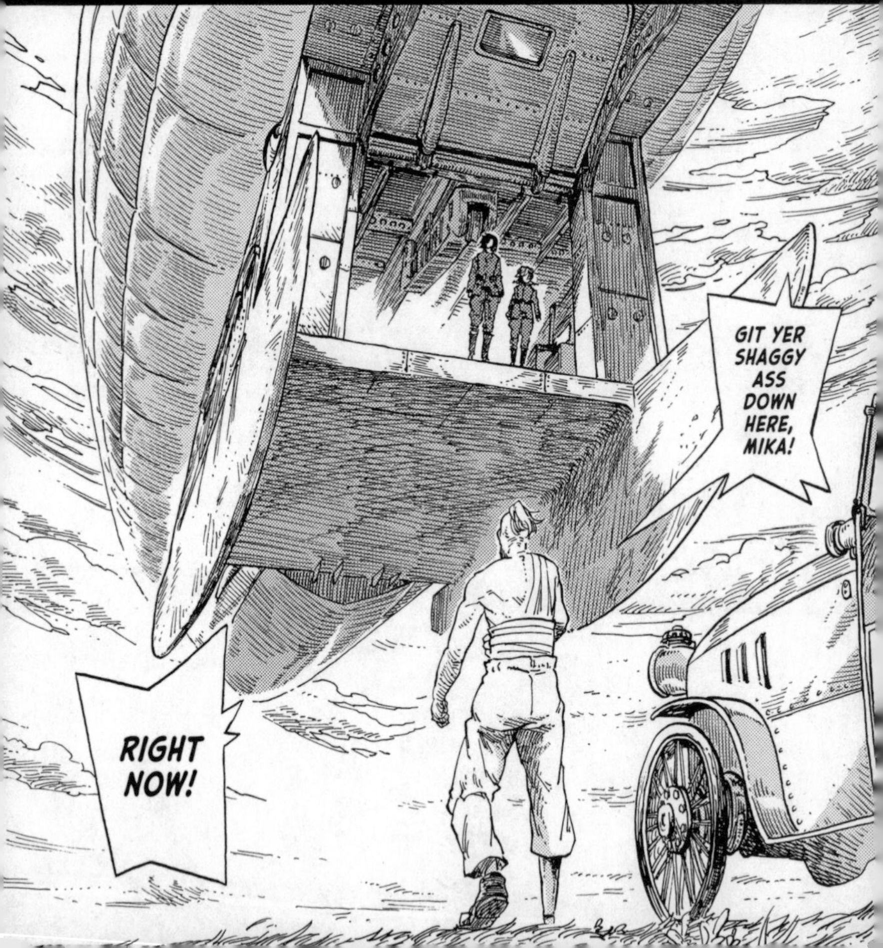
GIT YER SHAGGY ASS DOWN HERE, MIKA!
RIGHT NOW!

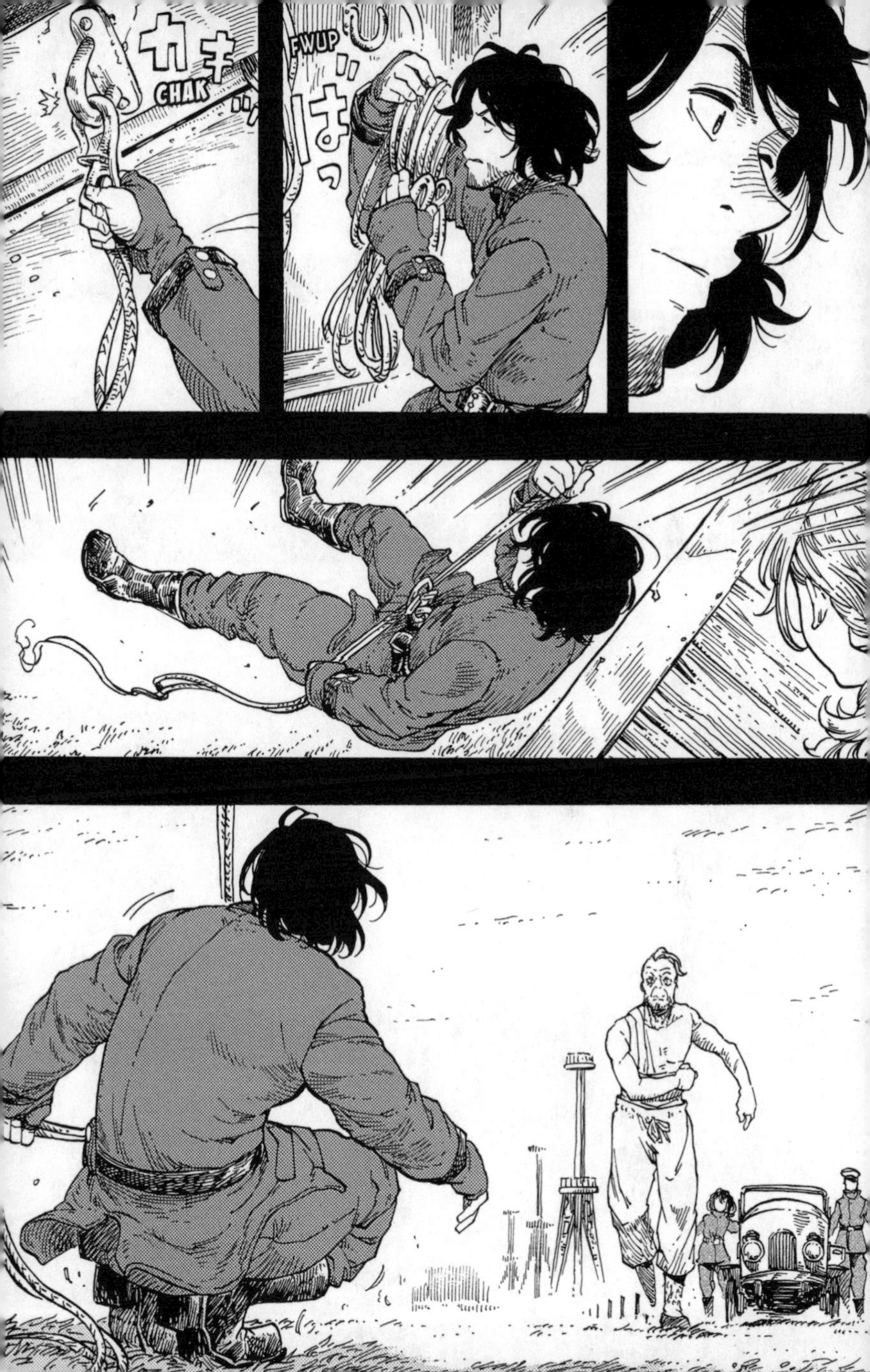
FWUP
はっ
カキ
CHAK

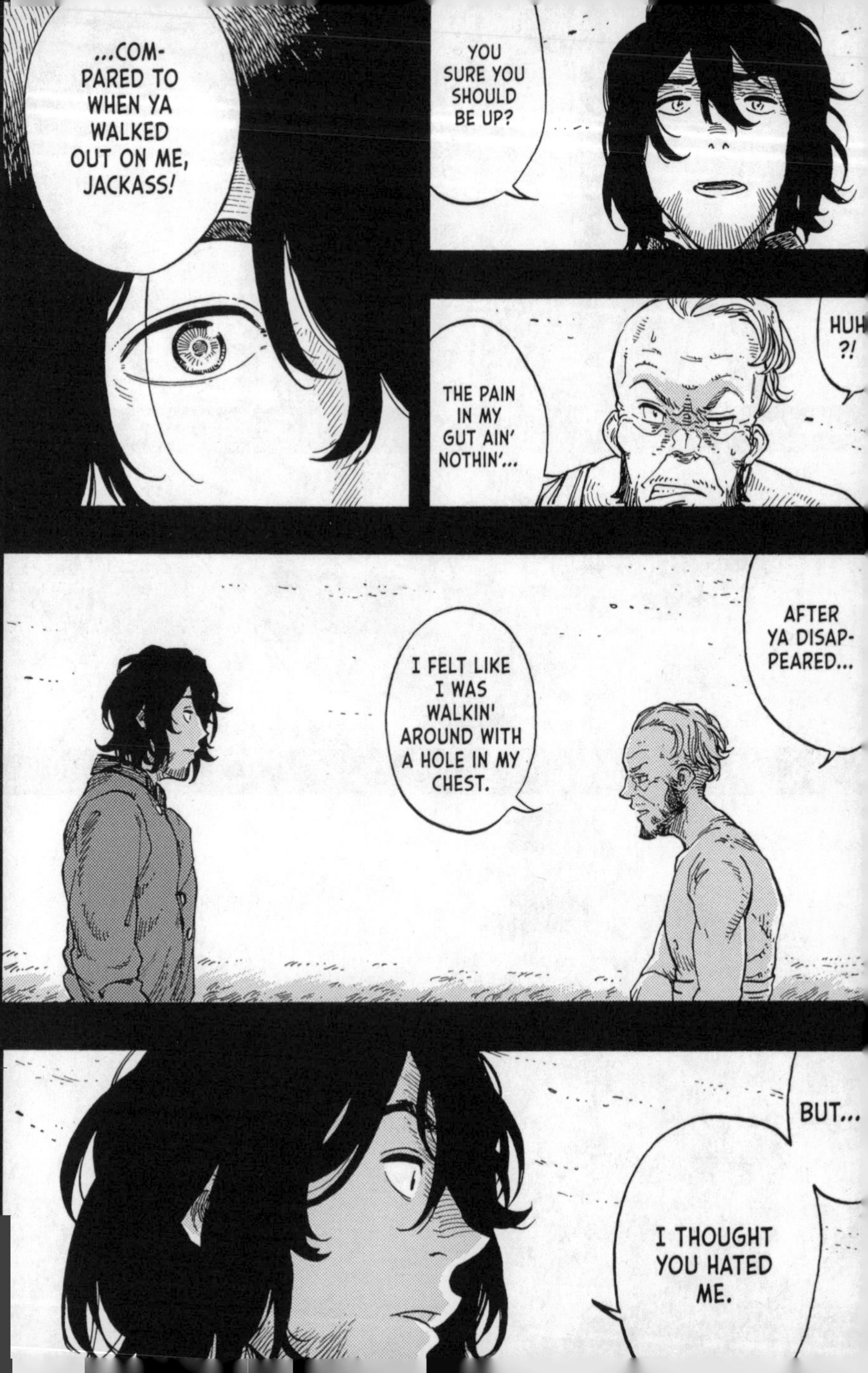
YOU SURE YOU SHOULD BE UP?
HUH?!
THE PAIN IN MY GUT AIN' NOTHIN'...
...COMPARED TO WHEN YA WALKED OUT ON ME, JACKASS!
AFTER YA DISAPPEARED...
I FELT LIKE I WAS WALKIN' AROUND WITH A HOLE IN MY CHEST.
BUT...
I THOUGHT YOU HATED ME.

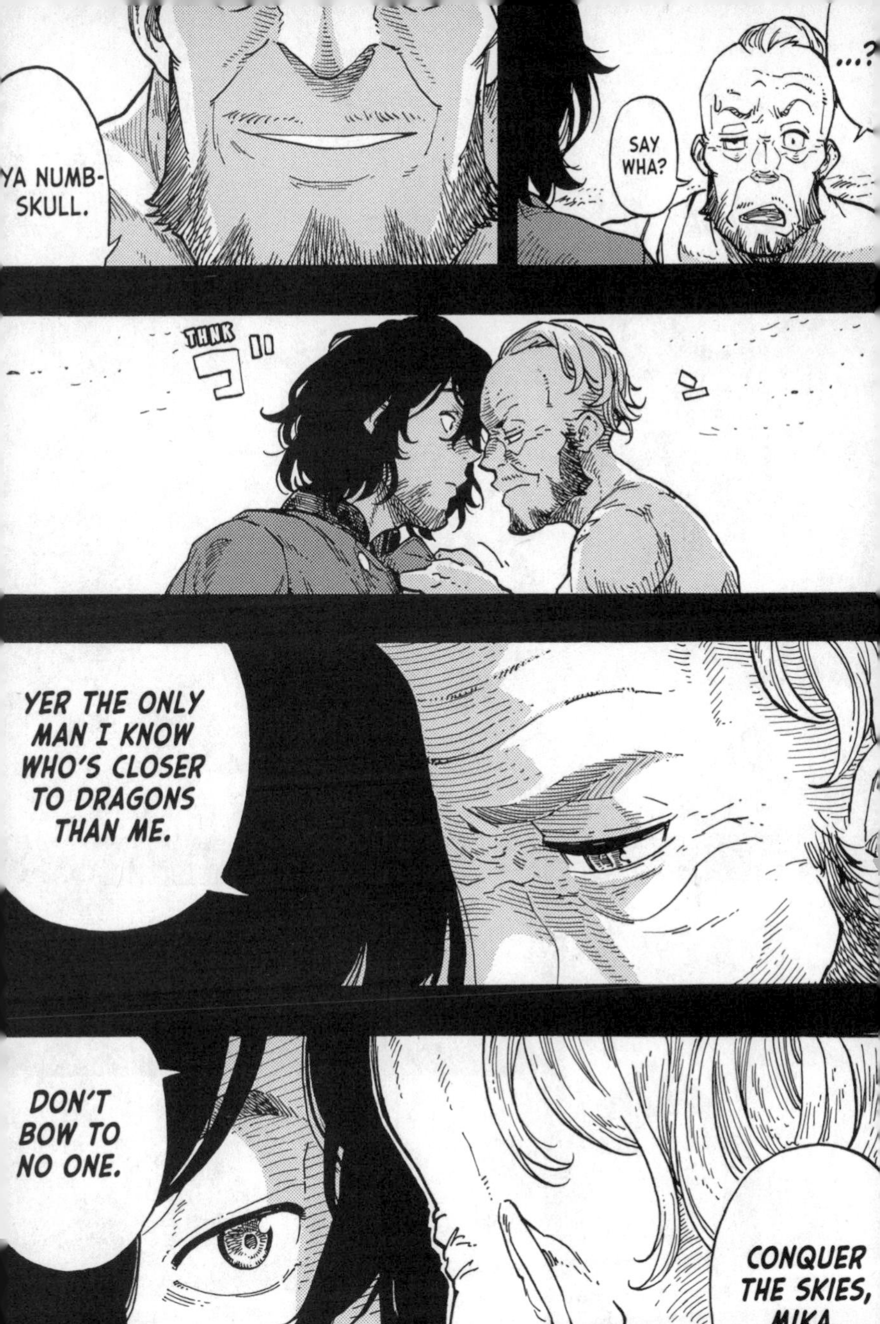
YA NUMBSKULL.
SAY WHA?
...?
THNK
YER THE ONLY MAN I KNOW WHO'S CLOSER TO DRAGONS THAN ME.
DON'T BOW TO NO ONE.
CONQUER THE SKIES, MIKA.

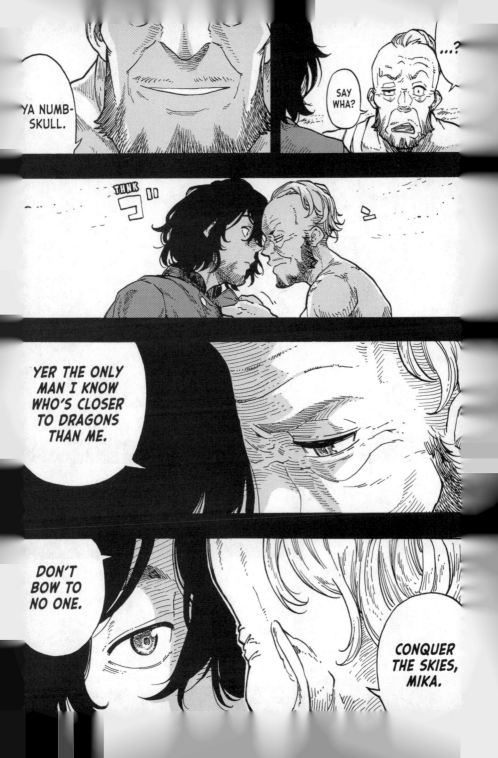

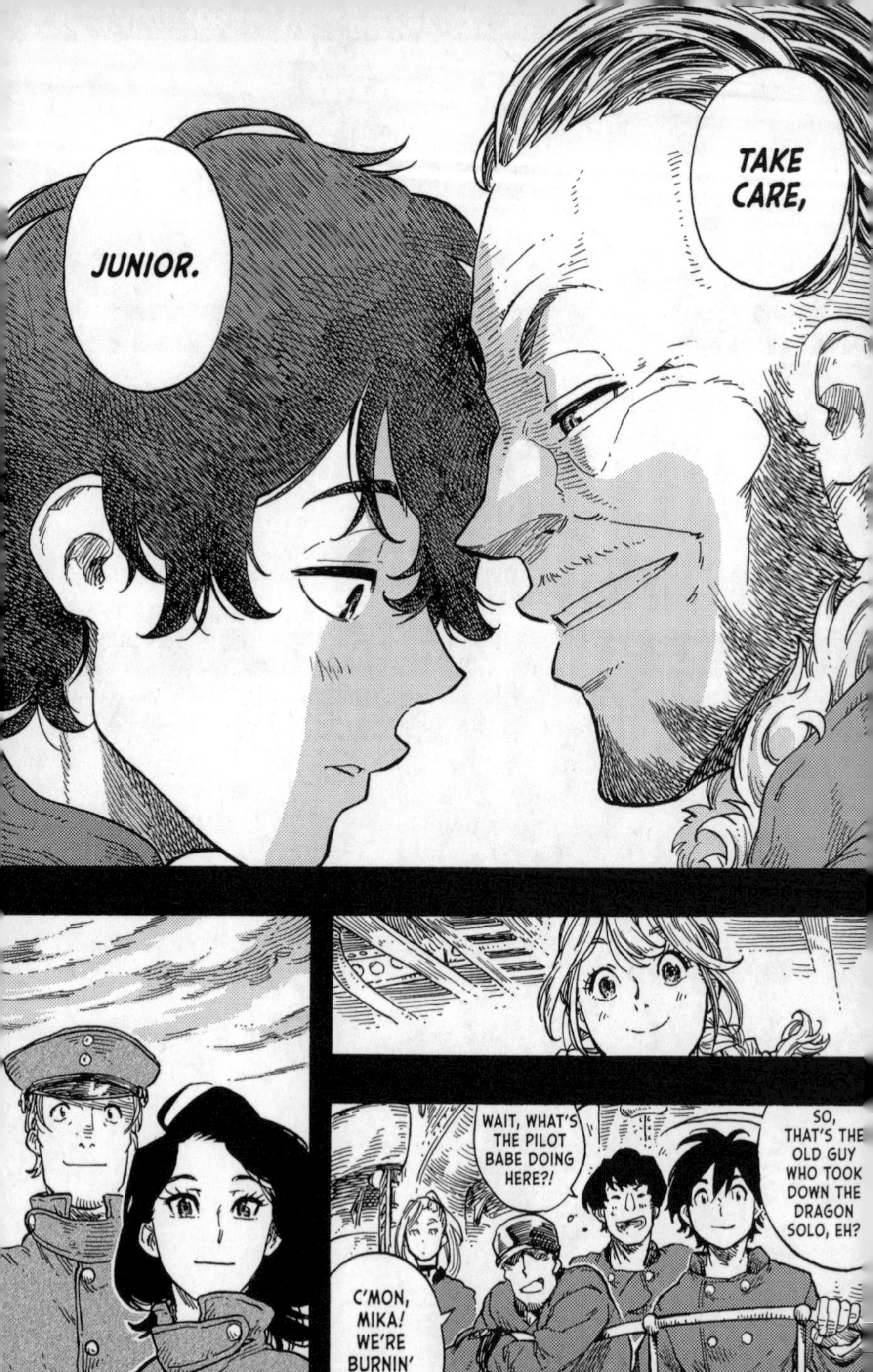
TAKE CARE,
JUNIOR.
SO, THAT'S THE OLD GUY WHO TOOK DOWN THE DRAGON SOLO, EH?
WAIT, WHAT'S THE PILOT BABE DOING HERE?!
C'MON, MIKA! WE'RE BURNIN' DAYLIGHT!

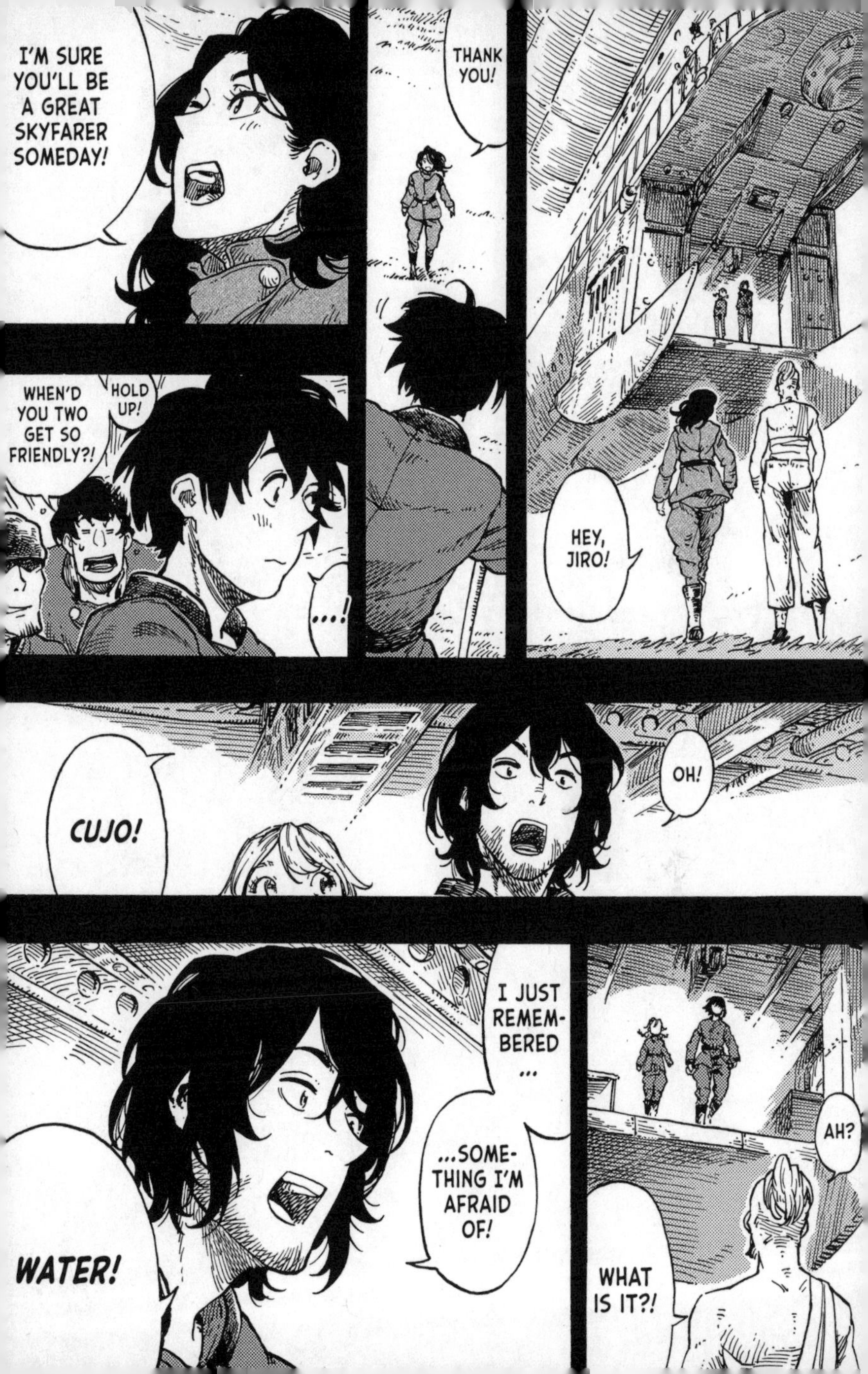
HEY, JIRO!
THANK YOU!
...!
I'M SURE YOU'LL BE A GREAT SKYFARER SOMEDAY!
HOLD UP!
WHEN'D YOU TWO GET SO FRIENDLY?!
OH!
CUJO!
AH?
WHAT IS IT?!
I JUST REMEMBERED...
...SOMETHING I'M AFRAID OF!
WATER!

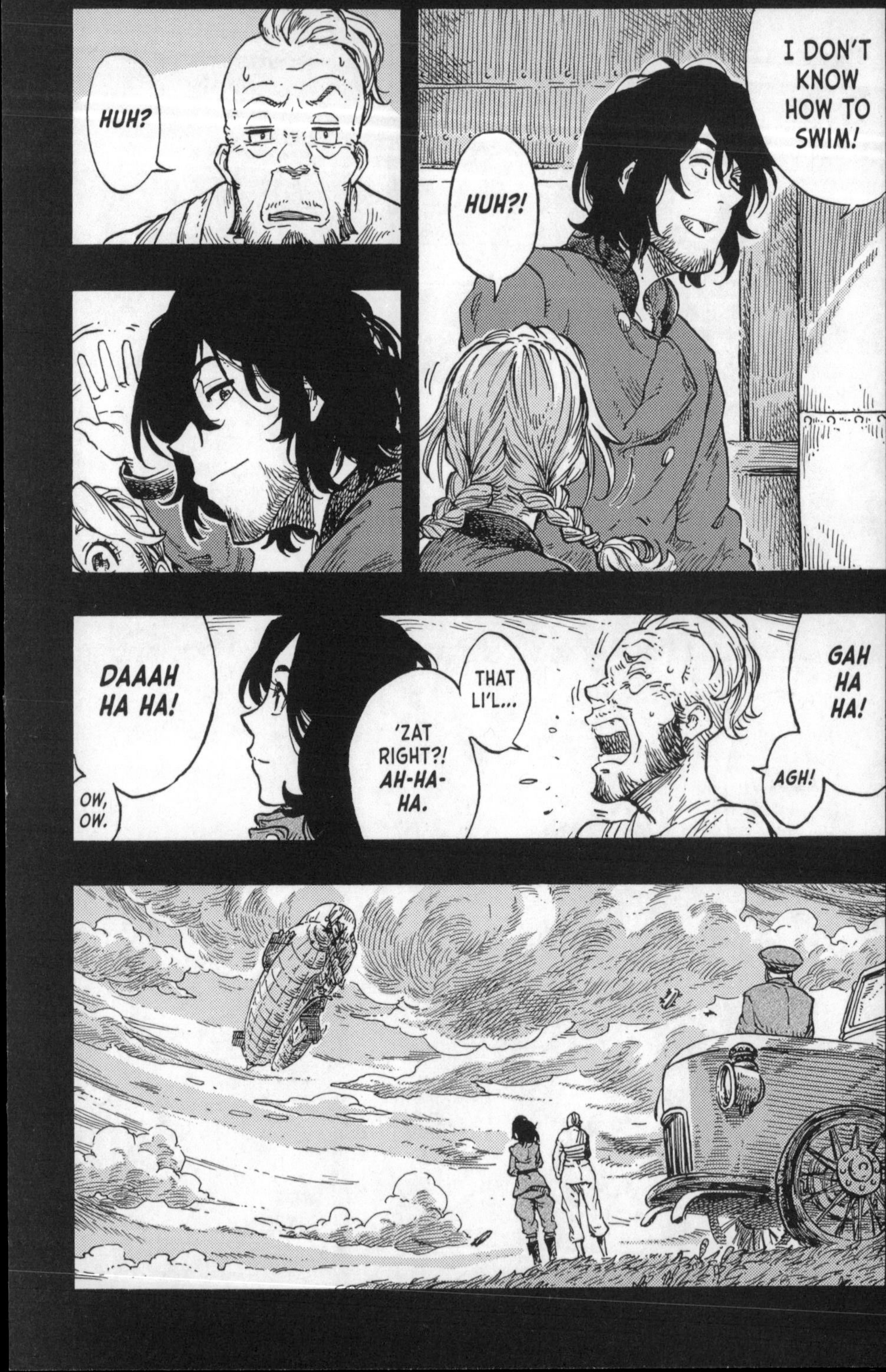
I DON'T KNOW HOW TO SWIM!
HUH?!
HUH?
GAH HA HA!
AGH!
THAT LI'L...
'ZAT RIGHT?! AH-HA-HA.
DAAAH HA HA!
OW, OW.

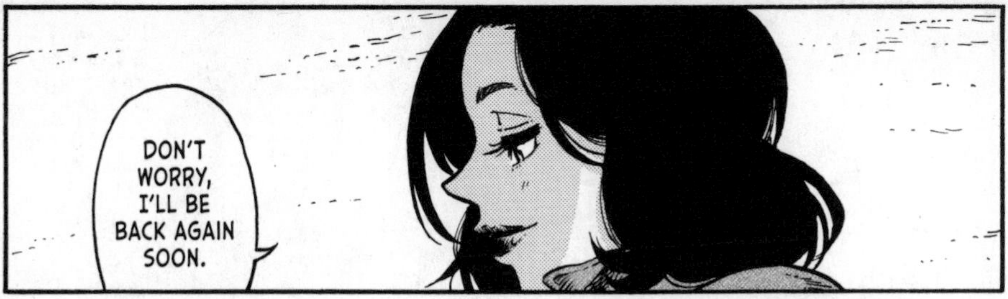
DON'T WORRY, I'LL BE BACK AGAIN SOON.
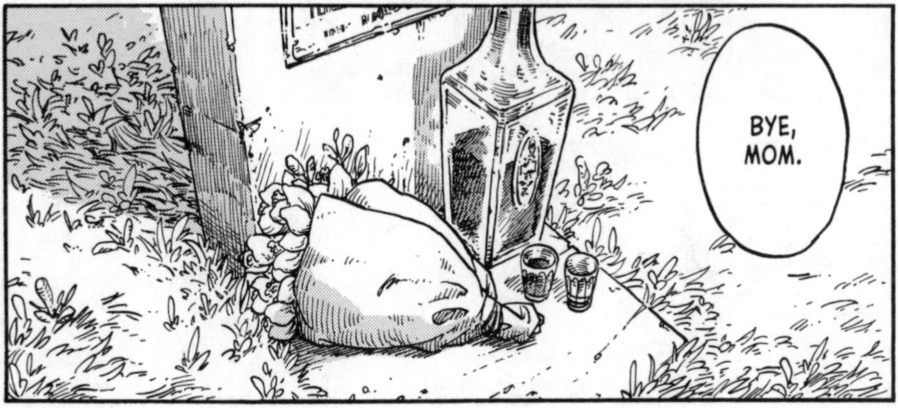
BYE, MOM.
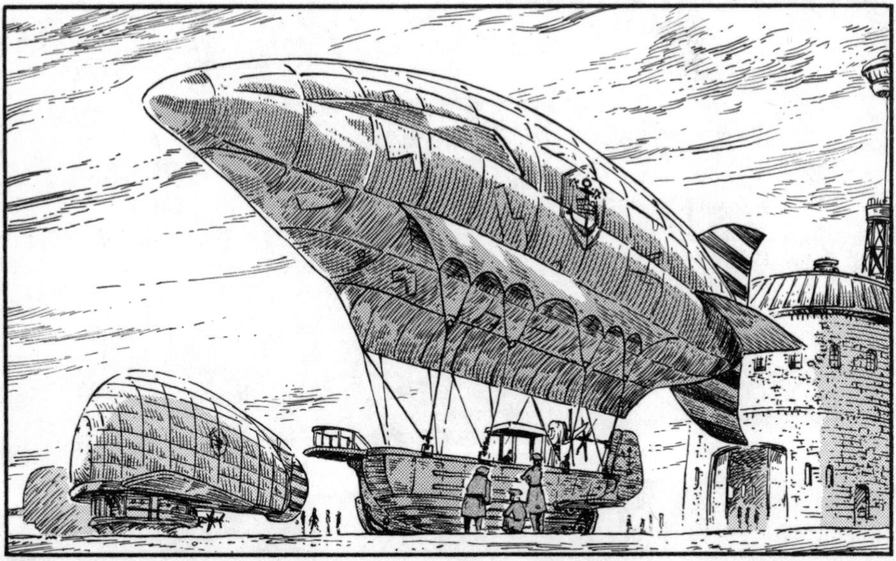

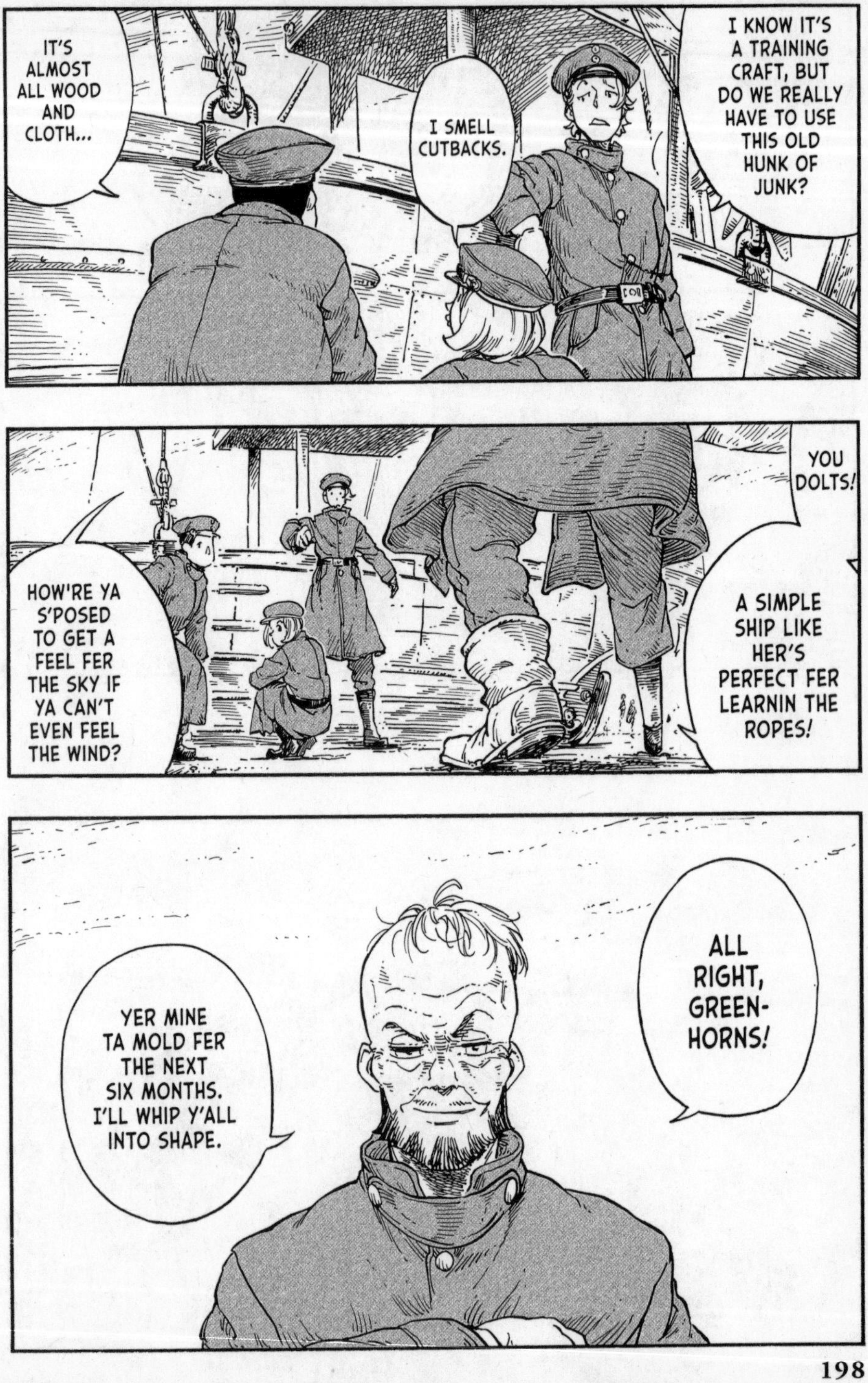
I KNOW IT'S A TRAINING CRAFT, BUT DO WE REALLY HAVE TO USE THIS OLD HUNK OF JUNK?
I SMELL CUTBACKS.
IT'S ALMOST ALL WOOD AND CLOTH...
YOU DOLTS!
A SIMPLE SHIP LIKE HER'S PERFECT FER LEARNIN THE ROPES!
HOW'RE YA S'POSED TO GET A FEEL FER THE SKY IF YA CAN'T EVEN FEEL THE WIND?
ALL RIGHT, GREEN-HORNS!
YER MINE TA MOLD FER THE NEXT SIX MONTHS. I'LL WHIP Y'ALL INTO SHAPE.

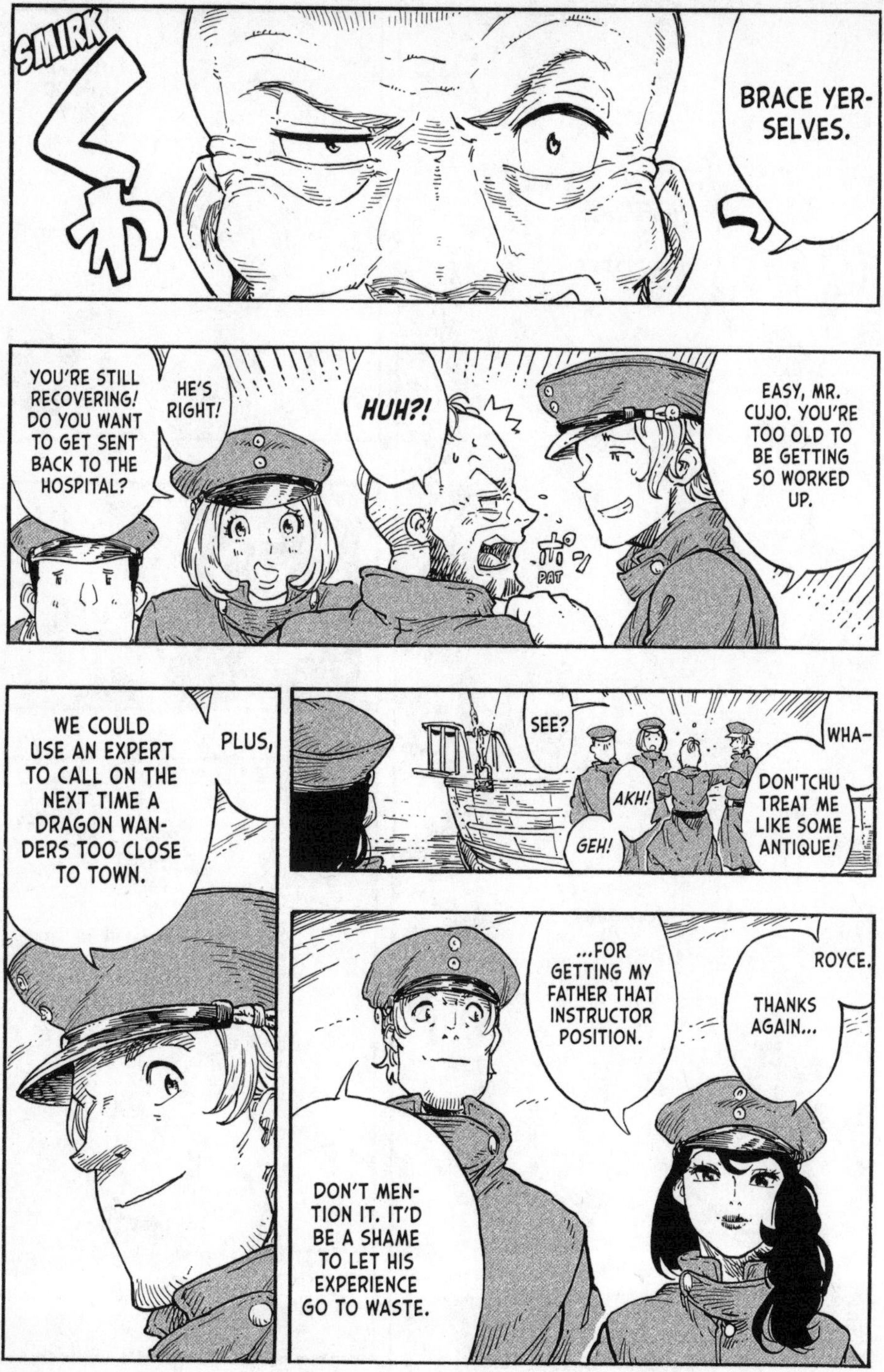
SMIRK
BRACE YER-SELVES.
EASY, MR. CUJO. YOU'RE TOO OLD TO BE GETTING SO WORKED UP.
PAT
HUH?!
HE'S RIGHT!
YOU'RE STILL RECOVERING! DO YOU WANT TO GET SENT BACK TO THE HOSPITAL?
WHA-
DON'TCHU TREAT ME LIKE SOME ANTIQUE!
SEE?
AKH!
GEH!
ROYCE.
THANKS AGAIN...
...FOR GETTING MY FATHER THAT INSTRUCTOR POSITION.
DON'T MEN-TION IT. IT'D BE A SHAME TO LET HIS EXPERIENCE GO TO WASTE.
PLUS,
WE COULD USE AN EXPERT TO CALL ON THE NEXT TIME A DRAGON WAN-DERS TOO CLOSE TO TOWN.

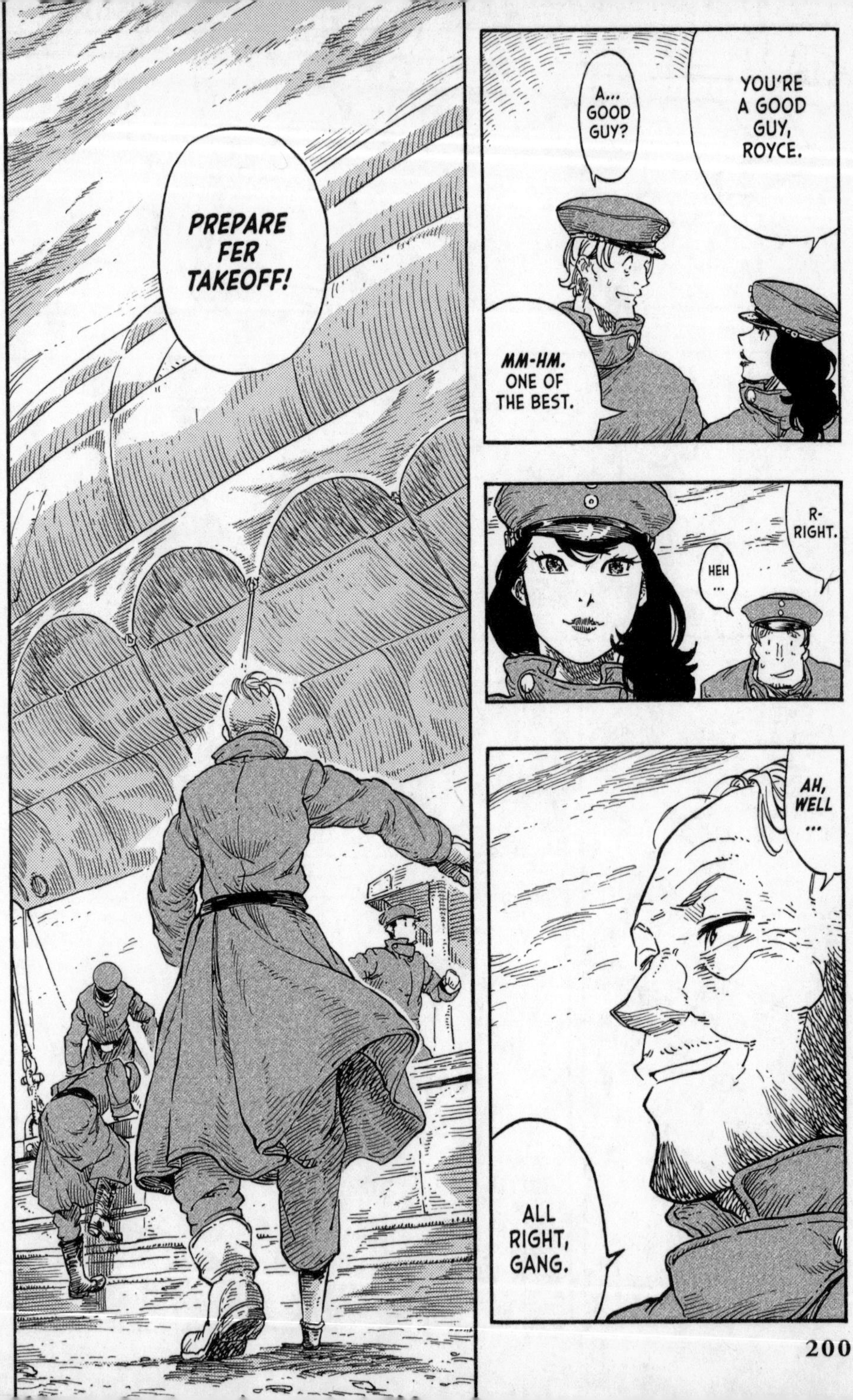
YOU'RE A GOOD GUY, ROYCE.
A... GOOD GUY?
MM-HM. ONE OF THE BEST.
R-RIGHT.
HEH ...
AH, WELL ...
ALL RIGHT, GANG.
PREPARE FER TAKEOFF!

Dragon Red Meat Casserole w/ Mashed Potatoes

Ingredients (serves 4)

+ 700g lean dragon meat   + 1-2 Tbsp flour
+ Salt   + Pepper
+ 2 Tbsp olive oil
+ 1 Tbsp brandy
+ 1 large onion   + 2 garlic cloves
+ 2 celery stalks   + 2 large carrots
+ Bouquet garni (parsley, bay leaf, and thyme bound with twine)
+ 700g mushrooms
+ 300 ml white wine
+ 2 tsp berry jam
+ 700 ml soup stock

01 Cut dragon meat into bite-sized pieces, lightly dredge in flour, and season generously with salt and pepper. Heat half of the olive oil in a frypan over medium heat. Place meat in the pan and brown on all sides for 6-8 minutes. Remove meat from the pan and transfer to a casserole dish.

02 In the same pan, add brandy, remaining olive oil, diced onion, and sauté until golden brown. Add diced garlic, celery, carrot, bouquet garni, and cook vegetables until tender.

03 Add quartered mushrooms. Increase the heat, add white wine and bring to a boil to cook out the alcohol. Remove the pan from heat and pour the contents into the casserole dish. Cover the dish with a lid.

04 Place the dish in a 180° C oven (350° F) and braise for one hour or until the meat is fork tender, adding hot water to the dish as needed. Serve with mashed potatoes.

Dragon Meatloaf

Ingredients (serves 4-5)

+ 900g ground dragon meat
+ 100g finely-diced dragon fat
+ 100g raisins
+ 100g walnuts
+ 1 garlic clove
+ 1 Tbsp balsamic vinegar
+ 1 Tbsp Yoshi's homemade ketchup
+ Salt
+ Pepper
+ Parsley
+ Olive oil
+ Mustard powder

01 In a large bowl, add ingredients through pepper and mix until well combined. Transfer the meat mixture to a loaf pan and gently press the meat down to form an even layer.

02 Using a bain-marie, bake the meatloaf at 200° C (400° F) for 40-50 minutes or until cooked through.

03 Garnish meatloaf with chopped parsley, olive oil, mustard powder, and serve.

Mika's Dragon Steak Tartare

Ingredients (serves 2)

+ 400g fresh dragon tenderloin
+ 2 medium jarred olives
+ 2 Tbsp finely-chopped onion
+ 2 tsp mustard
+ Salt
+ Pepper
+ 1 Tbsp capers
+ 1-2 Tbsp olive oil
+ 1 tsp Yoshi's homemade ketchup
+ 1 medium egg yolk

01 Slice dragon meat against the grain into thin strips then finely dice and place in a bowl (for a stickier texture, pound meat with the back of the knife before moving).

02 Finely chop olives and capers.

03 Add the rest of the ingredients besides egg yolk to the meat mixture and gently fold together with a fork or spatula. Season to taste with salt and pepper.

04 Dish tartare onto a plate, top with whole yolk and serve.

> CASSEROLE IS A CLASSIC GET-WELL-SOON DISH.

INTRODUCTION

DRAGONS

Dragon Diagrams

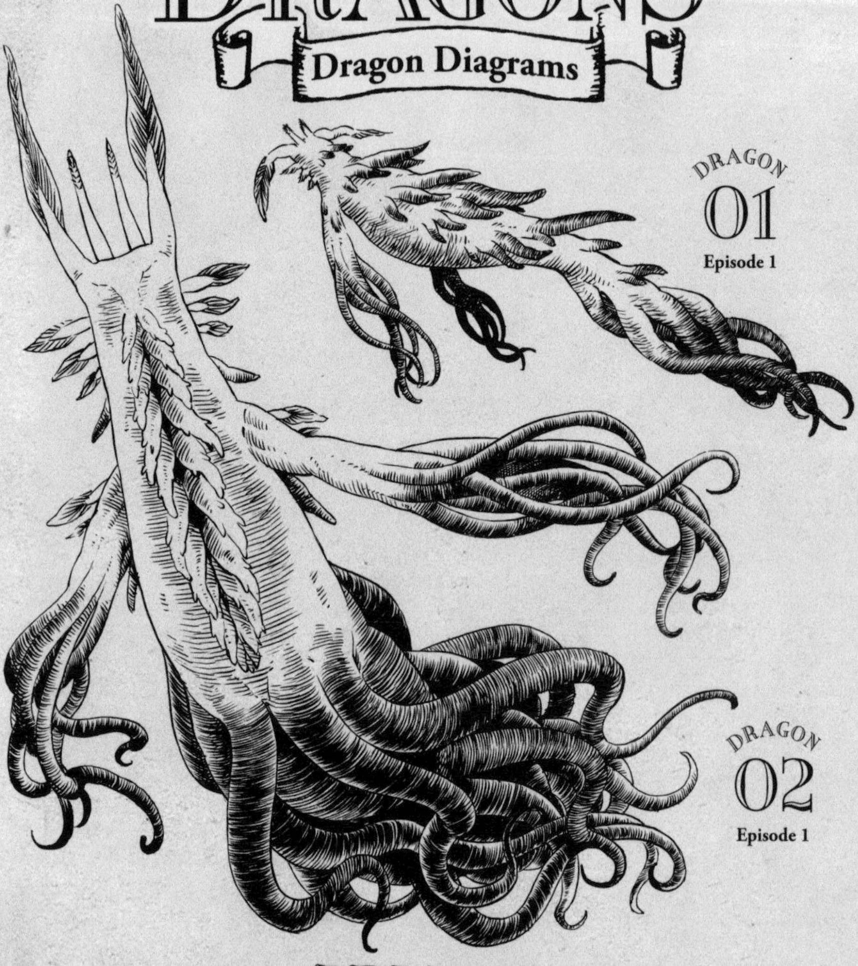

DRAGON
01
Episode 1

DRAGON
02
Episode 1

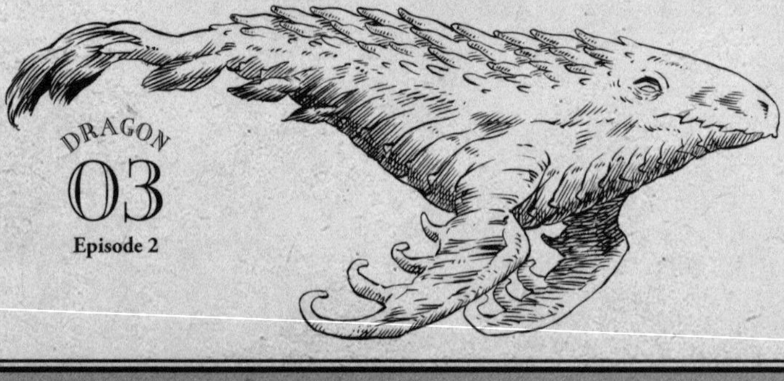

DRAGON
03
Episode 2

DRAGON

04

Episode 2

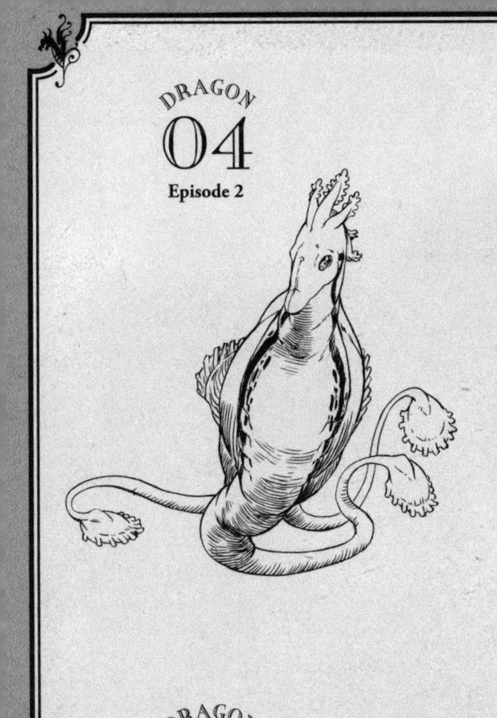

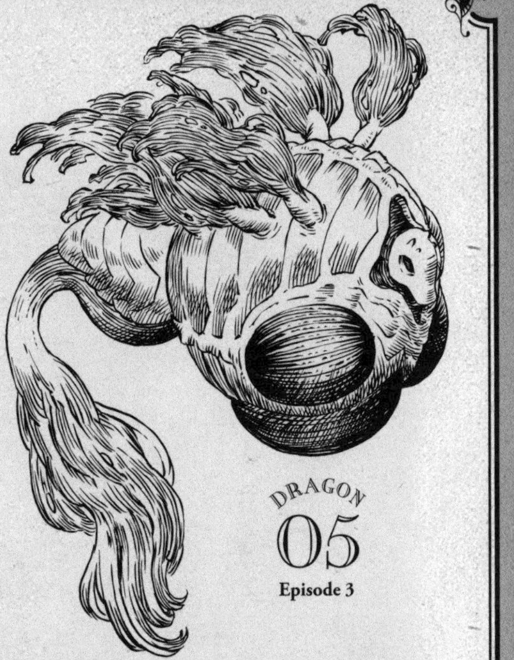

DRAGON

05

Episode 3

DRAGON

06

Episode 4

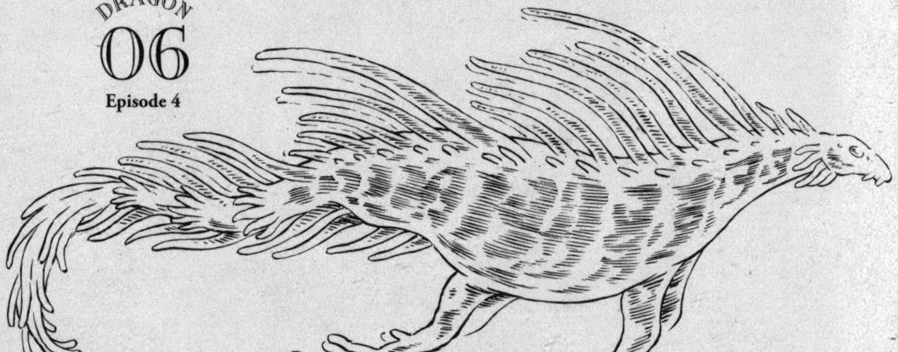

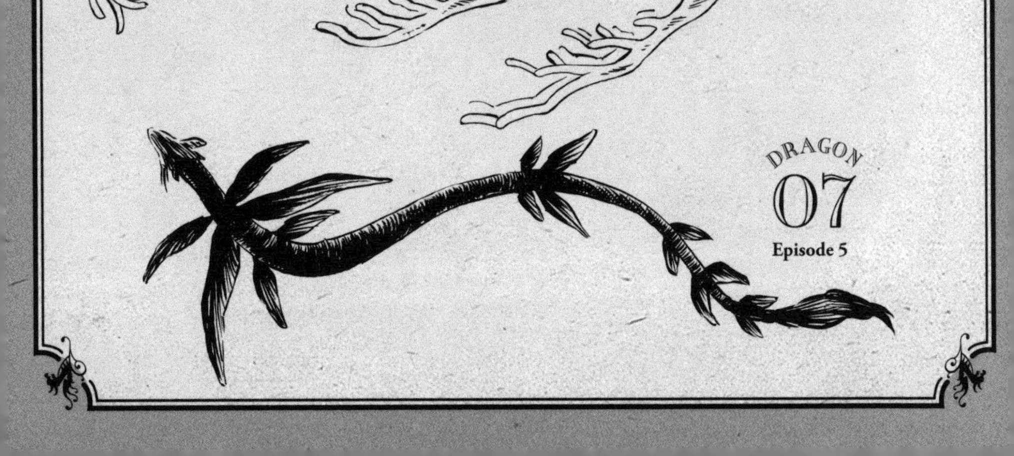

DRAGON

07

Episode 5

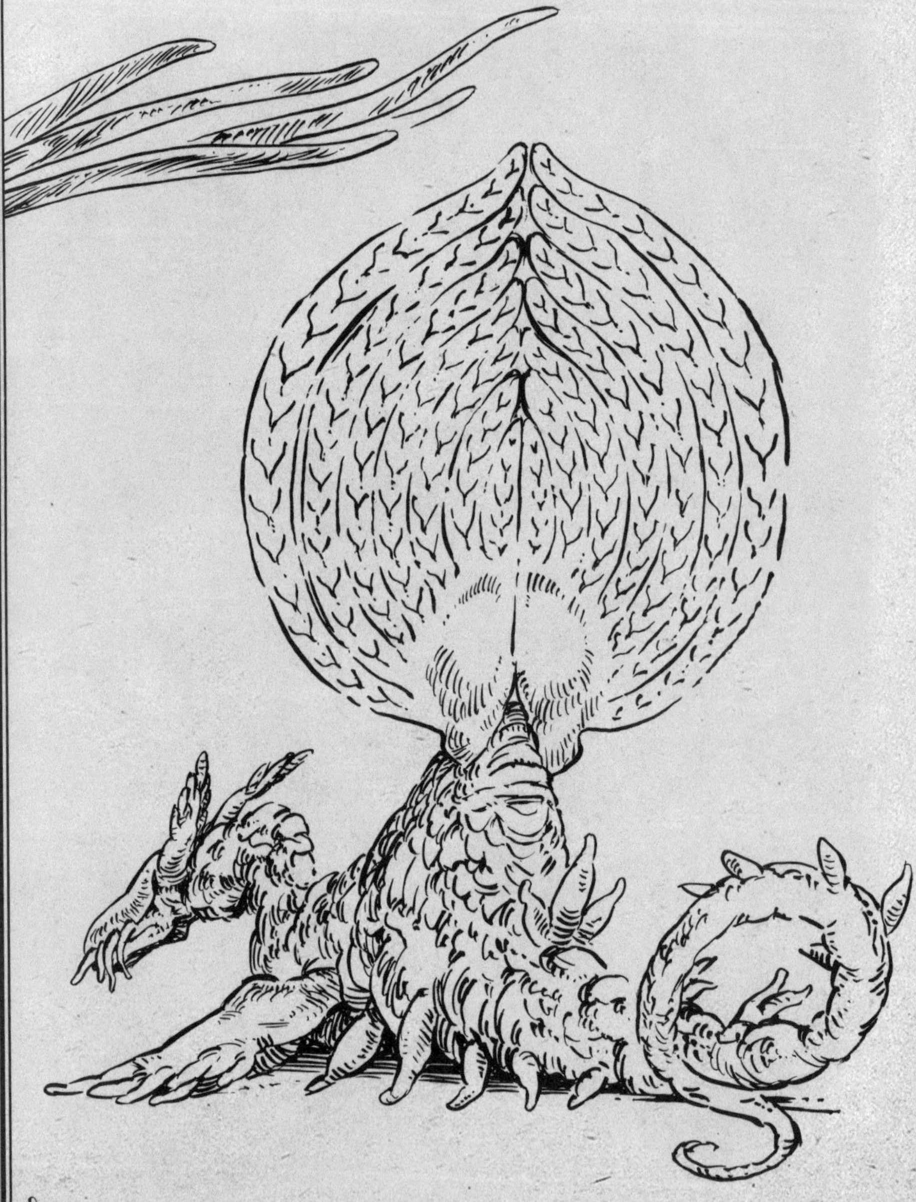

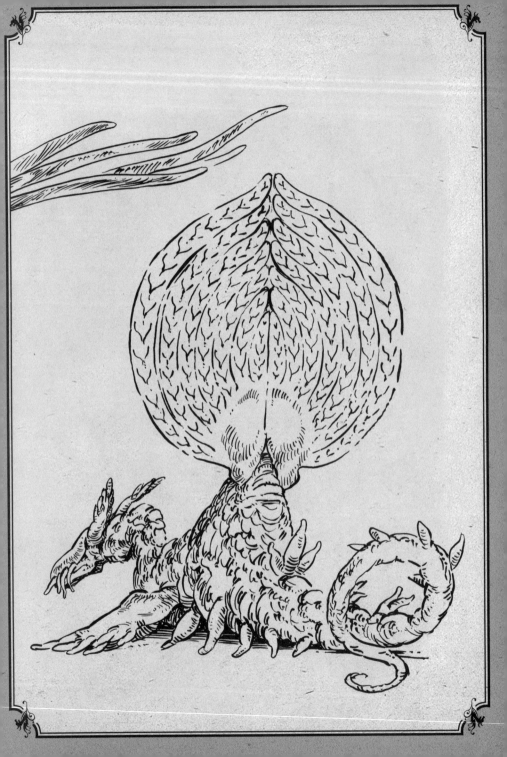

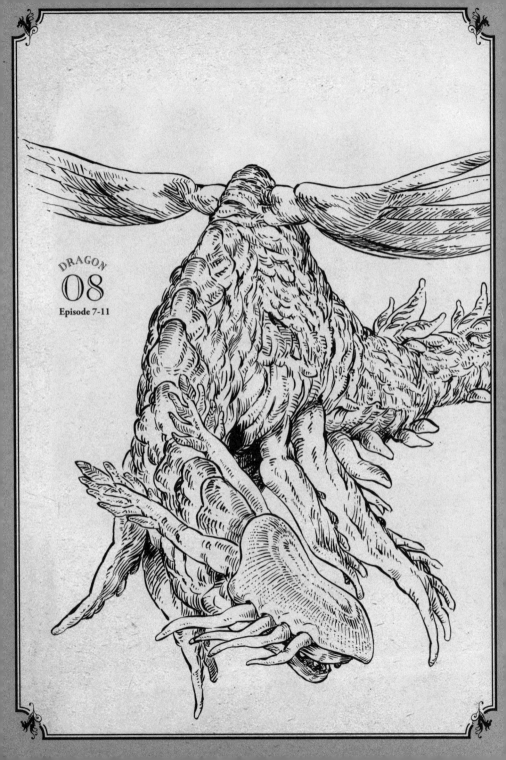

DRAGON
08
Episode 7-11

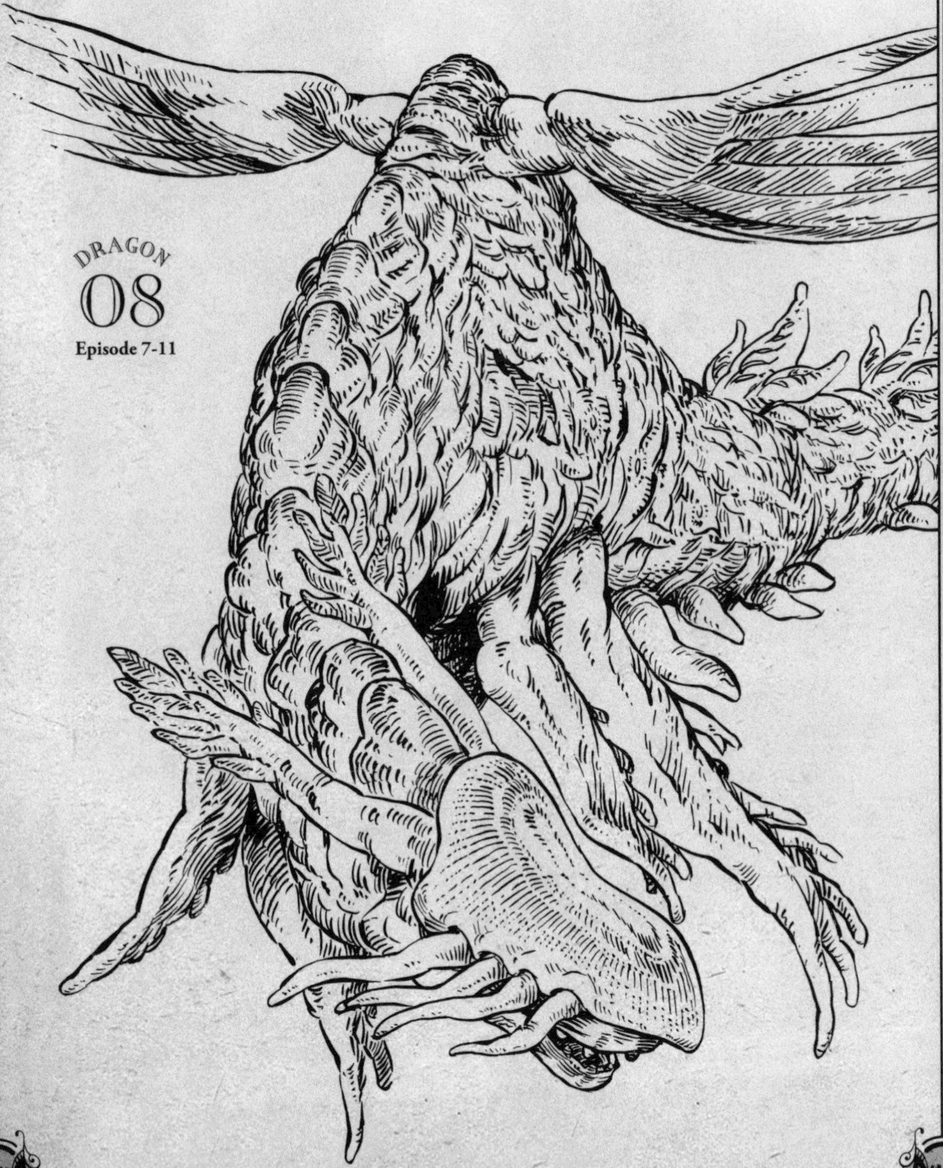

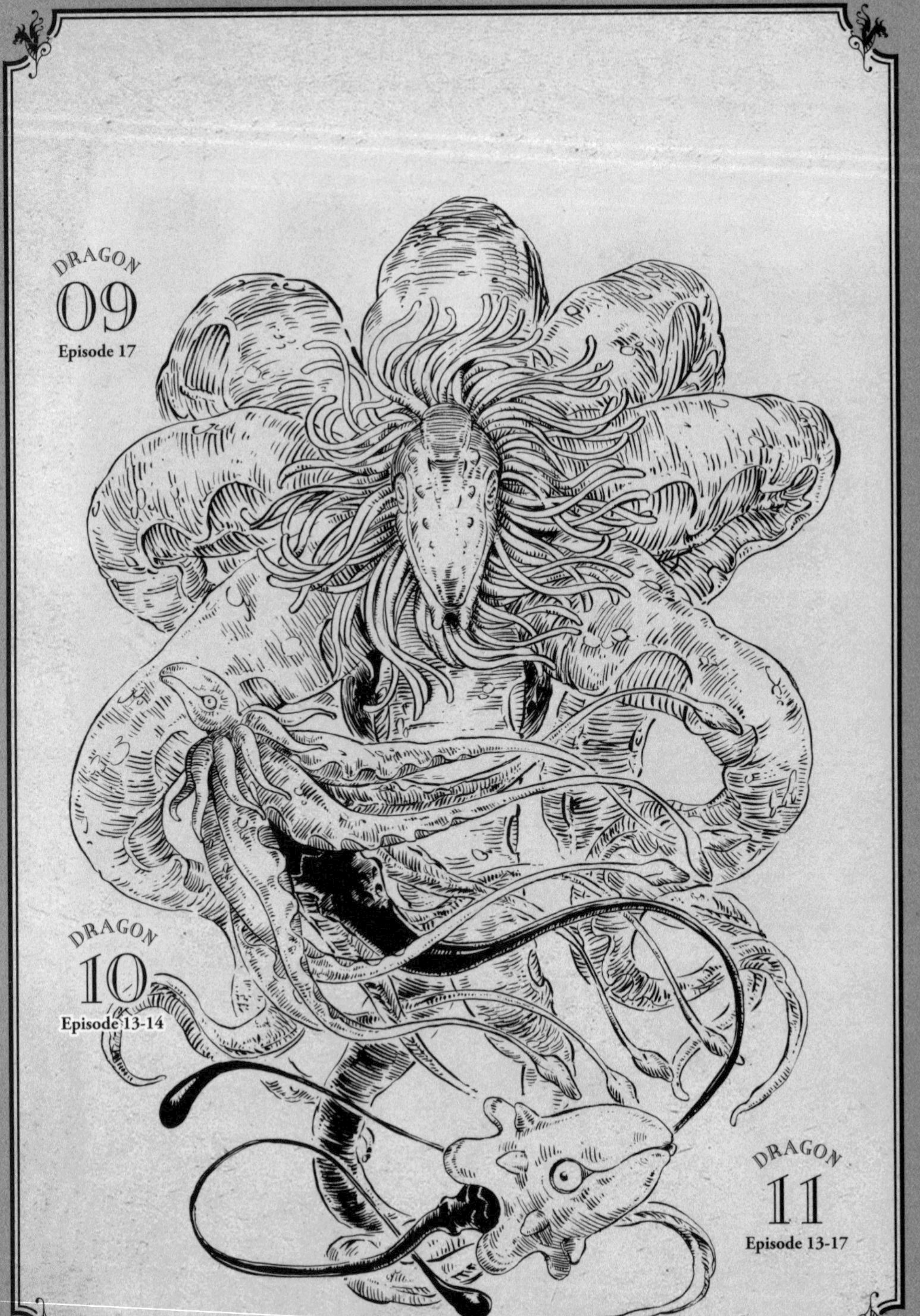
DRAGON
09
Episode 17
DRAGON
10
Episode 13-14
DRAGON
11
Episode 13-17

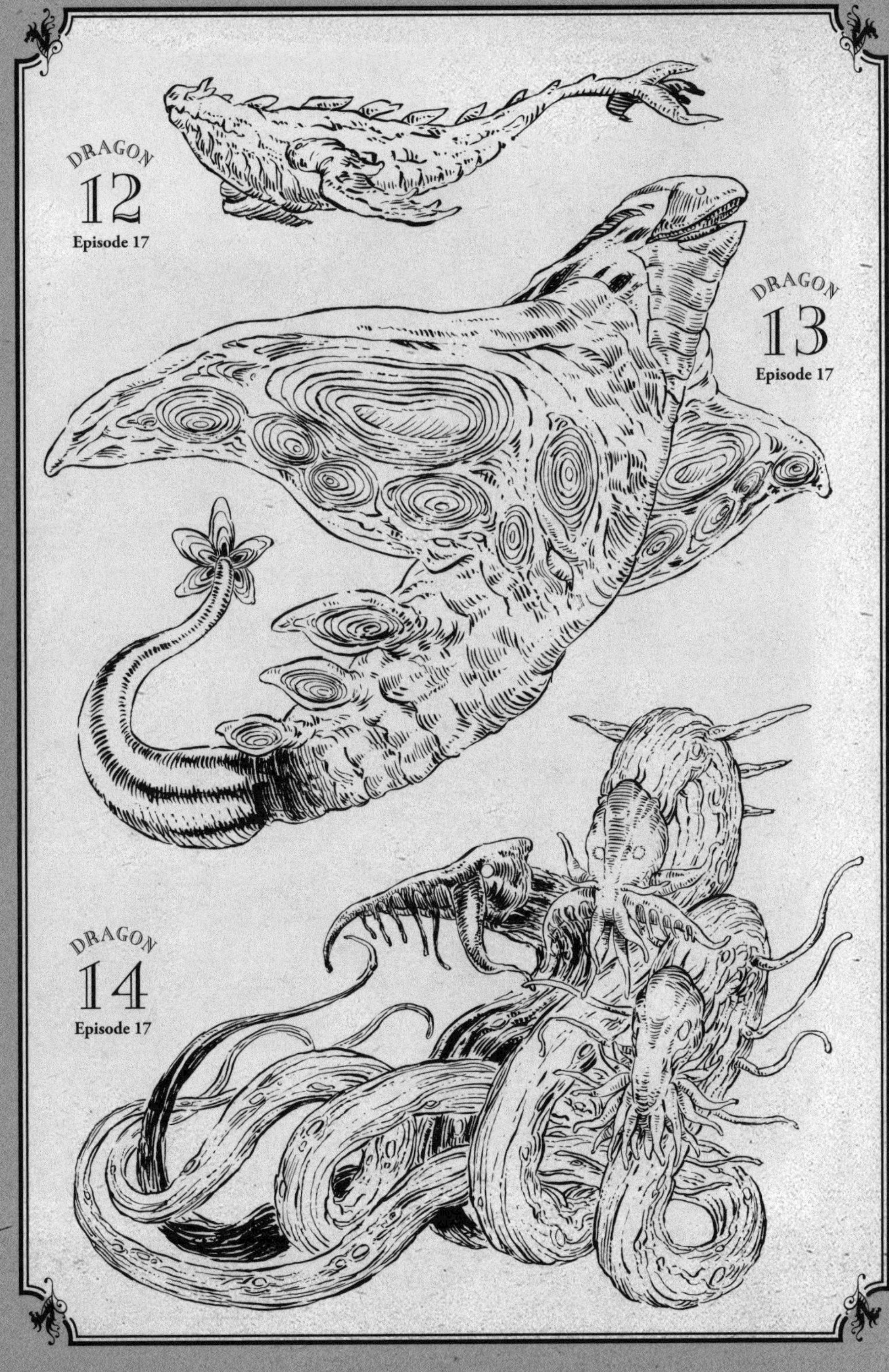
DRAGON
12
Episode 17
DRAGON
13
Episode 17
DRAGON
14
Episode 17

A Kodansha Comics Trade Paperback Original
Drifting Dragons 6 copyright © 2019 Taku Kuwabara
English translation copyright © 2020 Taku Kuwabara

All rights reserved.

Published in the United States by Kodansha Comics, an imprint of Kodansha USA Publishing, LLC, New York.

Publication rights for this English edition arranged through Kodansha Ltd., Tokyo.

First published in Japan in 2019 by Kodansha Ltd., Tokyo as *Kuutei doragonzu*, volume 6.

ISBN 978-1-64651-035-1

Printed in the United States of America.

www.kodanshacomics.com

9 8 7 6 5 4 3 2 1
Translation: Adam Hirsch
Lettering: Thea Willis
Editing: Jordan Blanco
Kodansha Comics edition cover design by Phil Balsman
YKS Services LLC/SKY Japan, INC.

Publisher: Kiichiro Sugawara

Director of publishing services: Ben Applegate
Associate director of operations: Stephen Pakula
Publishing services managing editor: Noelle Webster
Assistant production manager: Emi Lotto, Angela Zurlo